Own Me

Shayna Astor

Edited by Heart Full of Reads
Edited by Cruel Ink
Edited by Beth Hudson
Cover Designer Shower of Schmidt Designs
Formatting Caelan Fine

Own Me
Copyright © 2022 Shayna Astor

From the Author

Own Me is a full-length, stand alone that features strong language, mature situations, explicit sexual scenes, abandonment, drug and alcohol abuse, promiscuous behavior, non-consensual intercourse, and mental health struggles including: anxiety, depression, self-harm, suicide, attempted suicide, rage issues, and attending therapy. Reader discretion is advised, and this book is intended for readers age 18 and up.

Own Me has a very special place in my heart. Many of the mental health issues that Jules battles, are those that I also battle daily. This story began as a way to express myself and my daily struggles, and turned into one of my favorite stories.

Thank you so much for reading my novel! I hope you enjoy reading it, as much as I enjoyed writing it!

For those who feel alone,

Lost in the darkness,

Screaming, thinking nobody can hear their cries for help.

You are not alone,

There is a light out of the dark.

You are heard, there is help.

Introduction

The light flicks on, chasing away the all-encompassing darkness. I raise my head from my hands to see Zane standing with his fingers still on the switch, taking in the scene. Me, sitting on the cool tile of the kitchen, knees to my chest, heels of my hands to my eyes. Knife on the floor.

He kneels in front of me in half a second, grabbing my wrists and pulling them out straight, inspecting them further.

"What happened? Are you okay? Did you cut?" His voice is low, trying to be calm, but I hear the slightest hint of panic seeping through.

"No. But I want to," I whisper.

Crossing my arms against my chest, he curls around me, pulling me into his lap and wrapping his arms tightly around my waist. I let myself feel his strength. I wish I could steal it, or at least borrow some. I'm weak. So much weaker than he is.

We have similar problems, similar demons. But he's learned to control his urges better than I have. He doesn't end up awake at two in the morning, fighting himself like I do. At least not anymore. This isn't the first time this month. It's not even the first time this week.

"It's okay. I've got you." His deep voice is low against my ear.

Breathe. Close your eyes. Take in the moment. Go to where you feel comfortable, safe. The only problem with the directions my psychologist gave me when we practiced the exercise is that I don't know where that place is. Zane makes me feel safe, but I refuse to use him as my grounding visual.

Instead, I keep my eyes open, looking around to find five things I can see. *Toaster, magnet, coffee pot, moon, knife.* My stomach roils at the thought.

Deep breath, keep going. Four things I can hear. *Zane's heart, the tick of the clock, the hum of the fridge, the wind.*

Three things I can touch. *Zane's warm skin, the cool tiled floor, water from the faucet.*

Two things I can smell. *Soap, fresh coffee.*

One thing I can taste. *Tangy iron.* A shudder wracks my body.

"Are you doing your grounding exercise?"

"It's not working." The words come out through gritted teeth.

"Focus on me. See, hear, touch, smell...and taste." With a firm finger under my chin, he tilts my head up as his mouth meets mine, forcing it open as his tongue slips in. Mint crosses my taste buds as my hand splays open over his chest. It's a dual touch sensation—his warmth and the steady beating of his heart beneath my palm.

Zane understands me in a way no boyfriend of mine before him ever had or ever could. I hate that he does because I don't want him having the same struggles I do. But it's what makes us work as a couple. It also makes us toxic together. Kind of like how they say addicts shouldn't date each other. Sometimes if one of us falls off the bandwagon, the other does too.

When we moved in together, we had strict rules. No breakables of any kind, including glasses and dishes. We eat off paper or plastic dishes and only have plastic cups. No vases of any kind. We learned the hard way that mirrors aren't safe either when Zane connected his fist with one.

At the beginning, he locked up the knives, keeping the key with him at all times. My therapist had recently recommended he remove the locks so I could learn self-control. It isn't working, though.

When Zane urgently says "Jules" and shakes me, I snap to. Great, I'm dissociating too. When had he stopped kissing me?

"Huh?"

Pain, I feel pain in my shoulders. Zane's hands are gripping me so firmly it hurts. I try to shrug him off, but it only makes his grip tighten until I wince, making him realize how strong of a grip he has on me. It's like he's trying to hold on to my sanity for me.

"Feel the pain, Jules. Focus on it. Let it be enough."

Closing my eyes, I take more deep breaths. *Nails digging into my skin, warmth rolling off his body, mint lingering in my mouth, clean linen tingling my nose, a heartbeat.* At the moment, I don't know whose heartbeat I'm hearing, mine or his, but I try to focus on the steadiness of it. In the blackness behind my eyelids, I pull up visions of flower fields, the beach, a snowy mountain. Any place that may hold calm. Instead, my mind wants to come back to this apartment.

It seems to be working, as my shoulders start to slump against Zane's hands. He starts rubbing small circles wherever he can. I keep my eyes closed, trying to focus on his fingers, even willing myself to think about all the things they can do to my body. But that just brings up other impulses.

Shivers tingle through me as Zane slides his hand up my neck and into my hair, massaging my scalp. It's two-fold. It feels incredible and helps ease the tension from my taut muscles. But it's also a move he uses when he's trying to get me to take my pants off. I'm not really sure what his motive is at the moment.

When he tangles his fingers in my hair and pulls my head back as he fuses his mouth over mine, it becomes clear.

His lips are hungry, tongue forceful in my mouth. Without words, he's begging me to relinquish my body to him, to give him everything so he can clear the darkness. It's worked before, more than once.

But tonight feels different, darker, harder. Even as his hand slips up my shirt, all I can think of is shiny metal gliding across my arm. The pinch, the sting. The *feeling*. It was a hard day with my psychologist. Sometimes those make for the hardest nights. They bring up all sorts of feelings you've tried to bury for years.

Then at one thirty in the morning, you realize they're not so dead and buried anymore and find yourself standing in the kitchen holding a knife to your arm fighting yourself not to do it while the tiny voice in your head eggs you on. *Do it. You'll feel better. This pain will take away that pain, the hatred, the numbness.* But it never does. It's temporary, fleeting. And then you're left with the reminder of how stupid you were, how weak.

I have to tell Dr. Ptansky if I cut. I don't have to tell her if I have sex, at least not if it's with Zane. Sex with your boyfriend is not self-destructive. Sex in the bathroom at a bar with a man you just met, especially while in a relationship, is. But in the two years Zane and I have been together, I've never once even come close to cheating on him. Dr. Ptansky calls it progress. I call it finally being satisfied in bed.

It helps when that person understands you and doesn't belittle you. Even that they know when to add a little pain to the pleasure. In more ways than one, Zane just gets me.

A whimper rising from my own chest brings me back to what my body is doing. At some point, I straddled Zane's lap, and his mouth is against my throat, both hands cupping my breasts. He's pushed away from the counter, his back now resting against the fridge. Great, I dissociated again.

Focus, focus, focus. Has Zane not had a shirt on this whole time? I'm usually much more aware of his naked physique.

"If I get up, will you follow me to the bedroom?" His voice is low and gravelly.

Will I? I don't know. I want to. Oh, I so want to. But I'm also acutely aware of exactly where the knife is and how it would be to grab it. His hands on me feel so good, but I don't want pleasure. I want pain. I need it. It gives me a reason to hate myself; it reminds me I'm not numb, that I can feel something.

"Yes."

"You hesitated." Grabbing my wrists from behind his head, he pulls them forward, his grip tight. He leans away as I try to kiss him again. "It's not worth it, Jules. Whatever you're thinking, it's not worth it."

"You don't know that."

"I *do* know that. Don't do it. Come to bed with me, let me distract you. Feel me, not the pain."

I nod. "Okay."

Sliding me off his lap, he goes to stand, but he's not careful enough. He doesn't keep control of my hands and before he can stop me, I throw myself across the kitchen and grab the knife, dragging it across my forearm and watching the dark liquid blossom.

I barely hear the knife clank to the floor or Zane screaming behind me. He's suddenly at my side pressing something to my skin as blackness invades my vision. As I fall into darkness, I have one last thought.

Pain.

Chapter 1

Jules

"I don't like how much you're still struggling to control your urges, Julienne. What you're doing isn't working. You need more."

I'm only ten minutes into my weekly session with Dr. Ptansky. Her office is artfully decorated without anything that could be dangerous, also known as no glass, crystal, or sharp objects in sight. All tones are muted shades of blues, browns, and whites.

"It's not as bad as you think," I mumble as I twist a string at the hem of my shirt. It was a fight to convince myself to put on jeans today instead of wearing sweatpants. I wore them once. I thought Dr. Ptansky was going to commit me to a psych ward immediately.

"You just got finished telling me that you and Lance broke up because you disappeared for four days and woke up in Florida in bed with another man. If that's not as bad as I think, I'd hate to see what is."

"I already told you though that no—"

"Nothing happened. I'm aware. But you still dissociated on a massive scale. Which is *not* being in a good place."

She's right. Of course, she is. Dr. Ptansky is always right. It's been hard for me to admit that. Even harder to accept it.

"Okay. So, what does that mean? More sessions?"

"I think you'd benefit from group therapy."

All the blood in my body pools in my feet. *Group therapy.* I don't do well around other people. I don't *like* other people.

Daphne is my one and only friend; she has been since we were kids. I pick up and drop boys like a bad habit. Actually, it *is* a bad habit, one I've been working on breaking for over a year. Barring the brief excursion to Florida, I've been successful for a few months. But that's different, physical, a means to an end. Sitting around and sharing my feelings? No thank you.

"No, no, I'll do anything else. Commit me even!" Sometimes a white padded room sounds absolutely delightful.

"You don't need to be committed, Julienne. Yet. And even that has group therapy. I think it will help you."

I'm vehemently shaking my head before she finishes. "No, I don't like talking to other people. You know how I feel about people."

"Julienne, do you trust me?" Dr. Ptansky has been my psychologist for over four years. She's the first one who's actually sort of helped me, even if only a little bit.

"Yes."

"Then please, listen. Do what I'm asking you. Give it a few sessions. If it's really not working or making things worse, we'll re-evaluate. I can't force you to go, but I truly think it will be beneficial to you."

I start chewing the inside of my cheek as I look around the room. She's told me more than once that it's an avoidance tactic.

"Julienne."

My eyes flip back to her.

"Just try it. Here, this one will treat you right." She scribbles something on a small piece of paper and hands it to me. It takes me a minute, her hand hovering in the air, before I decide to reach out and take it.

"How will you know if I go?" Maybe there's a loophole here.

"I won't. I'll have to trust you if you tell me you went." Dr. Ptansky is the one person I've never lied to. I don't even think I'd know how. "You don't have to go this week, but I really think you'll see it's not so bad."

"It's a bunch of people, talking about their problems."

"You do that with me every week."

"Yeah, but it's the other people part that's an issue."

"Julienne. You don't *hate* people. You don't trust them." Dr. Ptansky is the only person allowed to call me Julienne. One of my ex-boyfriends tried it once. I left and never went back.

"You're right. And I don't like to be around them."

"For somebody who used to find herself in the bed of different guys fairly frequently, I'd have to disagree." I want to be offended by her statement, but I can't when it's true.

"There was a purpose to that."

"What about the ones you start a relationship with?"

"They're just slightly good enough to hold my attention momentarily." Slowly working towards folding in on myself to fight off the gnawing feeling in my chest, I lean forward and place my elbows on my knees.

"If you don't work on bringing down your walls, working through your issues, you'll never find somebody you want to be with."

"Who says I want that?"

"Don't you? You don't have to start actual relationships. You can have your fun and move on, keep it free and simple. No need to define things. Yet, you do. You let yourself be called girlfriend, call them your boyfriend. You stay that way for a few weeks or months." She says months like it's a long time. The longest I've been in a "relationship" was four months.

"But I've never loved any of them. I've never lived with them. Sometimes I just get tired, flitting from boy to boy." And it's lonely and scary being alone. That's when the darkness encroaches faster, easier. There are no distractions keeping it at bay.

"That doesn't mean you don't want it. You either don't allow yourself to have it or you haven't found the right person for you."

"I don't believe in *the one*, Dr. Ptansky." I hope my face matches the incredulous tone I'm using.

"I'm not necessarily referring to that. I'm thinking more along the lines of somebody who understands you, who can handle you, who can challenge you."

Oh, I do love a good challenge when it comes to men.

Since I remain silent, she continues. "All of the people at these meetings are going to be in similar situations. They may also have a strong dislike of other people, some even fear. You can always come up with a name for yourself if you'd prefer to remain anonymous. Many people prefer that.

"This group is quite small. Only allows at most ten people at a time. It's run by a colleague of mine, Dr. Shiner. I'm going to add you to the list and let her know that you will hopefully be joining the group."

"So, you're hoping I'm going to find my match made in heaven at this group?" The snarkiness is not necessary, but I can't help it. One of the many coping mechanisms Dr. Ptansky wants to eradicate.

She sighs heavily while looking down her nose at me. "Not even a little, Julienne. I just think it would be beneficial for you to find somebody, anybody, who you feel you can talk to. That doesn't have to be in a sexual relationship. It can simply be a friend."

"I have a friend." *Defensive. Good going, Jules.*

"Yes. You have *a* friend. More would be good for you. Especially one who understands your struggles and can be there for you when needed."

I'm fighting a losing battle. She doesn't back down. And she's not exactly wrong. While I love Daphne, she doesn't understand me. Not like somebody else would. Still, the prospect of meeting other people, getting to *know* other people, makes my stomach leap into my throat and my blood run cold.

"And for the record, Julienne, I'm not sure it would in fact be a good idea if you *were* to find somebody you were attracted to in the group. There are a lot of ways that can cause you to backslide."

All I can do is nod in agreement.

She's suggested I go. Hasn't demanded it, hasn't required it. She's basically pleaded with me but hasn't absolutely insisted. I see a little leeway here, and I'm not about to jump into it without a little fight. Waiting a few weeks can't hurt. Right?

Chapter 2

Jules

Ten weeks into group therapy and I don't feel any change. I've cut three times this week, which is more than usual. I blame the added stress of group, Dr. Ptansky says I'm not trying hard enough to use my coping mechanisms. She's probably right because my old coping mechanisms were just destructive behaviors. I haven't really found new ones.

But something changes that tenth night. Or, really, someone. I'm sitting back in my chair, people watching and avoiding talking to anybody, as I like to do, when a new person walks in.

He's tall, very tall by the looks of it, and startlingly handsome. From where I sit, his eyes somehow look both dark and light at the same time. Not quite blue but a color I can't pinpoint from afar. His hair is a dark brown, much like mine. It's cut close at the sides, but longer and styled at the top—the type of hair that you just love to run your fingers through. And he's wearing a suit that fits him so perfectly you'd swear it was painted on what appears to be a toned body.

When he flicks his eyes up and catches me staring, I know I should be embarrassed, but he's so gorgeous I'm sure he's used to it. He smirks and waves his hands slowly down his body before bringing them to his face and pretending to take a picture, then flipping me off.

Feisty. I like it.

New Guy seems to be the only person here with more than just a pulse. Possibly even a personality.

He grabs himself a cup of what he's about to learn is extremely bitter coffee and takes a seat opposite me in the circle. Putting his jacket on the back of his chair, he reveals a fitted powder-blue button-down shirt and a striped tie. He's dressed pretty fancy for a group therapy session, so I'd have to assume he came from work. Judging by the suit, I'd say he makes decent money.

When he waves at me, I realize I've been caught staring again, sure that drool is pooling in the corner of my mouth. Usually, I'm the one getting stared at, though, I don't really know why.

While he's incredibly good-looking, I'm more focused on what a guy like him is doing at a meeting like this. Pretty and wealthy people don't have problems. I know that's not really true, anybody can have problems, but why is he *here*? I guess I don't know he has money, but dressing like that, he *has* to.

I avert my eyes to look at the others filing into the too brightly lit room. It's a very nice space in a very bad location. Why they chose this building is beyond me, except that maybe rent is cheap. The part of town isn't the issue; it's a pretty good area. It's the physical location of the building, the alley off to the side that you have to cut down that makes my pulse jump and my hairs stand on end every time I walk through it. The lights are incredibly dim in that section, and the entrance is far back from the street.

Mary, Tim, and Seth are gathered in one corner chatting, while everybody else mills around. All of these people I've come to know a little about from what they share weekly. The guy across from me is the only new person in the ten weeks I've been here. Before him, it was me. And while I don't want to stare, there really isn't anything better to look at. I've read all the motivational posters plastered around the walls more times than any one person should read them.

A laugh catches in my throat as I watch New Guy basically choke on the horrible coffee. It didn't catch enough though, as he glances over to see me covering my mouth. He glares at me for a second before amusement glides over his features.

Reaching down, I lift my takeout cup from next to my feet and hold it up, raising my eyebrows. After my first session, I asked if I was allowed to bring outside beverages, prepared to make a stink if the answer was no. There was absolutely no way I could make it through these sessions without a large and *drinkable* cup of coffee.

He nods imperceptibly. Pulling his phone out, he types something in, scrolls, then spreads his fingers to zoom. Then looks back up at me and points to the right. If I understand what he's asking me, which I'm pretty sure I do, I shake my head and point to the left. He looks back at the screen, squinting slightly and nods.

I've tried both coffee shops that are right near our meeting location. The one to the left is far superior than the one to the right. There's also always Starbucks within a block or two, but I like helping small businesses when I can. Land of Lattes has become a weekly stop for me.

To be sure we're talking about the same place, he takes his hand and makes an L, O, L with his fingers, to which I nod in response.

This is becoming interesting. I've barely spoken, or even really interacted, with another person since I started, aside from Layla, who runs the meetings, when she tries to get me to talk. But New Guy has me intrigued.

My second session was the one and only time I shared. As far as I'm concerned, that's enough. Dr. Ptansky isn't happy. She says there's no way this will work if I don't talk. I don't know if I want it to work. I don't like group therapy. Simple.

It'd be nice to have somebody to talk to here. Maybe sexy New Guy will be that person. Though I'm not having random sex anymore, he would certainly jump to the top of the list if I was.

All those thoughts of communicating with him go out the window when we're partway into group and Layla asks me to share.

"No thanks, I'll pass," I say, giving her a tight smile. That's when I hear a snort and look around the circle to see New Guy rolling his eyes. I raise my eyebrows in challenge.

Which he takes, leaning forward in his chair. "I'll go. I'm not afraid to speak up." The low baritone of his voice does something not entirely unpleasant to my insides. He's barely taken his eyes off me since he entered the room.

"I'm Flynn. I'm here because I have issues with rage control." The look he flashes me is very akin to a see-that-wasn't-so-hard but mixed with something else. Superiority?

"Welcome, Flynn. Would you care to go into detail? This is a safe place; you can share anything." Sugary sweetness drips off Layla's words as though they were actually coated in honey.

"Sure. This weekend I got mad about something, threw a few mugs against the wall in my apartment." The way he says it, eyes still fixed on mine, is like he's trying to portray that he's...dangerous.

"Would you care to elaborate?"

"No." One very strongly spoken syllable and the door slams shut on his openness.

"Okay. Anybody else?" She drags out the okay and pats her knees before looking around the circle.

When Becky dives into a story about her family and why she chopped her hair off this past weekend, I find myself in some sort of staring contest with Flynn. Something tells me that's not his real name.

Flynn's eyes are scathing as they flick over my frame. One would think I caused him some great offense, just by existing. I'm pretty confident, just by looking at him, that nobody has ever challenged him. The way he wears his tailored suit, I'd bet he has some high-powered job, people flitting around after him, hanging on to his every word. I'm not one of those people. Maybe he can tell by looking at me and the hot mess that I am in my torn jeans and baggy, holey sweater. At least my hair's washed today and not piled on my head.

Or maybe it's because people shrink away from his gaze, which is completely understandable. I'm sure women melt in the street if he glances in their direction. The pulsation between my legs tells me I'm curious how he looks at women in the bedroom. My readjustment and squirming cause his lips to upturn and eyes to flicker. Well, that confirms he knows the reaction he has on women. I hate that he also has it on *me*.

Not being like others of my gender is something I pride myself on. I don't swoon. I don't fall at the feet of men and hope they'll take me home with them. When I fuck, I do so on my terms. I'm always in control. Always. Boyfriend, random hookup, I'm the one holding the reins. I have a sneaking suspicion with *Flynn* that things don't quite work that way.

Why am I even thinking about that? Why do I care? I have sworn off men and random hook ups. Besides, I've never been one to go for men like Flynn. They think too highly of themselves, like they're God's gift to the planet earth and women everywhere. I'm not about that. I don't want to have to stroke a guy's ego; I just want to get laid.

The staring contest continues as the meeting drones on around us. His eyes never soften and, more than once, rake my frame. If he even remotely likes anything he sees, he doesn't let on, his face remaining stoic the entire time.

It's such an odd exchange. Neither of us pay much attention to our surroundings, yet we're unable to tear our eyes from each other. He's cocky. I'm sure this is some sort of contest for him. If I look away first, he wins. Too bad I'm not a quitter. He's going to be disappointed when he loses. Or at the very least isn't the victor.

As Layla wraps up the meeting, we still haven't looked away. It has to have been at least a half an hour. If I wasn't so determined, I may be uncomfortable.

When people start standing, he looks away, gathering his coat and the untouched horrible meeting coffee. *HA! I win.* But he doesn't even glance my way again as he slips his sports coat on and walks to the exit.

Maybe I didn't win after all.

Chapter 3

Jules

T he following week, Flynn attends the meeting, again dressed in a suit. This time, he's holding a large cup from Land of Lattes. I wonder what his coffee order is. I'd imagine something dark and strong—like him.

Shit, what the hell kind of thought is that?

Every so often Layla will bring snacks, like donuts or biscotti. Today's one of those days. Normally, I don't partake, but when I see Flynn walking to the table, I weigh my options.

Biting the inside of my cheek and turning away for a second, I go through the choices. Try to start a conversation with him and maybe, just maybe, actually have somebody to talk to here. Don't say anything, be alone, and possibly continue to have weird staring contests.

I've already decided I'm going to let him hold my focus. There's nothing better to look at, and he certainly didn't seem to mind last week. Why torture myself looking at boring posters I basically know by heart instead of staring at his deliciousness?

Coffee still in hand, I jump up and wander over to the table. He's eyeing the snacks like he doesn't trust them. Sliding in next to him, I realize I only come to about his shoulder. Good to know I can still peg height from a distance.

"I see you trusted my suggestion today."

He turns to me the slightest bit and arches an eyebrow. "I'm capable of finding coffee places on my own, thank you." That deep voice of his vibrates through me.

"Sure, but I still suggested it."

"And do you think you deserve something for that?" Well, I was right about the asshole part at least.

"I don't know, maybe a thank you?" I don't expect it, and I certainly know better than to think I'll get one from a guy like this. But I'm bored.

Now, he turns to face me fully. Today, he's wearing a deep blue shirt, fitting just as perfectly as the one last week. I swallow the drool that's pooled in my mouth.

Looking up at him, I take in his eyes. They're not blue, maybe the slightest hint. But they're not brown or green either. If anything, they're almost...slate. Cold and hard.

My tongue flicks out to lick my suddenly dry lips. The glare coming from him is intense. I like to think I'm a tough-ass bitch, considering all I've gone through in my life, but this makes me falter, wanting to take a step back. I don't, standing my ground, but it's not so easy.

What is this effect he's having on me and why?

It must be the suit. Or the dark eyes. Maybe it's how he towers over me. Maybe the combo.

He rakes his gaze over me incredibly slowly, taking in every inch from toes to tip before meeting my eyes again.

"I don't thank people for things they didn't do. It's not a hidden gem, it's not the Holy Grail. It's a coffee shop. That I would have found on my own. I may have tried one or two other cafes with stupid kitschy names, but I would have found it." Disdain drips from his tone.

My eyes grow wide and my tongue slides along my teeth. "Well, okay then."

I turn on my heels and walk back to my seat, flopping into it. He takes the chair he had last time, practically straight across from me. As he sits, he slouches in the chair, legs outstretched in front of him. Nobody's walking around, which is probably a good thing, because they'd likely trip over his feet. Though I'm sure he doesn't care.

He holds his phone in his lap with one hand as he scrolls with one thumb while the other holds the top of his coffee near the floor. I watch him with narrowed eyes, not really sure what for. I mean, yeah, for the aesthetic purposes, but something about him intrigues me. I've met plenty of assholes, and I'm one myself most of the time. But it's usually deserved. Not just unadulterated hatred.

As Layla sits in her chair, everybody quiets down. Flynn slides his phone into his pocket, glancing up, right in my direction. The corners of his lips lift ever so slightly while a shimmer dances through his eyes.

Shifting higher in his seat the tiniest bit, he loosens his tie, undoing the top button of his shirt and running his fingers through his hair. It tousles the strands so a few stand at varying angles. It ruins his perfectly coiffed hair, but hot damn if it doesn't make him sexier.

Two can play at that game.

I reach down and grab my coffee, taking a nice slow sip. Once I've swallowed, I trail my tongue along my bottom lip before pulling it between my teeth while letting my eyelids flutter slightly. One hand gently rests at the base of my neck, fingers up stretched to caress the bare skin.

When I tilt forward again, taking another sip of coffee and glancing at him like nothing happened, I notice his eyes are wider and laced with desire. He's sitting forward slightly in his chair instead of resting back.

I got his attention at least. The only question is what kind?

Slowly he wraps one hand around his wrist, starting with his thumb and forefinger and then one by one, wrapping the others. Then he gives a squeeze, one corner of his mouth quirking up.

And my mouth drops open. I'm not fast enough to stop it, causing him to break into a full grin that's so devilish I think hell opened. It makes my heart race, heat rush to my face, and my panties wet.

"Flynn, would you like to share today?" Layla ventures. I hadn't even heard anybody talking until she said his name.

"No." He says the single syllable solidly, not turning away from me.

"All right. Serena?"

"No." My voice isn't quite as strong, a little flustered by the...teasing? I'm not quite sure what to call what we're doing. All I know is that I have a pretty damn good feeling if we ever ended up in bed together, it would be explosive.

I don't like how badly I want to find out.

Sitting back in his chair again, he gives me another once-over. I swear he does it so frequently he has me burned in his memory by now.

Maybe he's wondering how many different positions he can get me in.

No. Bad thoughts. Not going to happen. *No more random sex.*

He runs his finger along his lower lip which draws my attention to what appears to be a very kissable mouth.

There aren't any more antics as therapy draws to a close. Just more staring. People start to filter out, and Mary approaches me. We chatted once, she's nice. But she's quiet, and as I said, nice. I haven't quite figured out her deal.

She held me back the first day I shared. I'd talked about my promiscuity, and she'd looked at me with wide eyes and asked what it felt like to be with "all those different guys." I made sure she realized it wasn't at one time and was over the course of several years. I haven't spoken to her again. For some reason, tonight she's choosing to keep me back.

I'm barely focusing on what she's saying because across the room, Flynn has been retained by Shane. Flynn has a hand in his pocket while the other holds his coffee cup that he's swirling around. I'd been so caught up in our contest that I didn't finish mine either. He's making me all sorts of crazy.

He's at least four inches taller than Shane, looking down his nose at him. His jaw is tight, cheekbones sharp. I can't hear what they're talking about from here, but when Flynn lets out a sharp "No," I'm sure it's not going how Shane had hoped.

"Okay, well, I'll see you next week, Serena." Mary's voice draws my attention back to her.

"Oh yeah. Bye, Mary." It's her real name; she told me the first time we talked.

I turn to my chair, pulling my phone out of my purse to see if I have any work assignments or anything from Daphne.

The hairs on the back of my neck stand at attention and my skin is electrified when I feel somebody standing right behind me. A mix of linen, sandalwood, and coffee waft into my nose.

My heart races as a firm chest brushes against my back and lips ghost over my ear. "You seem to think you're good at playing games." I relax the slightest bit when I identify the voice as Flynn's. He seems much more bark than bite. Though, even if he isn't, I could get on board with that.

"I am. You certainly seemed bothered." I turn my head the slightest bit to the side, hoping he can't hear my heart as it hammers against my rib cage.

From this angle, I can see the slightest curl of his lips as a few of my strands of hair shift with his derisive snort. "You're playing with fire. Be careful you don't get burned."

He's gone just as quickly as he appeared, and as I spin around on the balls of my feet to retort, he's already across the room, his long legs carrying him quickly. With his hand on the door frame, he turns back to me...and winks.

That motherfucker.

He thinks this week was something? *Game. Fucking. On.*

Chapter 4

Jules

It's another week of this weird dance with Flynn. There have already been three more just like it filled with tiny things that seem like flirting or teasing. Few words are exchanged, but when they are, his tone is as if I'm the biggest bother on the planet.

Tonight, I dash out once the meeting is finished, planning to avoid him and removing his chance to sneak up behind me again. The others already seem to have gone. That's the one downside to sitting across from the exit.

On my way up the stairs, Tim catches up with me.

"Hey, Serena, how's it going?"

I'm a little skeptical. We've *never* spoken. "Fine. And you?"

"Good, good. So, I was hoping you could help me out with something." He's hoping I can help with something? I don't even know him.

I push the door open and breathe in the fresh air. The meeting room still holds the chemical sting of fresh carpet and paint, even though it's been used for these meetings for over six months.

Not being around people much and having social anxiety means I don't quite know what to do in these situations. "What can I do for you?" Ignoring him doesn't seem like the right answer.

"I have a little problem I need some assistance with."

He's stopped walking, and I'm feeling squirmy as I look around the poorly lit alley. Why does the only entrance and exit have to be here?

"See, things have been a little dry for me lately and hearing your history a few months ago, well, I was hoping you could throw old Tim here a quick one."

My eyebrows shoot to my hairline. A mixture of anger and disgust swirl in my stomach.

"No." One word. I say it firmly. There's absolutely no chance in hell I'll break my good behavior. Not for a guy like Tim, especially.

While I don't know terribly much about him, as with most people here, I've gotten creepy vibes off of him from the second I met him. Beady eyes that always fall to the chest of any woman he encounters, a greasy comb over far too intense for a man in his thirties, and an ever-present stench of his piney cologne. Though I try to keep my distance, it's so potent, smelling like he dumped a whole bottle on himself, that you can't be within two feet of him without being engulfed by the cloud.

"Oh, come on, just one time. I promise you won't regret it." He's trying to sound alluring. It's not working.

"I said no, Tim. I'm not like that anymore." I'm done with the conversation and start walking away.

My back hits the brick wall before I even realize he's moved behind me. It knocks the wind out of me.

"Oh, come on, baby. Just one time, for fun." The stench of burned coffee wafts into my nose, making me want to gag for two reasons.

Everybody handles their demons differently. Some use drugs or alcohol, some use sex, others self-harm. Some, like myself, use all of the above. Or at least, I did at one point. Most fell away before I hit twenty, leaving the self-harm and occasional random sex, though not usually while in a relationship. I stress the usually. And at this point, I haven't for several months.

When some guys find out about how wild I was, they're all too quick to think they can have a shot. They don't seem to understand that people can, in fact, change. Isn't that the point of therapy? To change our dangerous behaviors that we use to cover up some deep-seated pain? They think once a slut, always a slut. Maybe they're right.

"No. Leave me alone." He still has me pinned against the wall. I can throw a punch when I need to, but Tim is far bigger than I am. It's been a long time since I've felt fear, but I recognize it slithering through my body.

Instead of answering, he presses his mouth against mine. His lips are aggressive as I pinch mine closed as tightly as I can, trying to turn my head away from him.

"Oh, well, it's not as fun if you don't participate. But still *some* fun." He presses his mouth against mine as he slides his sweaty hand up under my shirt, the other boxing me in as he leans against the wall.

It frees my hands to push hard against his chest. He's caught off-guard, and I get him back a good foot. "I said no." My voice is low, but I can hear the waver in it. I'm sure he can too.

His lips pull back in a snarl, exposing yellowed teeth. My eyes dart from side to side, trying to find an escape route. Tim grabs me and throws me, hard, back against the wall when I try to dash. I wince as pain sears through my head.

"I didn't say you could leave yet, you little slut."

"Tim, don't do this."

"I'm not doing anything. You're going to say yes."

"No, I'm not." The resolution in my voice is fractured as it shakes.

"We'll see about that." His pelvis presses against mine as his mouth latches onto my neck. I can't move; he has me pinned against the wall. I could scream, but I'm afraid of what he'll do.

One of his giant paws starts aggressively grabbing at my breast. It's uncomfortable and unpleasant, only made worse when I feel his erection pressing against me. For a minute, I think I'm going to be sick.

"See how much I want you? You can feel it now, you know you want it."

"No, I don't. I'm not going to. Let go of me." My voice is loud enough that if anybody is nearby, they'll hear me. But it's late, dark, and the meeting ended twenty minutes ago. I wonder what Dr. Ptansky will think of me being the hunted instead of the hunter. On some level, I'm sure I deserve it.

"You'll change your mind. That's what sluts do."

"I'm pretty sure she said no." I turn to the new, deep voice. It's Flynn. He's standing a couple feet away with hands calmly in his pockets. Even through the dim lighting in the alley, I can see fire dancing through his irises.

"Go away, kid, this doesn't concern you." Tim is still pressed against me. In fact, he hasn't even moved his hand from my breast.

Before anything happens, I know that was the wrong thing to say.

The fire in Flynn's eyes explodes as he grabs Tim by the collar and throws him backward, punching him in the jaw, before he tumbles to the ground.

My hand flies to my mouth. I've had guys fight over me, but never *for* me.

Flynn turns to look at me, hand outstretched in my direction. "Are you okay?" All I can do is nod.

Tim starts to get up, spitting blood. "That was a bad move, kid. She's a little slut. I just want my turn." Before I can blink, Tim's on the ground again and Flynn's shaking his hand. Seems the second punch didn't land as gracefully as the first.

He moves to stand over Tim, looming with his height and wide frame. I have no doubt Flynn is nothing but muscles under his shirt. "If you come near her again, I'll kill you." His words are solid, forceful. It doesn't matter that he says it in a leveled tone.

Tim spits in Flynn's direction, which causes him to stomp, hard, on Tim's leg as he cries out in pain. Without another look, Flynn walks over to me and puts his arm around my waist, pulling me from the wall and toward the street.

Once we've walked a few blocks, he drops his hand with a pinch, sliding his fingers across my back before slipping into his pocket. "Are you okay?" he inquires again.

"Yes. Thank you."

"Don't worry about it."

"No really, thank you." I rest my fingers against his forearm. He looks down at them but doesn't pull away.

I don't know Flynn well; I don't even know if it's his real name, but I can feel the anger rolling off him in waves.

"Where do you live? I'd like to make sure you get home safely." There's a grit to his voice.

"That's not necessary. I'll be okay."

"Christ, would you please just let me walk you home?" I don't want him to be put out, but his voice has such irritation in it that I eventually give in.

"Why are you being nice to me? I thought you hated me. You've been an asshole every therapy session for the past six weeks."

"I may have done some pretty shitty things in my time, but pushing myself on a woman who very clearly said no is not alright and never something I've done. And I'm an asshole to everybody."

"Oh, so I shouldn't feel special?" I'm teasing, a playfulness rising in my chest.

"Do you want to?" He gives me a sideways glance that makes my heart race and the playfulness evaporate. I hate that my body responds to him at all.

"So, what's your deal anyway? Mommy issues? Daddy issues? Oh, maybe both?" I decide to glaze over his question.

"Tell me yours and I'll tell you mine."

We aren't exactly banned from telling each other our deep dark secrets, but it's definitely frowned upon. It's more about talking about our day-to-day struggles, and successes. Talking each other down from the cliff or celebrating a victory. Not the whys, never the whys. It doesn't make any sense to me.

"Why don't we start simple? My name's not really Serena. It's Julienne, Jules." I don't know why I'm being so honest with him. But he just saved me, so I feel like I owe him something.

"Zaneth."

That's it? "So do people call you Zaneth or..."

"Well, it is my name." Maybe opening up was a mistake. But he softens in the next moment, a sigh escaping his mouth. "Zane. Most people call me Zane." He stares straight ahead as we keep a steady pace toward my apartment.

"Oh. By most people, you mean, like friends, or..." Why am I wondering if he has a girlfriend?

"If you want, you can call me Zaneth. Or you can call me Zane. Or stick with Flynn. Your choice."

I nod, frustrated with myself at the disappointment filling my chest that he didn't answer what I really wanted to know. "Good deal, good deal. Please don't call me Julienne. I hate it. Only my psychologist can call me Julienne. It's Jules. Or Serena."

"Not even your mother?"

"Huh?" Red-hot rage flows through my veins at the mention of my mother.

"You said only your psychologist can you call you Julienne. I'm asking if your mother isn't even allowed to call you that."

"She'd have to be around to call me anything." Why am I spilling all my secrets to him?

"Hmm."

We walk in silence for a few minutes, but I don't do well with silence. "What do you do?"

"For?"

I look at him, brow furrowed, for a minute before his eyes flash over to mine.

"For fun, for a living, for my birthday. It's not a specific question." The irritation at my existence is back in his voice. Granted, he has that tone almost every time we exchange words.

"Oh. For a living."

"Finance."

My eyes grow wide as I do a slow nod. "Wow. Exciting." He doesn't seem to be very interested in opening up.

With a shake of his head and a sigh, he continues, "I'm a financial investor. I help people make good investments to grow their portfolios, help set up for retirement, or just save their money responsibly. And work with companies that are struggling and need help to get back into the black." That explains why he's always in a suit.

"So, you're good with money." I realize it came out more of a statement than a question, but it certainly seems better that way. I don't really feel like I need to question it.

"You could say that."

When it's clear he's not going to ask me anything, I decide to keep imploring further.

"Where'd you go to college?"

"I graduated from Harvard with my bachelor's in finance and went to Columbia to get my MBA."

"So, you're like super smart too." I'd gone to Columbia myself for grad school, but he'd gotten into an Ivy League twice.

"I guess you could say that." Seems to be a preferred phrase of his.

"You don't like to talk about yourself much, do you?"

"No."

"Well, you could ask about me. If you want to know, that is. I guess you're not asking 'cause you don't." I'm not exactly sure where this willingness to share is even coming from on my part. Must be my need to fill the gaps and my social anxiety. Dr. Ptansky would be proud.

"Or you could just tell me." He turns to look at me. His eyes have softened in the few blocks we've walked. They seem lighter. Maybe it's just a play of the streetlights bouncing off them.

"Okay. Well, I went to state school to get my undergrad education degree. I came to the city to go to Columbia to get my Master's in education. I worked at a private school as a first-grade special ed teacher. But they weren't exactly understanding when things got...messy. So, now I'm a freelance writer. I get to work from home."

"Does that happen a lot? Things getting messy?" Did he really just ask me a question? About me? And if I'm not mistaken, it was even with a touch of concern.

"More than I'd like it to." I think back to some of what Flynn—er, Zane—has said during group. "So, anger, huh? What does that look like? Was that what happened in the alley?"

He snorts. "Hardly. That was me protecting a beautiful, innocent woman who clearly said no." Beautiful. He just said I'm beautiful. I hate that it makes my insides turn to mush.

"Do you act that way if somebody hits on your girlfriend?"

"Don't do that."

"Do what?"

"Beat around the bush like that. If you want to know something, ask."

"Do you have a girlfriend?"

"Do you care?" It's a good question. Do I care? If he doesn't, what would that mean? And if he does, it's not like I'm planning to sleep with him. Though, I don't usually plan it.

"I don't know. I guess maybe it depends on your answer," I answer as truthfully as I can.

"No, I don't have a girlfriend. Or fiancée, or wife."

"Good, good, good." I appreciate that he extended it to include any sort of commitment.

"And you? Do you have a boyfriend or some sort of man at home?"

"Do you care?" I shoot his response right back at him.

"I guess it depends on your answer." When he does the same thing, a strange sensation settles in my chest. I can't explain it, and I certainly can't figure out what it is. It's like a combination of excited and scared and intimidated and turned on, all at the same time.

"I do not currently have a boyfriend. But one of my...issues...has been sleeping with random men. I shared that, once, with the group before you got there. That's how...that's how, uh..."

"That's how *Tim* came to have you up against the wall." Clear disdain drips from his mouth as Tim's name leaves it.

While I'd prefer not to look at him, I can't control my gaze and glance out of the corner of my eye to see a clenched jaw.

"Yeah. It's not really a problem anymore. I've been doing really well, with that weakness at least, and haven't been in a relationship in a few months."

"I break things."

"Oh." I try to contain the surprise in my voice. Not from what he said—he told us that in group already—but more from the fact that he's sharing without prompting.

"Literally anything. I get into these fits of rage and just destroy anything I can. I don't keep glasses in my apartment because they just end up broken."

"So, you drink out of plastic cups?" My eyes narrow as I ponder this and wrap an arm across my chest to absently scratch at my shoulder.

"Yup."

"Why did you start coming to group therapy?"

"Are we getting close to your apartment?"

"Yeah, like six more blocks. Am I taking you far out of your way?" I ignore the fact that he dodged my question.

"No." He doesn't turn to look at me and there's no softness to his tone.

Not knowing what else to say, I leave the uncomfortable silence. Well, it's uncomfortable for me. I have no idea how he feels about it. Maybe he likes it.

"Do you have other behaviors?" My jaw almost drops when I hear his voice.

"I do."

"You don't have to tell me."

I swallow hard. There's something about him that makes me want to open up. I don't understand it. Maybe it's because I barely know him and only see him once a week where he seems equally not so thrilled to be sitting in the meeting. Somehow, I know he won't share anything I say.

"I self-harm. A lot. I used to drink, a lot, usually to black-out levels, which often meant I was waking up in bed with some random guy because I also used sex as an escape. I stopped drinking completely over a year ago after a slow and steady pullback. But I dissociate sometimes. That's pretty scary when it's something big and not like I walked to the store and don't remember the walk."

"Sounds like it."

He's not really giving me a lot to work with. Maybe he's okay with silence. But it's part of why I don't like being around people, the pauses in conversation where nobody quite knows what to say. It makes my skin crawl and I feel awkward existing. I can't even have quiet at home. There has to be a constant stream of sound, whether music or the TV.

"I really can walk the rest of the way myself. It's not much further."

"I'm walking you to your door, Jules." The sound of my name coming from his mouth makes my heart race. Is he expecting something from me? I mean, he did save me from Tim. Does that mean he now expects me to give him some sort of favor?

"I'm not inviting you upstairs."

"I'm not asking you to. You were basically attacked tonight. If I hadn't have stepped in, I'm sure Tim would have followed through. You think you're tough, but you wouldn't have been able to fight him off. I'm making sure you get home safely. And I'm going to walk you home from group from now on." There's a resoluteness in his eyes that matches his tone. I know I shouldn't argue with him, but I wouldn't be me if I didn't.

"You don't have to do that."

"I do a lot of things I don't have to do." I want to ask why he does them then, but I have a feeling I'll either get another dodged question or another response of few words.

"So, this sex thing you do. Are you that selective or just not with guys like me?" Is he really curious? I'd jump on him so fast his head would spin. He'd by far be the best-looking man I've ever had sex with.

"Actually, I don't do that at all anymore. For about a year now." I choose to leave out the part where I somewhat recently woke up with a strange man in Florida. He doesn't need to get to know me *that* well tonight. The fact that I didn't actually have sex is harder to believe, which is why Lance and I broke up.

"Wait, you haven't had sex in over a year?"

"Not exactly. I don't have random hookups anymore. Instead of having a bad day and going to a bar and getting drunk and taking a guy into the bathroom or his apartment, I just...don't. I had a boyfriend, for a little while. I'm allowed to have sex with a boyfriend, or even somebody I'm developing feelings for or have interest in. Just no random hookups."

"Allowed?"

I can't help but snort. "Oh, yeah. It's a rule from my psychologist. I had to find something else to replace it with. I chose baking."

With a quirked-up eyebrow, he glances over at me. "Baking?"

"Yeah. Something about keeping my hands busy. I don't know. I'm not very good at it, but the attention it takes distracts me...enough."

"Is it like an addiction or something?"

"No, not at all. It's more a self-destructive urge. I need to do something...bad...to myself. It's not as big of an issue as it sounds. Even with all the randomness, it still hasn't been a lot of guys, just more than it would have otherwise been. I went a little off the deep end when I was younger, starting in high school and just kind of followed through. My methods to get out of my head work but are not at all healthy. It's been a long hard process and I'm nowhere near better. But I'm slowly able to replace one bad habit." Man, I'm really just laying it all out there.

"Isn't it just a bad cycle, though? Doesn't doing one of those things make it worse?"

"Sometimes, yeah. Which is part of why I'm trying to distance myself from them. It's hard." I've opened up more to him in the fifteen-minute walk back to my apartment than I have in sixteen weeks of group therapy. I don't know why, or how he's done it. Especially since he doesn't give much in return. Maybe that's why, my need to have no silence keeps my mouth moving.

"I don't know. I don't understand myself. I hate myself, frequently, so I do something self-destructive, which makes me hate myself more. I feel numb so I do something that makes me feel *anything*: sex to feel good, even if for a few minutes, or cutting myself to feel pain. Sometimes the internal emotions are so strong, they need some sort of external outlet so I don't have to think about them. But it just continues the cycle because then I hate myself for doing those things." I gesture frantically with my hands, as though I'm trying to make some sort of visual that he can grab onto.

"You cut yourself?" I watch as his eyes glance down to my arms, the look of disapproval I've learned to recognize so well.

"Sometimes." I absentmindedly tug at my sleeves, but he doesn't skip a beat.

"I put my hand through a wall. More than once actually. A few windows. I had really nice crystal decanters and glasses. I don't anymore." He doesn't have to tell me what happened to them. I can deduce. He smashed them.

"Do you do it for the pain? The pain that comes from breaking something?"

"No. Do you ever get the urge to just break something?"

"Not really.

"Hmm. Interesting."

"What's *interesting*?"

"We don't necessarily understand each other, yet we probably still do on some level. Especially more so than 'normal' people."

I know exactly what he's talking about. Prior boyfriends, Daphne, even Dr. Ptansky. They'll never understand me the way somebody who goes through the same struggles will. They can't. They don't have to deal with it, fight with it. Dr. Ptansky is trained in how to help with it, but that doesn't mean she knows what it *feels* like.

This is what she had been talking about all those weeks ago when she urged me to start group therapy. Yet again, she's right.

My apartment door comes into view. While I'd spent a few weeks not even wanting Zane's eyes on me, for some reason, right now, I don't want to be out of his presence.

"Well, this is me," I declare as we get to my building. "Thanks for earlier. And for walking me home."

"Anytime. You may want to consider switching meetings. He may hang around for a while."

"I'll think it over."

He makes no move to walk away.

"Do you, uh, do you want to come up?" I'm going back on my word of not inviting him upstairs. Though I won't let it lead anywhere. I don't think.

"No. Not tonight." Not tonight. Does that mean some other night, he might?

"Oh, uh, okay."

"It's just...It's probably not a good idea if anything happens between us."

"Who says that's what I'm looking for?" Considering our conversation, I could see how he'd come to that conclusion.

"Maybe it's not you I'm worried about." His gaze locks with mine in a way that makes me want to shrink into the door, into myself. How does he do that? One tiny look and I want to disappear. But at the same time, I can't seem to look away.

I already know this man is going to wreck me.

Chapter 5

Zane

There is something undeniably attractive about Jules. Sure, she's gorgeous with her dark brown curls and chocolate brown eyes that have golden flecks scattered throughout the irises. In certain light, you can make out the slightest hint of freckles speckled across the bridge of her nose and under her eyes. Her great rack and ass are just added perks.

No, it's not her looks that make her attractive. It's the combination of her outward strength and deep insecurity and vulnerability. She thinks she's tough as shit. And maybe in some ways she is. I don't know what she's been through in her life. She thought she was fine after what happened with Tim, but I saw the slight tremble of her hands. I'm not even sure she was aware of it, but I noticed.

Her voice was also different, shakier. She talked...a lot. Whether that was nerves from Tim, or being alone with me, or that's how she is; I'm not sure. I hate that I can't wait to find out.

I don't date. I haven't in a long time and have no intentions of starting now. But Jules has made it clear that random sex isn't something she does anymore. It's a destructive habit for her, and I don't want to feed into that. I know what it's like to battle against yourself daily. Making things harder on her won't help either of us.

But some part of me, one that I have to lock away, is dying to know what she tastes like, what she feels like.

Dropping her off at her door was a lot more difficult than it should have been. I wasn't ready to be fully open with her on our walk, though, I still told her more than I've told anybody besides my psychologist in years. I'm not sure why that is.

As soon as I get home, I contact Layla and let her know what happened. Tim needs to be removed from the group immediately, and if she can't handle it, I'll be contacting the police. I'd have already done that, but it's hard enough to get them to do anything for an actual rape. I'm sure they'd laugh at me about an attempted one. It's pretty disgusting.

By the weekend, I find myself looking forward to seeing Jules again. Group has been nothing but a joke to me, but she makes it better, easier. The little game we've created makes it fun. I wasn't even trying to do anything like that; just being my normal asshole self. But she seemed to enjoy it. That makes her all the more intriguing.

I wonder how far I can take this. At the very least, maybe there's a way to use it to my advantage.

Chapter 6

Jules

The following week, I think our game is going to be over, but I know Zane is playing hardball when he flops into the chair to my right and immediately rests his knee against mine. Shifting away would give him reason to think he's won, that he's made me uncomfortable, and I can't stand his nearness. Staying may send a message that I'm interested in him. Which I'm not.

My nose is infiltrated by the scent of linen, sandalwood, and coffee. He's holding a cup from Mocha Matty's. With an arched brow, I slowly raise my gaze from his cup to his face.

With a similar face, he turns to me, brow arched, as he takes a sip. Pulling out the drink in his hand, he examines it with narrowed eyes, licking his lips once. I told him Land of Lattes was better.

Not wanting him to know that I'm gloating, I have to bite my cheek to keep a smirk from spreading across my face.

My back straightens and my body stiffens as he leans close to my ear. I hate that his closeness makes my heart race and my palms sweat. "I'll deny saying this to the very end. But you were right. Land of Lattes is better." His voice is like velvet in my ear, and a shiver works its way up my spine.

Slowly I turn to face him, my eyebrows raised and eyes wide, sure I must be imagining it. When I do, I notice how incredibly close his face is to mine. My eyes automatically drift to his lips, which he immediately picks up on, causing them to pull up at one corner.

I may not be able to compete with his games.

Leaning back slightly, I keep my expression flat. "I told you, I'm a coffee snob."

"Among other things," he says quietly as he moves back into his own space.

"Excuse me? Don't pretend that from a few meetings here and one walk home, you know *anything* about me except where I like to buy my coffee and the fact that I'm here with all of you lovely people." My tone is biting, but I'm not sure it's as much as I'd like. Yeah, maybe I told him a few things about me, but honestly nothing too deep, nothing that I didn't say here the one time I shared, aside from my real name, which I'm quickly realizing I may regret.

"I know I've been here for a few weeks, and you haven't spoken more than to turn down the invite to talk. And according to Sean, or whatever his name is, you basically don't."

"Shane. And what are you doing talking to him about me?" This is part of why I didn't want to come here. My life is nobody's business.

"I'm not. Trust me, I have no interest. He brought it up, seeing our little...exchange, a few weeks ago."

Narrowing my eyes, I glare at him. "And why exactly did Shane talk to *you*? What exactly was his thought process?"

"His exact words were, 'She's barely said more than two words after her second week and doesn't talk to or look at anybody. Except you.' So, I guess he thinks that because I've had an effect on you, that I'd be able to convince you to share or something. Not that I care."

"An effect on me? No, not even close." The short breaths and fluttering of my heart beg to differ.

"Is that why you spent the past few weeks staring at me and are squirming right now?"

"For one, I've only stared at you because there's nothing better to look at. And you are equally as guilty. For two, I don't like people in my personal space. In fact, I don't like people, period." Why am I sharing all of this with him? It's like he has a key to my innermost thoughts. I need to find a stronger lock.

"Interesting place to be for somebody who doesn't like people, considering it's a room filled with them, wanting to share personal life stories."

"I didn't really have a choice," I mumble as I cross my arms tight against my chest and sink lower in my chair. "Besides, you're here and haven't exactly been very forthcoming."

"I shared my first day."

"Barely."

"More than I can say for you."

"You just missed it."

He opens his mouth to retort when Shane stands in front of us. Zane's eyes darken, and his face contorts into a scowl.

"Hey, Flynn, Serena. Glad to see you're talking. Serena, sometimes I wonder if you're even able to talk." He laughs lightly as he rubs the back of his neck, clearly embarrassed. He's not unfortunate looking, with light brown curly hair kept short and amber eyes, a few inches taller than my five-foot-four. But he's shy and nervous around girls, or at least around me. I can't hold somebody's hand.

I absolutely despise the raised eyebrow and smirk that crosses Zane's face as he turns ever so slightly to look at me. It screams *I told you so.*

"I'm very capable, just choose not to. Thanks for your concern, though." I shoot him a shit-eating grin, tightening my arms against my chest. When his eyes flicker down, I, too, adjust my gaze and notice that my breasts are peeking over my arms, hinting at what's pressed down and what would be a nice cleavage glimpse if I was wearing a low-cut shirt.

I'm eternally thankful I'm not. Gliding higher in my chair, preparing to bite back at Shane, Zane jumps in.

"It's a little difficult for all of us to open up in a room full of strangers, no?" Out of the corner of my eye, I notice his gaze also drift to my chest, almost imperceptibly and ever so briefly. He's at least better at hiding it than Shane.

"I guess that's the point. The more you come here and share, the less like strangers we are and the more like family." Shane's wide smile is as if he's trying to invite us to join his cult. I have to physically force myself not to gag.

"Well, it's just easier for some than others. I'm sure our *Serena* here will open up at some point." At this last part, he puts his hand on my thigh, just above my knee, and rubs up and down, reaching a little higher than halfway.

This gives me two thoughts. One, he's playing dirty. But two can play at that game. He wants to add touching? Sure thing, buddy.

Two, the way he said Serena makes me worry he may try to give me away and let others know my real name. Or at the very least, that Serena isn't it.

Before Shane can say anything, Layla takes her seat. I consider it the front of the circle, which is a weird thought because circles have no front. But it's where our attentions draw. Shane skulks to the other side of the circle. Everybody has a usual seat, except for Zane, who has taken Jenny's.

I like Jenny; she's quiet and doesn't try to talk to me.

"You're welcome." Zane leans slightly toward my ear, speaking quietly as Layla starts by talking about her week. He hasn't removed his hand from my knee.

I shift in my seat, closer to Zane, as I retort back out of the corner of my mouth. "I have nothing to thank you for. I can take care of myself just fine."

"You would have scared the poor kid."

"I'm not sure how old you think I am, but Shane is older, by two years."

"It's pretty clear he has a thing for you, maybe you should give him a shot." Our heads are almost touching, we've leaned in that close.

Turning to him, I raise an eyebrow before leaning forward, resting one hand on the back of his chair, my fingertips brushing lightly over his back as my lips graze his ear. "I eat guys like him for breakfast. He wouldn't be able to handle me." As I lean back in my chair, I cross my legs, effectively removing Zane's hand from my knee, and trail my fingertips along his shoulders and down his arm ever so gently.

In my peripheral, I see him rub his bottom lip as a corner of my mouth tips up. For a second, I think maybe I've won. Until he leans into me again, arm stretched across the back of my seat, his scent and warmth positively infiltrating my mind.

"So, what you're saying is that only a real man can handle you?"

Tilting back, I give him a slow once-over before returning to answer. "You're not man enough."

The snort that comes out of his mouth makes me look around the room to make sure we're not being disruptive. I may not take it seriously, but some people do.

Stretching his arm further over the back of my chair and encroaching in my personal space again, he speaks low and gravelly in my ear. "Don't flatter yourself, sweetheart."

I have to bite my cheek to keep my mouth from hanging open. He'd be so lucky.

Right now, I want both to punch Zane and drag him into the bathroom to wipe that stupid, self-enamored grin off his face.

Instead, I have to use my words. Which can be scathing when done right.

"Well, I guess you'll never know what you're missing. I don't fuck guys who think they're God's gift to women. I've found they never measure up." I give a quick flick of my eyes to his crotch before returning to his glare. There's no other way to refer to it than a *glare.*

It's not from this jab, or the conversation. Aside from trying to rattle me, I've only ever seen a glare on Zane's face. I'm not sure he knows how to arrange his features in any other way. Even when he walked me home, that look was plastered to his face.

Layla starts wrapping up the meeting and I'm shocked an hour has passed so quickly. I'm thankful she didn't call on me this time.

"Flynn, Serena, would you two mind staying back for a moment?" Uh-oh.

As everybody files out, I slowly gather my things and walk over to Layla, who's standing near the snack table cleaning up.

"I don't mind that people form friendships in this group, in fact it's encouraged, but please keep it outside of the meeting hour." It's hard to take her seriously. She has to be around my age, if not younger.

"Sure thing, Layla. Sorry if we distracted anybody." I can be a good liar when I need to be.

"You didn't seem to, this time."

"And just to be clear, we're not friends. We won't be friends. We were just having a..."

"Discussion," Zane fills in for me. My skin prickles when I realize how close he's standing.

"Yes. A discussion. Won't happen again."

"All right. I appreciate it. See you both next week." When she turns back to her task, the conversation is finished, and we're effectively dismissed.

We walk out in silence and it's not until we push through the door and I shiver that Zane even looks at me.

I start before he can. "Game over. I may not take this very seriously, but I'm not going to fuck it up for people who do. So, whatever, you win." With that, I start stomping off towards my apartment, but Zane falls into step next to me.

"Giving up that easily? I expected more."

Gritting my teeth, I bite back my anger. He certainly knows how to get under my skin. I hate it. I hate how much I love it.

"Well, I'm not willing to bother other people. Plus, you never would have won otherwise." That may be a straight up lie; he was holding his own and there were times I was ready to fold, but he can't know that.

"I don't know, I think I was getting to you pretty good."

Rolling my eyes, I turn to look at him, noting again how tall he is. He has to be over six feet the way he towers over me.

"Oh please, *Flynn*." I say his name with the same inflection he used saying mine earlier. "All I'd have to do is wear tight pants and a low-cut shirt and you'd be putty in my hands."

"Possibly. I won't deny that I'd certainly enjoy it."

My feet freeze in place on the pavement. "Are you really going to walk me home again?"

He kept walking a few steps, so he turns around to look at me, hands in his pockets. "I said I would last week. One thing you'll learn about me is that I don't lie, and I'm a man of my word."

"Okay, well, while we're sharing things, I don't like silence. It makes me feel icky. So, if you're going to walk me home, you need to stop being such a Goddamn asshole."

"Oh, come on. A little banter is fun." His shoulders actually loosen, and the glare leaves his face, maybe even a hint of a smirk crossing his lips.

"Banter is one thing. We both know what was going on. This stupid game we were playing? It's over. So, if you can't talk to me like a pleasant human being, bring music next time." I start walking again, brushing right past him and intentionally crashing my shoulder into his bicep.

My steps are quick, but even if I was running, I'm sure Zane would be able to catch me in a few strides.

"Well, to continue on this honesty train we've jumped on, I don't talk a lot. I don't like opening up. But you're welcome to talk as much as you like. I'll add commentary where I can or feel it's necessary and answer any questions I'm comfortable answering. Deal?"

"Whatever."

"Okay, now hold up." He grabs my bicep as he stops and spins me toward him. "If I have to be pleasant, you do too. I'm just trying to make sure you're safe, Jules. Men like *Tim*, they don't always take the hint the first time. Which is why I still think you should find a different group."

I take a deep breath and sigh, my breath tendrils into the air like smoke, and I start a slow trek again. "Fine. First question. How old are you?"

"I'm twenty-eight."

"I'm twenty-six."

"I know."

My brow furrows quickly. "How do you know?"

"Shane and I discussed a little more than just that you don't talk. He and I are the same age. You told me today that he's two years older than you. I wasn't referring to him as a kid because of his age."

"Where are you from?" I'm moving on. If he's going to be walking me home every week, I'd like to know a little about who he actually is.

"New York. Born and raised."

"Me too. City?"

"Various parts." I guess he's not willing to be more detailed.

"Parents?"

"Yes, I do in fact have parents."

Glancing over at him, I can tell he's not going to give me more. Which is fine because I'm hoping he now doesn't deflect onto me. Parents are a sticky subject for me, and I'm sure I'm not alone in that.

"You said your mom's not around. Care to elaborate?" Guess I'm not so lucky tonight.

"Not yet. How long are you going to walk me home for?"

"I don't know. Maybe until I feel like it's safe for you to go alone. Maybe once Tim's been gone for a while. Unless at that point you'd like me to continue to. I don't live too far from you, so it's no trouble. Or you could switch meetings and then I wouldn't be a problem anymore."

I don't know what to say to that. It's more protective than anybody's ever been toward me in my life. I thought about switching meetings, but this has become part of my routine, which I have trouble changing, and part of me deflates at the thought of not seeing Zane anymore. I loathe that part of me.

"Well, I appreciate it." It comes out low and strained. I'm used to taking care of myself, and I'm not sure how I feel that somebody else is doing it for me. And not just doing it but wanting to. I'm nobody special.

The icky silence fills the next block. But I'm too stuck in my head to talk. Why is he being nice to me? Why is he walking me home? It's great that he's a good enough guy to stop Tim, but that doesn't mean he should feel guilty or like he has to walk me home every week now. I'm sure he has better things to do with his time than accompany me.

"What's wrong?"

"Huh?" I'm drawn from my swirling thoughts by the sound of Zane's voice. If I didn't know better, I'd say I heard concern in it.

"You seem...distracted. Like you're in your head."

"Oh. I guess I am."

"I hope it's not because I'm walking you home. Really, Jules, it's on my way. It's no trouble at all. I don't want you to be uncomfortable, but I'd really feel better walking you to your door." There's a softness to his tone I've yet to hear outside of him asking me if I was okay last week.

"It's okay. It's fine."

The silence lingers for two blocks, and I let it. Out of the corner of my eye, I see Zane look over at me every so many steps. At one point, I think he wants to say something but doesn't. How could he not? I just told him I don't like silence, and here we are, shrouded in it.

When we get to my building, I thank him again for walking me home and scurry inside before he can say anything more than you're welcome. I burst through my door in a haste, wanting to get out of my own skin, my own head.

My heart is racing, I feel like I can't catch my breath. I drop my things by the door and walk into the kitchen to get some water when my eyes dash to the knife block. I gulp down a few big sips, my gaze never straying.

Draining the glass, I wipe the back of my hand along my mouth and take the two quick steps to cross the counter, pulling out a knife and dragging it across my skin. It's not hard, it's not deep, just a few pricks of blood. But remorse and hatred instantly wrap around my heart, twisting through my veins.

Throwing the knife in the sink, I walk to the bathroom and wash my face, my arm, and angrily brush my teeth.

I'm mad at myself. I'm mad that I let Zane get to me. He's being nice and I'm feeling bad that he's being nice to me. I don't deserve it.

It's early still, no later than six-thirty, but I crawl under the blankets and block out the world.

Chapter 7

Zane

Jules seemed different tonight. Halfway back to her place, a strange look crossed over her face. I can only think of it as vacant.

My plan worked. I was able to find out more about her today. Sitting next to her was a great idea. Not only does she smell fucking fantastic—a mix of lavender and jasmine wrapped around her and what seems to be a lingering scent of coffee—but she's aware of how sexy she is and knows how to use it to her advantage. I had teased her about the effect I had on her, hoping she didn't turn the tables on me.

Her zing about measuring up was a good one. She thinks she has me all figured out. She doesn't. I haven't decided yet how much I'll be sharing with her on these walks. I told her I won't lie to her, and I mean it, but not answering isn't the same as lying.

It's pretty clear she thinks I'm some kind of ladies' man, taking my pick of the women that throw themselves at me daily, possibly more than one. When, in reality, I'm a recluse. I prefer to be home alone with a glass of scotch, whiskey, or bourbon at the end of a day of work. I haven't been to a bar in years. I don't see people outside of work besides my psychologist and now group, aside from the occasional game of basketball.

It's been months since I've had sex with somebody. It's never worth the hassle. And that's exactly what it is. Sure, sex is great. But getting somebody to leave, to not want more, it's not worth it.

But things can't be like that with Jules. I wouldn't encourage her bad behavior, just as much as I wouldn't want somebody to feed into mine. I haven't figured out how I'm going to resolve this ever-growing need quite yet.

As much as I try, I can't deny my attraction to her. I didn't sit next to her today to play games. I wasn't entirely sure Tim was actually going to be gone. I also wasn't sure what others knew. If he'd have shown up, there was absolutely no way I would've let him near her.

Getting the coffee from the other shop wasn't a dig or anything. I really just wanted to try it, see how it differed. She took it the wrong way. Though the banter was fun, Jules can certainly hold her own verbally.

The fact isn't lost on me that I'm sitting in my living room, swirling amber liquid in my glass, taking slow sips while thinking about her. The tumblers I have are the only glass I have in the apartment, and that's because I refuse to drink my poison out of anything else. Everything is replaceable, but I keep them locked in the bar to prevent destruction.

For the past few weeks, Jules has been a heavy focus of my nighttime wind down.

Puzzling is the only way I can describe it.

Chapter 8

Jules

"Jules, that's crazy. How are you?" Daphne's voice is so low I almost don't hear her over the sputtering of the milk frothing a few feet away from us. The Starbucks we meet at weekly is busy this morning.

"I told you, I'm fine." I say this in a low voice that matches hers as I try to poke holes in my coffee cup with my stare.

"Bullshit. There's no way you're fine."

My eyes bulge out of my head at Daphne's tone. It's a good thing my cup is on the table, or I would have dropped it, spilling my coffee. Which is sacrilege in my book. She *never* talks with such authority.

"Look, I was a little shaken up that night. But Zane walked me home and handled it. I don't know; his presence was calming in a way." Admitting it is the first step.

"Then why'd you wait two weeks to tell me?"

Guilt wraps its icy tendrils around my throat, and I shrink down in my chair at her calling me out. "I wasn't ready."

"But if it was no big deal, then you'd have been ready immediately."

"Okay, well, maybe it was more than I'll admit to myself. And I didn't want to do *this.*" I wave my hand at her but can't meet her eye, picking at the strip on the edge of the table instead.

A stern look, a huff, and three sips of coffee and she's ready to move on. "So, tell me more about Zane. You seem...intrigued."

The urge to slap myself rises as I sit up a little higher in my chair at the prospect of talking about him. "Intrigued is actually a really good word for how I feel. He's such an asshole, like really and truly. But he's also kind of sweet? I think? I'm not entirely sure. I mean he was pretty damn protective, but like, was he just being a good guy?"

"Well, he *is* still walking you home."

"I think he's worried about something else happening. I'm not sure."

"It sounds like the back and forth has been pretty intense."

"It was. I put a stop to it. I think. I hope." *Do I?* I despise myself for even wondering that.

"What are you going to do on Tuesday?" Daphne starts kicking the leg she has crossed over the other. This is her I'm-getting-good-gossip move.

"I have no idea. It went from staring at each other, to him saving me, to sitting next to me and trying to make me uncomfortable."

"Well, that's certainly hard to do."

"It wasn't so much what he was saying, but how he was saying it. Low and right in my ear." A tingle crawls up my spine at the thought of his breath warmly caressing my skin.

"Sounds hot."

"Honestly? It was. And Daph, he's *gorgeous.* Like, by far he'd be the best-looking man I have ever been with."

"Jules." There, that's her warning tone.

I finally look at her. "I'm not going to, Daphne. As much as I may want to, because trust me I'm sure it would be worth it, I won't. I haven't done that in a long time, and I don't regret it or miss it. If anything, I regret those days, those actions. I'm not going to go back to that." There's a swelling in my chest and I sit up a little straighter at my words.

"That's great, Jules. Really."

"What about you? Tell me about you. I don't want to talk about Zane anymore." *I'd rather daydream about him.*

"There's nothing going on with me that's even remotely close to being exciting." Her tone is grim. Poor Daphne has been struggling in the men department lately.

"What about that guy you went out with last weekend?" I try to add some lightness to my tone to indicate hopefulness.

She waves her hand like she's flicking through a plume of smoke. "I told you, he was boring. And smelled weird."

"Well, they can't all be winners."

"How does Zane smell?"

"Really, Daph?" I can't help the tiny smirk that crosses my lips as my fingers busy themselves picking at the cardboard sleeve on my cup.

"I mean, sometimes a man's smell tells you everything you need to know."

I let it simmer for a second before I answer in a quiet voice. "Clean, like linen, with a hint of sandalwood. And usually, coffee because he's been bringing coffee to the meetings."

"So not like dirty feet?"

"No, not even a little." The thought of his scent makes my nose tingle and brings the memories from the last session rushing through my brain like a freight train. His nearness, the sound of his voice, his warmth enveloping me. My chest inflates like a balloon.

Clearing my throat, I take the last little sip of my coffee and stand. "Sorry, Daph, I have some work to get to before Monday."

"Oh, no problem. I expect some new information by Thursday. Friday at the latest."

"I'm hoping nothing interesting happens. Just a session and a walk home with neutral conversation. But yes, I will let you know."

We toss our cups and leave the shop, giving each other a quick hug before going our separate ways. Daphne is my sounding board. She has been with me through so much and so many ups and downs, often more downs than ups. I'm sure she can see right through me. And what she sees is way more than just intrigue.

I decide to do something that I think is nice for Zane. I bake him some muffins. It helps distract my mind from the swirling thoughts of him being kind to me for pity. I'm sure that's all it is, but the negative thoughts of why a guy like him would be interested in a girl like me sends me falling down the rabbit hole and into a dangerous area.

Slouching in my chair, sipping my coffee, I wait to see what tonight will bring. I have no idea whether Zane is going to sit next to me or take his place on the opposite side of the room. Will he taunt me and tease me with his nearness and sexy banter? I don't have to wait long for my answer as Zane strolls in, eyes locking on mine immediately. He holds a Land of Lattes signature sky-blue cup in his hands. My pulse quickens as he walks right over to me.

When he opens his suit jacket and lays it across the back of his chair, I note the gray shirt he's wearing today and how it matches his eyes almost exactly. My heart beats so erratically I'm sure he'd be able to see my neck jumping as blood rushes through my body.

The muffins are in a plastic bag in my purse, which is set on the floor. I'll give him some after the meeting.

So far, I'm met with silence. Before I have a chance to wonder how long it will last, he leans in slightly. Sandalwood, linen, coffee and warmth infiltrate my senses. "Hi."

That's all he says. One simple word, one syllable. So why does it feel like so much more?

"Hi." God, I feel like a silly schoolgirl. Suddenly I can't talk to him?

"How was your weekend?" Is he making small talk? I actually wasn't sure he knew how.

"Fine. Yours?"

"Also fine. Do anything exciting?"

"I have a standing coffee date with my best friend every Saturday. You?"

"Played basketball with a couple guys. Something I do every so often when I just need to get out of my apartment. I kind of prefer to be alone."

I lean back to check his face to make sure he's not trying to make fun of me. His brow furrows the longer I stare. "What's the look for?" He waves his hand toward me as he asks.

"Nothing. I just like to be alone too. I wasn't sure if you were making fun of me or something."

"For one, I didn't know that you also preferred to be by yourself, though it's glaringly obvious if I think about it. Two, I'd never make fun of you. At least not about something like that." There's the touch of snarkiness I've grown accustomed to. I readjust my position so I'm sitting normally again, his face still close to mine.

"Well, I guess I'm also surprised you played basketball with other people. You don't seem like you play nice with others."

"Never said I did. I just like the physical aspect. And I could say the same for you."

"I don't either. I basically have the one friend. She's been with me through a lot. Seen me at my worst." Admiration and love swell within me. Daphne has been my one constant, and it's nice to be able to tell other people about that.

"It's good to have somebody like that."

"Do you?"

His jaw tightens and he cuffs the wrist holding his cup. "Not anymore." The way he says it I know there's definitely a story there, but I won't press.

Taking a slow sip of my coffee, I'm not quite sure what to say to continue the conversation. When I adjust in my chair, I hear a quiet chuckle.

Turning to Zane, he's shaking his head while bringing his cup to his mouth, a slight smile gracing his lips.

"What's so amusing?" My eyes narrow as my nose scrunches.

"You."

"What about me exactly?"

"You mentioned on our walk home you don't like silence. Our conversation wanes for a second or so and you're squirming in your seat already. Yet, you spend most of the meeting not talking to anybody."

"Yes, but other people talk. They share. I have that to listen to during a meeting." Not that I typically pay attention or listen, but it is there.

"Ah, but there's the background din of everybody else right now, so, not silence. Listen Ju-Serena. There are people talking all around us."

My teeth clamp together and the blood pools at my feet when it hits me that he almost used my real name. Even though people are carrying on in their own conversations, I wouldn't want somebody to overhear.

"Or maybe you just enjoy talking to me and my company." I don't even have to look at him to know he has a smug smirk on his face.

I snort as I refuse to accept this as fact.

"Break anything this week?" I'm not sure why this is the first thing that jumps from my lips as I try to change the subject.

"No. Cut yourself this week?" He doesn't skip a beat. But his words are a shameful reminder.

Instead of answering, I look away, sliding low in my seat while I ball the hem of my sleeves into my hands.

"Jules, shit, I'm sor—" His voice is low, quiet enough where unless somebody was in my lap, only I can hear him. But he's cut off when Layla welcomes everybody.

We spend the meeting without any banter or conversation. I can't even look at him. It's going to make our walk home very awkward. Maybe I can get out of it.

Ha. That's funny. I don't know him well, but I have no doubt he'd follow me out if I were to get up and leave this very second.

Instead, I settle in for the meeting. Every so often, I'll feel him shift in his seat next to me. But I don't warrant even a glance in his direction. I can't. I'm afraid to see the disappointment that always exists in moments like this. It's the look I hate most, and I can't stand to see it from somebody who struggles like I do. That makes it worse.

It's one thing if it's Daphne or Dr. Ptansky. But not people like me. I do my damnedest to keep my face neutral when somebody in group says something about having a weak moment, when I'm listening that is.

And for some strange reason, it tangles around my ribs just a little more that I'm worried about it coming from Zane. I don't know what it means, but I can't stand that it means *something*.

I spend the better part of the meeting keeping my eyes on my clothes. In my right hand, I hold my cup, sleeve still pulled around my hand. With my left, I pick fuzzes off my loose sweater.

When an elbow jabs into my right arm, I jump, my face flying to Zane's. Eyes wide, he juts his chin imperceptibly toward Layla.

I turn to face her. "Sorry, what?"

"I was asking if you wanted to share today?"

"Oh, no thanks."

"You seem a little distracted. Is everything okay?"

Sitting up straighter in my chair, I sense Zane tense next to me. Maybe he's wondering if I'm going to share about my moment of weakness over the past week. Maybe he thinks I'm going to share about Tim.

I'm not going to talk about any of it.

"Everything's fine. I was just thinking about work. Please continue."

"Now, Serena, you know this is a safe place. You can talk to us." Layla's voice is disgustingly sweet and syrupy. *If* I was going to talk to people about what I was thinking or feeling, this room does not hold any contenders. Except possibly one who only talks to me out of pity. *Great choice, Jules.*

"I think you'll feel better if you open up. It takes one time to share, which may be uncomfortable, but once you push past that, I think you'll see that the flood gates open and—"

"She said no, damn it!" Zane's voice booms next to me and silence settles over the room like a leaden cloud. It almost seems like everybody stopped breathing, including me.

Clearing her throat, Layla continues, "I think that's enough for tonight. We'll end here. See you all next week." Her voice is low and shaky. I wonder if she's scared of Zane. I'm sure she knows all of our backgrounds, our diagnoses. She doesn't seem like she does well with being challenged or yelled at. I hope she doesn't cry.

But the thought pushing into the forefront of my mind is, why did he do that? I have a twenty-minute walk to find out.

Everybody around us starts to gather their things, but Zane and I sit back. He makes no move to get up. I still can't make eye contact with him, but when I shift and move to stand, he places a hand gently on my forearm.

Steeling myself, I meet his gaze. But I don't find the sentiment I thought I would. There's no sign of disappointment, no sign of sadness that comes from noting another's failure. Instead, I find irritation and concern.

"You ready?" No mention of either incident. He seems ready to move on. *Good.*

"Absolutely." Standing, I grab my coat and bag from the floor. Zane takes my cup from my hand as I slip my coat on. My gaze stays locked on his at this simple and kind gesture. This time of year requires more planning than I like. For mid-March, it's a cold day, requiring a sweater and coat. But three days ago, I almost got my shorts out.

Zane dons a charcoal peacoat but leaves it unbuttoned. He jerks his head toward the door and starts walking, tossing our cups into the trash on the way. He doesn't acknowledge Layla on our way out, even though she turns to us.

Holding the door open, I slip past him, brushing against his chest. Just the lightest of touches, but it shoots a current through my entire body. *Dammit, why is my body reacting in such a way?*

Once we're on the street, Zane stops, touching my arm so I halt. In his other hand, he holds out an iPod with earbuds. My brows bunch together as I look at him. "You said if I wasn't going to be pleasant, I should bring music. Since your definition and mine are likely different, I figured I'd cover my bases."

Rolling my eyes, I start walking again. He quickly catches up with a smirk on his face. He just thinks he's *so* hilarious. A part of me wonders what sort of music he listens to. But another part of me yells at the first part for having any interest in the first place.

Before he can say anything else, I procure the bag of muffins from my bag and hold it on one hand. "I made you something. As a thank you for walking me home."

"Jules, I told you it's not a big deal. You didn't have to do this."

I shrug. "You may not feel like it's anything special when you try them." I haven't yet, but I know my skills are pretty lacking.

He quirks up an eyebrow and stares at the bag for a minute before holding his hand out, palm up. I stop so I can open the bag and pull a muffin out, placing it gently in his hand. He eyes it carefully, turning it from side to side before taking a hesitant bite.

When he doesn't start sputtering or choking, I assume they're okay. Until I hear a loud crunch. That's not supposed to happen in a muffin. *Fuck.*

I quickly dig a napkin out of my bag, thanking myself for the forethought of taking my larger one and not just for carrying the muffins. This thing's a giant black hole and I always grab a handful of napkins when I get coffee.

Upon taking the brown paper, he promptly spits his bite into it, moving around the half-chewed food until he finds what he's looking for. Tapping it, he holds it up for my inspection.

"Typically, you don't include the shell with the eggs." He balls up the napkin and walks a few paces to the nearest garbage can, tossing it in the trash with the rest of the muffin.

When I reach him, I toss the whole bag in. "Well, I told you I wasn't very good at baking."

Brushing his hands off, he starts walking in the direction of my apartment. "Did you need a distraction that badly? It didn't seem to work if you did."

"Different days. And yes, I did."

"What made you decide to make muffins for me?" His hands have found their usual home in his pockets, only this time it's his coat pockets. The weather had been decent enough that he could get away with just his suit coat. We're in an unusual cold snap.

I'm colder than I'd like to admit.

"I told you, to say thank you. For walking me home."

"So, you were thinking about me?"

"Of course you would twist it as such." I was, though. All week. As much as I didn't want to, as much as I wished I could forget him, I've thought about him every single day since he said goodbye to me at my door seven days ago.

"I'm not really sure what to think. I've never had a girl bake for me before. Even if it was terrible."

"Hey! Don't be a dick about it. The sentiment behind it was nice. Be thankful it was only a piece of eggshell." While I want to be offended, it's hard to be when he's right.

"So, you had a rough week?" There's a tentativeness in his voice I haven't heard before.

"I don't want to talk about it." I turn away, eyes planted on the ground. A shiver racks through my body as my hair whips around my face, a tendril sliding to my lips. A moment later Zane makes the tiniest of shifts closer to me, and I sense warmth rolling in my direction.

With my next step, I move my foot closer to him, needing more heat. I should have worn a warmer coat. I wasn't expecting the temperature to plummet so much once the sun set.

The slight glimmer of extra heat stops the chill rattling my bones, but I pick up my pace, pulling my coat tighter around me.

"You can talk to me you know. About...anything. I know you have your friend and your psychologist, but I'd be willing to listen. I don't know anything about them, or your life really, but I do know how helpful it can be to have somebody who gets it in your corner."

"I thought you said you don't like people."

"I'm pretty sure I just insinuated it. But either way, I had a friend, and it was just nice to be able to talk to somebody who at least gets it on some level."

Had. The way his jaw is clenched and his eyes are narrowed, I can see it's still a sensitive subject.

"I appreciate that. But I don't really talk about it."

"Does your psychologist know?" He angles his body in my direction as he speaks.

"She does. It's one of my rules. I have to inform her."

"Have you ever tried to hide it?"

"Once. I have a bad tell, as you saw for yourself tonight." Habitually, I take my sleeves in my hands. The fact that he knows that little tidbit about me sets an unease in my bones.

"Not exactly discreet if you're trying to hide something, but maybe that's for the best."

"Well, after that, she told me I have to tell her. She and Daphne are basically the only people who I trust enough to talk to and be myself with. I don't feel like I have to hide. Dr. P has really helped me a lot. I was in a...*bad* place when I started seeing her. And it was from Daphne's begging that I sought help at all. After all she's been through with me, I had to do it for her."

"It takes a certain something to take that step."

I'm sure we both had our bottom moments. The ones that caused us to seek help in the first place. It's hard to admit that you need it, that what you're going through won't just pass. I've been cynical, anxious, depressed, numb, for almost as long as I can remember.

Early on with Dr. Ptansky, I tried a few meds, but they made me feel weird and off. I didn't like it. She was willing to let me try just therapy but said that if she didn't see a difference, she'd have to insist. It took a while, but I started making changes.

I don't know Zane well enough to tell him my bottom. And I certainly won't ask him his. Who knows though, by the time he feels comfortable letting me walk alone, maybe we'll know the answers to the deep questions.

When we get to my building, Zane hesitates as I'm about to burst through the door, ready to run upstairs and take a hot shower to thaw my frozen body.

"Here," he says, holding out a business card. "If you ever need, or want, to talk. Like I said, I'm happy to listen. Even if it's the middle of the night. People like us, we shouldn't have to struggle alone."

Carefully, I take the card. It's simple. Heavy, white, with a dark border. *Zane Montgomery*. So that's his last name.

"Kline."

"What?" His brow furrows and mouth hangs slightly agape.

"My last name. It's Kline. I, uh, I just realized we'd never really exchanged that until I got your card. I guess I'm just trying to keep the playing field level."

"Oh. Well, I appreciate that. Good night, Jules Kline." I'm suddenly not feeling so cold anymore as my name slides off his tongue.

"Thanks for the walk home, Zane Montgomery."

"Until next week." And with that, he turns and leaves. I can't tear my eyes from his back as he dips his head and walks away, hands in his pockets. I don't know why, but I'm already looking forward to next week.

Chapter 9

Jules

"What it sounds like to me is you're still not taking group therapy seriously. Julienne, it's been over four months." I've come to recognize the tone from Dr. Ptansky as disapproval. It's probably the one I hear most frequently.

"I feel like I've made some progress, though."

"You self-harmed a week ago."

"Yes, but only once." I hold my finger up as a sign of the one time, like it's a huge victory. The tightness in my muscles tells me I know it's not.

Dr. Ptansky pinches the bridge of her nose and takes a deep breath. I tend to have this effect on her. I often wonder why she doesn't dismiss me as a patient. I actually asked her once. She had said that it took something truly terrible for her to stop seeing a patient, not just frustration. I tried to joke about her admitting that I frustrate her. She didn't find it amusing.

"Talk to me more about this Zane gentleman."

"I don't have much to say." Looking down at my lap, I pick at the hem of my shirt.

"Well, his name came up several times in the last"—she looks quickly at her watch—"forty-five minutes."

I shrink into the couch a little bit. It irritates me that his name flowed off my tongue so easily and frequently. For two days, I've been trying not to think about him. And for two days, I've been failing.

"I don't know, our conversations are getting easier. He still seems like an asshole most of the time, but there was something...different on Tuesday. He said something about how he *had* a friend. I don't know, the word just stuck out to me."

"What did he mean by that?"

"He didn't offer. I didn't ask."

When she doesn't say anything, I know she's waiting for me to continue. But I don't know what to say. Nothing sounds right, nothing about it makes sense.

"I'm confused." It's the most basic of truths.

"About?"

My eyes roll to the ceiling. Orange streaks stretch across the length of the white expanse above me.

"All of it. I don't quite understand what's going on. Is it pity? Does he just feel bad for me? The sad girl who almost got raped in the alley, too weak to defend herself. Is he playing the long game, hoping to wear me down to have sex with me because he knows that was a weakness at one point? Or is there some other reason?"

"Maybe he just wants to get to know you."

I snort at her suggestion. It's crazier than I am.

"Julienne, there are people who want to get to know you. You may not always want to reciprocate, but this isn't the first time I'm telling you. What I am advising, though, is to not be so closed off to him. I know you've been sharing, but you seem to think he has some agenda that can't possibly be getting to know you. You're a lovely girl, Julienne. And after all this time of us working together, I wish you were closer to believing that."

I look at my hands knotted in my lap as I squirm under the scrutiny. I don't do well with compliments, worse when Doctor P scolds me. She just did both.

She's the closest thing I have to a mother. Her thoughts and opinions of me matter, as much as I wish they didn't.

"Our time is up for today. But Julienne, please give yourself a chance to be open. I'm not saying Zane is somebody you'll have an interest in, or that you even should date somebody who's in group with you, but give yourself the chance to get to know him, let him get to know you. Maybe you'll find a new friend."

"Sure. I'll keep that in mind." Standing, I walk out, feeling more confused than when I got here.

Things are no better once I'm home. I pace my apartment, thoughts jumping around from what Doctor P said, what Daphne's said, to Zane. Why is he sticking in my mind so much? It's not even his looks that come to the forefront, though those certainly help.

I consider baking again, busying my brain and my hands, but it just reminds me of the muffins I made for Zane. I should find another hobby; I'm not very good at this one.

Sometimes working from home has its disadvantages. I'm stuck in my apartment most of the time. Sure, I could go into the small office that most of my assignments come from, but part of why I started working from home is to not be around other people.

As I'm making what has to be at least my twentieth pass by the entrance table while trying to repurpose the current coursing through me, I spot the corner of a simple white business card. I pluck it from under my purse.

Chewing my lip, I contemplate the card, like it holds the answers to my never-ending questions. Before I can second-guess myself, I grab my phone from the counter and type out a quick text message.

Me: *Hi. It's Jules.*

When the phone doesn't immediately ping back, disappointment seizes my chest. Then my teeth clench together at the first feeling.

Growling at my phone and my stupidity, I slam it back onto the counter, heading down the hallway with the intention to take my emotions out on the bathroom. It could use a good scrub.

I'm about halfway down the hall when my phone dings. Flipping around, I almost trip over my feet as I run to grab it. *Stupid, stupid, stupid. Don't catch feelings. Don't be excited.*

Zane: *Well hi there. Everything ok?*

I understand why he'd ask that. He had given me his card saying if I ever needed to talk, I could reach out. All after finding out I'd cut myself. He probably thinks I'm having a bad day and need some help. I'm not. Yet, at least.

Me: *Yeah. Everything's fine. Just wanted to say hi.*

Zane: *Oh. So you were thinking about me then huh?*

My jaw hurts from the pressure of teeth against teeth. He would have a comeback like that.

Me: *I just wanted to let you know I decided to give up on baking. Going to find a new hobby.*

Zane: *That's probably for the best. For me at least.*

My whole body freezes. Why for him?

Zane: *Don't need any more thank you eggshell muffins. I don't mind walking you home. Some conversation is nice. I mostly only have it at work, which gets old.*

Me: *I'm mostly alone, so yeah it is.*

Me: *Any suggestions for a new hobby?*

Zane: *Hmm. Maybe give me a few days to think about it. I'm thinking anything involving cooking isn't the best idea. That's my go-to.*

He cooks? I'm finding that messaging him was a very good idea. Especially with the lightness in my chest.

Me: *I mean, I have to feed myself so I can in fact cook.*

Zane: *Well?*

Me: *I guess that's subjective.*

Zane: *Maybe I'll get to find out for myself some time.*

My eyes grow wide, and my pulse hastens. My fingers are far too shaky to type out a new response, not that I even know what to say to that.

Me: *Yeah. Maybe.*

I leave it at that.

Me: *I was about to scrub the bathroom. I just wanted to let you know about dropping the baking. I'll, uh, see you Tuesday.*

I don't wait for his response as I drop my phone on the counter, turning it to silent first.

Donning my yellow gloves, I start spraying the bathroom, scrubbing until a light layer of wetness coats my body. *Maybe I'll get to find out for myself some time.* That message plays over and over in mind.

I scrub like I'm trying to erase it from memory. What does it even mean? *What the hell does it mean?*

Chapter 10

Zane

Looking at my phone, I'm wondering if I said something wrong. Jules jumped off quickly and my last message sits unread.

When I first realized who messaged me, tension immediately worked its way through my muscles. Penelope had made sure everything was all right when a scowl took over my face. I'm not exactly sure why, it's not an unusual look for me. Especially at work.

"Mr. Linkston is on line one for you, sir." Penelope draws my attention from the phone in my hand as she pokes her head in. She prefers to give me the personal message instead of using the speaker. I'm pretty sure it's because on her first day, she walked in while I was giving myself a quick shirt change.

She's an attractive woman with long straight blonde hair and large round blue eyes. But not my type. And I definitely don't dip into the pool at work.

"Everything okay, sir?"

"Penelope, I've told you it's unnecessary to call me sir. Mr. Montgomery or even Zane is fine." My eyes flick up just in time to see her cheeks pink.

"Absolutely, si—Mr. Montgomery. Line one." She closes the door on her way out.

For the rest of the day, my mind is in a haze. And the primary focus is somebody I shouldn't want.

I 'm surprised I've never run into Jules at Land of Lattes. It's been a few weeks that we've both been coming here before the same meeting. I don't care to admit how long it takes me to realize she's always at the meetings before me.

Today, I'm going to go over early. As soon as I walk in, I see her delicate dark curls that fall halfway down her back. A lightness wraps around me.

Michelle, the barista, juts her chin toward me, and I nod, a silent question and answer. She flirted shamelessly my first day here and has since memorized my coffee order. A large black coffee isn't that difficult, I suppose.

Jules must have ordered something a little different as Michelle carries mine over to register, where Jules still waits. I stand behind her.

"That'll be two dollars." Michelle adds a little too much sugar to her tone but her eyes glance nervously between me and Jules, noticing that I'm standing quite close to her. Jules either doesn't sense my presence or is dutifully ignoring me. It's probably the latter.

"Hers, too," I say as I casually place my hand on her shoulder. I'm taking a risk and hoping it pays off.

As she spins around to face me, her warm eyes wide, I again note our height difference. She has to be around five-foot-five, max. I kind of like it. I shouldn't, but I do.

"You don't have to do that." It's the first thing she says. No hi, no thank you. But I'd expect nothing less.

"I do a lot of things I don—"

"Have to. Yeah, I remember. Buying my coffee doesn't need to fall into that category."

"Consider it a thank you for helping me find something drinkable for the meetings."

Her eyes narrow as she shifts on her feet. I slide my hands into my pockets, awaiting the comeback, and allow my eyes to slowly graze down her frame. It's warmed up a little compared to last week. Her coat's unbuttoned and she has on a deep maroon V-neck lightweight sweater with dark jeans. The twinge that settles in my pants doesn't surprise me. There's a very thin silver chain that hangs at her collarbone. It has a J hanging in the center. How have I never noticed it before?

"I seem to recall you saying that you would have found it just fine on your own."

"Ah, I did say that, didn't I. Well then, consider it a thank you for the muffins."

She cocks up an eyebrow at me. "You mean the disgusting muffins you spit out?"

I'm getting slightly frustrated. She certainly likes to challenge me. But can't she just take the coffee? Why does there have to be meaning behind it? There isn't. Right?

"Jules. Just accept the damn coffee, would you?"

"Fine." It comes through gritted teeth. At the moment, I echo her sentiment and wish I hadn't offered. Even more so, I wish I hadn't met her here.

After I pay and then hold the door to the meeting room open, her voice raises to my ears ever so quietly as she walks under my arm. "Thank you."

I raise an eyebrow, not quite sure what she's thanking me for, but she tilts her head and holds up the coffee. Maybe it's for everything. I kind of think she hates saying it. From the little I've gotten to know her, it seems like she's been relying on herself for a while. As have I.

We take our usual seats on the far side of the circle. My assumption is she likes being able to see the door, knowing her escape route. She seems like a flight risk.

Jules doesn't make eye contact, doesn't say anything, but her body is angled the slightest bit toward me. It's so subtle I'm not even sure she notices she's done it. I'm also not sure how I feel about it.

Okay, that's not true. I like that she's feeling more comfortable, but I know I shouldn't. I guess we could become friends or something. But it's probably better if we don't.

I should start putting some distance between us. Go back to just being the asshole I am. It'll be hard; she brings out that softer side of me that so few get to see.

The session goes by uneventfully. I fight not to look at her, my gaze drifting from the speaker to the posters on the walls. Every so often I'm unsuccessful and slide a quick glance her way. We say nothing to each other. It's better this way.

It's better this way.

As the meeting ends and people leave, I wait for Jules as she puts her coat on. When she tries to free her hair from the collar of her coat, a small section catches, and she winces. Feeling around, she touches what I can now see, as I followed her finger trail. Her hair is tangled in her necklace. She'd been running it back and forth during the meeting, sometimes tucking the J into her mouth.

She flinches back when I reach over, causing me to lower my hands slightly. Hardening my mouth into a line, I take a deep breath and reach out again. "Here, let me help you."

This time, she doesn't move away. Trying to assess the damage, I see that it's only twisted a few times, and working quickly, I'm able to set her free. My fingers only graze her skin twice. I swallow down the tingles that start in the pads of my fingers and shoot through my body at each gentle touch.

"Thank you," she says quietly as she touches the J that sits just above her sternum.

I hold my questions until we're out on the road, away from others and their always listening ears.

"That's pretty. I've never noticed it before." I point to the necklace to be sure she knows what I'm talking about.

"I don't always wear it."

"J for Julienne?" I'm taking a chance with this question. And using her real name.

She stiffens before she answers. "Sort of. It used to have two Js on it. One for me and one for my aunt. Her name was Juliette. I was actually named after her, obviously with the slightest change. She was my mom's older sister. They were really close when I was born, and my aunt had always done a lot for my mom growing up. My parents wanted to honor her. It was a present from her when I graduated high school. She used to call me her JuJu, a combination of our names." Turning to point at me, she very sternly says, "You are, under no circumstance, allowed to repeat that name. Ever."

I wouldn't do that with what is clearly a personal name. It's also impossible to ignore that she said her aunt's name *was* Juliette.

There's a question sitting on the tip of my tongue, but I have to bite it back. When I had referred to somebody important to me in the past tense a week ago, she didn't question me. It's only fair I do the same.

"Well, I like it. And that's a nice story. Also, sorry for using your real name. Don't hold it against me."

"I guess I can let it slide this one time." A smirk picks at the corners of my lips as I turn to look at her, but it's gone just as quickly. Her face is drawn, looking at the ground.

"How come you don't smile?"

"I don't do that."

"Do what, smile?" I'm confused.

"Happy." When she locks her eyes on mine and they're hard and serious, it's like a punch in the stomach. I suddenly feel like I can't get enough oxygen. She says it so resolutely.

Even if I wanted to ask for more, I wouldn't know what to say. How do you ask a follow-up to an answer like that?

A woman like Jules is too beautiful not to smile.

"Thank you again. For the coffee. And the hair. And walking me home. I guess for a lot of things." Her tone is rough and choppy. Like it's hard for her to get the words out.

I'm slightly taken aback by her words, still a little dazed from her confession. "Oh, uh, you're welcome. Happy to do all of the above."

I know she doesn't like the silence, but I don't know how to carry on the conversation. I'm distracted by the voice in my head that's screaming at me to do anything I can to make her smile.

It's a dangerous thought. I have to push it away. This is to make sure she's safe. Guys like Tim will try again. But that's all this can be.

Right?

Chapter 11

Jules

Zane and I exchange a few messages over the week. I hate that my heart flutters every single time my phone dings. I hate it even more when my chest deflates if it's not him.

This is bad. All kinds of bad. I know what Dr. P said, but I also know that I don't want to have feelings for him. And that's exactly what it seems is happening.

When I get to Land of Lattes on Tuesday, he's leaning against the building, one foot resting against the wall. There's a coffee in each of his hands.

"Here. I got your order." He holds a cup out to me.

Stopping in my tracks, I look at the coffee, then his face, then back at the coffee. I make no move to take it.

His eyes narrow at me. "What?"

"How did you know my order?"

"I asked Michelle."

"She doesn't know my name."

He sighs and shifts on his feet, the buttons on his shirt straining against his deep breath. "I didn't mention you by name. I just asked about the beautiful brunette with the curly hair who I was in with last time."

Beautiful. Did he just call me beautiful? Again? Is that why my pulse has quickened?

"I don't think I should take it."

"Why?"

"Because I don't know if I like the message it sends."

"And what is that exactly?"

Honestly, I'm not sure. But it doesn't seem innocent. I may have let him buy my coffee last time, but I was at least present for the purchase.

"Nothing can happen here, Zane."

"I'm not sure what you think is going on, but all I did was buy you a coffee. It doesn't mean I'm asking you out, developing feelings, or trying to get in your pants. It's just coffee."

"Well, maybe in my mind, buying coffee for me *is* like trying to get in my pants." Really, a sure-fire way to get me to at least consider it. Coffee is my love language.

He sighs audibly as he tilts his head to the side. The look on his face screams that he thinks I'm being ridiculous.

"Fine," I mumble as I snatch the coffee from his hand. Thankfully, it's still relatively warm. "Thank you."

"You're welcome. I know that's hard for you to say."

Taking what appears to be an angry sip of his coffee, Zane starts walking toward the alley, and I fall into step beside him.

"How do you know it's hard for me to say that?"

"Because you practically look pained every time you do." The scathing back and forth will help me put any sort of feelings out of my mind. It's perfect, exactly what I need.

While I want to continue to push his buttons, I don't know how far I can go until he snaps. Maybe I should try to get him to push at me.

Settling into my seat, I cross my legs, taking sips of my coffee as I glance around the room. I'm hoping he'll accept another session like last week where we didn't talk. A sideways glance and I see he's sitting low in his chair, hand in his pocket as he takes a sip of his coffee.

He's wearing a suit vest over his shirt today and I hate that a jolt runs through my body, a heaviness settling in my clit. He looks better than any man has a right to. It does not help things *at all.*

I clench my thighs a bit as I shift in my seat, trying to calm my mind and get this feeling to go away. A snort causes me to turn to look at Zane. He's shaking his head as he takes another sip, face pointing toward the ceiling.

"What?" I can't contain the irritation in my voice. He did just snort at me.

Instead of answering, he looks at me with an eyebrow raised. I must look confused because he lowers his gaze to my thighs and looks back at me with a knowing expression.

Though I'd love to shoot him back a snarky comment, tell him not to flatter himself, it's pointless. He looks like Goddamn sex in a tailored suit and I'm shifting my body, overheating at the mere sight of him. He knows exactly what's going on, and there's no point in denying it.

My choices are to run with it, ignore it, or try to turn the tables.

"What do you want from me? You know you're attractive, don't pretend you don't. You, in a suit, would be the same as me in a short skirt, tight shirt, and heels. And you can say it wouldn't do anything for you all you want, but I know I'm hot, so you'd be lying." I don't actually have that much self-confidence, but I can usually sell it pretty well.

A quick lick of his lips lets me know he's thinking about it.

"Not even ten minutes ago, you're jumping down my throat for buying you a coffee and saying nothing can happen between us, but you're thinking about fucking me?"

"I never said I was thinking about anything. All I insinuated is that you look good in that suit, and it's hard not to be a little...excited about that. It doesn't mean I'm going to try to act on it."

"So, you're just trying to get me to think about fucking you?"

My face burns and my eyes bulge. "No! Why would you say that?"

"You compared my suit, which I wear for work, to you wearing a short skirt, tight shirt, and heels. Which I'm sure you'd wear to a bar or a club or for a boyfriend for some extra fun. And I can promise you if you wore something like that here, I'd spend the hour thinking about nothing but how many different ways and places I could have you."

Holy hell. That shouldn't intrigue me as much as it does.

"So, you can see why I get a little frustrated when you're biting my head off and then putting images in my mind about your sexy body in—"

"Stop talking," I interrupt him, holding out my hand toward his face. "No more talking. We will not speak again during this meeting, and when we leave, we will not bring this up. Got it?"

"Sure thing, sweetheart."

God, this man knows how to get under my skin.

Chapter 12

Zane

Buying the coffee seemed like a nice gesture. I guess I was wrong. Jules didn't seem pleased. I wasn't entirely sure if it was because I had paid or if it was because I had done it without her. Either way, I didn't expect to have to convince her to take the drink.

Her little game of comparing my suit to her in a skirt? She can play dirty. The second she said it, an image emblazoned in my mind, and it's been there ever since. It's incredibly distracting and gets the best of me at night.

In my mind, she's wearing one of those short, pleated skirts, dark gray, with a tight white button-down shirt. Bright red heels with black knee highs. And her curls are full and cascading over her shoulders.

I have no idea what she looks like under the clothes, but there's no way it's anything short of amazing. I don't even know that I care. I'd bend her over every surface in my apartment.

When I start wondering what she tastes like and feels like, I get out of bed and into a cold shower. I refuse to pleasure myself to thoughts of her. That crosses a line, makes things murky. I'm trying to get her *out* of my mind, not make her a permanent fixture.

And if I use mental images of her in that way, she's never leaving. I only hope she's suffering with thoughts of me as much as I'm suffering with thoughts of her.

I have to dislodge them. I don't know how, but I have to. If Jud was still around, he'd tell me to go find somebody—or a few somebody's—to get her out of my system. But that lifestyle died with Judson.

I don't know what to do. I can't get her out of my head. A place she has no business being. Yet I feel like I have to keep walking her home.

Brian, my psychologist, says I need to be honest with myself about these feelings. Whatever the fuck that means.

The only reason I even told him about Jules was because I was so distracted thinking about her, I missed one of his questions. When he asked where my head was at my mouth answered before my brain could compute, and I said, "Jules." I had to dive into the whole situation.

He commended me for walking her home, protecting her, even saving her. I was disgusted when he told me some men wouldn't interfere. He also told me beating the crap out of Tim was a rage issue. Startled doesn't quite explain the look on his face when I told him I wanted to kill him, so only beating the shit out of him was me showing self-control.

I mostly talk to Brian over a virtual meeting platform. I don't have time to go to group and therapy with my work schedule. Plus, I have zero interest in sitting on a couch and talking about my problems. At least this way I can be at work or in the comfort of my own home. Usually with a drink in my hand.

Ridding myself of thoughts of Jules is proving to be more than difficult. I'm unnervingly disappointed when I don't hear from her by the time the weekend rolls around. As Saturday drags on and there's still no contact, I have to stop myself from reaching out to her. I have nothing to say, nothing of importance, no good ruse I can think up.

I'm in a bad mood when I get to work on Monday. Penelope notices immediately and stands a little further away. I'm not a very nice person when I'm in a bad mood. More than once she's had to clean up a glass mess from one of those moods.

It's only made worse when she informs me that I have a conference call scheduled for five thirty on Tuesday. That will feed right into group time.

We're walking to my office from her desk when she hands me the paper with the schedule of meetings for the week so far. I stop short when I see the late call.

"I need you to change this." I point at the meeting and then look down my nose at her. It's not my preferred look, I know it makes me look like an asshole, but right now I don't care.

"I'm sorry sir, I can't. I've already tried I know you have your meeting. But Mr. Jenkins is leaving for Europe the following morning."

"What about today? Or earlier tomorrow?"

"I'm sorry sir, I asked. They said he's completely unavailable, and that's the only time he has open. He feels it's integral to talk to you before he leaves Wednesday morning."

Staring straight ahead, my jaw hurts from biting down so firmly. My fingers twitch at the need to grasp something and shatter it. The paper crinkling in my hands informs me that I'm doing more than just thinking about it.

If I end the call early enough, I can at least make it to walk Jules home. I'll miss the meeting but that's fine. I know which investments he's wanting to discuss. I should be able to make it.

"Fine. But tell his secretary I expect some sort of penance for missing my previous engagement."

"Already done, sir."

"Excellent. Thank you, Penelope."

I don't wait for her response as I enter my office and close the door. One hour is all I'll have from when the call starts to finish the conversation before I have to leave to make it to Jules. It really gives me a little leeway because it only takes fifteen minutes to get there.

I can do this. *I have to.*

Chapter 13

Jules

Walking out of the meeting and into the alley, I pause to dig in my purse for my phone. Zane isn't here. I don't know what to call what we have, I don't know how to explain what I feel, but I have the urge to see him, and it unreasonably deflates me when I don't.

The sudden tight grip on my hair is the only sign I have that something is amiss. My eyes flood as the follicles set strands free. Trying to turn my head is pointless, the grip is too tight. I'm trying to piece together what's happening when a familiar cologne mingles with the wetness of the ground, sending a shiver straight down my spine.

I know who it is before he even flips me around and smashes me against the wall. My ears ring and my vision goes spotty as my head slams against the brick. His breath is warm in my ear, the stench of stale beer mixing with his potent cologne, making me want to vomit. The hand that was tangled in my hair has wrapped tightly around my throat, holding me in place against the wall.

"I've come to collect what ya owe me," Tim drawls against my ear.

Tears spring from my eyes as I try to twist away from him. My head is pounding, and I can hardly see.

"No, no, please no." I can't tell if my voice is barely audible or if it's just from the ringing in my ears that my voice sounds meek.

"Oh, but ya owe me baby." There's still a hand tight around my neck while the other slides down my body, stopping to roughly grab at my breast before ripping at the button of my pants and hastily pushing them down.

My hands scratch at his arms, the only place I can reach, but they have no effect; there's no delay or hesitation from him. I'm stuck against the wall, and the throbbing in my head is making me woozy.

"No, no, please, no," I repeat as I turn my head to the side, tears silently streaming down my face. It's dark, it's quiet. Last time Zane saved me, but he's not here tonight. I don't even know why; I didn't get a chance to check my phone before Tim sank his claws into me.

I keep my mantra going as I feel him at my entrance. He hesitates, and I think maybe he's going to stop, realize it's a bad idea, walk away. That thought is quickly squashed as he slams himself, all of himself, into me, causing me to shriek out in pain and violation.

My eyes drift shut as I keep my mantra going. I'm not even sure if I'm saying it out loud or in my head, but it's all I have to hold on to as my body goes limp. Behind the black of my eyes, I try to conjure a calming image, and I'm immediately met with slate eyes and can faintly smell linen and sandalwood.

With my eyes closed, I don't see what's happening when Tim is yanked from me, causing me to stumble to the ground.

Catching myself before I face plant onto the concrete, I cradle my neck as I cough. When I finish my spasm, I hear the pounding of flesh on flesh and words coming through gritted teeth.

"I thought I made it clear last time, when a lady says no, it means no. I should have fucking killed you." It's Zane. He's slamming his fists against Tim, anywhere he can. His face, his chest, his stomach. Tim's curled into the fetal position, blood soaking his collar, when Zane kicks him, repeatedly.

With one final kick to the abdomen, Tim groans and stops moving. For a second, I wonder if he's dead, then I realize I don't care.

Zane's next to me in a matter of seconds, but his hands don't touch me. Instead, they hover over my body as he kneels in front of me.

"Jules, Jules, are you okay?"

Am I okay? No, no, I am not okay. I have been with a lot of guys, but none of them have ever forced themselves on me. All I can do is shake my head as my lips tremble and hot tears start pouring out again.

Despite the hesitation I can sense from Zane, he wraps his arms around me and pulls me against his chest. Ignoring the wet ground, he sits and pulls me into his lap as I grab at his shirt and press my face into him.

"Shh, Jules. It's okay. I've got you." I don't know why but his arms around me, his voice, feeling his heart beating beneath my cheek, all bring me a sense of comfort. "I'm so sorry I couldn't make it tonight. I'm so, so sorry."

Why is he apologizing? None of this is his fault.

I have no idea how long we sit in silence before he clears his throat. "Did he...did he hurt you anywhere else?"

"My head." It's still throbbing.

"Do you want to go to the hospital?"

My grip tightens on his shirt as I push closer against his chest, hiding. "No. I just want to go home."

Without an answer, he pulls my pants up as much as he can, sliding off his coat and wrapping it around my body. Somehow, he's able to stand while holding me in his arms. He starts walking in the direction of my apartment. It's twelve blocks, he can't possibly plan to carry me the whole way. But I'm content and comfortable in his arms, his warmth running through my body and thawing my insides.

The smooth swaying of his steps and the steady beating of his heart are almost enough to soothe me to sleep. I'm kept awake by the tears, the body rattling sobs. If my eyes drift closed, all I can see is his face, and I'm brought right back to that moment, so I make sure I keep them open.

Zane doesn't set me down once. His arms have to be killing him, it can't be easy to carry somebody twelve blocks. But he doesn't complain, he doesn't grimace. He walks steadily, with purpose, on a mission.

I know I should help him when we get to my apartment. Try to lower my feet or get my keys out, *something*. But I can't.

I'm still clinging to him as he carries me inside my apartment. He's never been here, always leaving me at the door downstairs. But he doesn't stop, doesn't falter. Instead, he carries me to my room, laying me gently on the bed.

I know I'm safe at home, but I'm also alone, and I can't be alone right now. My grip tightens on his shirt before he pulls away, and I look at him with desperation in my eyes, hoping he sees my silent plea.

Please don't leave me.

Miraculously, he reads me loud and clear, sliding onto the bed next to me, pulling me close, as close as he possibly can. With his arm around me, the sensation and sound of his heart beating, I feel safe.

I don't understand it, I barely know him, but he makes me *feel*.

Chapter 14

Zane

T he sound of her shriek makes my blood run cold. My call ran later than I wanted it to, and even though I speed-walked, almost ran, all the way here, I'm still too late to stop it.

Turning the corner, my feet instantly glue to the ground, my whole body frozen. I'm pretty sure I'm not even breathing. He's got her pinned up against the wall, hand wrapped tightly around her throat, as tears pour from her eyes. Her lips are moving but I can't hear what she's saying.

I see red, and my body jumps back to life. He's so distracted violating her that he doesn't hear or see me coming as I grab him by the collar of his shirt and rip him off her. Some part of me is aware that she falls forward, but I can't focus on her right now. All I can think about is making sure this fucker never even so much as looks at her again.

I should have killed him the first time.

After pummeling him until he's bleeding and not moving, I turn my attention to the beautiful creature still gasping for air on the ground behind me. I kneel beside her, but I'm afraid to touch her. I don't want her startling, but I so desperately want to bring her comfort. She hasn't even lifted her eyes.

"Jules, Jules, are you okay?" *What the fuck, asshole. Of course, she's not okay.* How could I ask such a *stupid* question to a girl who was just raped?

The slight shake of her head and torrent of tears are enough to stop my concern over touching her, my need to comfort her winning. Hesitantly, I pull her against me. The ground is wet where I sit, but I don't care. It could be pouring, snowing, anything. In this moment, I just need to comfort her.

"Shh, Jules. It's okay. I've got you." Her hand is tangled in my shirt, wetting it with her tears. I'm vaguely aware that her pants are still around her ankles. I should have prevented this; I should have been here to make sure this never happened. Last time I told her I'd walk her home every week, to protect her. And I had one meeting, one stupid call, that threw it all out the window. "I'm so sorry I couldn't make it tonight. I'm so, so sorry."

It's my fault. I knew it was getting late, I knew Mr. Jenkins could get chatty, make calls last far longer than they needed to. It was why I had told Penelope to switch it. I should have just said *fuck it* and let him flounder. But I took it anyway, I stayed on anyway. And look what happened. I'll never miss another group again. And I'll be calling the police as soon as I'm away from Jules.

I do a quick inventory of the rest of her body. She looks mostly unharmed, which means it's primarily going to be mental, the hardest part for people like us. When I ask, she tells me her head hurts and I wonder if he slammed her against the wall or if it's just from the trauma. Maybe she has a concussion. I offer to take her to the hospital, but she doesn't want to go, I don't want to force her.

So, I do the only other thing I can do for her. I pull her pants up as far as I can, take off my coat and wrap it around her, and scoop her up in my arms. I do a quick check of the ground to make sure nothing spilled from her purse and start walking.

Carrying her twelve blocks is the easy part. Listening to her whimpers and sobs is anything but. All I can think about is her, comforting her, getting her to safety, to peace. It propels my feet forward.

She mentioned in passing once that she lives in 4C. Carrying her up the stairs with ease, I'm sure I'm running on adrenaline.

When we get to her apartment, I fish around in her purse for her keys, supporting her lower half over a bent knee as I unlock the door. She's calmed to just sniffles and ragged breaths.

I haven't seen the inside of her apartment; it's tidy and nicely decorated, nicer than I expected. Taking a quick look around, with the aid of the light from the hallway, I take in the granite counters in the kitchen, a tan fluffy sofa in the living room, and breakables everywhere. I would not fare well here in a fit.

Letting the door shut behind me, I pull her purse from her arm and set it on the small table by the door with her keys, flipping on a switch that illuminates the rooms around us. There's a small hallway a few feet ahead of me.

Quickly sliding off my shoes, I walk toward it and straight into her bedroom, laying her down on her bed. Her grip against my shirt prevents me from pulling away and I pause, leaning over her to look down at her face. Her eyes are on mine, pleading.

Untangling her hand from my shirt, I take it firmly in mine and slide up onto the bed next to her, as close as I can get, pulling our linked hands between our chests. She folds into me, forehead against my chest. My entire body rattles with her sobs.

Pushing my arm under her neck, I pull her tighter against me. I want to do anything I can to take her pain, her sorrow, her horror, away. She wants me to stay; she asked wordlessly, but the intent was clear. To not leave her. If she wants me to stay, I'll stay, for as long as she wants.

I don't understand the power she has over me, but it's there. And it's strong.

Chapter 15

Zane

I plan to stay with Jules as long as she needs me to.

Going to bed, I ease in next to her, taking my movements very slowly as I keep my eyes on her and her reaction. She curls right into me and quickly falls into a slumber. I wrap my arm around her and watch her as she sleeps.

She's restless, rolling out of my arms within minutes before she's flipping around again only moments later. This goes on for at least an hour. Every time I think maybe she's settled and will get some solid sleep, she's tossing and turning again.

The worst part about the fitful sleep is that she whimpers. Or at least, that's what I think, until she starts screaming. I quickly jump to action, looping my arms around her and pulling her into my chest, shushing her and running my hand over her hair until the screaming stops. That doesn't make it better because that's when the hysterics start.

My body tenses as I hold her against me, and she bawls into my chest.

By the time the sun is rising, she's had six nightmares, all of which I held her for, all of which tore my heart to shreds.

When she wakes up, her eyes are red-rimmed and puffy. Immediately, she snuggles into me.

"I'm going to go make some breakfast. I'll be right in the kitchen." I practically have to pry her fingers from my shirt.

I whip up some pancakes and bacon, hoping a good meal will help.

When the coffee's brewed, and the table is set with plates, I go to get her, my feet cementing to the floor in the doorway. She looks so tiny laying curled into a ball. Jules has never seemed small to me, despite our height difference.

I kneel on the ground in front of her and brush some hair from her face. "I made some breakfast. Come eat." When she shakes her head, I say what I hope will change things. "There's fresh coffee."

Thankfully I'm right, and she climbs out of bed and follows me to the kitchen, her hand twisting into the bottom of my shirt like she needs something to hold onto, an anchor.

She sits, but she merely pushes the food around on her plate, opting for a breakfast of coffee and coffee only. When it's clear she's not going to eat, and the food's likely ice cold, I clear the plates.

"You need to shower, Jules. Think you can do that?"

She nods and makes her way to the bathroom. I take the opportunity to walk around her apartment. Her bookcases are impressively filled. There's a picture of her with a wide smile standing with a blonde wearing an equally wide smile on one of the top shelves. Jules looks younger than she does now. I'd guess high school if I had to.

I stay with her for the day, watching her closely. We barely speak, but I'm not here for that. I have to make sure she's going to be okay. I have no idea how she possibly can be after something like that, but I have to do my best. And if it's as simple as making sure she isn't alone, that's easy.

Letting Jules lead, we spend a lot of time in front of the TV. At one point, she dozes off. I can't blame her for the lack of sleep she got last night. I know I'm exhausted, I can feel it in my aching bones, but I need to watch over her. I have to be ready to help her if she needs me. That's not possible if I'm sleeping or just waking.

By dinner the first day, she's able to eat. Not a lot, not for long, but a little something. For bed, she curls into me again. Having her against me makes me feel things that shock me, things I don't even know how to describe, although the word *comfort* drifts to my mind.

She falls asleep quickly. Watching the clock, I take note when it's been almost three hours and she hasn't had a single nightmare and hasn't rolled around too much. I'm able to drift off for a little bit myself, wrapped around her and holding her tightly, just in case.

Eternally an early riser despite the lack of sleep, I wake up before her. Feeling somewhat rested, having only had to soothe Jules twice, I hope for a better day.

I'm quickly rewarded with a slight improvement from yesterday when Jules rolls toward me.

"Good morning." Her voice is thick with sleep, possibly even lack of use over the past day and a half, but it's there.

My heart takes off racing at the sound of it. I hadn't realized I'd missed it.

By lunch, she's eaten some. A few bites of eggs, two pieces of bacon and now some of her sandwich. She's taking tiny, dainty bites, except for the bacon which she almost swallows whole. Apparently, it's something she likes, and I file that knowledge away.

It's nice cooking for somebody else. I like cooking, but it's not as fun when you're doing it for yourself and only yourself, day after day. Even though she doesn't eat much, the soft "mms" that escape her lips are plenty.

My phone is ringing off the hook. I've canceled more meetings and conferences than I ever have. Penelope was beside herself when I told her to clear my schedule for the next couple of days. The first few times it rang, Jules nearly jumped out of her skin at the sudden sound in the otherwise quiet apartment. After that, I turned it to vibrate. Every time it rings, Jules looks over at it, then at me while I send calls straight to voicemail. None of it matters right now, everything can wait.

That third night, about forty-eight full hours after everything happened, we're laying in her bed when her soft voice reaches my ears. "You can leave. I'm...I'm okay now. Sort of." She hasn't cried in at least eighteen hours. Not even a trickle.

"I'm good to stay. I'll be here if you need me to be." Why am I putting my life on hold for this girl? Yes, she has been through something horrible and traumatic, but why am I offering to stay?

"I—" She starts but stops just as quickly. I can sense her hesitation to finish. Does she want to ask me to stay? Or does she want to ask me to leave and doesn't know how to do it without sounding ungrateful? In this moment, I think I'd stay forever if she asked me to. And that thought scares the crap out of me. I barely know her.

"You should go." It comes out a strained whisper, and she won't look at me. I'm not sure if it's really what she wants, but I don't know how to go against her. So, I get my things to leave.

"Zane," her quiet voice stops me as I'm about to walk out the door. I turn to face her just before she plows into me, wrapping her arms around my waist. I'm taken aback for a moment before enveloping her in a hug. "Thank you," she whispers against my chest.

"Anytime. I just needed to make sure you were okay."

She's voiceless, but nods before pulling away.

As I force myself through the threshold, I have one large realization.

Leaving her is so much harder than it should be.

Chapter 16

Jules

Zane stayed with me for two full days. I can't believe he actually stayed. Especially because I barely talked to him. His presence was pleasant though. Calming. He's a good cook, from the few bites I took at least. It was nice of him to cook for me. Too nice.

I enjoyed having him here, and I don't like that fact. I've never really *enjoyed* being with men, unless we were having sex, including former boyfriends. Zane didn't try to touch me inappropriately once. I don't want to feel anything regarding his company, it makes things...complicated.

But I told him to leave, and he did. So now I'm alone again.

The nightmares get worse. I can barely sleep. Every noise has me jumping out of my skin. I've woken up in a cold sweat screaming more times than I care to admit. I know I should talk to Dr. Ptansky, but I can't bring myself to do it. I don't want her to make me work through it or figure out what it *means* to me.

I was raped. It means a sick bastard thought he was entitled to something he wasn't.

She'd also ask about Zane and want me to sort out my feelings, why he makes me feel comfortable, why I was okay that he stayed for two days after something so traumatic. I don't want to figure it out.

He's a nice guy, from what I've been able to gather on our walks home, despite my initial thoughts that he was a rich asshole. Maybe he's just protective, he's saved me twice now. But that's all it can be.

Being alone is a dangerous thing for me. The thoughts don't stop. They swirl and spread, the demons in my mind lingering in the shadows. I can't quiet them.

Days slip by without notice. My phone chirps one day with a text from Zane wondering where I am, if I'm alright, letting me know I missed group. That tells me it's Tuesday.

I wander through my apartment like a zombie, snacking on random things when my stomach feels like it's going to eat itself. I haven't showered since Zane was here, however many days ago that was.

I sleep so poorly at night that I fall asleep at random times, like while watching mind-numbing television on the couch, waking up screaming as I fall to the floor.

Dodging calls is easy, I just don't answer. It's even easier when my phone dies and I just conveniently don't charge it.

There's so much darkness, so much hatred. One night while the moon is high in the sky, I drag a blade across my arm. The pain barely registers. Not good.

I try again, harder. The sharp sting causes my breath to catch. Better.

Stupid, dirty girl.

Chapter 17

Zane

It's been two weeks since I've seen Jules. She's missed two meetings. She also hasn't returned my texts, the last showing as unread. I'm worried about her, which is a very strange feeling because I can't remember the last time I worried about anybody other than myself.

Sitting at home, at eight o'clock at night the day after the second session she missed, I can't get her out of my head. Images from that night flash like a movie reel through my mind. Her shriek like a soundtrack to it all.

My leg bounces so much I slosh the amber liquid out of my glass and onto my pants, pulling me out of my reverie. It sat untouched for so long the ice melted, filling the glass to just below the rim.

In that second, I make a decision that may alter everything. Giving myself a quick change of pants, I toss on shoes and head out.

I don't have any second guesses as I walk straight to her apartment. I try knocking gently at first. No answer. Trying a little louder, I say her name against the door. No answer. I doubt she's out. Pressing my ear to the door, I hear the TV. I'm pretty sure she's home.

She could have somebody over. She told me she used to distract herself with sex. Maybe she started again. Why does that twist my insides? My bigger fear is she's hurt herself. That she's bleeding out in the bathtub. Or already has.

My hands curl into fists before I realize and pound on the door. "Jules. Jules! Open up! It's Zane!"

I keep pounding, louder. If this keeps up, the neighbors will surely at least poke their heads out, if not just call the cops. At least I could probably convince them to open her door. Before they arrest me, that is.

"Jules, open the door, or I'm going to break it down." I'm going to what? My mouth is speaking with its own volition.

Filling my lungs, I'm preparing to slam into her door while also accepting I'll likely end up in the hospital with an injury, or jail, when I hear the lock flip.

A breath catches in my throat when I see her.

Baggy clothes, the same ones she'd changed into two weeks ago. Her face is gaunt, deep dark circles under her eyes. Her hair is piled on her head in a messy ponytail, parts are matted. She clearly hasn't showered since I left. Her hair's always beautiful, with shiny, perfect loose curls that are currently nonexistent.

Her eyes are the worst part of her. They're void of the light. That mother fucker extinguished her light. There wasn't much there, it was clear to see she struggled to maintain it, like we all do, but I could see it. Now it's nowhere to be found.

The sight of her hurts. It physically hurts, like being stabbed with a red-hot knife over and over. I don't know why; I can't begin to decipher it now.

I glance into her apartment, taking in what I can. There's a blanket bunched on the couch, random snack foods on the table, the counters in the kitchen. There's no sign that she's eaten an actual meal in days.

I reach out a hand to touch her, and she recoils.

I fall back on my heels. I can't leave her like this. So, I wait, anticipating the door to slam in my face. But it doesn't. She stands there, hand on the handle, not speaking. She's also not leaving. I take it as a good sign.

Especially when she glances sideways at me.

I try again, putting a hand out toward her. The internal struggle is plain to see in her delicate features. I'm not sure why she's struggling, maybe for the same reasons I feel like I both shouldn't be here but can't seem to leave.

Slowly and gently, she puts her hand in mine. I don't hesitate to pull her against me, my other arm wrapping around her shoulders. She's stiff at first, but after a minute she melts against me. She doesn't move her arms, doesn't wrap them around my waist, but she softens.

It's both exhilarating and extraordinarily confusing.

Chapter 18

Jules

I gnoring the knocking has become easy. Daphne's come by twice. She went away after about ten minutes. Both times. She knows me, knows my down times. I don't want to see her. At one point, after an especially bad spell, we agreed on a twenty-day period. If I don't answer in twenty days, she enters with the key she has.

But one night, I'm not really sure which since I have no idea what day of the week it is anymore, there's a harsher knocking. Then I hear a man's voice say my name. A voice I immediately identify as Zane's.

Though I try to ignore him, he gets louder and louder. When he says he's going to break the door down I fly off the couch. I don't know if he's serious, but I don't want to find out. My security deposit was too high.

His face falters as he takes in my appearance. I know it's bad. But I don't have the willpower to fix it. I have to turn my eyes away; I can't look at him and the expression that resides in his eyes.

When he reaches out to touch me, I flinch, pulling away. He's been nothing but kind to me, he's here, but I've been alone with my thoughts and nightmares for too long.

Watching out of the corner of my eye, I see he's not leaving. I expected him to leave. I could close the door in his face, send him away. But I don't want to be alone again. I want the comfort he brings me.

He notices my gaze and extends his hand again, almost like I'm a scared animal he's trying not to frighten, but his palm is up, hand open so I can take it. Which I do.

It takes me a minute to relax after he folds me into his arms. He's hard yet soft, warm, and smells damn good.

When he starts walking, I keep pace but stay pressed against him. He leaves one arm around me as he closes the door, slipping off his shoes. I like that he takes them off at the door, I usually have to ask people.

I'm not really sure why he's here, I'm not sure what he's planning to do. All I know is that I don't want him to leave. I don't want to be alone again. It's hard and scary being alone.

Arms still around me, he walks over to the couch and sits down, settling me next to him but not against him.

"You missed two meetings and didn't answer me. I got worried. Seems I had a right to be." His voice is low and calm.

I can't look at him, finding a nice spot on the floor to focus on instead.

"You didn't tell me you also have depressive episodes." There's a sense of pain laced amongst his words.

I shrink in on myself. Why does it matter? I don't know all his secrets.

"After what happened though I guess anybody could. I could have stayed. I didn't have to leave."

"You don't have to be here now." Wow, I'm such a bitch.

"Do you want me to go?"

"No." It comes out breathless and way too quickly.

"Looking around I'd say you haven't eaten anything besides junk for the past two weeks?"

I shake my head. I still can't look at him.

"Do you have any real food that can be cooked?"

My shoulders only lift slightly. I'm barely aware of what day it is, let alone when I last went grocery shopping.

"You have to shower Jules. You'll feel better with a shower."

"I can't." It's true. It's too exhausting to stand in the shower.

We're sitting close enough that his warm breath caresses my cheek as he sighs beside me.

Patting his knees he stands, pulling me up. "Come on."

Trailing behind Zane, my feet shuffle as he gently leads me down the hallway to the bathroom. When he turns on the light, I squint and duck away from its harsh brightness. I've mostly been existing in the dark and glow from the TV. When he reaches in to turn on the water, my heart races. Is he going to throw me into a cold shower? It's been done before.

I watch with apprehension as he puts his hand in the stream, adjusts the temperature, and feels again, before his gaze meets mine. He looks at me with a serious face, determined yet soft.

With slow hands, he reaches out and wraps his fingers under the hem of my sweatshirt. His eyes stay locked on mine as he lifts it above my head. My arms immediately cross against my bare chest but he doesn't falter. His gaze stays trained on mine as he takes off the rest of my clothes before easing me into the shower, under the stream.

The warm water feels nice, but I can't get myself to do anything but stand here. What comes next shocks me.

Zane strips down, quickly, and steps in behind me, holding me under the water, carefully easing the hair tie from my very knotted hair, trying to be as gentle as possible. When it's free, he turns me and dips my head under the water. My arms are still crossed at my chest, but now I squeeze my eyes closed. I shouldn't look at him, I know I shouldn't.

But I can't help it. His chest, abs, and shoulders are all lean and toned, with light muscle definition. How have I never noticed the tattoo on his forearm? Have I ever seen his forearm? There's another on his shoulder, yet another on each side of his ribs. I realize I'm staring and avert my gaze, inadvertently looking down which causes me to bite my lip as I look away. *Wow.*

When I hear him chuckle lightly, I decide it's best to just shut my eyes. Though that poses its own risks. But the water on my back feels good, his hands in my hair feels even better. Lavender fills the small bathroom as he works my shampoo through my hair. His fingers massaging my scalp releases the tension in my shoulders.

He's gentle with me, hands on my biceps as he dips me back toward the water to rinse. His hands never graze an inappropriate place. Jasmine wafts into my nose as he rubs conditioner through my mane, likely completely untamable. The last time this happened, I had to do a big chop.

"Do you have a comb or a brush for these knots?" His voice is low, soothing.

I shake my head. "Fingers." I finger comb my hair in the shower, but I'm sure he won't do that.

To my surprise, he puts his hands on my waist and turns me around so the water beats against my front, his fingers working gently through my hair. Any knot he encounters that tugs, he apologizes for. I know he's trying hard to clear the mess and not hurt me. After a few minutes, it feels like he's working through pretty easily. I'm sure his hands are covered in my hair, mine always are. But he doesn't complain.

Before he turns me around, he comes up close behind me, his chest brushing my back, and something else against my ass.

Part of me feels like his erection should bother me. That I should feel disgusted, especially with the events that transpired two weeks ago, the ones that brought him here while I'm deep in the midst of a depressive episode. But I don't. The second night he stayed, he actually slept. I woke briefly to feel him hard against me. It didn't bother me then either.

Right now, how could it? He's with a naked girl in the shower. Still, I'm surprised he's even turned on by my gross depressed self.

When he's done rinsing his hands and adjusting the water, which starts pouring out warmer, he turns me around again, leaning me back into the water. He runs a hand over my head as he ensures all the conditioner has come out.

I tilt my head back into the stream, feeling a little fresher than I had. I'm enjoying the water in my face, the warmth on my skin, when I tilt too far. My eyes have been closed through most of the shower, and I lost my sense of balance in that time frame.

Instinctively, my hands drop from my chest and reach out to steady myself, grabbing onto Zane's arm as it wraps around my waist to stop me from falling. I don't need to open my eyes to see how close he is to me, but I do anyway.

Though my breasts are now exposed, Zane's eyes are locked on mine, not wandering, not trying to sneak peeks. I can't say what happened while my eyes were closed, but something tells me he didn't look.

"Think you can wash yourself?" His voice is barely audible above the pattering of the water around us.

I nod silently, my voice stuck in my throat. Something about this moment, the closeness, the tenderness, the nakedness perhaps, makes it feel intimate.

With a tight smile, he climbs out of the shower, grabbing a towel from the stack and wrapping it around his waist. I stare as his muscles work. He doesn't face me as I wash, giving me the privacy to fully expose myself. The honeysuckle scent fills the bathroom and helps me loosen a touch more.

After rinsing, I take a few extra minutes to just stand under the warm stream, letting it run down my face. Good thing he's here, forcing me to shower. It helps me feel better. Something I never remember while I'm deep in it, is that showers help. It's like they peel away a layer of sadness, bring back a sense of normalcy, and make me feel human again.

The second I turn off the water, he's holding a towel open for me. I'm not used to this level of care. Nobody has ever cared for me like this, and he and I are just...what? What are we? Friends? Maybe?

Whatever we are, I'm thankful he's here.

Chapter 19

Zane

While I'm not sure she'll go for it, she needs a shower. It will help her feel better, more normal. The awkwardness is palpable. We have an odd relationship, and we're standing together naked in the shower while I wash her hair. She's a gorgeous woman, my body reacts in kind.

She seems thinner, not just in her face. And while I don't bring attention to them, I notice the cuts on her arm. Thankfully there are only two. When her eyes are closed, I do a quick scan to look for other signs of harm. The relief that pours over me when I don't find any confounds me. Everything about this and my feelings confounds me. I'm completely enthralled by her, and the magnetism is undeniable, yet I don't understand how when I have walls ten miles high.

To give her some privacy, I change back into my clothes in the bathroom and give her a few extra minutes. When I walk into her room, she's sitting on the edge of her bed, still wrapped in her towel.

Her hair is curling at the ends, refreshed from the wash. There's a pile of clothes next to her. She got the clothes, she just doesn't have strength to put them on. I don't understand it, but something inside me wants to be the strength for her.

I kneel in front of her, hands on her knees. Taking the shirt from the pile I slide it over her head, pulling her hair out of the collar, leaving her towel in place. I take her panties and sweatpants, sliding both over her ankles before pulling her to stand. I keep my eyes locked on her face the whole time, even as she drops her towel. It's not easy, but I do it.

The vacancy in her eyes helps me stay on task. It's absolutely heart-rending.

Once she's dressed, she plops back on the bed.

"Do you want to eat?"

As expected, she shakes her head no.

I climb onto the bed next to her and wrap my arm around her waist, pushing myself back toward the pillows, pulling her along with me. I slide her into my lap as I flip the covers back before slipping her in, joining her immediately.

Laying on my side looking at her, I don't know what to think, what to do. She's lost. She's in there somewhere, but she's lost.

I don't get depressed. I get angry. I get even. I break shit. This is foreign to me, I don't know what to do, I don't know how to fix it. I don't even know why I want to, just that I do.

She's just laying there, staring at the ceiling, hands folded across her stomach.

"Thank you," she says quietly as a single tear drips down the side of her face. She doesn't look at me.

My thumb grazes across her cheek at its own volition. I'm surprised by my audacity. Everything I've done tonight, from the shower, to dressing her, to now touching her tenderly, are far bolder than I have a right to be. Jules doesn't flinch away though. In fact, her eyes drift toward me. I see something flashing across her features, hesitation, an unsureness, before she rolls in my direction.

Her face is so close to mine, the scent of mint wafts through my nose. Somehow, I'd been able to also convince her to brush her teeth. She'd pulled out a new toothbrush and handed it to me silently.

I miss the fire in her eyes, the spark. I wonder if I'll see it again. I wonder why I want to, why I feel anguish that it may be permanently extinguished.

Her voice startles me. "I guess it's why you wanted me to change meetings."

All I can do is nod.

"I—I didn't want to switch because I like seeing you. I like our walks home. It's my fault. I was stupid." She chokes on a sob, and it nearly cracks me in half.

"No, no, no. *None* of this is your fault. I'm so sorry I wasn't there in time to walk you home. I never should have had that meeting. I should have postponed, canceled, rescheduled, anything." Though, I tried to do all those things, aside from telling Jenkins to go fuck himself. That's exactly what I should have done.

"It's not your fault, you have to work."

"I should have been there. I knew, I *knew* he was going to try something again. Men like him always do. He could have been waiting for you to be alone for weeks." I tense as a shudder tears through her. "I should have killed him the first time."

"I should have listened to you, switched meetings. Even though it would have meant I didn't see you again." I love that she skips right over the fact that I said, and clearly meant, that I should have killed him. Given the chance, I would have no second thoughts or regrets about taking his life with my bare hands.

I brush some hair out of her face with my fingertips, tucking it behind her ear. "Oh, Jules. I would have switched meetings with you." And I was prepared to. I'd already figured out how to adjust my schedule.

Anything to keep seeing those beautiful brown eyes, those gorgeous curls, to keep hearing her voice.

Chapter 20

Jules

He would have switched his meetings to be with me? Meanwhile, I didn't want to change *because* of him. When he brushes my hair away from my face, my heart almost explodes. His tenderness takes my breath away.

My lips are tingling at the thought of kissing him. I know I shouldn't be thinking about it, shouldn't be wanting it. But I can't help it.

My glance shifts down to his lips, briefly, so briefly I hope he won't notice. But he does.

Instead of reacting how I think he will, by bolting out of bed and leaving, his gaze drifts to my lips. And in that moment, I know a similar thought is passing through his mind.

Taking a chance, I shift my body closer. His hand slides over my stomach to rest on my lower back. He presses firmly, pulling me the tiniest bit closer to him. We're moving in centimeters, inches, nobody wanting to take too big of a step forward.

My heart starts hammering in my chest and I'm sure he can hear it, feel it. Curious, I stretch my hand up to rest against his chest, over his heart, to find his is also beating erratically.

I'm not sure if what happens next seems slow because it is, or if it's because time has all but stopped; Zane leans in, closing the gap millimeters at a time and making me ache to feel him before our mouths finally connect.

Fireworks explode through my body as his lips brush mine and start moving against them. His mouth is soft but forceful. He pushes my mouth open, his tongue curling against mine as his heart speeds up and his hand pulls me closer.

Slipping my hand behind his neck, my fingers scratch at the back of his head. He keeps his hair shorter here, nothing to tangle in. As our mouths move together, I shift myself to be all the way against him, pelvis to pelvis, chest to chest.

He slides his hand up the side of my body to come to a rest cupping my cheek. Alarms in the back of my head scream that this is wrong in so many ways. But everything about it feels so right. Like he's breathing life back into me, reassembling the pieces of what fell away weeks ago, months ago, years ago.

I have no idea how long we lay here for, mouths moving in sync. Every so often he'll slide his hand down my side to rest at my hip, squeezing while his thumb rubs against my hipbone. He doesn't do more than that, doesn't go further, doesn't try to slip a hand under the hem of my shirt.

My heart pounds against his, electricity tearing through my body at his touch, making me feel supercharged.

When he pulls away my lips are sore, my chin raw from his stubble, and all the air from my body resides in his. He rests his forehead against mine, swallowing loudly as a light laugh escapes him and a smile graces his face. His hand is resting gently on my hip, giving a squeeze as he pulls me tighter against him, though barely a hair's width of space exists.

"Not quite what I expected when I came over."

"Why did you?"

"I was worried about you."

Worried. About me. I'm not sure anybody worries about me. Except Daphne. But she worries about everything. Literally everything. She worries about seals in the Antarctic being eaten by whales, lions in the Savannah starving during dry season. She's been worrying about me for twenty years.

"Thank you for checking on me." It's basically a whisper and even though he just had his tongue in my mouth, I can't look at him. Instead, I focus on twisting my fingers into his shirt.

"You're welcome."

"You don't...you don't have to stay. If you don't want to."

"Do *you* want me to stay?"

What a loaded question. If I'm being completely honest with myself, yes, I absolutely do want him to. It's scary, and dark, and lonely by myself. On my own, I'm too weak to stop myself, to care for myself. But I also know having him stay isn't necessarily the best idea. The question isn't so much what I want, but what's right.

"Yes." I throw what's right out the window. I've been alone for two weeks. It didn't go well for me.

He snuggles into the pillows, closing his eyes, his arm still draped around my waist. He doesn't say anything, just hunkers down, ready for sleep.

I curl into him. I don't understand the comfort he brings me, don't know what to make of it. Yet I find myself not caring as I fall into a deeper sleep than I've had in two weeks.

For the first time since Zane left after the...episode...I wake up having had only one nightmare. Somewhere in the very early morning hours, I woke up to Zane shushing me and hugging me close, rocking slightly, suddenly aware that I was screaming. Once I calmed from thrashing and screaming to a gentle tremble, he loosened his grip. I fell back asleep in his arms.

Waking for the morning, to start the day, I feel somewhat refreshed. In front of me is the wall, the window. The sun is streaming through in bright streaks, illuminating the dust particles that float through the air, mingling and swirling. Reminding me I haven't cleaned in weeks. Sometimes I lay here and watch the particles, wishing I could just float away with them.

Rolling over, I find Zane, face propped on his hand, looking at me. I immediately wonder how long he's been awake, watching me sleep. I'd feel embarrassed if I didn't already know he spent an entire night watching over me a few weeks ago.

His face is serious, no hint of happiness. "Have you been having nightmares since that night?"

Shame washes over me, and I can't meet his eyes anymore, giving a slow nod.

The sigh that releases from his chest is too much and the tears erupt from my eyes.

"You haven't spoken to your psychologist, have you." It's a statement, not a question. He knows the answer. I shake my head anyway.

"Jules, you have to. You have to process what happened. You can't sit here alone for another two weeks falling deeper and deeper. What if I didn't come here? What would have happened?"

"I would have gotten out of it." My voice is low, quiet, barely above a whisper. It's unconvincing because the hollowness in my chest tells me I'm not sure I believe myself.

"Oh really? With how many more scars?"

I'm not sure if he means physical or emotional until he pulls my left arm from in between us and pushes my sleeve up.

"This isn't okay, Jules." His voice is soft but stern. A finger gently traces along the angry red lines. And then he does something astounding.

Pulling my arm toward him, he leans forward and places a gentle kiss on each cut. The heat that starts at his lips and warms through my entire body sends me into a tailspin; I want to pull his lips against mine again and tear all my clothes off. I know both are bad. But one is far worse.

Which is why when he looks up at me, I crash my mouth against his. He doesn't hesitate as he pushes my mouth open, tongue claiming mine. This time he slips his hand under the hem of my shirt, the same heat warming through me as his palm presses against my skin.

When his hand slides to my lower back and a pinky dips below the waistband of my pants, I know I should startle, should pull away, should say it's too much. But I don't. If anything, I inch myself closer to him, fitting into him like a puzzle piece.

All at once, I'm realizing that he may be everything I want, and everything I can't have.

Chapter 21

Jules

"I'll stay with you as long as you want me to, Jules." Zane breaks this news as we lay in bed the day after he comes over.

It's the oddest relationship I've ever experienced. I don't know what to label it. Are we friends who make out? Acquaintances who have seen each other naked? Two fucked up people in therapy together?

The last one is true at least. But otherwise? I have no idea what to make of it. He stays because he wants to. He stays because *I* want him to.

The longer he's here, the better I start to feel, even if it's in baby steps. He cooks dinner for me while I watch from the living room. Every meal we have together, I hear the same thing.

"You need to eat something Jules. At least a few bites. Your body needs fuel, energy. Please, just a little something."

Begrudgingly, I eat, if only just to get him to leave me alone. I'm not hungry, ever.

I offered him a pair of old sweatpants after breakfast the first morning. "Here." I held them out to him as he eyed them warily.

"What are those?"

"Pants. For you. I'm sure they're more comfortable than jeans."

"I won't fit in your pants Jules. I'm at least six inches taller than you."

"They're not mine, exactly. They're from an ex-some-thing-or-other."

He raised and eyebrow and looked the pants over with a new level of disgust on his face. Grumbling, he grabbed them from my hand and quietly thanked me.

Guilt rolls through me anytime I think about the fact that he's here and not home. The least I can do is make sure he's somewhat comfortable.

Everything about this is so incredibly confusing, but especially my feelings about him. I'm comfortable enough to share my deep, dark secrets, to lean on him, lay next to him. To kiss him...a lot. His presence makes me feel at peace. I can't describe it, maybe because I've never felt it before.

We talk for hours. He talks more than I do, which is so strange because I carried the conversation for weeks. But I think he remembers when I told him that silence makes me feel icky. Of course, there are lulls, but for some reason I don't have that icky feeling just existing next to him.

We're laying in bed the second day he's with me, and he's telling me a little more about his issues.

"I have serious anger issues that have an outward expression. It makes me break things, anything. IED, Intermittent Explosive Disorder, has been tossed around from time to time. I get these random bursts of anger, I don't usually know why or where they come from, but I also just get overly mad at things that maybe aren't quite as extreme."

His voice is so melodic, it's soothing to listen to him talk.

"See this scar, here?" He holds his right hand up above us. We're laying on our backs, heads tilted and touching, brushing shoulders. He's pointing to a white line between his knuckles.

"I punched a soap dispenser. Those stupid plastic ones, in like stores, and whatnot. I was in college, my girlfriend at the time was mad about something or other, and I went into the bathroom and connected my fist with it. The damn thing cracked, and the plastic sliced my hand. She flipped out.

"Oh, and this one?" He holds his left arm up and shows me a line. Squinting, I can't quite see it as it's hidden under a tattoo. The one I've come to find is a forest that wraps around his forearm.

"It can be hard to see, here." Taking my hand, he trails my fingers along his skin where I feel a long ridge, placed perfectly under the trunk of a tree. The feeling of his hand on mine sends tingles racing up my arm and through my body.

"What happened?"

"Put my fist through a window."

My eyebrows arch their way to my hairline. "But...your hand."

"I got a few small nicks on my hand but after it went through, my arm somehow dropped, and a big shard sliced right up it. First time I needed stitches."

"Not the last?"

He lets out a big sigh that seems like he's releasing his soul. "Unfortunately, no."

"Are they all covered by tattoos?"

"Mostly." He has another tattoo on his right shoulder, a Celtic symbol of some sort, and writing on his left rib cage. I'm not sure I understand how he could have gotten scars there from breaking things, but I don't ask. The one that confuses me most is the one on his back, which is a flock of birds that traipse from one shoulder to the other and down to his right ribs.

A question piques my interest, causing me to swallow hard. "Have you...have you ever, um." I'm really uncomfortable to ask the question on the tip of my tongue.

But he seems to know, taking a deep breath as he lowers his hand and links his fingers in mine. I glance down at our hands, another seemingly intimate moment that makes my heart race.

"I've hit people. I mean shit, you saw me beat the crap out of Tim. Twice. But I've never hit a woman. Really it has to be provoked for me to hit a person. Mostly." He clears his throat before I can spend too much time dwelling on *mostly*. "What got me into therapy, besides knowing I had a problem, was a stupid bar fight. I don't even remember what about, that's part of the issue, I don't usually know why I'm mad. I had to go to anger management, and they kind of felt like there was more going on, suggested a psychologist. That was five years ago and, here we are."

"Does it happen often?"

"I guess it depends on your definition of often."

"Oh, uh, I guess more than once a month?" There are times I cut more than once a week, but I figure a month is somewhat safe.

"Yeah, most of the time."

"More than once a week?"

"Not usually. Why, do things happen for you that frequently?"

I knew he was going to switch to me at some point. While he's been patient with my quietness, I knew this was coming. Eventually I'd have to talk to him. And he's just shared a whole lot.

"Sometimes." His fingers silently drift to the spot on my arm where the angry red lines still exist, asking a silent question. "The same day. One right after the other."

"And the other thing?"

I shake my head silently. "Not in a really long time."

His shoulder sags next to me, and I realize he's releasing tension and sighing from relief. "I don't like thinking about you hurting yourself."

"Why?" I hope he doesn't think I mean that I feel he's some sort of asshole that doesn't care about other people. Though honestly that isn't far off from my initial impression of him. But I've gotten to know him more since then.

"I don't know. I can't explain it. The things I feel around you, for you. It's...different. It's why I'm here. I was worried about you, what you were doing here, alone for weeks. To yourself, or...or with others." He seems pretty hung up on that last part, almost like it's hard for him to say.

"Just me. In the darkness. The pitch-black darkness." I didn't realize I'd started rubbing my fingers along the lines in my skin until Zane takes my hand in his, bringing it briefly to his lips.

"Let me help you out of the darkness." His lips hesitate against mine, like he's questioning if I want to kiss him again. How he doesn't know is beyond me. We've kissed many times by now. Hoping to leave no questions in his mind, I close the gap, parting my mouth for his.

We both turn to our sides at the same time. I don't flinch as his hand rests on my hip and slowly slips under my shirt. When his palm is barely brushing exposed skin, warmth easing through my body, he falters, his hand suspended. I know I shouldn't be doing this, shouldn't be kissing him or moving closer to him so he hopefully gets the message and slides further up my shirt, but I can't stop myself.

I won't let it go further, I won't let it lead to sex. I've done enough stupid things in the past few weeks. But I also have an overwhelming feeling that Zane won't even try.

Thankfully, he seems to get the silent message I send him, by sidling closer as his hand traces up my back, drifting forward to rest against my ribs, a thumb gliding gently over the swell of my breast. His fingers may as well contain a current for the electricity it sends through my body, a primal desire settling between my thighs.

I absolutely cannot and will not have sex with this man. At least not right now, while he's here with me. I can admit that I'm not making myself any promises I'm not sure I can keep. Breaking promises makes me want to do bad things to myself.

His mouth moving against mine, his warmth surrounding me, his crisp clean scent wafting in my nose, all have this magical way of making everything else disappear.

The darkness doesn't feel so dark, the nightmares don't encroach, there's even a little light, a sense of self.

Chapter 22

Zane

I'm standing against the brick exterior of Land of Lattes, foot against the wall as I stare at the ground, waiting. I got here even earlier than necessary, impatience and need drawing me here.

It's been a long and difficult few days without Jules. I wasn't expecting it. While I was with her, I finally accepted the feelings I'd pushed away for so long. It was impossible to deny them once her lips touched mine. Even more so when doing it again was all I could think about during our time apart.

I didn't call her; I didn't message her. She told me she was okay if I left, and I didn't want to argue. I left Friday night so she didn't have to worry about me in the morning before what is apparently a routine meet up with her friend. She'd missed a few and didn't want to miss again, said she was feeling better.

I hope she still is and will be here.

Before I can do too much wondering and worrying about how she is, I see her walking towards me, fresh curls bouncing around her. Everybody around her fades away, like she's parting the Red Sea and illuminating the world as she gets closer. There seems to be a little more pep in her step, a little more of the light in her eyes. It sets a fire in my chest. Maybe coffee with her friend did her well.

Pushing away from the wall, I'm about to ask how she is, but I don't get the chance as she walks right into me, resting her head against my chest, just under my collarbone. All the air eases from my lungs. I hesitate for all of one second before I wrap my arms around her and kiss the top of her head.

Her hands are between our bodies, but instead of looping them around my waist, she tangles her fingers into what she can of my tucked-in dress shirt. I squeeze her closer, no words necessary.

Slowly, she pulls away. I don't want to let her go, I don't want to feel the void of her being away from me again, but I don't fight her.

"I, uh...I," she starts and stammers.

"I missed you, too." When a twinkle flashes through her eyes and her lip turns up the slightest bit in one corner, I know I guessed her sentiment correctly.

I'm not really sure what the rules are here. Was it just a hug? A friendlier hello? Deciding to go for broke, I throw my arm over her shoulders as we walk into the coffee shop. When she leans into me ever so slightly, I know I made the right call.

This time when I pay for coffees, she doesn't argue. Turning the corner to the alley, she pulls away and looks around frantically. It takes me a minute to realize she hasn't been here since that night.

Taking her elbow, I pull her back to the street and around the corner, standing close so she's mostly against the wall of the building and I can box her in, resting my hand across her breastbone, making her focus on me.

"Jules, listen. I'm right here with you, okay? I will never miss another group session again. I will be here with you every single time. You're safe."

She swallows hard and gives the tiniest nod of her head, but her eyes are still wide and swimming with fresh tears. Glancing each direction, I make sure nobody from group is nearby and fold her into me. I could offer to take her home, but I know it's important for her to be here. Even if she doesn't participate, there's a reason she's here. It dawns on me that part of the reason she's here *today*, clearly sooner than she's ready for, may be for company, for noise, because she doesn't like silence.

Pushing her back, I keep one hand on her shoulder as I lower myself so my eyes to meet hers. "Do you want to go home?"

She looks around, worrying her lip between her teeth, bouncing on her toes a bit. There's clearly some sort of decision she's struggling with. I know she doesn't like group enough to worry about it. So there has to be a different reason.

Me.

It's a guaranteed hour plus of time with me. I haven't heard from her since I left Friday, but I haven't reached out either. I wonder if she was as nervous and unsure as I was. My heart plummets to my feet as I wonder if she's putting herself through this just to be in my vicinity. One text and I would have been there in a heartbeat.

Making the decision for her, I loop my arm around her waist and pull her in the direction of her apartment. Three blocks in and she hasn't said anything. I don't know how to break the silence, but I need to get something out of her. I've barely heard her voice today, and I miss it.

"How was your coffee with your friend? Daphne, right?"

Instead of a verbal answer, she nods.

Taking a sip of her coffee and fiddling with the lid for a minute she clears her throat. "It was good. She's been with me through basically everything. She's seen me worse. It was two weeks, that's nothing."

My heart twists into a knot at the thought of Jules going through that rough of a time for longer than the two weeks she had.

"Do you always hole yourself away?" I pull my arm from around her, sliding my hand into my pocket. While I want her close to me, this line of questioning may not go my way.

"For some of it. Daphne has a key. She only uses it for emergencies. She knows me better than anybody, she knew I was in there, that I was just having a hard time. I'm not suicidal, I never have been, so she wasn't worried about that. When she found out *why* I was in such a bad place, though, she was livid that I didn't call her immediately."

Relief instantly washes over and flows through my veins like a bursting dam when I hear that Jules has never been suicidal. The level with which it was concerning me isn't something I had registered until built up tension oozes out of me.

"I would imagine."

"She was actually pleasantly surprised to hear you were with me." She turns her head away from me and brings her cup to her lips, tipping it back slightly. That reaction tells me there's more to this.

"Why is that?"

"I've never let a guy be there for me before. Not that many have wanted to." Every so often she'll leave little tidbits like this without going into detail. All I can gather from it is that other men haven't treated her very well. It makes my blood boil.

"Well, I'm happy I was able to help."

The silence settles over us again like a dense cloud. It's somehow more awkward now. We know each other better; we shared some dark and dirty secrets. We kissed, a lot. Hell, we've seen each other naked. Things have shifted, and now we don't know how to act.

When we get to her apartment a few minutes later, we pause outside the door. She makes no move to go inside, and I have no intention on leaving until she does.

Looking anywhere but at me, she's biting her lip again. I so desperately want to kiss her, give her something to do with those lips besides chewing them.

When her eyes lock on mine, I can see the littlest bit of the fire that had been snuffed out. It makes me happier than it should.

"Will you, um. Would you mind staying with me again? At least for dinner?" My heart skips a beat. She wants me to stay?

"Of course, Jules. I can stay as long as you want. Would it be okay if I spend the night again?" Though I can't prove it, and don't necessarily have a basis to make this judgment, I have a sneaking suspicion she's scared. Maybe she's struggling and needs support. I wonder if she's having nightmares again. I hope not.

A look of relief washes over her face at my question. "Yeah, I'd really like that."

"Okay. I need to go back to my apartment to get some clothes. I have to be at work early for a meeting."

Her face drops a little.

"Why don't you come with me? I'll just pack a few things into a bag. If that's alright? I don't want to be presumptuous bringing some clothes. I can just wake up extra early and go back if you prefer."

"No, that's not necessary. It's fine. Besides I wouldn't want you to have to wear your suit again in the morning. Or the ex-pants."

A smile works its way to my face as I start walking toward my apartment. Jules falls into step next to me. "I appreciate that. They were a little too short."

"You're definitely one of the tallest guys I've kissed. If not the tallest."

"Interesting. So, you tend to go for shorter guys?"

"Actually, I don't usually go for guys at all. I let them come to me." She says it with confidence, but from talking to her, I know it's not. It's more likely just success.

"So, how is it? Being with a taller guy. Everything you'd hoped it'd be?"

"I wouldn't know yet." The look she gives me sends a jolt straight to my cock. This is the Jules I've grown accustomed to over the past few weeks. I'm glad she's making her way back.

As much as I'd like to make a snappy comeback about her finding out, I don't think it's the right time. Though I'd gladly show her a million times over.

Before I can answer, we're in front of my building. I hold the door open for her, watching as her eyebrows arch at the lobby. Leading her through, I have an unease settling in my bones.

I can't remember the last girl I brought back to my apartment. I'm not sure I've ever had one here at all. I try to avoid having other people at my place at all costs.

Hesitating for a second, I toss a quick glance back to Jules before I open the door and flick on the switch.

Her eyes grow wide as she looks around.

"You live here?"

"Yeah?" We are in my apartment. I just opened the door.

"I mean it's just...dark and depressing."

I don't have a lot of stuff. Her apartment has tons of clutter and artsy things like vases of fake flowers. Mine doesn't. I can't.

"Yeah, kind of like me," I deadpan.

She turns to look at me with a frown. "You're not depressing Zane. If anybody is, it's me. And my apartment is bright and colorful."

I shrug like it's no big deal. "I'm a guy. Guys don't do bright and colorful."

"Some do."

"Not this one." The brightest, most colorful thing I care about is standing in front of me. "Feel free to look around, I'm going to change and pack some things."

She nods as she starts to wander slowly through the space. It's set up a lot like hers, kitchen and living room feeding into one another with a hallway toward the bedroom and bathroom in the middle.

Quickly, I toss on a pair of jeans and T-shirt, packing some drawstring pants, boxers, socks, and more shirts in a duffel bag. I use one of my garment bags to pack a few suits and dress shoes. I don't want to be too forward, but I do want to be prepared for staying for a few days.

Walking back into the living room, I find her running her fingers along the bookshelves. I had a strong feeling she'd like them, having taken note of her extensive collection. She looks good in the space, right.

"See anything you like?" I do, but it's not on the shelf.

"Not really. Not my kind of books. But very impressive space. I'm jealous." Her bookcases are overflowing with books. Literally, she has them piled on top of the rows and in front of them.

"I'm all set."

"Can I help you carry anything?" She holds her hands out to take something.

"Nope, I'm good." I take a quick glance around, making sure I didn't forget something before flicking the light off, locking the door behind me.

Once we get to the street, I link my fingers with Jules's. She takes a sharp inhale, looking at our hands and then up at me with a perfect 'o' on her face. The shock quickly fades and changes to what I think may be the slightest bit of happiness as she gives my hand a squeeze.

"You can put your stuff in the closet, there's a little room. For both your suits and your bag."

"Sure. I appreciate that." We're a few blocks from her apartment, but I appreciate that she's thinking about it now.

"How long do you think you'll stay?" There's a touch of unease in her voice.

"How long do you *want* me to stay?" I give her a sideways glance and catch her eye.

"Honestly? I don't know."

"Let's take it a day at a time then. If you want me to leave tomorrow, I will. If not, I'll stay. And we'll try again each morning. Sound good?"

"Yeah."

Jules has shown me she's tough, she doesn't take shit. But I think right now she's thankful that I'm taking charge of the situation. I have zero doubt she'll kick me out the second she's had too much or I say something stupid, both of which are equally as likely to happen.

When we get upstairs, I put my things away and find Jules on the couch, her hands in her lap. Sitting next to her, I take her hands in mine. She looks up at me with a sadness in her eyes that sends ice spiraling through me.

"What's wrong?"

"I don't know. I just...I feel weak." She looks at her lap and shakes her head, her curls bouncing around. "I couldn't even walk in that alley. I asked you to come here. Though, that had been a plan before I couldn't make it to the meeting."

To hide my racing heart, I take a deep breath. "Jules, look at me." When she doesn't, I hook my finger under her chin and tilt her head up so my eyes can lock on hers. "You are *not* weak. At all. You are so strong. You went through something traumatic. It would rattle even the toughest of people, which is why it rattled you. Because, Jules Kline, from what I've learned of you so far, you're incredibly tough."

Her bottom lip trembles, and I pull her against me, leaning back into the cushions. "And you only want me to be here because you realized what good company I am. What a good cook I am. And of course, that I'm an amazing kisser." This earns a light laugh which makes me smile.

"I just feel better when you're around." The feeling is mutual. Should I tell her? I'll just revel in knowing she likes having me around for now.

"What do you say I make some dinner?" I offer, but I don't really want to get up.

"How about we order pizza and wings so you don't have to cook?"

"Sold."

While Jules sits curled up on the couch, the cuffs of her sleeves tucked into her fists as she stares a spot on the rug, I call and order dinner. She's coming out of it, but we're not there yet. I'll stay as long as she lets me, but my goal is to bring her back to herself as much as I can.

Chapter 23

Jules

It's a little weird having Zane here. Not a bad weird, just...different.

He moves around like he's lived here for months, not that he's stayed with me for a handful of days. For two days, he's been here, watching me like a hawk, and he cooked dinner last night. He even leaves me lunch.

Adding to the weirdness, before he's left the past two mornings he kneels in front of the bed, resting his chin on the mattress and brushing the hair from my face until I wake up. He gives me a smile and tells me to have a good day, that he left me a lunch in the fridge and to please try to eat it. Then he kisses my forehead before he walks out.

Every kiss makes my heart race. He does it so naturally, like he doesn't even have to think about it. I know he's asking me to eat because he sees I'm still struggling, and I was able to turn to him the first night he was here when I was warring with myself. He helped distract me by talking, by touching me—only appropriately—and by kissing me. I'm sure he thinks eating is a problem. It's not so bad, but I appreciate the concern and forethought.

The first day he was here, he had asked if it was okay that he brought some shampoo and conditioner over after grumbling that he had to use mine and was going to smell like a flower all day. I couldn't help but laugh a little. He was very sure to say he liked it on me, but not himself.

"Do I need a key, or should I meet you somewhere? I don't want to impose or be presumptuous. I could go back to my apartment until you let me know it's okay to come over." He was getting ready to leave the first morning and wanted to know the details of how this was going to work.

"Oh, uh, no I'll be here. The only time I go into the office is when I need to get new assignments, need a change of scenery, or have a meeting. None of which I need this week. Feel free to come right from work."

"Are you sure?"

"Mhm." I bite back the discomfort of telling him to come whenever.

I *do* want him here. That's part of the problem. I never have before. In reality, he's the first man to ever step foot in my apartment besides my Super, who I've only seen when he showed me the apartment and the one time I needed something fixed.

It's Thursday, which means it's therapy day. I'm going to talk to Dr. P about Zane. I've told her *about* him, but now I'm going to talk about my feelings for him. Because they're all sorts of confusing, and I need her to tell me what to make of them.

She won't actually do that, but she'll guide me in the right direction. I hope.

"J ules!" The shouting of my name and hand cupping my cheek make me snap to. It's Zane. Blinking quickly, I look around and realize I'm sitting on my couch, knees tucked to my chest. Zane's eyes are filled with worry as he crouches in front of me, one hand still on my face, the other on my knee.

There's a sharp sting in my arm and I know what it is before I put my arm out and raise my sleeve. An angry red line glares back at me, and hot tears prick the back of my eyes.

Zane rubs my cheek with his thumb. "What happened?"

"I...I don't know. I don't remember. I had therapy today, it was rough. I don't remember doing this. I must have dissociated." Fear flows through my body, wrapping around my lungs. At least I'm home this time.

Quickly he stands and moves to sit on the couch next to me where he pulls my legs into his lap. Wrapping an arm around me, he drags me closer and runs a hand down my hair. "Will you talk to me?" I like that he doesn't push but merely asks. Though his voice is as desperate and pleading as his eyes.

If I talk to him, really talk, I'm letting him in on all my darkness. What if he can't handle it? He'll run, like everybody else. But what choice do I have? I asked him here for a reason; he's seen me at an ultimate low.

After a deep breath, I take his hand in mine. I can't meet his eyes, but feeling him helps me steal some of his strength.

"Why don't you start with what you talked about?" He must sense my hesitation.

"You." I chance a quick look at his face and see his mouth hardened into a line, jaw tight, cheekbones sharp, and eyes dark as night. As he shifts uncomfortably in his seat, I notice he's still in his suit. I start to move my legs from his as I speak. "You can go change, be more comfortable."

Before I've shifted from his lap, he pulls my legs back to rest against his torso. "I'm fine like this."

I don't know if he sees my delay tactic for what it is or if he really is just fine. A sudden burst of strength courses through me, and I straighten myself, putting my chin up and meeting his gaze. "Once I share this, there's no going back. You can't...you can't disappear. I don't know what exactly this," I wave my hand between the two of us, "is, but if there's anything I might say that could scare you away, you need to decide that now, before I say anything else."

Leaning forward, he places the tiniest kiss on my lips, hand cupping the back of my head. "I'm here, Jules. I'm here for all of it." My eyelids flutter as my heart speeds up, and butterflies echo the sentiment of my eyelids in my stomach. He says he's here. Let's see if he means it.

I clear my throat, hoping to shoo away the nerves even though a tremble has set into my hands. "I talked to my psychologist, Dr. Ptansky, about you today. She knew a little bit. That you'd rescued me, that you'd stayed here and helped me earlier. But I had more to say this time. I wanted to talk to her about my feelings for you." At this part I turn away, I can't even look at my legs in his lap, choosing the coffee table.

"I don't know what to do with them, what to make of them. I've never had another guy in my apartment, I never *wanted* one in my apartment. For years. That scares me a little. But Dr. P, doing what she does best, pushed me to think about why, and it just brought up the whole reason I'm messed up in the first place."

Zane sits silently next to me. He doesn't push, he just waits.

Taking a deep breath, I continue. "My parents both left me before I even hit puberty. My mom basically decided she didn't want to be a parent one day. I came home from school, and she was just...gone. About a week later, my dad never came home. I called my aunt, Juliette. She'd always been a huge presence in my life. She came right over and packed a bag of my things, saying we were taking a little vacation to her place.

"For a week I stayed with her with no idea what was going on. I'd always felt safe with her, I knew I was okay, but I was worried something bad had happened to my mom and dad." Swallowing around the lump in my throat hurts. The fresh prick of tears in my eyes makes me hate myself. I don't want to let them have any control over me and my emotions anymore, but then again, they're the cause of all my problems, my day-to-day struggles.

"My aunt told me I'd be staying with her for a while. I didn't know then, being a kid, but she'd finally gotten a hold of my mom, who told her she couldn't do it anymore and wouldn't be coming back. That she'd spoken to my dad who also wasn't coming back. See, he loved her more than me and wanted to be with her more than he wanted to be my father."

Silently, Zane brushes a runaway tear from my cheek.

"My aunt was great. We had a great life together. She had no kids, never married. She couldn't have her own children, so she'd always been sort of motherly to me anyway. She just stepped it up a notch and fully took over. We did so much together. She was always supportive of everything I did. When I started to unravel in high school, she found me a therapist."

The hint of fresh tears burns my eyes, but this time because the next part shatters my soul. "I gave her such a hard time in high school. I stayed out all night, I went to parties, coming home drunk at all hours of the night. I slept around. When she found out, she didn't even yell, just took me to get on the pill so she wouldn't have to worry about me getting pregnant at least."

I hang my head and shake it, curls creating a curtain for me to hide behind. Zane's been quiet and still this whole time. Now he runs a hand along my calf, squeezing slightly. It doesn't feel like an urge to continue so much as reassuring me he's here. He's listening.

"When I was in college, my aunt got sick. Cancer. It was already very advanced. She'd spent so much of her time taking care of me, that she completely ignored her symptoms until she passed out in a drug store. I was too self-absorbed to notice she was different. She was gone within six months. I fell off the deep end. Hard. I'm pretty sure the only reason I even finished college, let alone am still even alive right now, is because I had Daphne with me. She'd been through *all* of it with me. We were neighbors growing up."

A deep breath helps me buy a second to gather myself and clear the tears. Aunt Juliette's been gone for almost ten years, but the pain never gets easier. My hand flutters to my collarbone, and I realize I didn't wear my necklace today. As it falters against my chest, searching for something that's not there, Zane links his fingers in mine and brings them to his lips.

I make eye contact with him for the first time since I started talking, saying a silent thank you.

"The necklace? I had said it had two J's. Well, my aunt gave it to me before I went away to school as a token to remember her, remember our life. To remind me that I had somebody in my corner because she knew, so often, I felt alone. The day her J fell off, it was a different design, so I knew it was hers, was exactly three months after she died. It was the first time I ever dissociated. Daphne was terrified." A shudder runs through me as I remember that time and the very lowest of lows I had resided in. Even to this day, it's a haze of drugs, alcohol, sex, and self-loathing.

"Dr. P says I have some abandonment issues, though it's not really that hard to figure out. But a lot of it goes to my self-worth. I don't feel worthy of people, of their support, their love, their time. I didn't even have that from my parents, the two people who were supposed to love me no matter what, without reason. I mention it to Daphne all the time but she's such a staple, I know she's not going anywhere. She's the only positive constant in my life. But that's where things went today with Dr. Ptansky. How do I balance these feelings of...interest...with the fear of abandonment and feeling unworthy?"

My eyes flutter shut, and I squeeze them tight as the harsh reality sets in. While my parents may have been the first to leave, they certainly weren't the last or most recent.

"Nobody sticks around for me, Zane. I've tried to do relationships in the past, they always end up leaving when things turn dark, which they will, they always do. Usually sooner rather than later. I haven't developed feelings for somebody in...well, I'm not sure I ever have. I try to guard myself, but I couldn't this time as hard as I tried."

I meet his gaze with a hard-set line on my lips. I just shared big time. Now it's do or die.

He looks right at me and shrugs. "I don't know what you want me to say to that, Jules. It's a tough life, a sad story. But if there's anything I hope you know from the time we've spent together, it's that I have feelings for you, too. And yeah, they scare me because I don't let people in either. I have my own set of issues, and it's easier if I keep other people away. But you barreled through my defenses and obliterated them. I'm not just here because you asked me to be. I'm here because I can't imagine *not* being here." All of the air rushes from my lungs as my heart hammers against my breastbone.

Taking my arm, he slides my sleeve up, running his finger gently across my puckered skin. "I want you to talk to me about this, confide in me. I want to be here to help you. Will you let me do that?"

"I can try." It comes out a whisper. Nobody's ever wanted to be here for me before. Even with Daphne, it's different. I'm not sure I know what it looks like. I'm also not sure he'd stay if he knew how frequent of a problem it is. I'd told him, sometimes more than once a week, but seeing it, experiencing it, is very different.

Straightening up and adjusting his tie he clears his throat. "I guess it's my turn to share."

"You don't have to. You asked, I had a bad day, I did something stupid. I had things to answer for. You don't owe me anything."

"We've done a lot of honesty and a lot of level playing field so far. Let's keep that going. I knew what it meant by asking."

Leaning my head against the couch, I run my fingers through his hair. It feels good, natural.

"Same rules though, Jules. There's no backing out of this, especially now that we laid it on the line. I don't know what *this* is either, but I hope it's heading where I think it is."

"I don't know what you're thinking, but I'm pretty confident we're in agreement. Especially since I asked you to be here, and you've stayed. I'm not going anywhere."

"Okay, if you're sure. Here goes nothing."

Chapter 24

Zane

It's been a really long time since I've told anybody about my life, aside from everyday basics.

Taking a deep breath, I steady myself. "I grew up with money, very privileged. My dad worked hard to provide for us, and he was a very successful attorney upstate. He billed hundreds for the hour. But he was an asshole. Through and through.

"He never wanted kids. My mom did. And he was willing to do absolutely anything for her. That was his only redeeming quality, the way he loved my mother, who was an absolute shining ray of light. My dad could get...physical...at times. Not severely so but rougher than a parent should be with their child." Needing the comfort she provides me, I adjust myself a little, pulling Jules's legs closer to my body. I haven't even started to unravel what it means to me that she reciprocates my feelings for her. I can't right now with this heavy weight on my chest.

"I had a friend, Judson. We grew up together, kind of like you and Daphne. I'd always been an angrier kid. My dad pushed me to let it out in sports, swearing there was nothing wrong with me when my mom worried. He probably just thought I was like him. But in private, he'd tell me to get it under control, to 'figure it the fuck out'. He started saying that when I was twelve." I adjust my head from side to side like I'm cracking my neck. The slightest hint of anger lingers when I talk about him. I wish it didn't, but I can't help it.

Before the rage builds up and erupts, I have to take a minute to calm myself. "When Mom died, things got worse. Dad was just nasty, telling me it was my fault, that worrying about me caused it. She had a brain aneurysm. It was so sudden, there was nothing anybody could have done. She was there one second and gone the next." I startle as a hand cups my cheek and a thumb rubs across my temple. Leaning into her palm, my eyes drift closed. Comfort wraps around me like a warm blanket, dousing the fire that was starting to burn.

She's staying quiet, just like I was for her. I appreciate it, because it only gets harder, and I'm not sure I'd be able to continue if she started asking questions. I need to get it all out.

"I was sixteen at the time. Home was the last place I wanted to be, so I spent most of my time at Judson's. Dad didn't care, he was happy he didn't have to deal with me. I just had to show him my report cards and keep my nose out of trouble. It was absolutely expected that I would go to a good college and get a job that made good money. That was easy, school wasn't hard for me, and I wanted *out*. I'll never be able to repay Judson's folks for letting me stay with them all that time. They took care of me like their own son for nearly two years.

"Dad had said if I got into an Ivy League school, he'd pay every penny. When the acceptance letters started rolling in, he kept true to his word. He even bought me an apartment off campus. He'd said, 'No son of mine will live in a dorm.' I'd been disappointed at the time, but it turned out to be a gift. I never had to go home again. I sent him transcripts in exchange for money deposited into my bank account. Instead of going home over breaks, I stayed behind. Judson visited sometimes, even his parents."

I glance over at Jules to get a feel for her state right now. She's looking at me intently, softness in her eyes and encouragement in her features.

"Judson and I moved here together after our undergraduate years. I went to Columbia, and he started working. I had Dad's money to buy a nicer apartment. Somewhere along the way, something changed in Judson. He'd always had it a little rougher...emotionally. Struggled a bit. He didn't get mad like I do, he got quiet. Pulled in on himself. He always worked his way out of it, it was short lived. Looking back now, I realize he was severely depressed."

My teeth grind against each other. "One day he'd had enough and OD'd on Oxy. His neighbor found him and called me. He'd never said anything to me, never confided in me even though he'd been there for me to talk to constantly. Just quit one day."

Talking about Judson goes one of two ways. Either I can talk through it, or rage boils under my skin. Today, it's the latter. I often don't have control of my outbursts. But today, I bite back the urges to destroy everything in sight.

Quickly sliding Jules's legs off my lap, I get up. "I'm sorry, I have to go."

Without another word, I leave a stunned looking Jules on her couch as I slam out of her apartment and speed walk home.

There's an urge to demolish anything I can get my hands on, and I hope I didn't just destroy my chance with Jules along with it.

◦⧒◦

I shouldn't have left. I know that. But I could feel the over-the-top rage seconds from bursting out of me, and I couldn't let Jules see me like that. When I get home, I put my fist through the wall in my closet—a few times. I'll fix it tomorrow. When you have a tendency to put your fist through things you learn how to repair walls pretty quickly.

Sitting on my couch with my head in my hands, I know I just royally fucked everything up. I told her I could handle it, I told her I wouldn't run. We both said there's no changing of minds now that we've told each other how we feel. Or at least sort of told each other. Neither of us said any words regarding actual feelings besides that they exist.

And I left. Basically, without a word. I'm sure she's thrown my stuff on the street by now. I deserve it.

I can't even bring myself to reach out tonight. I'm sure she has about a million words for me, and I deserve to hear them all, but I can't right now.

Instead, I wander my apartment in misery. Jules is the first good thing in my life in years, and I'm pretty sure I just fucked it all up.

Chapter 25

Jules

I don't hear from Zane for five days. I'm conflicted. He said he'd stay, that he was in it. But then he stormed out. It wasn't while I was talking though. Or even after. It was while he was. I could be wrong, but I'm giving him the benefit of the doubt that it had nothing to do with me. It leaves a hollowness in my chest all the same.

Not hearing from him doesn't help. I don't reach out because I get the feeling he needs to be alone. When he finally does, my heart breaks a little.

Zane: *Hi. I don't know what to say to make up for what I did. I'm sorry. I shouldn't have disappeared on you like that. Especially after I promised you I wouldn't. I need you to know that it wasn't you. At all.*

It takes me a few hours to answer him, not being entirely sure what to say. He hasn't explained why, but when I pick up my phone, there's another text from him waiting for me.

Zane: *Can we talk? Please? Jules I'm so sorry.*

Me: *I need a few days. I'm not shutting you out. I just, I don't know what to make of things right now and I need to work through it on my own.*

Zane: *Please don't do anything to yourself. Not because of me.*

Me: *I'm not struggling in that way Zane. I just don't know what to feel or how to grapple with things. I need to make heads and tails of it. I'll talk to you when I'm ready.*

Zane: *I know you're mad but if something happens please reach out.*

Me: *I'm not mad. I'm confused.*

It's the truth. My plan is to talk to Dr. P. She never just *gives* me answers, but I think she'll help me work through my conflicting thoughts.

Thursday afternoon I'm sitting on her couch hoping to do just that.

"It's not so much that I don't know if I want him back, I definitely do. It's more that he left. Without a word. What does that say for the future?" I pick at the fringe of the throw pillow in my lap to distract myself from the dark hole trying to swallow me.

"Julienne, he didn't leave because of you. If he was going to, he would have when you were talking or after you finished. You said he tensed, grit his teeth, clenched his fists. That tells me he was dealing with his own emotions."

"But it doesn't change that he left. And hasn't told me anything." Angrily tossing the pillow to the side, I lean back into the couch and cross my arms against my chest as irritation filters through me.

"You said he wants to talk. He probably just wants to say things in person."

"I don't know that I can handle it. I'm afraid seeing him is going to cloud my judgment."

"Don't let it. Nothing he said or did seems that egregious, Julienne. I know it's difficult because he left after saying he wouldn't, after you got deep with him."

Dr. P always sees right through me.

"Can I..." I clamp my mouth shut as I refuse to let the words pass my lips.

"I'll wait until you're ready, but we'll discuss this." Dr. Ptansky crosses her legs as she adjusts in her chair.

"I feel silly even asking you this." Heat prickles the back of my neck and a bead of sweat drips down my spine. "Can I sleep with him?"

"That's your decision, isn't it?"

"I guess I mean... do you think it's alright? Is it...safe to do?"

"Again, that's your decision. You need to think about the ramifications of what it would mean for you, both of you. I can't tell you the answer Julienne." She keeps talking, but I tune in and out. The thought of what Zane would feel like inside me is suddenly in the very forefront of my mind, invading the rest of my body as my nipples pebble and my clit heavies.

I'd pushed the thoughts aside for weeks, refusing to let myself go there. As he wormed his way into my heart, the thoughts started flooding in. I've been denying them, fleeing them from my mind any way I can. But now that I've voiced it, I can't erase them.

There's no question that I *want* to find out. The question is whether or not I should.

Chapter 26

Zane

I almost ignore the buzzing on my desk. I'm elbow deep in paperwork for an acquisition when it buzzes again.

When I flip the screen, I'm happy I didn't ignore the alert.

Jules: *Will you come over tonight?*

Jules: *Please?*

My pulse skyrockets. I didn't think I'd hear from her for a while longer, possibly ever. I'd given up on any hope of getting those clothes back. My fingers are almost shaky as I type out a response.

Me: *I'd love to. When?*

Jules: *Whenever you want. You can come straight from work. I washed the clothes you wore and you still have what was in your bags.*

Wait, she didn't throw my clothes out?

Me: *I'll be there as soon as I can. Big account problem I'm working out. Hopefully I won't be too late.*

Jules: *I'm ordering Chinese. I'll save you some if you're not here in time.*

That feels very *relationship* to me. But instead of scaring me like I'd anticipated, I have a need to get to her place and hold her.

I've missed her, more than I probably should at this point. After admitting I have feelings for her, to her, they've been stronger than ever.

"Penelope!" I holler louder than I usually do. There's a new urgency in my movements.

"Yes, sir?"

"I need to get out of here as soon as possible. Let's see if we can speed this up."

We set to work getting everything put together, calls made, money exchanged. I take a quick look over the numbers, the contracts, making sure I didn't make a mistake while I rushed through it so I can leave.

Even speeding through things, Penelope being a huge help, I don't get to Jules's until almost seven. Looking up at her apartment, seeing the light illuminating into the night like a beacon, I take a deep breath before opening the door and walking up the stairs. There's absolutely no way to know what I'm about to walk into.

I owe her another apology, an explanation. And if she'll let me, a lot of time with my arms wrapped around her.

I shake myself out as I knock on the door. She answers almost immediately. Her eyes are wide but soft. She seems as lost as I am. Stepping aside, she allows me entrance. I barely have my shoes off when she presses herself against me.

The breath that releases from my chest is one I hadn't realized I'd been holding since I walked out a week ago. The tension eases right out of me as my arms loop around her.

Pulling away far too quickly, she looks up at me. "Food should still be warm, I waited until about six to order." The thoughtfulness makes warmth spread through my chest. While my job is supposed to be a nine to five, I'm not usually done until six at the earliest.

"Thank you. I'm going to change quick. Have you eaten?"

She shakes her head, curls bouncing around her face. "I wanted to wait for you." This is a very different Jules than I'm used to. Soft, thoughtful.

"That wasn't necessary. I'll be quick." I disappear down the hall. It's not lost on me that I move through her apartment like it's my own. I'm comfortable here. I *have* had to notice every single thing that would be dangerous in rage, but I think I've found them all. If I'm lucky, I'll be able to get myself out in time, like last week.

My clothes are neatly folded on her dresser, the rest hanging in her closet. I change as quickly as I can. When I get back to the kitchen, she's set out plates and waters.

"What'd you order?" I ask as I slide into the seat next to her. I'm still on edge. I have a lot to answer for, and the Jules I've known is not against putting my balls in a vice to get to the bottom of what happened.

"Sesame chicken and lo mein. I hope that's okay."

"Yeah, I'm not picky."

We sit and eat in silence for a little while, and tension is building within me as I wait for the onslaught. When I can't take it anymore, I drop my fork. "Okay, Jules, what's going on? I haven't known you terribly long, but I think I know you pretty decently at this point. You've never given me a slide. On anything. Why are you not ripping my balls off?"

She shrugs slightly but doesn't look at me, fork moving her fried rice around. "I don't know. I guess I get it on some level? It became too much, and you needed to get away, be alone for a little. I get that." Her voice is soft.

I'm about to respond when she opens her mouth again. "I just kind of wish you had turned to me like you've asked me to do for you." My heart sinks.

"It's different, Jules. You have to know that. I left because I didn't want to scare you. Over the years I've gotten better at being able to control the outbursts in regards to Judson. I left before I exploded. I don't want you to see me like that, not yet, maybe not ever."

Her eyes lock on mine. "You've seen me at a low. Depressed, dirty, broken, scarred." She holds her arm forward, and I see the red line from last week has faded. Despite her self-harm, her arms are mostly unmarred. I take in a few faded lines but can tell they'll be gone.

"It's different," I say again. "I can help you. I can restrain you if I need to. You can't do that for me."

"Would you hurt me?" I wince at the thought of possibly ever hurting her.

"Not intentionally. That's the problem, I don't know what I'll do, even if it isn't on purpose."

She sighs heavily and looks back at her food, contemplating a piece of chicken. "I had a session with Dr. Ptansky today and had some time to think after. If we're going to make a go of this, which it seems like we are, we need to talk to each other. You want me to come to you when I'm struggling, that goes two ways."

I run my tongue over my teeth, considering what she's saying. She's right. I can't expect something from her and not give the same in return.

"Alright. Are you going to continue to be this pleasant as well?" I'm only sort of teasing.

"Don't worry, I'll start giving you shit again tomorrow." She doesn't exactly smile, but there's an amusement in her eyes.

"Looking forward to it." I really am. One thing that immediately attracted me to Jules is that she challenges me.

We finish eating and talk about our days. She says therapy went well which is good. I didn't like how things went last week.

After we eat, we lay on the couch to watch a movie. It's so unusual for me, and I can tell Jules feels slightly uncomfortable as she keeps shifting and fidgeting. "I probably shouldn't ask, but when was your last relationship?" She tenses on me. Her head is resting in my lap while I twist some of her curls. "Never mind, I shouldn't have asked."

Pushing up, she sits next to me. "No, it's fine. It was a few months ago. But we didn't really do things like this. It was more of a, um, physical relationship."

My jaw clenches on its own accord. I'm not an idiot, she told me she used sex as a way to cope. But that doesn't mean I like knowing or thinking about it. Especially since feeling her has been all I've been able to think about recently, but still have yet to experience.

I rub the back of my neck, the awkwardness palpable. "Oh. We don't have to watch a movie."

"No, I want to. It was different before. Really just somebody to pass the time." Looking away from me she tucks some hair behind her ear. One of the many nervous habits I'm finding she has.

"And that's not what this is?" I raise an eyebrow as I ask.

"No, it's not. How about you?"

"Relationship?" I make what I'm sure is an unattractive face as I bare my teeth and lean back. "A few years probably. But physically? Almost a year."

Her face widens in shock, her mouth making a perfect 'o.'

"Really?"

I just nod in response.

"Wow. I had you pegged *way* wrong."

"I get that a lot." I don't really. Nobody else asks, nobody cares.

"I mean, you *have* to know that you could have any woman you want. Right?"

I can't help but laugh. "I'm aware. That doesn't mean that's what I'm interested in though."

"Am I?" I narrow my eyes at her. I'm not sure if this is a test or some of her vulnerability and low self-worth. Either way, the answer's easy and the same.

"Yes, Jules. You are." Cupping her cheek, I pull her toward me as my mouth meets hers. We haven't kissed in over a week, and I've missed her lips on mine.

When my lips part hers, tongue sliding in to curl against hers, she climbs into my lap, straddling me seamlessly. My hands automatically lower to her hips.

Something snaps in my head, and I pull away. My dick—which had hardened the moment our lips locked—jumps in protest. "What are you doing?" I ask somewhat breathless, sure my body is asking me the same thing.

"What I want." Leaning toward me, she latches her mouth back to mine as her arms loop around my neck.

When a tiny moan vibrates against my lips, I've had enough. I have to know what she feels like, how soft her skin is, what she sounds like when she comes.

Sliding my hands under her thighs, I stand up from the couch, and carry her down the hallway. I'm about to find out.

Chapter 27

Jules

Z ane is about to ease into me when he stops and pulls his mouth from mine, keeping the rest of his body pressed against me, a hand by my head supporting his weight.

"Jules, if you want me to leave, if you don't want to do this, you need to tell me. Right now." His voice is tight and clipped. Restrained.

When I don't respond, he moves a hand to my chin, holding firmly so my eyes can't move from his exceptionally dark ones.

"Jules. I mean it. If we do this, there's no going back."

"I know."

"I need to hear you say it."

"I want this, I need this. With you." When I talked to Dr. Ptansky, earlier she didn't strictly rule against it, just suggested it maybe isn't the best idea. But Zane isn't just a fun roll in the hay, he's not a distraction. As much as I've tried to deny it, to push it away, I truly like him. Dr. Ptansky knows this.

His resulting groan tells me he does too as he doesn't hesitate any longer, pushing into me.

Holy shit.

He feels amazing inside me. And he's not even moving yet. It's almost like he needs a second to set himself as well.

When he starts, I have to take a very deep breath to keep from imploding.

"Are you okay?" He clearly heard my sharp inhalation.

"Oh yeah. Very much so."

The smile that passes over his face only makes me shudder more.

He starts slow, really slow. In and out, very rhythmic. It's not the sort of sex I'm used to, I'm usually a little wilder and always in charge in the bedroom. But this isn't the sort of situation I usually find myself naked in, though it has been a very long time.

Either way, I find my eyes rolling to the back of my head with every thrust. It takes him all of five minutes to get me close to orgasm.

"Oh God, Zane, don't stop. Fuck, don't stop."

"Fuck, Jules," he says it into the crook of my neck, his hair tickling next to my ear.

The way he says my name does something to me. The sheer desire behind it, like my name is the last name he ever wants to say. Before I can even catch up to what's happening, I'm tightening around him and screaming as I scratch my nails down his back and arch my chest to his. It's probably the fastest I've ever come in my life.

While it's been a long time since I've been with somebody, he must be doing some sort of magic because *if* I can get off with a guy, it usually takes much longer. This gives me high hopes. Especially when I feel the smirk against my neck.

Quickly followed by teeth, causing a jolt to shoot through me and a yelp to explode from my mouth.

"Do you want to stop?" Is he serious?

"God no." I'm so glad he's putting my needs before his own but there is absolutely zero part of me that wants to stop. If he can make me come like that five minutes in, I need to see what he can do after more time.

With a half smirk spreading across his face, one I've come to know as devious, he starts pumping into me, hard and fast. I squeak and whimper and arch and tilt and grab. God, it's so good.

Just as the pressure is starting to build again, and I'm starting to wonder if he's actually human, still holding out, he pulls away, leaving me reeling and whining at the loss of him.

Before my head can wrap around what's happening and why he pulled away, he flips me to my stomach, looping an arm around my waist and pulling me to my knees before pushing back into me. Immediately, my hands twist into the sheets as a long, deep moan escapes my throat.

A shuddery breath escapes him as his hands grip my hips, and he stops for a minute, pushed so deep inside me. "Holy shit, Jules. You're so fucking tight."

When he starts slowly pulling out and pushing back in, I swear I think I'm going to lose it. And then he starts really getting into it, and I'm convinced I'm going to just disintegrate below him.

Pushing up on my hands, my hair flies around my face, into my mouth. I'm combing it back from my face as Zane tangles his hand into the strands, pulling me up so my back is pressed against his chest, his hand sliding up to cup my breast. All while still thrusting hard.

Fuck, it's hot.

When he starts twiddling my nipple between his fingers, it's all over for me. My head tilts back to his shoulder and my fingers dig into his thighs. If my nails were any longer, I'm sure I'd draw blood.

His grip around my body tightens as I start to shudder and cry out. A low groan against my neck tells me he's coming too. His movements slow as he sits back on his heels, still holding me against him, as his teeth dig into my shoulder.

He keeps his hold on me as we fall sideways to the bed. I can't move, I can't think, I'm not even sure I'm breathing.

I'm slightly aware of light lips and breath at the nape of my neck. My whole body is tingling so much that I barely feel it.

We lay here for a few minutes, my faculties slowly returning, making me aware of his still slightly ragged breathing and his arms still tight around me. There's a thin layer of sweat between us. As he kisses from my neck along to my shoulder his arms loosen slightly. Enough for me to turn to face him.

Smirking, he brushes some hair from my face, sticky with sweat. "Are you okay?"

Okay? Is he serious?

"Oh, yeah. I'm way beyond the land of okay. Why, were you unconvinced?"

"No, not at all. I'm just making sure."

"And you?"

"Oh, I can definitely say that I am fantastic. I just know it's been a while for you. I want to make sure you're good. Not triggered or anything." He's referring to two things.

"Yes, it has been a while. And *that* was certainly well worth the wait. And I'm good on other fronts too. No triggers. I'm not going to run out and find some random hook up. Trust me, I doubt anything could compare."

"And the other?"

I push up to press my lips against his. "Willingly and happily being with you is very different. I'm good. I promise."

My eyes flutter closed as he brushes his knuckles over my cheek to collect my hair in his hand, holding it loosely at my neck. Opening my eyes, I can only describe the way he's looking at me as lovingly.

"You'd tell me?"

"Not only would I tell you, but I wouldn't lie to you. I promise. I mean it. One thing I've never done with you is hold back."

He seems to accept my answer as he leans in and kisses me. "I wasn't expecting this when I came over."

"No? You haven't been thinking about it for weeks?"

"Well, I didn't say *that*. You mentioned something about a short skirt, which I'd very much like to see by the way, and I haven't stopped thinking about it since. I just didn't expect it." I knew that skirt was going to stick with him.

"Maybe if I'm feeling generous, I'll let you see it some time." I told him I'd start giving him shit again. Guess it's already starting. "So, what *did* you expect?"

"You know how I asked why you weren't ripping my balls off? That. Or yelling. Or really for you to not want to see me again." Tracing down my face with his fingertip, he talks quietly. "I'm happy you let me come back."

I shrug nonchalantly. "I had to know what sex would be like. I'm good. You can go now."

Holding my wrists in his hands he rolls me to my back, hovering over me. He's already hard again. I can't remember the last time I was with a guy that had the stamina to go for another round so quickly. This is going to be fun.

"The hell I can." As he starts kissing along my neck, a low whimper eases from my lips and my chest rises to meet his.

He's already shown me he knows what to do with his hands, his fingers, his mouth. God every part of himself really. My only curiosity is if it was a one-time thing or not. I can't wait to find out.

Chapter 28

Zane

S ince I arrived twelve hours ago, we've had sex ten times. Ten. Every single time has been fucking amazing. She's so tight and wet. *Fuck*.

We've barely slept. We're completely insatiable for each other. I woke up one time to her perfect mouth around my dick. By far the best blow job I've ever gotten. As soon as she noticed I was awake, she climbed on top of me and rode me for twenty minutes, coming twice and stopping anytime she thought I was close until she'd had her fill.

I woke her up once flicking her nipple with my tongue. She moaned in her sleep until her eyes opened.

She's vocal and loud. The way she says my name is enough to push me over the edge. She screams when she orgasms, each and every time, just as loud if not louder than the last. She knows what she wants, and she isn't afraid to ask for it. It all makes it even better.

The fact that she just may be the most gorgeous woman I've ever seen is icing on this very delicious cake.

Things had progressed so quickly from the couch, we were already in bed ass naked when the thought of condoms came up. I can't even remember the last time I bought some, and I certainly wouldn't ever be so presumptuous to bring any with me even if I had cases of them at home. I was ready to walk to the nearest drug store with a hard on the size of the Eiffel Tower when Jules told me she's on some several-month-long birth control. That was all I needed to hear.

It's early, the sun is just starting to stream in through her gauzy curtains, but I find myself wide awake, just staring at the beauty laying next to me. I'm thankful to remember I don't have to work today, first Saturday in weeks I haven't had a conference call. I'm far too exhausted to talk numbers and investments.

The cuts on her arms have all but faded, the slightest hint of a mark, or maybe it's my imagination knowing they were there. I'm relieved to see no new ones. Her impossibly long eyelashes flutter as she dreams.

I fight the urge to reach out and run my fingers down the curve of her spine to the top of the sheet, resting just above her perfect ass.

Her nose starts to twitch, and I notice a curl has fallen in her face. Ever so gently, I brush it back to join the rest. I've never really dated a girl with curly hair before, or if they had it, they straightened it. But she loves her hair, embraces it. There's about a million different hair products in the bathroom, but I love that about her. The curls suit her.

Fuck, I'm getting hard just watching her sleep. I'm not sure how much more she can take. She has to be at least *getting* sore at this point. I don't want to hurt her.

Continuing to take in and track her body, I see the slightest hint of redness peeking through her hair on the soft track of skin between her neck and her shoulder. Carefully brushing the strands away, I find the round, red marks of bites. Two, given at different times. If she rolled over, I know I'd see another at the crest of her breast and another on her inner thigh. I'm not usually a biter, but something about her, I just couldn't help myself. She didn't seem to mind. I'll have to double check.

Without thinking, my fingers delicately brush over the marks. They don't seem too bad, just a little pink. I can't remember which was the hardest though. A sudden movement makes me quickly pull my hand back, not wanting to wake her.

Too late.

Jules looks up at me and smiles, stretching. God it's hot to watch, as she arches her back, forcing her ass in the air.

"Were you watching me sleep?"

"Maybe. I woke up not too long ago, was just admiring the beautiful creature lying naked next to me."

"Don't. It's weird."

"Well, maybe you should wear some clothes next time."

She turns on her side and sidles up to me, pushing from her chest to her pelvis against mine.

"Is that really what you want?" She practically purrs.

"No. But if you're going to be naked, you're going to get stared at." My mouth chases after hers but she pulls away, a smirk playing across her lips.

My fingers gently trace along the marks on her shoulder.

"It's okay, they don't hurt." She answers the question in my mind.

"Are you sure?"

"Definitely sure."

I like to think she'd tell me. That our conversation last night—God was it really just last night?—would be fresh in her mind that she'll tell me everything. But I also think I'm an idiot to believe that's reality. She's not one to shy away from giving me shit, but she tends to hold back the things that hurt her. Last night, she said she doesn't do that with me, but I know it's not true. I can't blame her; we don't know each other that well yet. But I won't risk hurting her.

"Zane. I'm good. I'd like to say I'm so good I could go for a few more rounds, but I'm a little sore." There's some honesty.

I wrap my hand around her hip and start to rub my thumb along her hipbone, fingers tapping along her back.

"Mm, that feels nice." She's still pressed up against me and starts kissing my chest. I swallow hard, trying to keep control of myself.

"Here, roll to your stomach." I pull back a little and glide her down, sitting up to massage her back. She relaxes and sinks into the mattress below my hands.

I start at her shoulders, thumbs rubbing over the muscles. As I slide my hands down, they wrap her ribs, thumbs massaging by her spine. Her skin's soft and warm beneath my palms. I can only get to her mid-back before I have to move, sitting on my knees between her legs.

"Mm, that feels so good Zane."

"I like to make you feel good."

"I can tell. You certainly did last night." Fuck that's sexy. So few women are willing to talk about sex in general, let alone how they feel about it. Or at least in my experience.

I keep working her muscles, running my hands up and down her back, adjusting the pressure, moving my fingers in slow circles. When I reach her lower back, my hands cup her hips, pressing firmly against the bone in front and back, sure it's where she's most sore.

I can't help myself as my hands slip lower and massage the upper part of her ass, hands right at her hip joint. If I wanted to be playful, I could dig my fingers in and tickle her. But I'm not exactly feeling playful.

I keep going until I get to the junction of her ass and legs, my thumbs resting just under the hump. I have to take a deep shaky breath to stop myself. She's made no protests, no signs or words to stop. But I can't let myself go there when she's sore.

"Why are you stopping?" Her voice is low, seductive. It's not helping.

"I just need a second."

"No, you don't. I know what you want, I do too."

"You're sore. I don't want to hurt you."

"Zane, I'm telling you what I want. And I want you to fuck me."

I've never really been a giver in the bedroom, or in relationships, probably why they never worked. But I didn't care before. With Jules, I care. I want to give her what she wants. But I know sometimes she doesn't know what's best for her. Still. Maybe if I'm gentle.

"I don't know, Jules."

"Please," she begs, wiggling herself toward me.

I glide over her, sliding my tip along her warm wetness. Fuck, so wet. I slip the head in, just a little, making sure she really is okay to do this. Before I can even read her, she pushes back against me, taking me further in. The girl certainly knows what she wants.

Tilting my hips, I ease the rest of the way into her as she moans low in her chest. Hot damn, this girl. I start out slow, gliding in and out, keeping an eye on her reaction, ready to stop at the slightest hint of discomfort.

I don't find any. Not as I increase speed, not as I go harder, not as I knot my fingers in her hair. The whole time she's whining and mewling and panting, fingers kneading the sheet by her face.

"Mm, fuck Zane, go faster." It comes out strained and between breaths.

Hiking up her hips slightly, I adjust my position, letting go of her hair and pushing my arms straighter, but not before giving her a nip at the base of her neck. I pick up the tempo, and she starts to fall apart. Her breathing increases as her voice rises and she starts to shudder.

"Just like that...don't stop."

I lean down close to her and lick her earlobe before pressing my mouth against her ear. "I want you to come for me baby, and I want to hear you, nice and loud."

That's all she needs as her hand grips mine and she tightens around me, screaming a string of obscenities with my name thrown in a few times. I slow slightly, kissing along her jaw as she works through her tremors before I push up straight again.

Three more hard thrusts and my balls tighten as I come right behind her with a low 'fuck' and a groan, resting my forehead against her head. I stay like that for a moment as I catch my breath, kissing her temple before rolling to my side.

Her eyes are closed but she has a small smile pulling at her lips. I gently brush some of the hair from her face as her eyes flutter open.

"You good?"

"Oh, yeah."

My face must not be very believable because she throws her arm around my shoulders and pulls herself against me, settling into my chest.

"I promise you, I am good. Even if I couldn't walk, I would be good, and it'd be very well worth it."

"Are you sure you *can* walk?"

"Well, no but I'm pretty sure. By far the best sex I've ever had."

I start tracing a fingertip lightly down her spine like I'd wanted to earlier. "Which time?"

"Oh, every single one. I mean, I could get technical and split hairs between the several times and pick a favorite, but overall, each time was far better than any other time. If that makes sense."

It makes perfect sense. And it's the same for me. I nod at her, like a fool. "Yeah, I get it. Same." Did I suddenly lose all brain capacity?

Shaking away the inability to think, I squeeze her waist, pulling her closer. "Let me make you breakfast."

She jerks her head back. "You want to make me breakfast? In *my* kitchen?"

"Well, I could throw you over my shoulder and carry you back to my apartment and make you breakfast there but we're already here."

"I mean, sure. Nobody's ever made me breakfast before." She hesitates for a second before quickly interjecting. "Besides you, of course, when I was, um, less than capable. But never on a typical Jules day."

"Really? Nobody?" She shakes her head. It makes my blood run hot that nobody has ever treated her the way she should be treated. Something I plan to right immediately. "Well, that's just unfortunate. Clearly the men you were with previously didn't appreciate what they had. Definitely their loss."

"I'm nobody special." It twists my heart strings when she says things like this.

Hooking my finger under her chin I tilt her face up so she's looking right at me. "You absolutely are Jules. And I know that your mind tells you otherwise, but I promise I will make sure you know that you are, in fact, very special." I know it's hard for her to accept praise, to see herself the way I see her. But I have every intention of helping with that.

Maybe those other guys didn't understand her the way I do. Maybe they didn't see her the way I do. Either way, I'm thankful none of them worked out.

Chapter 29

Jules

Days tick by uneventfully. For the most part. Zane and I spend our nights together. He comes straight from work, letting himself in when he gets here. It's the closest thing to a real relationship I've ever had, though no titles have been thrown around.

We had gotten into our first true argument about two weeks into his stay.

"Jules! What the hell?"

I jumped awake to the sound of his voice. "Huh? What?" I rubbed sleep from my eyes as I tried to get my bearings.

"Why is this door unlocked if you're asleep?"

"I don't want you to have to knock. I must have dozed off."

"That's not okay, Jules." His whole body was tense with his words. I wanted to feel some way about this situation, but I was still in the throes of sleep.

We'd been up extra late the night before having ridiculously hot sex. Zane does something to me that nobody else has done before. He can read my body like it's the alphabet.

"I'm sorry. I'll make sure to stay awake."

Striding over the couch he took my face in his hands. "I'm just worried about you. That's all. Your safety is not something I take lightly."

"I know. I'm sorry." I yawned at the end of my words and shook my head, deciding I'd have to get a key for him because another night like the one before, and we'd be in the exact same situation.

It took me another ten days, but I did have a key made for him.

He'll swing by his apartment as needed to get different clothes, to swap things out. We've stayed over at his place a couple times, but I don't really like it there.

Zane's had a few nights where he's felt a little on edge and decided it was best to stay at his apartment. I miss him those nights. It's a weird sensation, to miss somebody I haven't known terribly long but spend the majority of my time with. I don't sleep well when he's not around.

We haven't been back to group. Dr. Ptansky knows what happened, of course, and she doesn't push me to return, understanding the unease I have surrounding both the building and the experience.

One unremarkable Saturday morning, seven weeks after Zane and I have really started together, I'm at coffee with Daphne while he plays basketball with...whoever he plays with. He doesn't seem to have actual friends, says they're some guys from work.

"Hey Daph, can I ask you something?" I jump in before we've even sat down.

"Always, Jules. What's up?"

As we ease into our seats, I cross my legs, taking a sip and allowing the cold liquid to slide down my throat, which sends a shiver down my spine and through my veins. It's a sticky June morning and the opposition of the two in my body make for a delightful tingling. I use it to push away the nerves.

"Remember when I took you to therapy years ago? Dr. P had thought it'd be good for you to get some insight?"

"Of course. I still remember a lot of what she said and suggested. Though, you've really come a long way since then."

"What was it like?" I meet her eyes to look for any sign of hesitation or any non-truths. Daphne doesn't really lie to me, but she alters reality to better suit me. I don't need that now.

Narrowing her eyes at me she asks, "What do you mean?" before taking a sip of her coffee.

"I mean was it weird? Awkward? Did you feel talked down to or anything?"

"By Dr. Ptansky? No, she's wonderful. I didn't feel weird about it at all. I was happy to go, get more insight into you and how I can help you more. Why? Where is this coming from?"

I don't answer and she inspects me for a few minutes before realization slowly takes over her features, rearranging them as her mouth opens, her eyes widen, and her eyebrows raise. "Oh, you want to bring Zane!"

Heat prickles at the back of my neck and kisses my cheeks. "Shh. Yes, Dr. P thinks it might be a good idea if he were to come to one now that he's clearly a pretty major factor in my life. She thinks it'd be helpful if he knew some things about me, knew what he could do in a really low moment. Though he's been through a few already and has faired pretty well on his own."

"What does he do?" I realize I haven't talked to her about Zane recently. Or at least not more than a quick update as to what's going on. I mostly shift the conversation to her.

"A week or so ago he literally restrained me until it passed. Then made me talk to him."

"Good." She nods as though it's the best news she's heard in days. "I do still think it could be beneficial for him though. It wasn't even so much that I learned how I could help, but just more about you, why things are hard for you. I don't know, personally I just think maybe it could help in some way. And at the very least, it can't hurt." She raises a single shoulder before taking a sip of her coffee.

I bob my head slowly, digesting her words and trying to make my thoughts complete. "I guess I'll mention it to him later."

Our morning continues with much lighter conversation which helps me ease into my chair and loosen my muscles.

Messaging Zane on my way out the door, I let him know I'm finished, and I'll meet him at home. I figure today is as good a day as any to bring up therapy. I'm in a halfway decent mood after coffee, and Daphne's words are echoing in my mind, keeping the momentum going.

When I get back to my apartment, Zane's already freshly showered. One thing that's become increasingly sexy, is that he doesn't style his hair when he's not going to work. The loose tendrils fall more over his forehead, sometimes drooping into his eyes. He lets his ever present five o'clock shadow grow out a bit more over the weekends as well.

The very best part about seeing Zane when we've been apart for a few hours, is the absolutely beaming smile he sends my way. It makes my knees weak, and I want to melt into the floor. I don't tell him how much that reaction truly affects me; I need to keep a few things to myself, including how much of a hold he has on me already. There are too many dark marks on my record to trust him completely—especially so soon.

"How was coffee with Daphne?" The clean linen and sandalwood scent wraps around me to warm me from the inside out as he pulls me against him.

"It was good."

"I'd like to meet her sometime."

Resting my hands on his chest, I push myself back slightly, Zane's arms tightening so I stay in his hold. "You would?" None of the guys I've ever been in a "relationship" with in the past have ever had interest in meeting her.

"Well, yeah, of course. She's a huge part of your life, Jules."

"I'm just surprised is all." I shake away the thought and decide now is as good a time as any to broach the subject. But I can't meet his eyes, so instead focus on the collar of his gray T-shirt. It matches his eyes. Twisting my shaky fingers into the fabric gives me a place to put the nervous energy rolling through my body. "Speaking of meeting people important to me, I was um. I was wondering, hoping, if maybe you'd be willing to come meet Dr. Ptansky with me?"

When he stiffens and doesn't answer, I keep going. "I mean, you don't have to, I just, I was hoping you'd consider it. I guess I uh—"Tilting my chin to meet his eyes, I don't see what I was expecting, which was resignation and refusal. "Jules. I'm happy to go with you. Any time you want. But did something happen? Is there a reason that you're bringing this up now? I'm not against going with you, I'm worried something happened today or recently that's bringing this forward."

"Oh. No, nothing. I was just thinking about it, she brought it up on Thursday. Daphne has come with me, and I asked today what her feelings were about it." I'm trying to look away but he's keeping the hold firm on my chin. This conversation is making me itchy in my own skin. "They just think it might be helpful. Is all."

"I agree. So, you let me know when you're ready, and I'll be there. Okay?"

"Okay. How were your 'not really friends'?"

He laughs and releases my chin. "They were fine."

"Did they kick your ass?"

Scoffing, he narrows his eyes at me. "You should know better than to think somebody could be better than me at anything. Plus, I save the ass kicking for you."

"Smart man."

Tucking some hair behind my ear as he keeps his hold on me, he looks at me softly. "You've been nice lately."

I snort but can't look at him as he sees right through me. "I have not." In reality, I have been, dialing things back a lot and biting my tongue. Even though it's playful and all in good fun, most of the time, I don't need to take any risks of him leaving. Knowing it will happen is one thing. Having it happen when I'm just trying to have some fun is entirely different. It will be because of me no matter what. That I know for certain.

"Enough to make me think you might actually like me."

"Oh no. Well, I'll have to stop immediately. Wouldn't want you thinking that." Pushing up on my toes, I brush my lips against his.

"I don't know if you're just in a better mood or if you're holding back. If it's the first, I'm glad. If it's the latter, please stop."

My shoulders curl in as I try to fold into myself.

Zane puts a hand on one and pushes back. His lips are turned down in one corner, as are his eyes. "Why, Jules?"

The familiar fluttering of an anxiety attack settles into my chest as I look anywhere but Zane's face. His hold on me has strengthened as he pulls me closer and tightens his hand. I don't answer him. I can't. The words won't come out. And even if they would, I don't know what to say.

"Jules, listen to me. I'm not going to leave you just because you give me a hard time. You've done that since day one, remember? And things only got stronger between us. If you *want* to be nice to me, be nice to me. But if you want to give me shit, I'm here for it. Don't hold back just because we're seeing each other."

"You may regret saying that." It comes out low, on a wisp of air as I feel like I can't catch my breath.

"I won't. Besides, I don't want you having to think about what you're going to say or do around me. Be yourself."

"Myself means being a bitch and hurting myself when I have a bad day. And I have a lot of them. Do you really want that?"

"Yes, I do. Because I'm *here*. Bad days and all. Have I done something to show you I can't handle them? I mean I'm not an expert, in your life or the mental health field, but I like to think I've done a pretty damn good job as of late. Am I mistaken?"

"No." My eyes are locked on the floor by our feet as my fingers rest gently against Zane's stomach. I can't get my voice louder than just above a whisper thanks to the lump that's taken root in my throat.

"Then please stop. Jules, if something happens that I can't handle I'll tell you. Okay?"

All I can do is nod as he sighs and pulls me into him, closing his arms around my shoulders and head so I'm enclosed. His familiar scent engulfs my senses, and my heart rate starts to return to normal, my muscles loosening as I ease my arms from between us and loop them around his waist.

In every single way Zane is showing me that he's so different from anybody else. But at the same time, I can't get myself to fully believe it, to fully let down those walls; if I do, there's no going back, and no way to protect myself from the inevitable pain.

Chapter 30

Zane

Sex with Jules is unlike anything I've ever experienced. Not only is it far superior to any encounter I've ever had, even in my wild college and early adult years, the whole experience is on a different level. There have always been certain things I've enjoyed doing that many girls are not interested in. I've been slapped more than once for suggesting cuffs or ties. Seems a little over the top if you ask me.

Jules, on the other hand, embraces it. She's willing to try new things, many of which she's admitted to wanting to try herself.

There are few sexier things than seeing Jules sprawled out and tied to the bed. But there's no greater sight than my hand wrapped around her delicate throat. Especially when she gets the hazy look in her eyes of pure lust.

Jules is always up for something new. I wouldn't say my proclivities are too out there, but the fact that Jules loves them just as much, only makes me want her more.

I'm thinking all of these things as I sort through papers to close out an account for a client, eager to get to Jules. I could go home, could leave it for tomorrow, but I hate leaving things unfinished.

The fact that I consider Jules's apartment home these days doesn't even feel awkward anymore. I'm there far more often than I'm at my own.

A buzzing draws my attention.

Jules: *When will you be home? I'm hungry.* I can't help but shake my head and laugh. She's really given over the reigns for cooking to me. I don't mind, I enjoy cooking, even after a long day of work. Sometimes I think it's better she's not in the kitchen around the knives.

Glancing around at the papers I take in what's left to sign, sort, and seal away.

Me: *Working on closing something out. Should be able to get out of here in about twenty.*

Jules: *Ok. See you soon.*

Focusing my attention back to the task at hand, I organize everything into the proper stacks, signing where needed. I leave the three piles of papers on my desk with a note left for Penelope to handle the rest in the morning. She'll add tabs where my client needs to sign and get them to where they need to go. I let her leave at five tonight and it's now a quarter after six.

The second I walk through the door at Jules's, I know something's off. "Jules?" She's usually waiting for me in the living room, reading a book or typing frantically on her laptop.

Panic bubbles in my stomach, until she appears at the end of the hallway. I freeze as the air sticks in my lungs and my pulse skyrockets. My dick is immediately standing at attention. Leaning her shoulders back against the wall, as the rest of her body tilts forward, is Jules.

She's wearing a pleated dark gray skirt that ends just below her perfect ass. Her tight white button-down shirt is tied just under her breasts, exposing her midriff with her big bouncy curls hanging perfectly. A pair of red heels and black knee highs complete the look.

Months ago, I told her about the image she had brought forth after she had compared it to my suit. I've never gotten it out of my mind. Sure she'd pushed it aside, I haven't brought it up since. Especially because I don't want her to think I'm not satisfied or that something is lacking. It's not. At all. But Jules can be quick to turn something into a negative. I don't want that on her conscience.

My feet are glued to the spot near the door as I can't stop drinking her in. I'm sure my mouth is open; my erection is pressing against my zipper. But I can't seem to move.

"Aren't you going to come give me a kiss hello?" The sultriness in her voice makes me swallow a groan.

"Hot fuck, Jules." No other words will suffice. The vision in front of me is even better than I ever imagined. As much as I want to lick every square inch of her body, I need to take another minute to make sure this image is perfected in my mind.

When I start to undo my tie, Jules reaches a hand out to stop me. "Wait! Leave it." One corner of her mouth ticks up before she pulls her bottom lip between her teeth.

That's all I need as I cross the room in big strides, one hand finding her hip while the other tangles in her hair as I close my mouth over hers and pull her flush against me.

Turning, I box her in against the wall. The heels give her an advantage, but I still tower over her. But Jules doesn't shrink with me, instead, she stands taller.

Sliding my hand up her thigh I find a nice surprise as my eyebrow quirks up. "No panties Jules?"

One shoulder ticks up as she rests her hands against my chest. "I didn't see a need."

"You are the perfect woman." There are a million reasons she's perfection, but this is a major confidence booster for her.

Before she can respond, I claim her mouth again, sliding my tongue against hers. I want to devour her, right here, right now.

But I don't know when this outfit might come out to play again, and there are plans I'd made for it a long time ago.

My hands find their way under her skirt to grab her perfect ass, giving it a squeeze before I lift her, pressing her against the wall as my palms glide up her frame. Her body is my shrine.

Closing my hands over her breasts, I massage them, running my thumbs over the centers until her nipples turn to hardened peaks beneath her shirt. Her legs tighten around my waist as I kiss down her neck, scraping my teeth and tongue along her soft skin. I want to mark her, claim her as my own. I know it's not necessary, she shows me she's mine every single day—without words—but the urge is still there.

I start to work her buttons but they're increasingly frustrating with their tiny circles, refusing to shift back through the holes. Instead, I grab both sides and pull, the buttons clicking to the floor around us. I'll buy her a new one, or a dozen, so I can do that again.

To go with her cherry red heels, she's opted for a lacy red bra. I don't know how I didn't notice it through the shirt, aside from sheer distraction. Licking down her chest, I move my mouth over her nipple, sinking my teeth in, causing her to arch toward me and wrap her arms around my head.

Finding her mouth again, I move away from the wall, carrying her to the bedroom. Once I reach the bed, I throw her down onto it, furiously undoing my tie, my shirt, and my pants. I don't take anything off, just leave my shirt open, tie loose, and pants undone.

Grabbing her ankle, I yank her back to the edge of the bed as she giggles. The light airy sound sends a jolt through me, making my cock bob in my pants and my heart race. It's so infrequent.

Hastily, I flip her to her stomach, setting her feet on the floor so she's perfectly bent over the edge of the bed. Flipping her skirt up, I take a step back as I free myself, giving a few rough strokes as I enjoy the sight in front of me.

Pushing up on her hands with a huff, Jules looks over her shoulder at me. "What are you waiting for?" Irritation drips off her words.

"I'm just enjoying the view a little."

"Well, stop."

I quirk up an eyebrow at her boldness. Taking a step closer, I line myself up with her, slipping along her wetness as a growl settles in my throat. She's always so ready for me.

Before I can react, she pushes back, taking me in halfway. "Fuck. So greedy, Jules. Patience will serve you well." Who the hell am I kidding, it's a Herculean effort to wait just to tease her a little.

I ease myself the rest of the way into her before she can answer with more than a moan. God, her noises are the most amazing sounds. Her velvety smooth tightness is enough to make me weak in the knees, and I always have to take a second to set myself.

We've talked about fitting together like puzzle pieces, the way her body folds into mine when we lay together, how my chin fits into the nook of her neck, and how I can rest my chin comfortably on her head. But when I'm inside of her, I swear her body was made for mine, and mine was made for hers.

As I start moving inside her, she pants, her head tipping forward. My hands wrap around her hips as I start thrusting without restraint. Every sound and eye flutter from her fuels my fire, my need to get her to the finish line over and over. Her refractory period is astoundingly short, it's even made mine shorter.

Needing to feel more of her silky skin, I glide my hands up her back, sliding under her shirt as I keep slamming into her, leaning over her. Laying kisses up her spine, I move my hands to her breasts, cupping them and taking her nipples between my fingers, through her bra. I should have taken it off.

Reaching back toward me, Jules wraps my tie around her hand a few times as she pulls herself up against me, hooking her other hand around the back of my neck and pulling my mouth to hers. We moan in unison as our tongues collide.

Standing straighter, I pull her with me as one hand wraps around her throat and the other circles her waist, supporting her weight as I hold her against my chest. I love her like this, caged to me.

My mouth finds her ear as I murmur in it breathlessly. "You belong to me Jules. Tell me you're mine."

"Only if you tell me you're mine." She always pushes back. It's sexy as hell.

"I am. You know I'm yours."

"And I'm yours, Zane. Only yours." Fuck. That admission does things to me. Heat starts licking up my spine.

Dragging my tongue down her neck, I throw her back down, pressing my hand between her shoulder blades as I slow my movements. Her whine tells me she's not happy about it, but I can't release, not yet.

Leaning back over her, my free hand glides between her body and the bed, my finger finding her swollen clit. My mouth rests against her ear as I start circling it, talking low as she starts moaning. "Whining isn't nice, Jules. You'll get what you need."

Straightening to watch her, I continue with easy glides in and out of her as I swirl faster and harder. Within seconds, she's moaning and gripping the sheets. Picking up momentum, she starts shuddering beneath me. As she tightens around me and screams my name it sets off my own orgasm, the heat racing through me. A groan halts in my throat and comes out a strangled sound.

Slowing to a stop, I fold over her, kissing the nape of her neck and resting my forehead against the back of her head. With one more kiss on her ear, I stand, pull out, and take off my clothes before flopping on the bed next to her.

With my arm around her waist, I pull her up next to me and brush some hair from her face as she curls against my side.

Putting my hands on her shoulders, I push her back slightly so my eyes can lock on hers. "I love you." It's the first time either of us have said it. After sex may not be the most romantic, but it's us.

I steel myself for a look of shock to cross her face, for her to panic, even to run. But none of those things happen. She just simply responds.

"I love you, too."

Tension releases from my shoulders as my heart starts hammering in my chest again. I expected resistance, fear, something. But she said it seamlessly, easily.

"So, how was your surprise?" She's already moving on.

"Huh? Oh, it was amazing. Couldn't top it if you tried. You know I've been thinking about this outfit for months, right?"

"I do, in fact. Why do you think I assembled all the pieces just as you described them?" Her finger traces along my chest, and I can't help but revel in her perfection.

Instead of answering, I take a few minutes to stare into her warm eyes. The fire is back, full force, possibly even stronger than when we met. Her struggles are still part of our life, but she's doing well enough to control them for the past few weeks. She'll come to me most of the time, let me know, let me talk her down, let me hold her to prevent her from doing something she'll regret. I know it may not last, but I'm enjoying where we are right now.

"Are you hungry? I can go make something." While I don't want to leave the bed, she had mentioned being hungry when I was still at work, and my need to care for her takes over.

"A little. Mostly it was a ruse to get you here. And so I knew roughly how much time I had to get ready."

A small laugh seeps through my smile. "Very clever." Tracing along her hairline, I glide my fingers down and collect a handful of hair as I draw her mouth to mine. Pulling away the slightest bit, I lock my gaze on hers. "I mean it you know. I love you."

Still no startle, no draw back, no color drainage. "I know. I mean it too. I love you, Zane."

My body fills with warmth as I hug her close and kiss the top of her head. Hearing her tell me she loves me is the most amazing thing to come out of her mouth. I never in a million years would have imagined feeling this way, finding somebody. *Especially* in group therapy.

I almost didn't go, I almost said *fuck it* and decided to find a new therapist, figuring I could bounce around any time somebody suggested it. But I'm eternally grateful I quieted that voice and decided to show up that day. The gorgeous brunette who stared and gave me shit for weeks now loves me. Life works in interesting ways sometimes.

Chapter 31

Jules

The unease gripping my body and tightening my muscles hasn't ceased in the four weeks since Zane said he would come with me to therapy. It's only gotten worse since we decided on a day, which happens to be today.

While I sit on the couch, leg bouncing incessantly, Zane putters around in the kitchen, whipping up some lunch. Therapy is in a few hours, and he wants to make sure I'm at least full, of both food and caffeine.

He took the day off to be with me all day, not trusting that I wouldn't hurt myself if left alone. It's a strong instinct, and it makes my stomach roll when I think about how much I'll miss it when it's gone.

Dr. Ptansky has been on top of me about those thoughts recently. She says Zane has done nothing but show me he cares. She reminds me that he told me he loved me first, not in response, checks that I truly love him, and has me reiterate that he tells me daily, with more than just his words.

None of that helps chase away the voice in my head that tells me I'm not good enough, that he's going to wake up one day and realize that, love or not.

"Jules, please calm down." I jump out of my seat when Zane joins me on the couch, placing a fresh cup of coffee on the table in front of me. Immediately, I grab the mug and hold it up to my face, inhaling the sweet scent that instantly has calm snaking through my body.

"What if it's too much? What if she tells you something that pushes you over the edge?"

"She won't. Jules, what could be more than what I've already seen, already experienced? You were worried that it would be too frequent for me, and while there have been many times I've had to help you lately, I don't mind. It doesn't scare me away, it makes me *worry* about you. That's why I'm excited to go—so I can learn." He takes my hand in his, linking our fingers and bringing my knuckles to his lips.

Though I nod, I look away, focusing instead on a spot on the carpet where the sun shines in. Maybe I should get a cat, I bet they'd like that spot. Who am I kidding? I can't take care of a cat, I can barely take care of myself certain days. Plus, Zane doesn't really strike me as the cat type.

"Jules." The sternness of his voice makes me look at him. When I do, he cups my cheek, running his thumb under my eye. "I don't have to go if you don't want me to. I don't want to cause you more stress or anxiety."

"No, no, I'll get over it. I think it's important, despite my discomfort and concern." I think.

"Are you sure? Maybe we can try again in a few weeks." The fact that he speaks in future terms, that we both do, never really does anything to control my fear. It wouldn't be the first time. I've even had plans made.

My eyes drift shut, and I lean toward Zane when he starts twirling my curls around his fingers. A heavenly scent wafts from the kitchen, and my stomach rumbles. I've been so nervous and so distracted with nerves bubbling inside me that I not only forgot Zane was making lunch, but that I skipped breakfast, which he scolded me for.

"I'm sure. What's for lunch? It smells delicious."

"Chicken parm."

"You're making chicken parm just for me for lunch?" When he doesn't answer, I open my eyes and turn to look at him while he shifts his hand to massage my scalp. His eyes are closer to blue today, and he's looking at me with a softness in them that makes me melt.

"Of course, I am, Jules. Besides, we may want to just order for dinner, you may be feeling a bit down, I want to be prepared for that."

Words elude me when he talks like this, plans ahead, and so clearly just...*gets* me. I'm fairly certain that by this point he's become accustomed to my awkward silence after he's so sweet to me. It never seems to bother him, but I'm sure he'd appreciate some sort of return sentiment. The problem is that I never know what to say, and anxiety steals my words before I can get them out.

After a delicious lunch, we cuddle on the couch where Zane plays with my hair and trails his fingers along my skin. Normally he'd try to distract me in other physical ways, but I think he knows even sex won't cure my gripping anxiety this time.

At a quarter to four, we leave and start our walk to Dr. Ptansky's office. Zane holds me close against him, despite the early August heat and stickiness thick in the air.

When we get to the building, I freeze outside the door, looking up at the window I know is hers. Zane cups my face with both hands and turns me toward him, running his thumbs over the apples of my cheeks before he leans in and rests his lips against mine.

"Hey, everything is going to be fine. I'm here because I want to be, because you want me to be, and because I love you. You've got this."

Closing my hands around his wrists, I shut my eyes and fill my lungs, the wonderfully calming scent of linen and sandalwood filling my nose.

After a deep exhale, I meet Zane's graying eyes. "I'm ready."

There are polite introductions and a handshake when we get upstairs, and I sit close enough to Zane to feel his warmth, but far enough that it won't feel like he's ripping away from me when he gets up to leave.

Dr. P does most of the talking, which I tune in and out of. It's nothing I'm not already aware of, nothing I haven't heard before. My attention is drawn a little closer anytime Zane's deep voice registers. This meeting is mostly for them to discuss, as was the one that I brought Daphne to. I'm mostly just here for my comfort, so I know they're not saying terrible things about me behind my back. Also, her doctor laws or whatever.

"Julienne." My real name pulls me from the haze I've been settled in, and I focus on Dr. P. "I'd like you to join us in the conversation now."

"Okay." Hearing the hoarseness in my voice, Zane tries to take my hand, but I pull it back and look at him. He's eyeing me carefully, trying to figure me out, and I see the moment he decides what he's going to do, as he reaches for my hand again, linking our fingers. I don't pull away this time.

"Now, Zane, normally I'd say that if Julienne pulls away, she's trying to tell you she doesn't want that right now, but I can see how well you know her, and that you took a moment to inspect her, to read her, and to determine not only how she's feeling, but what she may need. You seem to have a strong grasp on her emotions."

"I mean, I like to think I've been doing a pretty good job getting to know her, how to figure out her emotions and her needs."

"Julienne, would you agree with that?"

"I suppose." My voice is quiet, and when Zane squeezes my hand so I can't pull it from his grasp, I start playing with a pillow with the other one.

"Since I'm fairly certain you weren't listening while Zane and I talked, I'll repeat a few things. Zane went over what he's been doing so far and how you've been reacting to that, which to me sounds fairly positive. We discussed some things that may lessen your urges to self-harm, which are all things you and I have talked about over the years.

"The biggest one we talked about is you finding your safe place, Julienne. Your place to bring up in your mind while you do your grounding exercises or when they don't work. I went over the exercises with Zane, so he knows what you're supposed to do. The rest is up to you."

She crosses her legs and puts her notepad on the top leg, pen in hand but not ready to write. The way she's looking at me, I'm sure she's waiting for pushback. While some part of me wants to give it, wants to say something, I can't conjure the words and none of them really feel right anyway.

Once we've thanked her, said goodbye, and are effectively dismissed, we head out and start toward my apartment. Zane throws his arm around my shoulders the second we're out the door, pulling me in and giving me a kiss on the head.

"How about we pick up Japanese at that place you like on the way home?"

"That sounds nice." It warms my heart that he knows I don't like to eat in public.

We take all of two more steps before he stops, taking my face in his hands and standing pressed right up against me. He pulls my mouth to his and slides his tongue along the seam of my lips, which I part immediately. Peppermint tingles across my tastebuds, and my entire being is overwhelmed with Zane.

When he pulls away, he keeps his hold on my cheeks and makes sure to catch my eyes. "I love you. Nothing in there changes anything. I'm here, Jules, I'm in this."

My shoulders sag as the weight of today releases from them, and I fall against his chest. A burn settles behind my eyes as relief pours through me that he's not leaving me.

Yet.

Chapter 32

Jules

Eagerly awaiting Zane's return from work, I'm pacing back and forth in front of the door. It's a little after six, he should be here any minute. I fight the urge to bite at my cuticles.

A breath catches in my throat as I hear the familiar sound of metal on metal and the flip of the lock. It's still a little weird that he has a key to my apartment.

He barely has the door closed when I push myself up against him. I loop his tie around my hand a few times and pull him down toward me. He hesitates for all of a second before his mouth moves against mine, tongues meeting in the middle. Wrapping his arms tightly around my waist, he yanks me flush against him as my other hand hooks to the back of his neck.

Walking backward, away from the door, I pull him with me as he stumbles removing his shoes.

"Something's gotten into you today," he says with a smile against my lips.

"Not yet," I return with my own coy smile.

A growl rises in Zane's chest at my words, turning into a groan as I glide my hand down his chest and along his erection.

I love how fast his body responds to me. There's no delay, no waiting. He just came home from what I'm sure was a long day of work, and he's ready to go. I've found that's not often the case with others.

Sliding his hands to my thighs, he lifts me up. As he carries me toward the bedroom, I wrap my legs around his waist, and he adjusts his hold to lose a hand in my hair as he keeps our mouths together. It's moments like this where I know he needs me as much as I need him.

Once we're in the bedroom, he tosses me onto the bed. He loosens his tie and throws it off to the side, but when he starts undoing the buttons of his shirt, I scramble to my knees. Pushing his hands away, I work them myself while he grabs onto my hips.

My fingers fumble against the solid little circles as his hands tighten. "Faster, Jules." His voice is clipped and urgent.

Finally fishing the last button through the hole, I tear his shirt away from his chest, trailing my fingertips over his muscles. If my panties weren't wet before, they certainly are now.

Reaching the top of his pants, I work furiously at his belt, which seems to mystify me and requires more attention than necessary. My mind is elsewhere, eager to reach what's inside the pants, making my hands clumsy.

Tangling a hand in my hair, he tugs my head back to lock on his eyes. Leaning down, he licks from my neck to my ear where he whispers, "Hurry, Jules," before sliding his mouth over and closing it on mine. I don't know how he expects me to go faster when he's kissing me like he's about to devour me.

Pulling my mouth from Zane's, I try to focus on the task in front of me, which is getting his pants off as fast as possible. It's hard when he's kissing down my neck and sliding his hands up my shirt.

Finally, I free his belt from the loops, quickly tossing it to the ground with a loud clang. I hurriedly unbutton his pants, pushing them down once they're loose.

When my hands reach for the hem of my shirt, Zane clasps onto my wrists, stopping me. "No. My turn."

His gaze slowly rakes over my frame for the first time since he's gotten home. I'm suddenly self-conscious, realizing I'm wearing a ratty long-sleeve T-shirt with no bra and yoga pants while he is—was—dressed in one of his expensive suits.

Thankfully, it doesn't seem to matter as his eyes meet mine and I see pure fire flickering in his irises. It also helps that I see the twitch in his boxers.

Pulling my shirt over my head, Zane's eyes grow wide as his hands cup my breasts, thumbs running over my nipples as a moan eases through my lips.

"God, you're so damn sexy, Jules," he says as he lowers his mouth to close over the hardened peak. My hand loops around his neck as my head tips back.

Keeping my nipple in his mouth, his tongue swirling around and sending pulsations rocking through my body, his hands find their way to the top of my pants and slowly push them to my knees. As one hand loops around my waist, the other settles between my legs.

He groans as he slips along my entrance. "Fuck, Jules. So ready for me." Finding my neck with his mouth, he presses two fingers into me as I arch backwards, my chest meeting his.

Slowly, he lowers me to the mattress as his fingers work inside me and his lips meld to mine. As my back hits the blanket, he leans over me, hooking his fingers as I latch onto his shoulders, writhing beneath him.

"I want you to come for me, Jules. Are you going to do that for me?"

"Yes," I breathe out. Of course, I am. Sometimes I think all he has to do is look at me the right way for me to come.

Moving his fingers faster he murmurs, "Let me hear it, baby," before pulling my nipple back into his mouth.

"Fuck, Zane." I tangle a hand in his hair as I pull him against me, dragging the other one down his back as my nails dig in and I cry out, shuddering beneath him.

Kissing his way to my mouth, he slips his tongue in, curling it against mine. "That's by far my favorite sound," he says against my lips.

"Me screaming?"

"You, falling apart around me. I hope you're ready for it to happen again." *Oh.*

I don't even have to answer as I lick my lips, and he frees his erection, stepping out of his boxers and releasing my ankles from my pants. He runs his open mouth up my leg, blowing gently, leaving a trail of coolness on my burning skin as he moves all the way up my body to my mouth, easing himself into me as he sucks on my neck.

As he starts moving inside me, I'm clawing at his back, the fullness so blissful. His slow steady thrusts—so different than what I was expecting but yet exactly what I need—bring me closer and closer to the edge.

"Zane." It's all I can say. It's low, laced with pleasure.

Leaning on his elbow, he locks his eyes on mine while he's still moving inside me. His lids are hooded, echoing my own which are fluttering. I expect to see sheer desire in his eyes, but instead I find love.

It makes my heart race more than it already is. Running his thumb tenderly along my lower lip, he pulls it down slightly before closing his mouth over mine.

As his tongue moves against mine, he adjust his hips, thrusting deeper and harder, his kiss turning hungrier. His mouth becomes more forceful and stays against mine as I start to tilt my head backwards.

Every movement inside me brings a whine or whimper that dies against his lips. When he becomes hurried, I tear my mouth away as I cry out, digging into his shoulders. Three more thrusts and he's groaning into my neck.

He lays on top of me for a minute or two, catching his breath before rolling to his back. I immediately curl into him, and he wraps his arms around my hips. In a clear hurry, we've ended up on top of the blanket, near the bottom of the bed.

When a shiver runs through me, Zane pulls me to the top of the bed, tucking us under the covers. Kissing the top of my head as I snuggle into his chest, he starts twisting some hair around his fingers.

"Are you hungry?" His voice is low and quiet, vibrating against my palms.

"A little. But I just want to lay here a little longer."

"You should be careful, I may get used to greetings like that."

"Not a problem, I'll gladly do that every day." I shake with him as he laughs.

Giving me a kiss on the forehead, he squeezes me gently. "I love you."

Though my heart, which had just settled to a normal rhythm, races in fear at his words, I respond. "I love you, too." It's not that I don't mean it. I absolutely do. It's the implications that come along with it. The history of those who have loved me in the past. The fact that none of them are still here, whatever the reasoning may be.

"I'm going to go make dinner. Any requests?"

"No. Anything you want. Should we order instead? I'm sure it's late, been a long day." Guilt pangs in my chest. I should have cooked. I should have made something for him to come home to. I was consumed with remorse, wanting to distract myself, wanting to hide the fresh marks from him the only way I know how.

"I don't mind. I can throw something together quick."

"I'm sorry, I should have thought about dinner before you got home." I trail my finger along his shoulder.

"Don't worry about it. Come out when you're ready. I'll wake you up if you fall asleep."

Climbing over me, he gets out of bed, making sure the covers are still around me. I roll to watch him get dressed, his muscles moving as he pulls on boxers and drawstring pants. He foregoes a shirt and heads into the kitchen.

Taking a deep breath, I slide out of bed. I pull one of his long-sleeve shirts over my head, letting it fall to my mid thigh. It's big and loose and warm. The fact that it smells like Zane is an added perk.

Walking down the hall, I know I should tell him about my moment of weakness today. I should be honest, let him be there. I always have before. But it's been a lot the past few weeks. I don't want him to leave me because it's too much.

As I get into the kitchen and see him moving seamlessly around, preparing something that smells delicious with a slight smile on his face, I decide I *will* tell him. But later.

Chapter 33

Zane

Laying in bed with Jules as she sleeps peacefully next to me, I can't help but wonder if I should leave and go back to my apartment. It took until she fell asleep for me to notice the two new angry red cuts on her left arm. They add to the two faded ones on her right. That's four in one week.

The problem, besides the fact that she did it in the first place, is she didn't tell me. She tried to distract me the second I walked in the door, and it worked. She's good at that.

I should have known something was up with the way she clung to me until I got up to make dinner, and she came out with *my* shirt on. I thought she was just being sweet and sexy. She was in bed before I was, also unusual.

She's been spiraling since I told her I love her five weeks ago. I get it, I'm not hurt by it. But this is the first time she hasn't confided in me. Before *or* after the fact. I don't know what to do with that.

Three weeks ago, I went with her to that therapy session. Dr. Ptansky seems nice enough, seems to have a good grasp on Jules. They both wanted me to go, thought it'd be beneficial if I had a little more insight into Jules, things Dr. P could tell me and things Jules is maybe too nervous to share herself.

One thing that stuck with me is that downfalls and setbacks are to be expected, they'll happen. My role is to help her through them, help her not feel worse about herself. But how can I do that if she won't talk to me?

She's laying on her stomach, her arm curled in front of her, but not under her. Gently, I pull her arm straight out. A frown immediately pulls at my lips as my chest seizes. They're not deep, but enough to have scabbed.

Maybe my being here is a mistake. Maybe I've put too much pressure on her, smothered her. She told me she loves me back, she didn't even hesitate, doesn't ever hesitate. But it could have been too soon.

Dr. Ptansky had mentioned it may bring up some of Jules's negative feelings about herself. That it can lead to more self doubt. All things Jules has told me herself. It confuses me. I'm here, telling her I love her, and she feels worse about herself. But one thing Dr. P made clear is that it's not for me to understand. Just to support.

I just don't know that being here all the time is the right thing. She said she's fine with it—that she wants me here. What if she's lying?

Should I tell her I love her less often? I don't even think about it, it just comes out. Maybe I should pay more attention.

When Jules stirs a little, I realize I'm still holding her arm. I want to yell at her, scream at her, tell her it's not okay, that she can't do this and especially that she can't keep it from me. I can *say* those things, but I can't yell. I have to keep my temper in check.

Tracing the lines with my fingers, I glance at her peaceful face before I lean down and kiss each one.

She pulls her arm from my grasp, tucking it under the sheets. If she had a long-sleeve shirt on, I'm sure she'd be pulling it down, tucking the cuff into her hand. I'm thankful she's not, it's the only way I was able to see anything in the first place. How I missed it earlier, I don't know, and I may never forgive myself for it.

Her beautiful brown eyes are wide, full of fear and sadness. Her lips tip down and the bottom one trembles slightly.

"Jules, what happened?" I keep my voice low and calm. I have to tread lightly. I'm not sure this is the right way, but I feel like jumping straight to her being wrong isn't right.

"Nothing." It comes so fast I know she didn't even consider telling me.

"Obviously something happened. Why aren't you talking to me? You've been doing so well communicating with me. I had to find out once you fell asleep."

She doesn't say anything, but her eyes drop to the mattress. I pull her against me and cup the back of her head. She feels so small when she's like this.

"Jules, this isn't okay. You need to talk to me. Even if it's after the fact, I need to know."

"I'm sorry. I just—I..." She doesn't finish her thought. I don't want to push, so I give her a minute to get there herself.

When she doesn't answer, I press. "You just what, Jules?"

"I don't want you to leave me because I'm struggling with you telling me you love me." She lets out a deep breath.

My heart stops in my chest. She thinks I'll leave her? "Jules, why would you think that?"

"Because everybody who's ever loved me has left. And I'm struggling with it, which I'm afraid will make you think that I don't love you or don't believe you and it's not that, it's just...I'm scared." Her voice drops off at the end to barely a whisper.

"I understand that. But I'm not your parents. I'm not any of those other assholes who said it but didn't get you. I'm here. And I'm not going anywhere. You're not going to scare me away so easily."

"But what if I have more bad days?" Is she serious?

"So what if you do?"

"You'll leave if they get to be too frequent." I hug her tighter to me as her voice cracks. How could anybody leave her because she's struggling to be happy?

"I won't. Would you leave me if I had a bad day?"

"No."

"Then why would I leave you?"

"Because they're more frequent. I'm more broken than you." The moisture I feel on my chest almost destroys me.

"Jules, you're not broken. I don't see your bad days as anything more than that. You're not weak. Some days are worse than others, while some are much better. And I love you in spite of it all. But you need to talk to me. You need to let me in, let me help you. And *don't* hide it from me. Ever again." I think for a second and add a little more. "New rule. When you're struggling, you tell me. Even if it's the middle of the night. Even if I'm at work. Deal?"

She nods against me as she sniffles. I'd give everything I am to be able to put her back together, make her whole again. I was able to once, but that was a recent damage. Not years in the making, not a lifetime's worth of hurt.

"I love you. I'm not going anywhere. Good days and bad." I run a hand down her hair to soothe her. "And *don't* use sex as a ticket out again. Understood?"

"Yes."

I let everything settle for a minute, let her calm. But I have to know. "Jules, is it too soon? Did I...did I scare you? Do you think you have to feel the same way? Because you don't. I just—"

She pushes away from me so she can lean up on an elbow and look at me. "No. No it's not your feelings that scare me. Nor is it mine, because I *do* love you. I really do. I wouldn't lie to you about that."

I choose to ignore the *about that* and not take it to mean that she'd lie to me about other things. Kind of like how I'm choosing not to look at her keeping her new cuts from me as a lie of omission and just something she needed time for.

"Do you want me to leave? Am I here too much?"

She throws herself down and wraps around me as much as she can. "No, please don't leave. It's not anything you are or aren't doing. Yet. It's what I'm scared is going to happen. It's me not feeling worthy. I don't deserve for you to love me. I don't...I don't understand why you do." My eyes flutter closed at her confession. It's like a knife twisting in my chest to hear her think so poorly of herself. How could she feel like she doesn't deserve my love? It's me who doesn't deserve hers.

"Jules, I'm not going anywhere." I squeeze her to me as her body rattles. I don't know how to convince her that she's the most amazing woman I've ever known. How to make her believe in all the reasons I love her, her looks being lower on the list because she's just that wonderful otherwise. Even if I tried, she wouldn't listen. Or at the very least wouldn't *hear* it, wouldn't absorb it. I'll tell her every day if I have to.

Though, maybe I should start tomorrow. It's late and as her breathing levels out and slows, I know she's drifting off to sleep. My insides constrict thinking about how she cried her way there, but at least she's safe in my arms.

Chapter 34

Jules

I thought Zane and I were having a nice evening. We were eating a pasta dish that he'd made, something Italian I can't remember the name of. Probably because he said it *in* Italian. I've recently learned he speaks three languages, other than English, fluently.

We had started talking about the weekend. But now he's screaming. I don't know why. I don't know what happened. The yelling has happened before. That's not the scary part. No, the part that's scaring the shit out of me, making me flinch and move away from him, is the fact that he's throwing things. Breaking things.

My things.

Everything and anything he can get his hands on. It started with his plate, which he slammed on the ground. I haven't made the change from ceramic. He's suggested it, said it only takes once, but I haven't yet.

We fight like normal couples, but he's never been like this.

I move away, keeping my eyes on him until my back is flush against the wall. He's not even screaming *at* me so much as just screaming.

With a hard swallow, I reach out a hand. "Zane, baby, you're okay." My voice is shaky, I don't think it's going to help. Because he's not okay. I see that he's not. But it's what he says to me when I'm struggling. It doesn't always help, but I'm hoping it will draw him back to me.

When he's upset, sometimes there's a build up he can identify, I wrap tightly around him. But this is different, and I'm honestly scared to approach him.

I can't even make sense of what he's saying. He seems to be slipping in and out of languages. It'd be impressive if it wasn't so terrifying.

He's mostly storming through the apartment, but I'm too scared to move from my spot. I don't think he'd hurt me, he said he's never hurt somebody before; at least not someone who didn't deserve it. But he's also never been in a relationship this long. What if that makes things different?

There are broken shards of various materials all over my apartment. I've inched closer to the bedroom. It's been five minutes at most, but you'd swear it's been an hour with the state of things.

The next object to join the fray is an oval glass bottle with a pinkish liquid inside of it, which is thrown against the wall, not far from my head. That's when this all becomes too much for me and I collapse into myself, sliding down the wall.

A warm wetness flows down my cheeks as I tuck my knees to my chest, curling myself into the cool plaster as close as I can, trying to shrink away and watch through my hands.

And what I see is Zane, immediately deflating as his eyes lock on mine.

I know he can't control it. I know he's trying to be better, just like I am. But this is scary. I'm not sure what to do, what to feel.

Being with Zane is the only time I feel safe.

Right now, I feel anything but.

Chapter 35

Zane

The look of absolute fear in her eyes is enough to snap me out of it. Glancing around, I see what I've done. None of it matters, none of it's important. But she is. And she's sitting crumpled on the floor as tears pour down her cheeks.

I did this. I made her feel this way. And it slices through me like nothing ever has before.

As I kneel down in front of her, she shies away, eyes wide. "Jules, baby, I'm so sorry, please." I reach out a hand but she flinches back. Cold fear and dread twist their way through me.

She's scared of me.

She's watched me beat a man to within an inch of his life, twice, and she wasn't scared then. Though, then, I was her knight in shining...whatever. This time, I'm the villain, the one causing her fear. Not the one saving her from it.

How do I fix this? I need to fix this. She's the only thing that matters to me, really, truly matters. I can't let this ruin things, ruin us.

So, I sit right in front of her, as close as I can get without touching her, and rest my arms across my knees as I wait. All the anger seeped out of my body the second I saw her face. How could I do this to her?

Watching silent tears flow down her cheeks, I feel completely helpless. Aside from the Tim situation, I don't think I've ever seen her truly cry before. Somehow, she's still stunningly beautiful.

Stretching my fingers to her knee, I try to touch her again. She doesn't shrink away. Instead, her eyes drift toward me, and I'm acutely aware that it's the first time she's looked at me since I threw the bottle.

But it twists my heart. Sadness, fear, and hurt are all sitting in her perfect, tear-filled eyes. I broke her. She'll never trust me again. I don't even remember what triggered this outburst. And now she's shattered.

I've shattered her.

I need to hold her; I need to feel her in my arms. What if it's the last chance I get? Slowly leaning forward, I try to wrap my arms around her. She shifts away, closer to the wall, so I sit back on my heels. Her eyes are still on me, but they're softer, accepting.

Trying again, I lean forward, and she lets me slip around her, resting my chin on her shoulder. She's tense, a tiny ball of tightness. Wrapping my arms tightly around her, I sit back, legs crossed, pulling her into my lap. Instantly, she collapses against me, crying and clawing at my chest.

I know I didn't hit her with anything, I know it was far enough from her that she's not injured, but I have to fight the urge to pull her away from me and look for any wounds. There are some though, but they're not physical.

I let her claw at me, my skin rubbing raw, as I squeeze her and rock gently. Taking her face between my hands, I kiss the trails of tears from her face. The salt is bitter on my tongue. "I'm sorry, Jules. I'm so, so sorry."

I've hurt a lot of people in my time. Mentally and physically. This one is the hardest, by a long shot.

How can I protect her from herself if I can't protect her from me?

It's this very moment, sitting here with the one person I love in this whole world—who is broken and sobbing in my lap over something *I* did—that I decide I need to find a new way. And she's my motivation to be better.

Chapter 36

Jules

The overwhelming scent of my perfume jolts me awake. Memories of the night before are hazy at best. But as my eyes open, my mind gets to work, flashing through images like a movie playing in my head.

Zane was mad, so mad. I can't seem to remember why. I feel like we were arguing over something trivial, and then he exploded, literally. He started throwing things, breaking things. I had backed to the wall when he threw my perfume bottle against it. Not close to where I was, but it scared me all the same. That's why I smell it so strongly. The bottle smashed just outside this room.

I remember the anger, rage, and fire that flooded his eyes. Until he threw the bottle and looked at me. Then it was like I watched all those emotions fade. I watched the fire extinguish and the calm, the *sadness*, overtake.

Rolling over, I find Zane, face perched on his hand, looking at me with such pain and turmoil in his eyes.

"I told you I don't like it when you do that." It creeps me out when he watches me sleep. At first, it was sweet, especially when he was watching over me and keeping me safe from nightmares. Maybe he thought I was going to have a few. I hadn't.

"I'm sorry." Pain seeps through his voice and straight into my heart as he reaches out to touch me. Instinctively, I flinch away, my eyes fluttering closed, and I instantly hate myself. It's not his fault. I understand it more than others. I don't want him to be upset.

"I'm so sorry." It's barely a whisper this time. I open my eyes to see his are closed, his face tilted down. Without hesitation, I slide against him, my head resting below his chin, forehead at his clavicle, nose nuzzled to his chest.

His breath catches as I press against him, hesitating a moment before wrapping his arm around me.

"I'm not scared of you, Zane. I'm scared of what you *did*. Not of you. I know you'd never hurt me." Honestly, I *don't* know that. I know what it's like to not be able to control the urges. But he's protected me more times than I can count, both from others and myself. Most importantly, I saw his face when he registered mine. Seeing me crumpled against the wall, he stopped immediately.

"Maybe you should be."

"No, I shouldn't be. You stopped yourself. I watched as recognition registered on your face, and you stopped."

"It shouldn't have gotten to that point. It shouldn't have taken seeing you balled up on the floor in tears because of me." A shudder wracks through his body as he remembers.

He's calmed and comforted me so many times, even before we officially started dating, that I have to try to do the same for him now. I know he's beating himself up, angry at himself. I don't want him to be.

Pointing my finger under his chin, I tilt it up, so his eyes meet mine. "Hey. Do you love me?"

Confusion scatters his features. "Of course, I do."

"Would you hurt me?"

A wince pulls at his lips. "No." It comes out a breath.

"I know these things, Zane. Truly, I do. I know you love me. I know you wouldn't hurt me."

"What if I can't control it?"

"But don't you see that you did last night? You stopped yourself."

"Jules. I can't ever see you like that again. I can't."

"So, what are you going to do about it? Are you going to break up with me?" Is this what causes it to finally happen? Because I'm sure it will. Someday.

His eyes flash to mine. "What? No. I don't know. I don't want to."

"Then don't. Figure something out. Figure out a better way."

"We're not doing so great here, are we?" I know he means with our outbursts more than with our relationship. But part of me still questions it.

"It's a process. I haven't had random sex in four years. That's a good thing." "I've had to talk you out of cutting six times in the past two weeks. And you did twice the week before. That doesn't seem like progress to me."

"Okay, but how many times have you flipped out recently? Besides last night obviously."

"A few. But even if it was none, last night alone was too much."

"Listen, if you think breaking up with me solves everything, fine. I won't stop you. I'll be heartbroken, but I won't stop you. I think we both just need to find a better way."

He presses his forehead firmly against mine, his eyes closed tightly, like he can't look at me versus won't. "I can't hurt you." It comes out a strained whisper. I've never seen him so vulnerable, so raw. It's comforting in a way since he sees me like this far too often. His rage episodes are so vastly different than when I'm ready to fall apart and hurt myself.

I reach my hand to the back of his neck, scratching my fingers in his hair the way I know he likes. "You won't."

He wraps his arms around me and pulls me tightly against him. So tight I almost can't breathe. It's like he's holding onto me for dear life, afraid I'm going to slip away from him.

I'm not entirely sure what to do. I keep scratching at the back of his head, every so many passes his muscles loosen slightly. I decide to nuzzle into his chest. He smells good, like Zane. It helps my own muscles ease, even though I didn't realize I was so tense.

This, right like this, is my favorite place to be. My heart races at the notion. We haven't been together that long. It doesn't feel right so soon. It shouldn't be my favorite place.

Zane slowly pulls his arm from around me. "Let me make you breakfast." It's not so different from a typical day, but the way he says it, that he does at all versus just doing it, is what pains me.

"You don't have t—"

"Please."

"Okay, Zane."

He stays close to me as we walk into the kitchen. I almost feel like he thinks if he's not up against me I'll float away and be gone. Looking around, he's already cleaned everything up. *When did he do that?*

While everything is still foggy, he had put me in bed. I can't think of him leaving, but he must have at some point. A chill runs through me, and I notice an open window in the living room. It's mid-December, and getting quite cold out, but I'm sure it's to help with the smell. A smell that I'm sure will linger for days if not longer.

"I'll—I'll buy you a new one." His voice is grim. Like the perfume is all that matters.

"It doesn't matter. It's not important," I say as I put my hand on his chest. I need him to hear me, feel me.

He stops in his tracks, covering my hand with his, eyes fluttering closed, his other hand wrapping to the back of my neck. His muscles are taut, like he's trying to stop himself from something.

When I realize what it is, I fold into him. He wants to be close to me, but is afraid to push it, afraid I don't want it. I'm worried he's never going to forgive himself.

"Zane. Zane, look at me." When he still doesn't open his eyes, I tilt his chin toward me and squeeze gently until he opens them. They're slits, pained. "It's *okay*."

"It's not, Jules. It's not okay."

"Maybe you're right. It's not okay. But *I* am."

"How?" It comes out a whisper.

"Because I know you love me. I know you won't hurt me." I've said it all already. I'll say it a hundred, a thousand, more times if he needs me to.

"What if that's not enough?"

"It will have to be. You need to make it be."

His arms tighten around me, hugging me to him like he's afraid I'm going to turn and run. "I can't lose you."

"You're not losing me. You're squishing me a little, but I'm not going anywhere." He loosens his grip around my waist. "I know you're worried, please don't be. I know you're sorry, I know you didn't do it on purpose. Was it scary? Fuck yes. But I also watched you take in the situation, take in my reaction, take in *me*. And you stopped. Completely halted. It wasn't a wind down, you didn't finish destroying things and then stop. It was like somebody hit the power switch. *That's* why I'm not scared. I know something registered with you."

Taking a deep breath, a hand slides up to cup my head, fingers tangling in my hair as he pulls my head against his lips. He holds me there for a few minutes and I'm sure his eyes are closed as he breathes me in.

Nothing I said to him was a lie. Yeah, I was scared shitless last night. But I saw the change in him, and it's what I'm holding on to.

"I'm hungry. You said you'd make me breakfast."

"Just...just one last thing. I don't want you to hurt yourself because you're scared or upset or anything. I'm barely going to forgive myself as it is."

I have to push hard against him so he releases me enough that I can look at him. "I'm not going to. Zane, please, listen to me. Please. I'm *okay*. Just hungry. I'm not going to kick you out, I'm not going to hurt myself or randomly burst into tears. I'm ready to move on. Please."

His lips are pressed in a tight line, but he nods, slowly lowering his arms from my waist, trailing his fingers down my legs.

I follow him into the kitchen, my kitchen, which he owns so much better than I do, and hop up on the counter near the stove while he looks in the fridge, deciding what to make for breakfast.

"In the mood for anything in particular?"

"Hmm, let's see. I could really go for some pancakes. With chocolate chips."

His mouth twitches, fighting a smile as he pulls out the milk, butter, an egg, and the bag of chocolate chips. He hates that I like chocolate in my pancakes. Says I may as well just eat candy for breakfast.

"I think I have an acceptable banana too. Over there." I point from my perch on the counter to the fruit basket.

He barely glances at me as he starts the coffee and sets to making breakfast. His movements are smooth and easy, like he's done this in my kitchen forever. He's even smoother in his own kitchen. It's a bigger turn on than I'd let him know.

"Bacon?"

"Um, I think there may be a pack in the meat drawer." Though he practically lives here, I do almost all the grocery shopping or ordering since he works long hours.

Once the batter's done and the pans are on the burners warming, he comes over to stand in front of me. Fisted hands rest against the counter on either side of me as he stands between my legs and rests his head against my shoulder.

Zane's not a crier. It's not something he's ever had to tell me, I just know. But this is a moment where I'm wondering if he might.

"Will you kiss me?" I ask him gently.

Slowly, he pulls his head from my shoulder, close to my level. "You want me to kiss you?"

"Of course, I do. I'd let you fuck me right here, right now if you wanted to."

He keeps his head at my level but tips his face to look at the ground. "Be serious."

"I'm being very serious. You need to see right now that you're way more affected by this than I am. Which is probably a good thing because it will hopefully prevent it from happening again. But I love you, and I want to be close to you."

Zane doesn't answer as he gives me a kiss on the neck and goes back to cooking. I watch his seamless movements as he pours the batter, lays the bacon, flips the pancake. Sometimes when he's feeling cocky, he'll flip the pancake using the pan and toss it high in the air. He doesn't do that today.

Once he's plated everything, he gives me a quick peck on the lips as he carries the food to the small table just outside the kitchen. Pushing off the counter, I pad over to the table, a shiver jolting my body as I wrap my hands around my arms.

"Sorry. I can close the window if you want. I was hoping to air it out a little."

"It's fine. Coffee will keep me warm."

He doesn't look convinced and gets up, walking down the hall. I take a bite of my pancakes, delicious and chocolaty. Zane walks back over to me and wraps a blanket around my shoulders. Tilting my head up, I look at him, a small smile on my face. I can force it when necessary. It helps that it makes me warm and fuzzy inside when he takes care of me.

Which in turn makes me hate myself a little, I've never needed or wanted anybody else to take care of me. I've never wanted to drag anybody down with me. I'm not worth it. I'll drag him as low as he'll hold on for and then he'll leave me.

You can't think about your own shit now, Jules, you need to focus on Zane.

Shaking the negative thoughts away, I try to work through how I'm going to get him back to normal. First things first, I put my attention into eating my breakfast and getting caffeine coursing through my veins.

We're eating in silence, which I still hate despite our comfort level with each other, but I don't know what to say that won't make him shut down.

"This is really good. Thank you for making it for me." It's worth a shot. I try to thank him any time he cooks. I tell him it's unnecessary, but he insists that he likes to. Since I hate cooking, I don't argue. Plus, he can always make the bacon chewy, just how I like it. Whenever I cook bacon, I overcook it, and it's crispy.

"You're welcome." He won't even look at me.

Do I push? Or do I leave him be?

I'm about to say something, anything, the first thing that comes out of my mouth when he beats me to it.

"I think I'm going to go for a run in a little while. It helped in high school. Maybe it will just be good to clear my head." Clear his head. Of me? Is he running to work out his thoughts and feelings? "Is it...is it okay if I come back after?" He tips his head up to catch my eye.

"Of course, Zane. I want you here. Or I guess I should say I want to be with you because I'd go with you back to your apartment if you wanted to. So, you have to know how serious I am because you know how much I hate your apartment."

I'm trying to get a little laugh out of him. A smirk. A look that contains anything but anguish. It doesn't work.

I take a few more small bites before I'm not hungry anymore, pushing my plate away as I watch him move the food around his plate. His torturing himself is making me more upset than the incident itself.

Chapter 37

Zane

I run until my body burns, and my lungs feel like they're going to burst. I want to run away from the image that's etched into my mind. Running around the world wouldn't be far enough to get away from it.

When I was in high school and had anger surges, my dad would push me to run it out. To run until the feeling was gone. It helped. Sometimes. It was probably the only thing he was actually good for. And when I say he would push me, I mean he would literally push me out the door.

She's willing to let me go back. I don't understand it. It doesn't make sense that she's allowing me to be in her apartment, be near her after *that*. I'm terrified she's going to hurt herself while I'm out, but I need to move, I need to go.

And yet, I need to be close to her. I want to do nothing but hold her close, make sure she's not going anywhere. She says she's fine, she says she forgives me. But how do you forgive something like that?

What if I had hurt her? It plagues my thoughts. I don't think a second has passed that I haven't had that thought paired with the vision of her crumpled on the floor. I lean my hand against the building I stopped in front of and dry heave. It's not from the run, it's from what's working through my mind.

Spitting, I wipe my mouth on the sleeve of my long-sleeve tee. Running in the winter has always sucked. The cold works and effects your body in a different way, and it's been a long time since I've used these muscles in this way. I'm going to feel it tomorrow.

Maybe that's a good thing. Just another reminder. *Hey, you fucked up, buddy. Don't forget it.*

Like I could.

Taking a deep breath, which sends needles through my chest, I turn around and slowly start back. I don't even know how far I ran. If my body would carry me farther, I'd go. I just hope she's in one piece when I get back.

I try to focus on the sound of my feet hitting the pavement, thankful it hasn't snowed more than a light dusting yet, as I make my way back to her apartment.

When I get upstairs, she's sitting on the couch, twirling a curl, tucked under two—no, wait three—blankets while she reads a book. I so desperately want to walk over to her and kiss her. I'm not sure it will be well received. Not sure that I should. I shouldn't. I shouldn't even be here.

Bending down, I unlace my sneakers, leaving them by the door. I had to swing by my apartment to grab both them and gear for running in. Walking in alone left a sinking feeling in my chest.

I toss the paperwork for the gym I joined onto the end table by the door.

Closing her book, she turns, resting her chin on the back of the couch. "How was your run?"

"Fine. I'm going to shower."

"Oh. Okay." She seems disappointed. *Why?*

Tilting my head back, I let the hot water pour over me. I run my hand up the back of my head to my forehead and back again.

My hair is getting long. I should cut it. Or maybe I should let it grow. I don't know. Maybe I should ask Jules.

Cutting or not cutting my hair is the least of my worries right now. I shouldn't even be thinking about it.

A cool burst of air and the perfume scent float into the room. Seconds later, Jules is climbing into the shower with me.

"Jules. You shouldn't be in here."

"Why? If it's because you're sweaty and want to shower alone, I'll leave. But if it's because you're upset with yourself and still think I should be scared of you, I'm not going anywhere."

"I'm sweaty, and I want to shower alone." There. That wasn't so hard to say. I'm just not sure if it was believable.

When Jules takes a few tentative steps closer and runs her fingertip along my chest, I know it wasn't.

"Is that really true? You know I can tell. And I don't really believe you. Or maybe, I've decided I just don't care." She's practically purring.

Fuck. I want to be inside her.

Hesitantly, I reach my arms out to rest on her shoulders. Instead of pulling away or batting at my hands, she looks at me with a scrunched-up face. Taking my wrists in her grasp, she places my hands on her waist as she wraps her arms around my neck and closes the gap between our bodies.

I release a slow shaky breath, trying hard to contain myself. "Jules, I don't think this is a good idea."

"Why? Zane, you didn't hurt me last night, you're certainly not going to hurt me in here. You need to forgive yourself." Sliding a hand behind my head, she pushes on her toes to kiss me. But I pull away. Hesitating, but not lowering to flat feet, she searches my face.

She must decide she's okay with what she sees because she pushes back on her toes, pulling my face to hers with a firm hold. When she presses her perfect soft lips to mine, the tension oozes out of me, right down the drain.

I force her mouth open, my tongue seeking hers. When she falters and starts to lower, I loop my arm around her waist, pulling her flush against me, supporting her weight.

There's no denying my need for her as my dick throbs, needing to feel her. Shifting my hands to under her thighs, I pull her up, spinning around to push her against the side wall of the shower. Her legs wrap around my waist immediately as she twists her fingers into my hair. She's never been able to do that before, a small smirk coming to her lips.

"What?" I ask against her mouth.

"I like this," she murmurs as she runs her fingers through the wisps. I guess I have my answer about whether or not to cut it.

"I love you." I press my forehead to hers. Saying it doesn't seem like enough.

"I know. I love you too." I start to slowly lower her to the ground when she tightens her grip around my neck, basically crawling back up me. "I came in here to get something, and I'm not leaving until I do." To further enforce her point, she reaches her hand between our bodies and wraps it around my rock-hard dick, giving a few slow slides along the shaft.

A groan catches in my throat. She's certainly persistent when she's determined. Following her lead, I move my hand between her legs, slipping two fingers along her before pressing inside. *Fuck, she's soaked.*

I stop hesitating, afraid she's going to change her mind and lift her slightly before settling the tip of erection against her. Giving one last check of her face, looking for any sense of regret, that she doesn't want this, I find nothing but desire, and I ease into her.

I don't think there's a single sound that Jules makes that I don't love, even the various tones of her voice. But the sounds she makes when we have sex all rank at the top. Right now is no exception. The tiny whimpers as I start slowly thrusting into her make my head spin.

My legs start aching as I pick up speed, supporting her full weight. Her fingers dig into my shoulders as her head tips back against the tile and the whines start slipping through with every single thrust. I know she's getting close.

If I hadn't just gone for the longest run I've had in years, I'd be gripping her hair and pulling her mouth against mine. As it is, I'm hoping we don't fall before we're done.

"Ahh, Zane." The way she says my name. It's Goddamn perfect.

"Fuck, baby." Three more thrusts and she tightens around me as she screams, setting off my own orgasm as my dick pulsates inside her. I keep thrusting, slower, releasing every last drop.

I rest my head against her shoulder for a minute as I catch my breath, and she clings to me. Sometimes I joke with her that she's like a little monkey with the way she holds on. But right now, I just want the closeness.

When my legs start to tremble, I set her down but refuse to let her away from me, keeping an arm tight around her waist as I quickly soap us both up. I guide her under the water to rinse and once the stream runs clear of suds I climb out, wrapping a towel around my waist before I reach in and turn the faucet off, holding one outstretched for Jules to step into.

Once it's wrapped around her, I pull her against me and kiss the top of her head. I can't lose this. I can't lose her. I'll do whatever I have to, to make things better. To make sure I don't lose her. I can't ever scare her like that again.

Chapter 38

Jules

"I don't know Daph. I've never seen him like that before." I'm playing with the lid of my cup, not wanting to meet Daphne's eye because I'm not sure I'll like what I see there. We're having our weekly coffee at a Starbucks downtown. Same time, same place, every weekend. Except when I can't get out of bed.

"Aren't you scared?"

"Yeah, I was fucking scared. I've seen him angry but that was a different level. He threw anything he could reach." He also connected his fist with a mirror I had in the hallway, but I keep that to myself.

"No, I mean, like, aren't you still?"

"Of course not."

"How? I would be."

"Because he's still Zane. He's still the same person."

"But that's scary."

"It was. But he's not like that. Like, he's not abusive or crazy. He has a problem, so do I. His is just different. You wouldn't get it." I flip a hand in her direction. How could she understand? I feel like the biggest impulse she can't control is eating a donut.

But her narrowed eyes and drawn face makes something inside me snap.

"You don't get it, Daph. You can't possibly. You never can. I know you love me, I know you're there for me every single step of the way, that you'd drop everything for me if I needed you to. But you don't get what it's like to fight yourself each and every day. To fight the impulses, the voices in your head. I lose the fight far more often than he does, and his support of me has never once faltered." I take a deep breath as the words finish spilling out of me at record pace.

"Jules. He could *hurt* you." Her voice is low and fear trails along her words.

Shaking my head at the thought, I refute her. "I don't know how to explain it, because you're right, he could. He definitely could. And I wouldn't be able to stop him. But he didn't, and I trust him completely.

"He's beside himself. He went for a run, said something about how it used to help when he was in high school or whatever, joined a gym on his way."

"Did he at least make sure you were okay first?"

"Oh absolutely. Many times, and every day since. And he made me breakfast. He didn't even want to leave, he asked if he could come back after his run. Which surprised me because I thought he'd want to go home. I swear he looked shocked I said yes."

"Are you sure you're okay?"

"I'm positive." I meet her eyes so she knows I'm serious.

"Are you going to tell Dr. Ptansky?"

"I already did. I told him that I need to be able to talk to her about it. It's not triggering me, it's not making me feel angsty or anything. I don't feel an urge to do anything stupid."

"I'm actually really proud you haven't slutted it up in a while."

"Well, gee thanks for wording that so beautifully." I roll my eyes at her.

We both laugh a few minutes. Daphne can be blunt at times but she's typically much more manicured. I'm the blunt, no filter person.

"But seriously Jules, it's been a long time since you've hooked up with some rando. It's a big step. Any feelings while with Zane?"

"Honestly? If anything, I'm even more against it than I had been. I know there's always a chance I can't control it during a dissociation episode, but I hope that because it's not something I really do anymore it won't be an issue. I almost feel like before it was like an autopilot thing. I was bored, feeling self-destructive or bad about myself, I'd hook up with a random guy. Boyfriend be damned. But it's just not like that with Zane. I care if I hurt him."

"He's got you loopy. I don't think I've ever seen you like this." The smile that spreads across her face and makes her green eyes sparkle is almost more than I can handle.

"I know. And it's scary."

"Why? I mean I know it's scary in any serious relationship, I know there's the fear of getting hurt and whatnot. But I'm wanting to hear your specific *why*."

It's something Dr. Ptansky had mentioned when I had Daphne come with me for a session. She had said to make me voice my fears, my worries, instead of letting them swirl round and round in my head where they only built up.

"I'm afraid we're volatile together. I mean, we're in a good place relationship wise, but we're both damaged. I'm afraid we'll just drag each other down at some point." And that he'll leave me like everybody else.

"You're not damaged, Jules. You've been through a lot in your life. It makes sense you didn't come out of that completely unscathed." My attention is drawn back to her—and away from the lid I've basically obliterated—when she puts her hand on mine. "And he won't leave you."

"How do you know?"

She shrugs. "I guess I don't really. But I see how strung out you are. I can't imagine he's different. You say how nervous he's seemed about losing you. I think the dude's just as crazy about you."

"Yeah?"

"Oh yeah. Don't you guys, like, talk about this?"

"I don't know, it's all so weird. We didn't like, date, or anything. If you remember, at the beginning I thought he was a douchenozzle. And then he saved me, twice. But after that first time, when he started walking me home, I don't know, we just got to know each other." My head tips even closer to my cup as I shake my head. The memories of how we started send a swirl of butterflies through my stomach.

"It's the most intense I've ever felt about somebody, especially so early and like not even dating. Or something. I don't know. We kind of just...are. Like he's never asked me to be his girlfriend, but we're definitely exclusive. I mean we love each other for God's sake. He spends just about every night at my apartment, and if we're not at mine we're at his. I can't remember the last night I spent alone. Yet we don't really live together. I don't know. It's confusing at times."

"If you're happy, who cares?"

I snort. "Happy?"

"I know the concept of happiness seems so foreign to you, but I'm pretty sure that's what's going on here. I mean, I'm not you, I can't speak for you. But it certainly seems like happiness. Or at least close to it."

"Happy. Huh. I don't know." I'm hesitant to accept this as a valid feeling.

"Listen, I've only ever seen you...content. At most. And that's being generous, I'd say. I think what happened is scary, and I definitely think something even a little close to that, with anybody else, would have sent you running for the hills. In fact, less has."

"I don't know if that qualifies as happy, Daph. Maybe it's just comfort."

"It's definitely more than that. Yes, you're comfortable of course, but it's more than just comfort. I see the way you talk about him. Your whole face lights up."

"It does not." The incredulous tone matches my furrowed brow and wide eyes. My face doesn't *light up*.

"Well, whatever your version of that is. Either way. You're definitely way more than content. If you don't want to accept that as happiness, then that's your choice. But you've never really stayed with a guy for more than just loneliness or sex, and this is way beyond that. And you've *never* let a guy stay with you. Not to mention, it's been over your four-month marker." Ah the notorious Jules exit sign at four months.

"Yeah, but you know he started at my place. Things began a bit reversed so it kind of stayed that way."

"That's part of it though. You felt something early on. Enough that when you were having a rough time you let him stay. You *asked* him to. I mean, shit, you ignored me the three times I came by. But he comes by, and you open the door?"

"He threatened to knock it down." My voice is low, and I trace the top of my plastic lid with my fingertip, not able to meet her eyes. I'm lying about the true reason, and she'll know.

"But you didn't push him away or slam it in his face. You let him in, you asked him to stay. For *three* days. You could have asked him to leave at any point and you didn't. And now things are just even further along because you started spending all of your time together. I'm surprised you even come see me anymore."

Now I make eye contact with her, my head tilting to the side. "Daphne. Of *course* I'm going to come see you. That won't change. The only time I've missed our coffee sessions are when

I'm sick or not able. I would never sacrifice our time together for time with Zane. And he wouldn't ask. He knows it's important to me."

"Really? Is that why you were late today?" The bite to her tone clenches around my heart. I apologized profusely when I got here, she seemed okay. I wasn't paying enough attention to see she was lying.

"I was late today because he started going down on me in the shower. Is that what you wanted to hear?"

"I mean I'm not getting any lately so you may as well."

"That's never been a problem between me and Zane, but it wasn't that. Since that night, he's been doting on me every second of every day. He offered to walk me here today. Like I need an escort or something. I mean sometimes it's sweet, like when he wakes me up with breakfast in bed. But today I was just trying to shower. And while yes it turned out to be pretty hot, I just want him to forgive himself."

"Should he?"

I narrow my eyes at her. Daphne has been my opposite for so many years I often feel like I wouldn't exist without her. "Yes, Daphne. He should *change,* but he should forgive himself. And it's not even change, it's..." I shake my head, not sure how to verbalize what I want to say.

Looking at the table and releasing a short breath, I raise my head back up at her. She's always patient with me. "I don't know how to explain it. I guess, think about my self-harm. It's not so much that I need to change who I am, as that I need to find a better way to handle the situations. It's the same thing for Zane. He needs to find a better way.

"We've been...together...for a few months now. This is the first time anything even close to this has happened. At least in my presence. I know he's had some other moments, but they've all been at his apartment, or work, or somewhere that I'm not.

Meanwhile, I've hurt myself while he's in the apartment. It's an impulse control. We're both learning ways to navigate it better."

"Don't hate me for asking this. Okay?"

"I make no promises."

"Jules." Her tone is serious. I'm not sure what she's about to ask, but fear snakes through my body.

"I could never hate you, Daph." I couldn't, it's impossible, but I sit back in my chair, awaiting the onslaught of whatever she feels is bad enough to say that I may hate her.

"Is it okay for you two to be together? Like, does Dr. P think it's okay?"

I lean forward in my chair slightly, brows knitting together. "We've discussed this already, Daph. Why are you questioning it now?"

"Because he just flipped out and broke a bunch of shit in *your* apartment." Her eyes are wide as she throws her hand out and her voice raises an octave.

I take a deep breath and lean forward, my fingertips open on the table. I keep my voice low and level. "He couldn't control it, Daph. You've never experienced it, you don't know what it's like. I fight myself constantly. And I lose. A lot. Up until the other night he has *never* lost it in front of me. Not even a little."

Leaning back in my chair, my fingers rub my lips as I look out at the street, people milling about, the sidewalk never empty. "I mean, shit, he beat the crap out of a guy, twice, and turned the switch off to take care of me. Everybody's allowed one fuck up."

"I'm just worried about you, Jules. He could have hurt you."

"I know. I get it. Trust me, so does he. As much as you don't want him to hurt me, he wants that even less. He loves me, Daph. Like he really, truly loves me." It makes my heart flutter as I say it, and all I want to do is go home and curl against him.

Daphne sits back in her chair with a self-satisfied smirk on her face. Tenting her pointers and pulling her hands to her mouth.

I pick up my cup and swirl the little bit of coffee leftover. I'm in an off mood since there's something left. I'll have to get a refill on my way home.

"What's so amusing?" I ask with a hint of irritation.

"Oh, you're welcome is all." She flips her golden locks behind her shoulder.

"I'm sorry, say that again? I'm what?"

"You're welcome."

"What for exactly?"

"Well, you went from defending Zane, to worrying you were going to self-destruct, back to defending him and getting all pleased when you told me he loves you. So much so, that I bet you're dying to get back to him. Which I hope makes you realize that you're happy. Even if this was scary, even if you're worried about the longevity and getting hurt, you're happy. If anything, those fears I think only lend to that."

"You just think you're *so* smart, don't you?" As much as I'm teasing, I can't help but smile. It's rare for me, but Daphne has seen me at my best and my worst. She's been my rock for so many years. I don't know how I haven't chased her off yet.

"You should go. Get back to your man. I'm *insanely* jealous because it's been a long draught for me. I miss having somebody to snuggle up to." She looks wistfully at the ceiling, as though imagining her perfect man in the grains of the wood above us.

"Who says we snuggle?" I give her my best devious look as I glance up at her through my eyelashes while my tongue pokes out the corner of my mouth. I'm sure I just look ridiculous.

She throws her hand out to playfully smack my arm as she stands and throws her coat on. "Of course, you snuggle. After what I'm sure is wild kinky sex."

I shrug. "I'm not going to deny it." Standing and tugging my coat on, Daphne pulls me into a hug.

"I'm glad you're okay, and I'm happy for you."

"Thanks, Daph." Taking a step back, I put my arms on her biceps. "See you next week."

"You're not leaving?"

Picking up my cup, I shake it. "Refill."

Nodding her acceptance, she blows me a kiss and heads out the door. I toss my cup into the trash, the lid too far gone, and stand on the end of the line. Whipping out my phone, I shoot a quick text to Zane.

Me: *Grabbing a refill and heading home. Meet me there?*

My phone pings back immediately.

Zane: *Are you sure?*

I take a deep breath and sigh heavily. Part of me wants to reach through the phone and shake him. But he needs love and support right now.

Me: *Very. I could come to you if you prefer.*

My need to see him outweighs my dislike of his apartment.

Zane: *No, that's ok. I'll be there in fifteen.*

Looking at the line and how slowly it's moving, with a ten-minute walk home, I figure fifteen isn't enough. I don't want him waiting and thinking I'm avoiding him.

Me: *Long line. Make it twenty?*

Zane: *Sure. See you soon.*

Pocketing my phone I bounce on the balls of my feet. I'm antsy to get home, to see him. It's only been a few hours since he left, his head hanging low, to let me have my routine Saturday with Daphne. I miss him. If that doesn't make me a smitten kitten, I don't know what does.

Chapter 39

Jules

"Well, from what it sounds like, Zane is doing much better and you're...not." Leave it to Dr. Ptansky to just lay it flat out like that.

"I guess." I pick at a string on the hem of my shirt, irritated that she's pointed out my shortcomings...again.

"He hasn't had a breakdown since that one time?"

"No. Exercising seems to help him."

"And what about you? What helps you?"

"Nothing." I've memorized the disapproving face Dr. Ptansky is giving me. I see it in my mind every time I say something I know she'd chastise me for, every time I do something I regret.

"I think maybe we should try some grounding exercises."

"What's that?"

"The concept behind it is to be able to ground yourself to the moment, bring you back to the present, to relax and soothe your mind from the swirling thoughts and bring you more peace."

Chewing the inside of my lip, my curiosity boils over. "How does it work?" Zane's been doing so well, I want to also.

"There are two I'll tell you about. Both utilize your senses. First, you can look around the room you're in. You'll look for five things you can see. Then four things you can touch, three things you can hear, two things you can smell, and one thing you can taste. You won't actually do these things, the smelling or touching or tasting, but it redirects your mind. You may even get a sense of that feeling or scent as you do it."

I take a few quick glances around the room as I think this over. It doesn't seem terribly difficult right now. But I know that things are very different when I'm deep in it.

Nodding resolutely, I turn my attention back to Dr. Ptansky. "Okay, that seems fine. What's the other one?"

"This one dulls your visual senses and calls on your memory or imagination. You'll do all the same five senses you did earlier, but you'll have your eyes closed while imagining your happy place."

"Happy place?"

"Yes."

"I don't have one."

"It can also be somewhere you feel safe, calm."

The blank stare she receives has her shifting in her seat and pressing her mouth into a line.

"What about Zane? Do you not feel safe with him?"

"I do. I just don't want to use him." My voice picks up intensity.

"I understand your concern. But Julienne, he is not your parents. He loves you." The tone of her voice is the one she uses when she's trying to convince me, but I'm standing firm on this one.

"And my parents were supposed to love me, too. Eternally, unconditionally. And where are they? I haven't heard from either of them in over a decade."

"It's not the same thing."

"I have never once had a meaningful or lasting relationship. At some point, all this shit just gets to be too much to handle, and they bolt, like everybody else." I'm pulling at my shirt sleeves, a sure sign I'm getting worked up. I fidget like crazy when I'm anxious or avoiding.

The pointed look from Dr. Ptansky alerts me she's clued in. I stop.

"You have Daphne."

"Yeah, and she's the only one. I'm sure she's just still around out of pity."

"Your aunt didn't leave you Julienne. She died."

"Well, she's not around, is she?"

"It wasn't a choice she had. You know this."

I do know that. But it doesn't change the fact that she *still isn't here.*

The reality is, I'm scared to let Zane in, all the way in. Being with him, in his arms, is the safest place I've ever been, despite his outburst a few weeks ago. But I won't be able to handle it when he inevitably decides to leave me. The thought of what I'd do to myself truly scares me, in a way nothing else has before.

It would be more intense than when Aunt Juliette died, because Zane is with me because he *wants* to be. Yes, my aunt loved me, beyond measure, and I know that for certain. But she was still family, still had obligations to take me in and care for me, even if she went above and beyond the call of duty.

If I can keep that one piece of myself, that one thing that keeps Zane from encompassing all of me, from rooting himself into the very foundation that is my soul, then maybe I ward off some of the hurt when he inevitably leaves.

The heavy sigh in front of me pulls me from my thoughts, and I glance up to see Dr. Ptansky's disapproving face. "Julienne, just think about it. Please. You may be surprised at how much relief it brings you, how calm you feel yourself become just conjuring the image of Zane when you're in a crisis. You already allow him to hold you, to intervene, this is not much different."

"It's different because he's physically right there, and often he doesn't give me a choice."

"It feels nice though, doesn't it?"

Even if I try to deny it, I'm sure my face would show my deception. Zane *is* comforting. But having him physically hold me, to feel him against me, is very different from being alone and thinking of him to calm myself. In a weird way, it feels almost more intimate than sex.

Maybe it's because sex was always just physical to me, a means to an end, an itch to scratch. And this, this lets him take up head space, lets him be something for me that nobody ever has.

I've given myself over to Zane completely—physically, emotionally, sexually. But mentally? It's the last piece, the last part of myself that I'm holding on to.

Because if I let go, I'm scared of how far I'll fall into total and utter darkness.

Chapter 40

Jules

"I want to go to group this week."

I flip around to face Zane, my eyes wide and mouth slightly agape at his declaration. "I'm sorry. You *what?*"

"I want to go to group this week. No wait, I want *us* to go to group this week," he repeats himself, making what I consider a pretty major amendment to his first statement.

"Why?" My eyes narrow as I tilt toward him. I haven't stood from my spot in my desk chair as he leans against the doorway. The way my heart is racing, I'm not sure I could stand.

"I just do."

"Uh-uh. I need more than that to go back. And how do you even know we can? We haven't been in months."

"I already called to find out."

My eyes bug out of my head. "You already called?"

"Yeah. Please, Jules, do this for me."

Before I answer I give him a quick once over. He's still tense, as he has been for a few weeks now. While my heart is hammering away in my chest and all I can hear is whooshing in my ears, I agree to go. "Sure, Zane. We can go if it's what you really want."

With tight lips and a curt nod, he turns on his heels and walks away. Today's Sunday. I have two days to prepare myself. It's clearly important to him if he already called. He needs this, for whatever reason, so I'll do it for him. If it can bring back some semblance of self for him, some sliver of the Zane I know and I love, I'll bear an hour in a place I hate.

He's been distant, quiet. More than once in the past few weeks he's asked if he can come back after work, though he's been doing it for months now. The few times we've had sex I've had to convince him, which is a strange and somewhat dirty feeling. I don't want to have to coerce my boyfriend into having sex with me.

Tuesday morning, Zane gives me a kiss on the forehead, not the lips, and says he'll meet me at Land of Lattes. Just as he's about to walk out the door, he spins around and takes three large strides toward me, cupping my face and kissing me passionately. Pulling away, he keeps one hand on my cheek while the other loops around my waist, keeping his face close to mine.

"Please come today, Jules. I know you don't like it, but please come."

"I'll be there. I agreed to go." As much as I hate it, I will.

"I love you."

"I love you, too. I'll see you this afternoon."

Just before five o'clock, I find Zane standing in line inside Land of Lattes. I make my way to him, excusing myself to the people also waiting. Once I reach him, I curl into his side. He wraps his arm around me, but he doesn't look at me, doesn't kiss me, doesn't say a word. Looking up at him, I notice his clenched jaw, narrowed eyes, taut neck. His lips have the slight downward turn they've had for days on end.

When we get to the meeting, Zane holds the door open for me, silently, and I make my way across the room. As I sit, I realize Zane's not behind me, having settled in the seat he first chose all those months ago. I try to catch his eye, unsure of what he's doing and why he's sitting so far away.

A cold panic settles into my body like a cool mist rolling in off the lake. It slowly penetrates every inch of me, drowning out everything else.

When Mary plops in the chair next to me, I try to tune in but can't tear my eyes from Zane. Is he going to break up with me? In this very public, very not happy place? Maybe he thinks it will lessen the blow, that I'll have these other people here to console me, that's the point of this after all.

"I've been worried about you, it's been so long since you've been here." I catch the tail end of what Mary's saying to me.

"Huh? Oh, uh, sorry. Yeah, I just needed a break." I'd been so distracted by Zane and his mood that I'm just realizing I had no issues walking through the alley, which was the initial reason I stopped coming. I can only hope it will be the same leaving.

"I guess I can understand that. But how are you? Doing alright?"

"Yeah. I'm fine." I'm anything but right now. Yet there's no way I'm going to actually say that to Mary.

Before she can say anything else, Layla starts the meeting. "Welcome everybody, I'm glad to see we have Flynn and Serena back with us tonight." I start to drown her out like I usually do.

Not having Zane next to me is weird. We spent several weeks right next to each other, flirting, bickering. In a lot of ways, it turned out to be some pretty extensive foreplay. Things are so different now, being so far into our relationship. I'm used to his company, having him be in my bubble whenever we're in the same room. But right now, he's sitting opposite me and intentionally avoiding meeting my gaze.

I look around at the posters I know so well, wondering if maybe somebody changed it up a little, got a new one, anything. Unsurprisingly there are no changes.

I'm pondering a particularly awful poster when a voice draws my attention, and I snap forward, sitting up straight and stiff in my chair.

"I'd like to go, Layla. If that's okay?"

"Sure, Flynn, go ahead."

"Uh, hey everybody. Sorry I've been gone for a bit. I had a life change and got a little busy and distracted. Actually, I started seeing someone. We've been together for quite a while now, we're happy overall, in love. Things were going really great." I swallow hard at the *were* as my throat starts to close. My eyes have not left his face, but he hasn't so much as glanced in my general direction.

"About three weeks ago, I had an outburst, in her apartment. Any time I felt something coming before that, I either wasn't with her or would leave. But this time, I couldn't control it. I don't even know what happened, I don't know what I got mad about. I went from zero to exploding in a half second."

His gaze drifts to the floor as he plays with his fingertips in his lap. "I scared her. Throwing things, breaking things. I grabbed her perfume bottle and threw it against the wall, that she was curled against." Zane gives a deep swallow, his Adam's apple bobbing up and down. My eyes flutter closed as a single tear slides down my cheek.

"I don't...I don't know what to do to fix things. She's acting like everything's fine, like it's normal. But it can't possibly be. I scared her, I truly scared her, to tears. And she's acting like it's fine. But it can't possibly be. I just don't know what to do to make things right. And I need to." The repetition of his words is just another sign that he's not okay.

My chest aches. It feels like there's a pull against my body straight toward Zane. Right now, I want nothing more than to climb into his lap and throw my arms around his shoulders, but he sat on the other side of the room for a reason. Probably because he doesn't want me consoling him.

"I just...I need her to forgive me, I need her to know how sorry I am."

Tears pour from my eyes without reservation. I couldn't swipe at them fast enough if I tried.

"Looks like she already has," Mary's voice is quiet in my ear as she leans in to my side.

When Zane's eyes finally lock on mine, my breath halts at how dark they are. Tilting my head to the side I give him a tight-lipped smile that I'm sure tips more down than upward. I don't hear what the other people are saying, I don't hear the advice he's getting. I'm focused solely on Zane and trying to express with my eyes that I forgive him, how much I love him. To come back to me.

"What have you done to change since then, Flynn?" The mention of his alias draws my attention back.

"I've started going to the gym every day to try to get ahead of it. I've also started using the grounding technique a lot of people use, with the closing your eyes visualizing something, thing. And I think of her and things about her. Sometimes I just physically go to her and hold her. If none of that helps, I do an extra gym session. It's only been a few weeks. I'm not sure if it will work long-term." His voice dies off at the end as he looks down at his lap.

I don't know how to get him to stop torturing himself over this. I've tried everything I can think of. This was why he wanted to come, it makes perfect sense now. He's hoping somebody, anybody, will say something worthwhile, something that will make him see the way out of the darkness that I know all too well.

Chapter 41

Zane

Everybody is filtering out, and I'm stuck with Shane as he yammers on about who knows what. I just want to get to Jules. Sitting across from her seemed like a good idea at the time. I'm still not sure how she doesn't hate me, how she's not scared of me. I just thought it made sense. Not to mention I didn't want any attention drawn to the fact that she's who I was talking about. But the second I recognized her tears, my heart sank and all I wanted to do was rush to her.

The meeting ended ten minutes ago, and we're both stuck. Mary is talking her ear off, and every few minutes Jules glances in my direction.

I put a hand on Shane's shoulder, effectively cutting him off, and walk over to Jules. "Hey, Serena, haven't seen you in a while." I don't know who I'm trying to fool, Mary perhaps, Shane if he's still behind me, Layla who's always lingering.

Mary isn't fooled though, clearly more aware than I've ever given her credit for, as she looks up at me with a knowing smile and a glimmer flickering in her eyes. Jules is trying hard not to turn in my direction. Part of me is worried it's because this conversation brought up too many negative emotions and it's the end for me.

"Call me, let's do something." Mary puts her hand on Jules's arm, and with one final look between the two of us, smile widening, she leaves.

"You ready?" To fight the urge to run my hand down her back and pull her against me, I grit my teeth until they squeak. She still doesn't look at me, just gives a solemn nod, eyes trained on the ground.

My hand lingers behind her back, hovering behind her until we get through the door. Her fingers grasp at my shirt which causes me to look down. I'd been so distracted on our way here that I didn't even realize where we were. Now, seeing her stiff and looking frantically around the alley, it plows into me, and all the air is knocked straight from my lungs.

Turning toward her, I lean down and take her face between my hands. "Jules. Look at me, Jules." When her beautiful browns are focused on me, wide and wild, her neck fluttering with her racing pulse, my heart slides to my feet. This was a bad idea. I shouldn't have brought her here. I'm weak right now, I could have just opened her up to the same thing. Both of us, struggling at the same time, it won't go well.

"I will *never* let anybody hurt you or touch you again. Do you understand me? I promise you they would die trying." It's an easy promise to keep. I still hate myself for not killing Tim the first time. I've mentioned it to Brian. He says it's part of what helped bring Jules and I together, the catalyst moment. It would have happened without her suffering. We were too pulled to each other, too magnetic, for it to not.

Slowly she nods as her hands slide up and wrap around my wrists. She's fighting tears, and I know she's doing it because of me, because of what I said in the meeting. Damn this perfect woman of mine. Trying to be strong for me when I don't deserve it.

My hands still hold her cheeks, her beautiful, perfect face. I run my thumbs over her delicately soft skin and pull her mouth to mine. There's no hesitation, not even for a second, as she melts into me, her whole body collapsing against me in one fluid motion. Sliding a hand to her waist, I pull her flush against me as my lips part hers, my tongue seeking its companion.

Her fingers tighten in my shirt as a tiny moan rises in her chest. It flows into my body and straight down to my cock, which rises to the occasion.

Smirking against her mouth, I kiss to her ear, keeping her cheek cupped in my hand. "I'd gladly give you some happy memories of this alley if you wanted." The resounding shiver is one of my favorite things about Jules. Anytime I talk nice and low about sex in her ear, that shiver runs through her body, and Goddamn...it's just one of the sexiest things about her. It's like her body knows what's coming and can't control the reaction it's having to the anticipation.

"Just take me home?" Pulling back to look at her there's still fear in her eyes. "Then do whatever dirty things you want to me." The fear dissipates and is replaced with lust.

Pressing my pelvis against hers, wanting her to feel the reaction I have to her, I talk in her ear again. "Very, very dirty things."

Once again Jules's fear is able to pull me from my own bullshit. By no means is it a habit I want to get into, but right now the light in her eyes is showing me the way back. I'll take it for now, and once I've found my way, I'll never get lost again. A little for myself, but mostly for her.

Chapter 42

Jules

I'm later getting home than I planned to be. It's after six, and Zane's likely already home, wondering where I am, and hopefully not freaking out that I've run away. Or dissociated and am currently in another state.

With a deep breath, I open the door.

Zane pounces on me before I've even taken my coat off.

"Where were you?"

"Out."

"With somebody tall, dark and handsome, I'm sure." Irritation bordering on anger drips from his words.

"Nobody can be more tall, dark and devastatingly handsome than who I have waiting for me at home," I say as sultry as I can while I run a hand through his hair and down his cheek.

Instead of softening, he grabs my wrist and pulls it away from him, dark eyes boring into mine. They seem to darken when he's mad, almost like they absorb his mood. When he's happy they're light, almost blue, but when he's mad, they're that dark slate, almost black. It's fascinating and makes my panties wet.

"I was with Mary. Feel free to call her and check up on it." I pull my phone from my pocket and hand it to him.

He doesn't say anything.

"Wow. You really don't trust me right now do you?"

"You've been spiraling lately." He's not wrong. I've been having trouble finding some level ground since his outburst, even though it was over ten weeks ago. I'm trying my hardest to hide it, but I'm clearly not doing a very good job.

"I'm not going to self-destruct and ruin this."

"Maybe not intentionally."

"I won't hurt you."

"You've dissociated and woken up in another state with another man before. It can happen again." The mention of it makes my stomach churn. Sometimes I wish I hadn't told him *everything*.

"I'm not dissociating."

"Yet."

"I could never do that to you." My heart is pounding against my sternum, and sweat is starting to bead along my hairline. How he doesn't know that he's so different yet, despite the way I've been acting, is incredibly frustrating.

"What makes me different? How could you even control it?"

"Because I'm happy with you, asshole!" Happy. Not a word I often use to describe myself. And never in terms of a relationship. Zane knows this. Even though he knows I love him, that I tell him daily, the word *happy* rarely crosses my lips.

Which is probably why he yanks me so hard and fast that I almost lose my footing as I fall against him.

"Say it again," he whispers. His arm is so tight around my lower back I'm afraid he might crush me. But his other hand is gentle, brushing down the side of my face, tucking hair behind my ear. Finally, his eyes have softened, slate with the slightest hint of blue, like a sky clearing after a storm.

"I'm happy with you...asshole," I murmur, my heart still hammering against my ribs.

The smile that spreads across his face is infectious as I feel my face contort to one so foreign to me.

"You should smile more, Jules. It looks good on you." His mouth closes over mine, blocking out any ability for me to respond.

One hand cups my ear while the other slides down my body. A flick of his wrist has the button of my jeans undone as his hand slips under the waistband of my panties. My legs part for him on instinct as he gives a quick whorl of his fingers over my clit before sliding into me.

My head tilts back with a gasp as he kisses to my neck, slowly pushing me backward until my spine hits the counter. Melding his mouth to mine, he moves his fingers faster and with more pressure as he swallows my moans.

Pulling his hands away, they wrap to my waist, giving a tight squeeze before removing my pants and panties. Returning to my hips, he grabs tightly, lifting me up and setting me on the counter. My fingers fly to his belt, but he swats them away, freeing himself faster than I would have been able to.

Grabbing the tops of my thighs, he pulls me to the edge of the counter as he presses into me. I wrap my legs around his waist, a hand curling behind his head and tangling into his hair, to hold tightly to him as he grips my waist.

He thrusts into me hard and fast as my head tips back, and a loud moan rises from my chest. A groan escapes his lips as his head also tips back slightly. His eyes hood as I fight mine from fluttering closed.

"Fuuuck," he draws the word out. I want to respond in kind, but my mouth can't form words. A strange "mph" leaves my lips instead.

With the slightest adjustment of his hips, Zane starts hitting different points inside me. Pleasure ricochets through my body as I tighten around him and twist my fingers into his hair, leaning back and screaming his name.

At the same time, a breath and moan stick in Zane's throat as he comes with me. As he slows, he rests his head against my chest, his breath ragged. Kissing his way to my mouth, one hand cups the back of my head as he tilts me forward and into a deep kiss.

Zane's the only man who's ever been able to kiss me and make everything else disappear. I've never told him this of course. He holds enough power over me without knowing it himself. It's something about his mouth, how it's soft but forceful. Like he's tender but claiming me as his own with every kiss. But he doesn't need to claim me. I've given myself to him willingly.

He owns me, every facet of me. But I can never let him know.

Chapter 43

Zane

J ules is a tiny ball of tension to my right, her knee bouncing incessantly. Without looking at her from my spot slouched in my chair, I cross my ankles under the table and reach over to place a hand on her thigh. The movements stop, and I turn to her just as she meets my gaze.

Her eyes are wide with a hint of pleading.

"Jules, it's going to be fine." With my other hand, I push the paper cup closer to her. Maybe a few sips of coffee will help. While coffee amps up most people, it seems to have a calming effect on Jules. Where some people relax with a glass wine, or like me, an amber liquor, she drinks a cup of coffee.

"Sure."

Before I can answer, she jumps to stand, and I join her as a busty blonde walks over and wraps her arms around Jules. Where Jules almost never smiles, Daphne seems to be the opposite, a wide, full-toothed grin plastered on her face.

After what I'm sure are the only hugs Jules allows besides mine, Daphne takes a step back and gives me a quick once over. Her jaw drops and her blue eyes widen. "Whoa." A hand immediately flies to her mouth as she turns to Jules, who glares at her, and then turns on me when I chuckle.

Daphne is a beautiful woman, but I only have eyes for Jules. The reaction is nothing short of routine for me, and I've grown accustomed to ignoring it, just as I did today, aside from a little amusement.

"Hi, you must be Daphne. I'm Zane." I extend my hand to take hers, and she falters for a moment before clearing her throat and placing her fingers in mine. She seems timid.

"Nice to meet you, Zane. Jules has told me a lot about you, and I'm sure likewise about me."

"She has." I nod my confirmation in addition to stating it. This would be less awkward if the woman of the hour would pitch in to the conversation, but I'm not entirely sure I can expect her to even open her mouth more than to let coffee in.

It's been a few months since I mentioned wanting to meet Daphne, and since meeting with Dr. Ptansky, who I've spoken to a handful more times and has agreed that meeting Daphne is a good step. My stubborn woman though, she just wasn't ready. So, I was patient, mentioning it every so often. I'm pretty sure the only reason she agreed today is because I told her I'd only hang around for a bit to meet Daphne and then had a monthly basketball game.

While the guys meet weekly, I can only really tolerate the interaction once a month. They're a little too crude for my liking. Half of them are married, but frequent the strip club and are all too happy to talk about their escapades and who they fucked that night. I could never imagine treating a woman I'm in a relationship with like that, especially if I was married or had kids. And the thought of ever cheating on Jules is not something I can even wrap my head around.

The promise of limited interruption of her weekly coffee date, plus me getting off her case to meet Daphne, was the only reason

Jules agreed. That, and the stars must have aligned in just the right way.

We all sit, and I notice that Jules is still tight and curled into herself as much as the table will allow. I bump her with my elbow, drawing her attention from the window, and jut my chin toward the coffee in front of her. "Drink."

With a grumble and a roll of her eyes, she angrily grabs the cup and takes a few large gulps. "There, happy now?" Even as she says it with all the attitude I've come to know and love, her back is straightening, and her shoulders are pushing back.

Leaning in, I place a small kiss on her temple. "Yes, very. Thank you." I shift in my seat so I can face Daphne but have my arm around the back of Jules's chair, my fingers getting lost in her sea of curls and twisting different spirals.

After a few minutes, Jules adjusts herself and her knees point a little closer to mine, her body turned in my direction. I'm not even sure she notices.

Daphne's able to bring a smile to Jules's face in a way I wish I could. It's infrequent, but it creeps up far more often than I've ever seen. She's funny too, is quick with a witty comment and talks openly about her abysmal dating life, which is today's topic of conversation. Some part of me is sure that Daphne talks about things like this because she knows it makes Jules feel more comfortable, allows her to relax by taking the pressure off her.

Jules made it exceptionally clear that there would be no retellings of embarrassing stories or childhood memories. This was solely so Daphne and I could get to know each other. Apparently, that involves being included on the very intimate details of Daphne's not so stellar sex life.

"Okay, I've rambled enough about me and things I'm sure Zane doesn't care to know about. So, it's your turn. Zane, tell me about yourself." She turns her large blue eyes on me, and I can see the dilation of her pupils. I know she's Jules's oldest friend, but I don't know what their history is like with guys. Has Daphne ever stolen one from Jules? Would she try?

Just to make it extra clear I'm not interested, I slip my hand around Jules's shoulder and pull her a little closer, which earns me a tiny smile.

"What would you like to know? I'm a pretty open book."

"You are not." A quick glance to my right, and I find Jules looking up at me with her brow bunched together and lips pointing down.

"I can be, when I want or need to be. I have been with you, have I not?"

"And how hard was it to get there? I carried the conversation those early days."

"I promise to answer any question Daphne asks."

Silent communication happens between us as Jules searches my face, looking for any sign I'm being dishonest. But when I told Jules at the beginning that I don't lie, I wasn't kidding, and never have lied to her.

When she turns away, I know I've come out successful and look back at Daphne with my brows raised, ready for the inquisition.

"Where are you from?" Well, that's not too hard.

"New York, born and raised. Not the city until college though."

"Job?"

"Finance." These questions seem too easy. And things I'm sure Jules has already told her.

"Siblings?"

"None."

"Parents?"

"More complicated, but none." She doesn't need to know that my father is in fact still alive somewhere, or at least as far as I know. It was five years ago when I hired the private detective to find him. Sheer morbid curiosity had me shelling out cash to find out if the douchebag was still living somewhere or had finally kicked it.

A clearing of the delicate throat next to me draws my attention, and I find Jules with a hardened stare on her face.

Daphne's lip tips up and her eyes alight. My assumption is she's amused at Jules trying to be forceful without words.

"Okay, real talk. What are your intentions with my best friend?"

"Daphne."

I put my hand over Jules's to calm her. "It's okay, Jules. Daphne, I love your friend, very much. Those are my intentions. To love her and take care of her and be there for her whenever she lets me, and even sometimes when she doesn't." I wait a second to let my words sink in. "We're on the same team here, Daphne."

Though her eyes are narrowed at me and she's chewing the inside of her cheek, I think I'm winning her over. At this point, Daphne not liking me could still sway Jules's opinion of me.

Without another mention of it, she perks up, eyes wide and bright, smile back on her face. She turns to Jules, talking about some guy like nothing happened and as if I don't exist. I'm not sure if it's a good thing or a bad thing.

I listen intently, sliding my gaze over to Jules every so often to gauge her reaction and see that she's smiling, though still curled into herself.

"Well, I'm not as lucky as you are to find a great guy like Zane. Really, Jules, he's wonderful." Finally, she turns back to me. "It's been really nice to meet you, Zane. I can tell you love my best friend and that you're going to look out for her. Don't make me regret saying this."

"I won't. Jules means a lot to me Daph—" I'm cut off by the alarm Jules made me set on my phone, indicating it's my time to go.

Her eyes are wide as she readjusts in her chair so she's facing me. Turning myself, I put my legs on either side of hers and slide to the edge of my seat, pulling her closer and tilting toward her. My hands rest around her hips and her palms sit on my thighs. I've barely heard her voice since we got here and it's killing me.

"Hey, I'm going to go play ball for a little while. I'll meet you back at your apartment?" The little up and down of her head is plenty, but when she grips my legs, I know she's going to miss me. "Have fun, try not to talk about me too much."

She lifts a hand to poke me in the ribs, causing me to flinch.

I place a tiny kiss next to her ear before pulling back and laying a lasting one on her forehead before dipping to meet her eyes. "I love you."

"I love you, too." One more kiss to her cheek and I stand to leave, her eyes following me as I move.

"Zane, I think it would be a good idea if we had one another's phone numbers, just in case something was to ever happen and we needed to contact each other about Jules." At the mention of her name, she bristles next to me, but Daphne's right, it's a smart idea. I have Dr. Ptansky programmed into my phone, Daphne should be too.

"Yeah, that's a great idea." I hand over my phone so she can program herself in, then immediately send her a text so she has mine.

"It was really nice to meet you, Daphne, I'm afraid my warranted time has expired."

"It was nice to meet you too, Zane. Enjoy."

On my way out the door, I hear, "He's incredible Jules, really," and it adds a little extra bounce to my step.

Chapter 44

Jules

Why do you do it? Are you really that starved for attention? Do I not *give you* enough attention? Sheesh Jules, didn't you ever grow up? Are you sure you're not still in high school? *You're weak.*

All just things I'd heard from previous boyfriends. Zane has always been different. Not only has he never once uttered a single sentiment remotely similar, but he can tell I'm having a bad day by a quick glance. He doesn't ask me why I do it, but instead asks me what he can do to help. He'll cancel plans, call in from work, come home early if he needs to. "Fine" is never an acceptable answer to how I am. He'll sit on the floor with me at two in the morning to keep me from doing something I'll regret immediately.

That's why it will hurt so much more when he inevitably ends things.

Despite all of this, there's no quieting the voice that tells me he's going to leave me, the one that tells me I'm not good enough for him, or anybody else. Sometimes it's enough to wake me at four in the morning. When that happens, I do one of two things. It always starts with turning and looking at his perfection, highlighted in the moonlight.

Everything about him still takes my breath away. All the clear-cut lines of his chest and abs, more chiseled than when we met now that he goes to the gym at least once a day. The sharp edges of his cheekbones and jaw. Based on how much I said I like it, he's grown out his hair a little and let his five o'clock shadow become more of a thick stubble.

At first, I wasn't sure what to make of the tattoos that mark his skin. They just didn't seem to fit the picture I had. Even though I had gotten to know him far better than just the new guy at meetings, they didn't feel right. But as time has gone on, I've found they are him to a tee, and now I couldn't imagine him without them.

Some nights, I'm able to just enjoy looking at him, feeling him right next to me, and snuggling into him. Without even waking up, he'll make room for me to curl against him and hold me tight until I fall asleep.

But other nights, I find myself unable to quell the negative thoughts, unable to tell the voice to shut up and leave me alone. That may mean I'm battling myself not to cut at four in the morning or waking Zane up so he can talk me out of it, or at least hold me until I pass out from exhaustion. On the better of the bad nights, I can find sanctuary in a book on the couch.

That's where I find myself tonight. After staring at Zane for what felt like an hour, I finally realize that the negative voice isn't going to stop haunting me tonight. It isn't loud enough that I need to self-destruct, thankfully, but enough that I can't sleep. Part of me wants to wake up Zane; he's said I should any time I have these thoughts. But he needs his rest. I may not have to be up for work tomorrow, but he does. And in only a few hours.

Tonight, I feel confident that everything will settle, I just can't sleep. Escaping into another world sounds like the perfect solution to take my mind off it.

With a grunt, I hit the floor. Blinking rapidly, I look around, finding I've rolled off the couch. I must have fallen asleep at some point.

Getting to my hands and knees, I find my book squished underneath me, and my lips turn down. The spine is cracked, not something I ever do when reading. I'll have to buy a new one tomorrow.

Pink is just starting to paint the sky, so I know I haven't been asleep for too long. The book did its job of not only helping me get out of my head, but calming me.

Now the trick is to sneak back into bed without Zane realizing.

He's exactly how I left him, not one who moves around much in his sleep. I must drive him crazy because I know I toss and turn a lot, my mind unable to quiet down, even in sleep.

Now that the truly negative thoughts are gone, I scoot close to him, his arm lazily moving for me to rest my head on his chest before enclosing around my waist.

This is my comfort zone, my happy place. Dr. Ptansky has all but begged me to use it as part of my grounding exercise, but I can't. It will hurt too much to grow accustomed to it when it'll be taken away. She tries to tell me that sometimes in life we have to take risks, and this is one that I may need to take in order to make strides in my mental health. But I can't.

The self preservation part of me needs to keep some things to myself. It's the same part that won't ever let me tell Zane how much he really means to me, beyond just loving him.

Dr. Ptansky wants me to take risks, and I am. Because I'm letting Zane into my heart at all. Deep in my soul, I know it's only a matter of time until he hurts me, possibly beyond repair.

Chapter 45

Jules

Even though Zane and I have been together for several months now, I haven't spent a lot of time at his apartment. After Zane started staying with me, it was clear he took a liking to mine. I think he also knows that I'm just more comfortable being in my own space. Who wouldn't be? Though some part of me feels guilty that he's at mine all the time and I'm not at his, I know he doesn't care as much, and likes to make me happy.

While this may be my fifth time here, I'm always a little taken aback by the simplicity. Where I have art and decorative things around, including vases of fake flowers—I can never keep real ones alive—and other things cluttered on counters, Zane has none of those things. Surfaces are basically bare. I know he can't have glass, but he can have *something*. The décor is all dark, the walls a shade of gray. I'd feel uncomfortable here if it didn't scream Zane. He himself is warm and sweet, but his apartment reminds me of who I thought he initially was. I've just broken him from his shell, and he shows me a different level of himself.

Wordlessly, he takes my coat as I slip off my shoes. "I know you don't really like it here, but I wanted to be here for a day or two. If that's okay." He must see my wide eyes as I continue to take in my surroundings. I can't help but have the same reaction every time. I'm not sure I'll ever get used to it.

"I don't mind it." It's a weak lie, and I'm sure he knows it but isn't about to argue.

Our time apart is incredibly minimal these days. Zane goes to work and the gym, we have our therapy appointments, and I have my weekly coffee with Daphne, but other than that, we're together. I fall asleep next to him every night, wake up next to him every morning. Up until his explosion, there'd be the occasional night he went to his place if he was having a rough time. There have been a small handful of arguments where he felt it was best to spend the night here, after making sure I was in a good head place of course. Those nights, I was too furious at him to think about harming myself.

"I have big meetings coming up the next few days. My bed's more comfortable than yours." It's a frequent topic of discussion. His *is* more comfortable, but I could never actually admit that. Zane says I like to be difficult. He may be right.

We've already eaten dinner, so there isn't much to do besides watch TV, read, or go to bed.

"I have an early morning. I'm going to go wash up and head to bed. You're welcome to stay up if you want to." Zane kisses my temple as he walks down the hallway toward the bathroom. I'm sure he knows I'm not going to stay up without him, but I let him wash up in peace. And a little bit so I don't seem desperate to follow him around.

To distract myself, I walk over to the bookshelf and peruse what he has. I complained the second time I was here that he didn't have anything I'd read. While he'd made an argument that we don't spend much time at his apartment, and the time we do spend shouldn't be occupied with reading, he still went out and bought a few things he thought I'd like based on authors he found on my own shelves.

I'm still looking over a few titles, brushing my fingers along the spines, pulling some out to skim a quick blurb, knowing full well I don't have any intention of reading, when the bathroom door opens. I wait a couple minutes to make sure Zane's in his room before heading down to the bathroom myself.

The first night I spent here, he handed me a new toothbrush. I don't really need clothes; I just spend my time in Zane's. The last time I spent the night, I'd worn a dress to dinner at Zane's request and not wanting to wear it home, I wore a pair of his sweatpants and a T-shirt. I may have looked like a bum walking home but at least it wasn't the walk of shame look either. Now I have a few shirts, bottoms, and panties tucked away in the back of his closet.

Quietly closing the door behind me, I notice a dark blue T-shirt folded up on the corner of the vanity. My heart flutters at the sweet gesture, Zane leaving it for me to change into. Also, probably so I don't wake him up when I go into his room. I'm a bit klutzy in the dark, and he tends to fall asleep the second his head hits the pillow. Lucky guy.

Looking in the mirror, I let out a large puff of air. This is such a different feeling for me. I'm not just here for sex, like had been the case in previous relationships. I'm here just to be with Zane, to be close to him, to sleep next to him. It rattles me a bit every time I realize not only how real, but how strong my feelings are for him. And it makes me pull into myself a little each time. I've never wanted to be reliant, dependent, or emotionally vulnerable with a man.

I brush my teeth with the still somewhat new toothbrush Zane had handed me all those weeks ago. It's in a brush holder right next to his. Seeing them next to each other makes it seem like we live together, which sets butterflies loose in my stomach. At my apartment, we put them in separate cups. I push the thought from my mind and change, leaving my clothes stacked on the end of the vanity.

Decked out in Zane's T-shirt, that falls to almost mid-thigh, I walk out of the bathroom, and freeze in the bedroom doorway. The room is mostly dark, except for a slight ray of light shining in through a crack in the curtains. What gives me pause is Zane, sitting on his desk chair, completely naked. I can see his outline, his erection pointing straight up, and the slightest bit of light hits his chiseled torso, illuminating the devious smirk on his face. He has his fingers steepled in front of his chest.

I know that face, and it usually means very dirty things are in store for me. It instantly makes me wet, and the corner of Zane's mouth twitches as he notices me squirm.

"What's going on here?" I try to ask without a shaky breath. I fail. Zane's the only one who's been able to be in control of me, both in the bedroom and life. It's frightening and exhilarating at the same time.

"You're going to walk over here, and you're going to slowly sit on my dick, and then I'm going to fuck you until I'm satisfied."

A chill shivers down my spine as a throb settles between my legs. He said it so casually, like he was reading off a list. "And I get no say in this?" Not that I want one.

"None." Through the low light I can make out the amusement on his face, knowing exactly what his words are doing to me. His eyes darken, and for a second, I'm sure I can see fire dance behind them as he glares at me, probably waiting for me to walk over and obey him.

He raises an eyebrow at my defiance as my feet stay glued to the floor. For years I had been so used to being in control, and I've never relinquished it easily, though I'm sure Zane would refute that fact since I always have with him. And right now, I desperately want to. But I'm not sure I want him to see how easily I hand myself over to him just because he *says* so. That he can say jump and I'll ask how high.

My brain loses control to what my body craves, and my feet move on their own. I'm thankful I chose to forgo panties.

The smile broadens on his face as I stand between his legs. His hands move under the hem of my shirt, sliding up my thighs to just below my ass as he gently nudges me closer.

My breathing is shallow at best as I rest my hands on his shoulders and place my knees on either side of his. Sometimes it intimidates me when he's basically eye level with me as I sit on his lap. Other times it invigorates me. Tonight, I fall somewhere in the middle.

His hands glide up to grip tightly around my waist as I raise up on my knees, grabbing the base of his erection as I lower myself down. My breath catches in my throat as I get lower, my head tipping backwards.

Zane grabs my ass and stops me, making my head snap forward and eyes pop open. "I said, *slowly.*" His voice is low and gravelly, eyes dark. It sends a trill straight to my core.

"Not slow enough for you?"

"Would I have stopped you if it was?" One hand releases from my ass and tangles in my hair as he pulls my head toward his. He licks slowly up my earlobe before his lips rest against my ear. "I want you to feel every single inch of me as I slide deeper and deeper until there is nowhere left to go." *Holy shit.* He's saying the wrong words if he wants me to go slow.

With a deep breath, I latch my lips to his and try to go even slower. A moan rises from deep within me and settles against his mouth. My legs want to tremble at the tension from how slowly I'm easing myself onto him and the pleasure I'm feeling at the same time. He's right, slow is *way* better.

Once I'm flush against him, I cling to him, taking a few deep, shaky breaths as I try to steady myself. He brushes some hair behind my ear, his other hand on my lower back. "You okay?"

"Mhm. Golden. I just...I need a minute." The rattle of his body as he laughs pulsates his cock inside me, sending thrills of pleasure through my body.

He melds his mouth to mine, tongue slipping in seamlessly, as his hand wraps into my hair. Tugging my head backwards by pulling on the strands he holds, he latches onto my throat, sliding his parted lips from my chin to the space just above my ribs, and over my collarbone. He traces his teeth over my sensitive skin back to my neck where he bites down, causing me to yelp. I haven't even moved yet, and I swear he's going to make me come.

That's probably his game tonight. See how many orgasms he can give me before exhausting one of us. He's going to win. He always does. Not that I mind. I'm far from a loser with these sorts of games.

I'm *sure* that's what he's trying to do as his fingers lace below the hem of my shirt and trace lightly across my skin as he slowly lifts the fabric over my head. The second he drops it, his hands cup my breasts, thumbs rubbing over hardened nipples as he catches my gaze, one corner of his mouth ticking up when he elicits a whimper from deep inside me.

How he's not struggling is something I can't comprehend. I still haven't even moved, my body remains stationary, pressed against his, but I'm ready to burst. When his mouth closes around my nipple, it's all over for me. A few quick bucks of my hips as my arms wrap around his head, fingers tangling into his hair and I'm screaming his name, as I tremble on top of him.

Goddamn this man and his prowess.

He keeps his mouth around my nipple, tongue moving expertly, hands tight on my hips, as I ride out the waves. Once I've all but stilled, he releases me and moves to smile against my mouth.

"That's one." His voice is low and teasing. I'd laugh if I wasn't already feeling the tingling sensation of another orgasm building at just the thought of what's still to come and the fact that he's still pressed deep inside me.

I'm stuck in limbo—not quite down from the high while climbing back up the mountain—when Zane slides his hands under my thighs and stands. All while staying inside me.

Gently, he lays me down on the bed, disentangling my arms from around his neck as he runs his palms along the sides of my body. He doesn't stop as he runs them down my legs to my ankles, which are linked behind his back. Leaning in, he presses his mouth against mine, tongue running across the seam of my lips, a silent request for entrance that I quickly grant. He unhooks my ankles, taking one in his hand as he straightens and rests it against his shoulder.

One of his hands slides down the outside of my leg while he gently kisses along my calf, the hand settling against my hip. The other slides up my body to curl around my throat. The corners of my lips perk up as I wiggle against him, begging for more, for movement. Something, anything, but preferably hard and fast.

Ever so slowly, he pulls himself out until just the tip is left. Then as he tightens his fingers, he slams back in, causing me to pull my lower lip between my teeth. He does it five more times before I'm reaching for any skin I can find, grabbing onto his arms.

"Faster." It comes out a desperate whisper.

"I thought you got it, baby. I'm in charge."

"Fuck, Zane. *Please.*" I've resorted to begging.

That just makes him smile widely. With the sliver of light in the room, he looks devilish. Right now, I'm not entirely sure he isn't.

"Do that again," he says as he pulls out excruciatingly slowly.

"What?" I squeak as he thrusts back in.

Staying plunged inside me for a moment, he gives a slight tilt of his hips and moves my leg to the side so he can lean over me to whisper against my ear. "*Beg.*"

Leaning back the slightest bit to rake his eyes over my features, he starts shifting his hips before standing up straight, replacing my ankle on his shoulder, the grip around my throat tightening slightly.

But he doesn't make me say it again, my face must express enough. He starts slamming into me, hurriedly, frenziedly. I grip his forearms, nails digging in as my breath hitches and tiny whimpers escape with every thrust. Within minutes, my back is trying to peel away from the bed, but he pushes harder against my throat, keeping me down.

When I try to buck my hips up toward him, he holds tightly to resist me. He has me pinned against the mattress, under his control, just how he likes me. And fuck it all if I don't love it too.

Though I don't have the ability to move, I'm so close Zane has to know. It's clear he does when he slides his hand from my hip to settle his thumb against my clit and starts making slow circles. "Come." He practically growls at me.

Fuck.

It's enough to send me flying over the edge again, nails scraping down his arm, as I tighten around him and scream obscenities. He slows, but doesn't stop, easing in and out as I work through the whole-body trembles.

Once I'm nothing more than a pile of mush beneath him, he pulls out, slowly lowering my legs as he licks from my belly button straight up to my throat where he closes his mouth around my fluttering pulse point.

My whole body is tingling, my brain fuzzy. But I know he's not done yet.

As he climbs over me, he wraps his arm around my waist, lifting me and pulling me higher on the bed. He leans down and places tender kisses along the inside of my neck, along my shoulder and back again. On his third pass, he sinks his teeth in, and I arch against him, my chest meeting his.

Leaning back, he brushes some hair from my face, trailing his thumb down my cheek and across my lower lip. His eyes are filled with hunger, desire.

"You doing okay?"

All I can do is nod. It's exhausting, exhilarating, but I'm good. "How are you holding out?" I'm basically breathless. I don't understand how he's edging himself so expertly.

"Trust me, it isn't easy," he says as he runs a hand down my side, trailing a finger over my nipple, causing a tiny moan to rise in my chest. "But I love seeing like you this."

"And how is that?"

"Vulnerable. Exposed. Blissful. But tonight, I'm aiming for euphoric."

"Think you can last that long?" I'm trying to tease him but it's failing.

"Think *you* can?" He's already got a score of 2-0 on me. And I'm at a point where I'm too weak to fight back, even if I wanted to. I like when he takes care of me first, so few guys do. I know if he wants to, he'll fuck me until I pass out from exhaustion.

"No. But I'll enjoy the journey."

"Mmm." He trails his gaze slowly down my body biting his lip. I can almost see the gears working his head, figuring out what he wants to do to me next.

When his eyebrows do a quick quirk up, I know he's landed on something.

His lips meet mine with passion, a deep seeded desire, as he thrusts his tongue into my mouth. For a minute I think he's going to ease into me, make it sweet and gentle, a rarity for us.

I realize I'm wrong when he pulls away and puts his hands on my hips, flipping me to my stomach and pulling my ass into the air. He's on his knees behind me immediately, rubbing his tip over my wetness, teasing me.

As he slips into me my hands grip at the sheets, my breath catching mid-moan. Once he's pressed all the way inside me, he runs his hands down my back, lowering his chest to rest flat against me. He kisses his way back up my back, toward my ass, then licks back down along my spine. I'm pretty sure he's invented a new form of torture tonight. Probably for both of us.

His hands settle on my hips as he rights himself and starts thrusting into me with purpose. I prop myself up on my hands, pushing my ass higher into the air as my back slopes down in the middle.

The air around us is thick with warmth, the sounds of heavy breathing and skin slapping against skin.

Sex. The room is filled with sex.

Tangling a hand in my hair, he pulls my head back so my face is pointing straight ahead.

He has me so lit up from two orgasms, the dirty talk, and touches in between that it doesn't take him long to get me to a tipping point again.

Zane makes the slightest adjustment as his hand slides from my hip to cup my breast, taking my nipple between two fingers. "Fuuuck, Zane."

"That's right, baby."

A few more hard thrusts and I'm falling apart around him. My arms and legs are too shaky and weak to support me, and I pull away as I collapse to the bed, breathing heavily.

I bounce as the bed rocks as Zane flops down next to me. He flings an arm over his eyes, breathing heavily, but with a large smile spread across his face. My jellyfish resemblance pleases him.

Rolling to his side, he smoothes what I'm sure is my frizzy, wild hair back, as he moves closer and presses his mouth against mine, opening it as his tongue slides in and slips along mine.

His fingers glide from my cheek down along my back to my waist, where he grabs tightly and turns me to my side before pulling me flush against him. I'm putty beneath his hands. At this point, he can mold me however he wants.

As much as this passionate make-out session is nice, I know there's more to come, and my body thrums with anticipation of what's next.

I don't have much time to think about it as he flips me to my back and slides over me, resting on his elbows so he's right on top of me, but not pressing his weight down. Taking hold of my calf, he wraps one leg around his waist as he eases himself into me, my hands gripping his shoulders as my chest makes the tiniest tilt up to push against his.

As he starts pumping into me, slow and steady, he pries my hands from his back, pulling them above my head, linking his fingers in mine. He's playing dirty tonight since he *knows* I like to be able to grab at him, touch him, *feel* him, which I obviously can't do when my hands are restrained. I'm just lucky he's using his hands and not tying me up.

Pressing my hands into the mattress, he starts moving faster and harder. He switches his grasp to have both of my hands in just one of his while the other wraps around to hold my ankle against his back.

My eyes are fluttering shut as the pressure builds again.

"Look at me." His voice is low, tight, and gravelly.

I do as he asks, fighting the urge to roll my head back. His lips tip up as he slides his hand from my waist to settle between where our bodies meet. I'm so sensitive from going so many rounds, the tiniest touch has me writhing under him.

"Zane. Fuck. Don't stop." There's another little uptick of the corner of his mouth as he pumps faster and swirls his thumb over my throbbing bud, his hand pressing mine further into the mattress. It takes all of two minutes before I'm pulling him against me with my leg, which is still wrapped around his waist, and screaming out his name.

"Fuck, baby." His voice is low and husky. Three more pumps and he releases a moan, breath catching in his throat as he comes.

Resting his head against my chest, he breathes heavily, slowly releasing my hands as he trails his fingers down my arm. He tenderly places his lips against my sternum, kissing upwards slowly until he attaches his mouth to mine. Cupping my cheek, he parts my lips with his, kissing me tenderly and passionately.

I still can't even move, my body and brain unable to make a connection. Hell, my brain can barely make coherent thoughts or words. My leg is still wrapped around his waist, my hands still above my head.

With a nip on my lower lip, a harder one on my neck, and two more quick pumps, he slides away and rolls to his back next to me, my leg flopping to the bed.

Turning his head to look at me, the whole bed moves with his laugh. "Can you move?"

All I can do is shake my head, unable to create words.

It's returned with another laugh as he turns to his side, leaning on his elbow as he takes my hands and brings them to my chest. Pushing his arm under my neck, he pulls me against him, my cheek resting on his chest as he kisses the top of my head and takes a deep breath.

"I guess I achieved my goal then."

"Of euphoria? Oh yeah." Words are starting to return with the slow calming circles he draws on my hip. "If that's what's in store when I stay here, I'll have to stay more often."

"Or you could just move in with me." Ice runs through my veins, slowing my heart. Is he serious? He hasn't hesitated, his fingers still making smooth circles.

"Really?"

"You've never thought about it?"

"I have." And every time I've wondered if it's a good idea. We have our issues, what if it doesn't work as well when we're living together? Even though we're together almost all the time anyway, we have our own apartment to go back to if need be.

"You can think about it more if you need to." He must sense my hesitation. Or he's using that direct access I swear he has to my mind. "I love you, Jules. We're together basically all the time. I can't even remember the last night we spent apart. It makes sense to me. It's something I want with you."

"I want it too, Zane. I'm just worried. What if something gets to be too much? What if one of us has a really bad day or we need space? Now we have our own apartment to get away to. We won't have that."

"It'll be like a real adult relationship, Jules. What, you're never going to be in a long-term relationship? Or ever get married?" *Marriage.* My stomach flips at the word. Not something I've really ever put much thought into. I guess I want it someday. Just never expected to find somebody who could deal with my issues. And I've certainly been convinced *I'll* never be able to get a real handle on them.

"I don't know. Things are so...different, with you. I didn't think I'd really ever find somebody who'd be able to put up with me for the long-term so it was really a moot point. Not something I wanted to spend too much time dwelling on."

"Well, I can deal with you and your issues."

"Yeah. Yeah, you can. Okay. Let's do it."

"You sure?"

Resting my hand on his chest, I push up to look at him. "I'm sure." There's not a shred of doubt in me. I feel safe with Zane. He saves me from myself. He's saved me from others. He's changed to keep me safe from himself. "But do we have to live here?" I don't really want to take on changing his apartment.

A twinkle skitters across his eyes as he chuckles. "Why don't we find a new place? We'll make sure there's a gym for me. A twenty-four hour one. What's important to you?"

I snuggle back in against his chest, excitement coursing through me. Zane can be tough, difficult, and is an asshole to people he doesn't like, which is just about everybody else. But he's always been kind and sweet to me, putting me first. "Hmm. I don't have too many needs. And I *guess* we can bring your bed."

"So, the truth finally comes out. I mean, I knew it all along, but it's good to know I'm right. How about this, we can go bed shopping if you want."

"I mean, if you want to that's fine but I do in fact like this bed. Very comfortable. I like it a little more after tonight."

"Well, I was thinking of getting a new frame. Something with at least some posts to the headboard."

"Oh really? What for?"

When he's silent, I tilt my head to look at him. One corner of his mouth is upturned, as is one of his eyebrows. It suddenly hits me and heat creeps up my neck and tears through my body.

"Oh, so you can tie me up. Gotcha."

"Any opposition to that?"

"Absolutely none. In fact, I was surprised it wasn't on the menu tonight." It's definitely not my favorite thing, removing the touch I so desperately need, but he likes it, and I want him to be happy.

"No time. I had a goal and personally was running out of time to achieve it."

"Well, mission accomplished." I can't help the yawn that breaks as I finish my sentence.

The resounding chuckle from Zane makes my lips turn downward in a scowl. I don't like how much he's enjoying this.

He disentangles himself from me and gets off the bed, pulling on a pair of boxers and scooping his shirt off the floor. Climbing back onto the bed he sits on his knees in front of me. I sit up on mine as well and face him.

"Arms up."

I do as he asks, and he puts the shirt on over my head, cupping my cheek and tangling his fingers in the back of my hair, pulling my lips against his as the shirt falls around me. As his other hand cups my ass under the hem of the shirt, he pushes me down, staying against me as we fall to the bed.

After a few minutes he pulls away, resting his forehead against mine. "I love you, Jules."

"I love you, too." Zane tells me regularly that he loves me. Yet every time it makes my heart skip a beat. He's not the first man to tell me. But he is the first man where I've truly meant it in return.

I roll in his arms as he presses himself to my back, an arm wrapping tightly around my waist. I'm asleep within seconds, exhausted from reaching euphoria.

Chapter 46

Zane

She said yes. I told her we should move in together, and she said yes.

Three days later and I can still hardly believe it. She hesitated for a second, questioned it, but she hasn't wavered, hasn't backed out. I expected her to fight it, fight *me* on it.

I know she's worried, I am too. It's going to mean a lot of changes for her and how she lives. Her apartment is still cluttered with breakables despite the outburst I had a few months ago. But when we live together, those things will have to be packed away or completely discarded.

The past few months haven't been impossible at her apartment, but in the back of my mind, I've always known I can escape if I need to go home. When we're living together, I won't be able to do that.

I know she's going to talk to Dr. Ptansky about it at her appointment this week. I know she'll talk to Daphne at their weekly coffee on Saturday. But I think both will lean in my favor. I know her opinion can be swayed by either.

"So, any chance you'd want to go apartment hunting this weekend? After coffee with Daphne, of course." I broach the subject tentatively. Sometimes I swear she's like a feral animal, ready to bolt or attack at any second.

Her shoulders rise and fall quickly. "Sure," she says nonchalantly. Hmm.

"That's it? Sure?"

She looks at me, her chocolate eyes still make my heart skip a beat. "I'm not sure what else you want me to say. Sure, let's go. I'm sorry I'm not jumping up and down? I mean, I kind of feel like we basically live together anyway. It will just be a new place with all of our things in the same spot instead of some of yours here and some of mine there."

God, I love her.

"Besides, I don't really *do* jumping up and down."

I can't help the smirk that pulls at my lips. No, Jules is definitely not the jumping up and down type. It's part of what I love about her. She's a little sadder, a little darker, and more troubled than most. But she's real. There's no fake happiness, often not even real happiness. But I always know where she stands. Sure, I know there are things she keeps from me, feelings especially. But I never have to wonder if she's hiding sadness beneath a smile.

"Alright. Well, I did a little looking into some of what's available. Any particular neighborhood you like or want to avoid?"

"No, not really. I mean my funds are kind of limited. I got lucky finding my apartment, and that it's rent controlled, because I probably wouldn't be able to afford it by myself."

"Don't worry about the cost."

Her brows furrow and her mouth presses into a line as she looks at me. I'm not sure she realizes how sexy it makes her look. "What do you mean *don't worry about it?*"

"I mean I'll pay the rent." We haven't really discussed finances before, not being together terribly long and it's just not something I like to bring up. Her not knowing means I know she's not with me for my money. It's a change from most.

"I'm not sure I'm comfortable with that."

Of course, she wouldn't be. I knew that and anticipated this conversation. "Why don't we just look and see what we find."

Her eyes are narrow as she glares at me. I'm sure it's intimidating to others, but not me. "I'm not going to agree to a place I can't afford. I know you make more than I do. I'm not sure how much exactly since you refuse to talk about it. But I'm not willing to get myself into a position where I can't afford my share and you resent me for not paying it."

I take the few strides to be next to her and wrap my arms around her waist. Sometimes our height difference strikes me as I have to look down at her. I love how she fits so perfectly in my arms.

"I could never resent you," I say quietly.

She raises her eyebrows. "Really? You know for a fact you absolutely could." She hasn't relaxed, hasn't eased into me. Nor has she wrapped her arms around me. I'm patient, she can be like this, aloof, standoffish. So can I, but she brings out the softer side of me. One I wasn't sure even existed.

"Well, I would never resent you for something like that."

"What about when money gets tight because I can't pay my half?"

"Money won't get tight."

When she starts to pull back, I tighten my grip around her. "Okay. Time for some real talk. How much are we talking here?"

"Enough."

She shakes her head, the curls around her face lightly shaking back and forth. "Nope, not a good enough answer."

Hooking my fingers into her belt loops so she can't get away, I pull one hand from her waist, pointing at her. "Fine. This changes nothing. Understood?"

The glower she shoots at me doesn't intimidate me like she expects. Instead, it makes my dick pulsate. "Yes." She says it through gritted teeth.

"I average about three hundred and fifty thousand a year. Great years can be upwards of five hundred, bad years can be as low as two hundred. But I've been at my job for seven years, and while I had to climb the ladder for the first few, I've been making good money for at least five of them. And I don't really travel or buy things I don't need so it's mostly saved."

Her eyes slowly grow into saucers. "So, you're rich. Like, rich, rich." She says it as a statement.

"I guess you could say that. Finance in New York City can be a fairly lucrative career. I'm good with money and numbers. And as you know I'm very charismatic."

I fight a laugh at her eye roll and scoff. "Charismatic is not exactly a word I'd choose to describe you." She doesn't mention the money. Is that a good thing? "I still don't know that I'm comfortable letting you pay more than I do."

Taking a deep breath, I steel myself, not sure now's the best time to dive into my next thought. "Well...I was actually thinking that I'd just pay it myself.""That makes it *your* place."

"No. I don't look at it that way. Especially because I asked you to move in with me." I haven't released my hold on her but now she's moved her hands to close loosely onto my biceps. "I want to do this, Jules. For us. If it makes you feel better you can take full control of decorating, within reason. We'll have to make certain changes, for me. But otherwise, you can do whatever you want."

The slight downturn of her lip tells me that's not enough. I know what's available in Manhattan, and it's not much, especially with a gym.

Chewing the inside of her cheek she looks around. I can practically see the gears turning in her head. "Okay."

My eyebrows shoot skyward. I was in the process of preparing for more of an argument. "Really?"

"Yeah. Just know the first time you bring it up in a fight we're going to have some serious fucking issues."

"I won't." I'd never do that. Especially because this is my choice. I'd be fine if she didn't want to work at all. She loves her job, but sometimes it stresses her out, makes things worse.

She slowly slides her hands up to my shoulders and down my torso to wrap around my waist and she draws herself in closer, leaning her cheek against my chest. I start twisting a few curls in my fingers as I rest my chin on the top of her head. Our height difference is perfect for these close moments.

"I can really do anything I want in terms of decorating?" She murmurs against my chest. I try not to cringe, knowing she's going to torment me a little bit. Jules wouldn't be Jules if she didn't. It's part of what I love about her, she challenges me, calls me out, and isn't afraid to tease me. She even pushes me, my buttons—sometimes to my limits. The one time I went beyond my limit, was when I changed, for her, so she's also made me a better person.

"I suppose."

"Pink everything it is."

"You don't even like pink."

"You're right, I don't. But I'd tolerate it just because I know how crazy it would make you. Bright pink, too. So very opposite of your depressing and dark apartment."

"If that's really what you want."

She leans back and scrutinizes my face. "It's not. But it's fun to torment you. You should tell your face what your mouth is saying next time."

I press my mouth into a hard line, jaw sharpening. The corners of her mouth twitch and I think for a second that I may get one of those rare Jules smiles that lights my insides on fire. Disappointment fills my chest when her routine look settles over her features, the one where her lips have a slight downturn, and her eyes look a little sad. It doesn't matter to me, she's always beautiful.

Running my fingers through her hair and tangling by her ear, I pull her into a kiss. "I love you," I murmur against her mouth. I've never really told another person I love them, aside from my family when I was a kid, but Jules makes me want to tell her every second of every day.

It works and I get the faintest smile as she says, "I love you, too."

Chapter 47

Jules

"I like that one," I say as I catch up to Zane on our way out of the third apartment we've seen so far.

He closes his peacoat, stretching his arms out as he adjusts the buttons at the wrist of his collared shirt. I'm not sure why he wore it. I don't typically see him in any dress clothes outside of working hours, but it pairs with his jeans in a new, sexy way.

"No." It's his only response.

"Why not?"

Throwing his arm around my shoulders and tucking me into him, which I'm thankful for, as the cold is a bit more biting than I expected, he looks down at me. "Not every room had ceiling fixtures."

My brows knit together as I wrack my brain for what that can possibly mean.

"Lamps. We'd need lamps."

"I have lamps in my apartment and you have no issues with those." The night he broke things, the few I have went unscathed.

"Let's not test that theory shall we?"

I sigh internally, not wanting him to know I'm feeling upset or frustrated. It was the nicest apartment we've seen so far, and he told me we're going to five places today. There's not a huge selection with twenty-four-hour gyms and in a neighborhood not too far from his office.

He must sense my frustration because he squeezes my shoulder. "We'll find one, babe. Don't worry. We could always buy."

"You mean *you* could always buy. And it's enough that I'm willing to find a place where you pay at least the lion's share of the rent if not all of it. I'm not about to let *you* buy a place because it would be just *you* buying it."

His body tenses, and I don't need to look at his face to know his mouth is pressed into a hard line, cheekbones sharp, eyes swirling in darkness. "Why are you making this difficult? *If* I were to buy a place, it would be for us, Jules. And it'd be something *you* like. I don't know what I've ever done or said to make you think that I'm going to suddenly kick you out or pull some 'this is mine and not yours' bullshit. I may be an asshole, but I like to think I've always been very giving and honest with you. Not to mention, I've never once lied to you."

Halting in his tracks suddenly, I take an extra couple steps before he grabs my wrist and pulls me against him. Cupping my face with one hand while brushing hair behind my ear with the other his eyes lock on mine. They're slate, swirling with darkness and frustration. "I need you to trust me."

"I have a hard time tr—"

"I know. I know you have a hard time trusting people. But have I ever given you any reason not to? Have I ever given you any reason to think that I'm not being honest? I need you to have a little faith in me, no matter how hard it may be for you. Because I've done nothing to give you a reason not to. At least not in this sense. If you want to be wary of me when I'm frustrated or mad, fine. That I can understand. But in all other aspects, it's unwarranted."

Taking a deep breath, I tip my chin up and set myself. "Fine."

He quirks up an eyebrow. "Fine what?"

"I'll be patient to find one. And if it comes to it, I'll consider accepting you buying it." It's not exactly what he wants but letting him pay for it isn't exactly what I want.

"And trusting me?"

"I do."

Clenching his jaw, he narrows his eyes at me, staring down his nose. It's my least favorite face of his. One I'm certain he uses on clients and poor Penelope. He's sizing me up, deciding if he believes me. He can wonder all he wants. I trust him. At least in some aspects. I know he has my best interests at heart. I know he'd never cheat on me. But I don't trust that he won't disappear from my life like everybody else has. Well, except Daphne. It's part of why I'm worried about him paying. What happens when he decides I'm too much? Then I'm left without being able to afford an apartment if we share that. If he pays for it? Then I'm homeless when he kicks me out.

One thing he's right about is that he's never given me a reason not to trust him. But that's how you get hurt. You let that wall down, you believe it won't happen, then it does. With others, I didn't care. I had my contingency plans, which was why I never lived with them. With Zane? My heart would shatter, and my world would fall apart. That one wall is all that's left keeping me sturdy. I've let all the others down with him. It's scary as hell.

He still hasn't said anything. I try my luck of tipping up on my toes and laying a delicate kiss on his lips. It only sort of works. He's going to need the gym when we're done. Oops.

Hastily, I unbutton his coat and slip my arms around the back, sliding my hands up to his shoulders and pressing my cheek to his chest, closing the tiny gap between us, and pressing myself to him.

It takes a minute, but he inhales a deep breath, and I feel him loosen underneath me and his arms tighten around me. There's a rumble in his chest as he growls the slightest bit.

"Hey," I say as I lean back. "This is frustrating and stressful for me too, okay? You have to remember that things like change, and letting other people take over, and trust, are not easy for me. It makes my anxiety jump sky high when I think about all the possibilities with letting you pay. The least of which is that you'll resent me for it."

His features soften, the peaks of his cheekbones not quite as severe, and his muscles are less taut under my fingertips. "You're right. I want to live with you, I'm excited about it. I just don't get that from you. And I know you're nervous, but Jules, I won't resent you. I'm not asking you to pay. That's not going to change. This isn't about sharing or splitting. This is me, wanting to be with you all the time, in our shared space. No more yours and mine. No more wondering where we'll spend the night, even though it's usually yours. I want more. More time, more space, just more. Let me give that to you. Please."

My heart beats so erratically I'm sure he can feel it. In a short period of time, we've both developed stronger feelings than we ever have before. What's always been about sex and loneliness with others has become an inability to be apart from him. A few weeks ago when he mentioned he may have to take a business trip for a long weekend, I nearly had a panic attack, not sure what I'd do without him. It wasn't any better when he said I could tag along; I don't like flying. He was thankfully able to send somebody else.

"I'm excited for that, too. I'll try to be better. I'm sorry if I'm ruining today for you." This whole experience is making me feel icky in my skin. Which doesn't usually end well. The shudder that runs through me gets a squeeze from Zane.

"Let's get some coffee."

Well, he certainly knows the way to my heart. Instead of removing me from clinging to him and closing his coat, he shifts me slightly to his side, wrapping his coat around me. It's a lot colder than I had anticipated, but I prefer walking over taking a cab or the subway, no matter how cold. The fact that I get this extra closeness is just an added perk.

Chapter 48

Zane

I need a trip to the gym. This day is turning out to be a lot more frustrating than I anticipated. That was my first mistake. Sometimes I'm not sure if Jules makes things difficult on purpose or if it's how she is. It doesn't usually bother me this much, but I'm trying to do something nice for her, for us. It's a little extra frustrating.

I just need her to have patience and faith in me. We've seen four places, and she's only liked one. I expected this, even planned for it. The last place is the one I'm fairly certain she's going to like the best. The third one was my error. It was nice, sure, but I hadn't paid enough attention to the light fixtures, or lack thereof.

It doesn't help that it's colder out than we expected this far into March. She's cold, clinging to me for whatever warmth I can give her. I'd planned to grab lunch anyway, but after the third appointment we made a pit stop for some coffee, always a plus for Jules. It helped both her mood and her temperature. For a little while anyway.

"Alright Jules, this is the last one. And if you don't like it, we'll try again next week or the week after."

She nods morosely. Clenching my jaw, I tighten and loosen my fist. Giving my eyes a quick close, I pull up the image permanently emblazoned in my mind of Jules, crumpled on the floor in tears. That one image alone makes all the tension ease right out of my shoulders as my hand slackens at my side. It's the biggest reminder of why I need to stay calm.

Hugging her to me, I kiss the top of her head, getting a whiff of her jasmine-scented hair product. When she relaxes into me, the rest of the tension falls through my feet and out of my body. I've beaten back the angry monster, for now at least.

When the elevator pings open on the twelfth floor there's a staff member waiting for us.

"Mr. Montgomery, Miss Kline. Welcome to The Waters. I'm Paul, and I'll be assisting you today. The apartment you inquired about is this way," he says with a smile and outstretched hand. I link my fingers with Jules's and start down the hallway.

This apartment complex is swankier than any of the others we've seen. I glanced at Jules while she took in the large lobby with chandeliers and the café. Her eyes grew wide, and I could tell she was biting her cheek.

As Paul opens the door, he starts diving into details. "So, this is a two bedroom, there's laundry in-unit, all appliances are stainless steel. There's a twenty-four-hour gym in the building, and on the grounds we have an athletic building that has some other features including a pool, hot tub, a larger gym, a basketball court, a tennis court, a sauna, and a steam room. There's also a small building with spa amenities including a nail salon and hair salon."

I'm nodding away as I listen to Paul continue to ramble on about the things that are readily available on the website while I watch Jules walk further into the apartment. Her eyes are wide, and her mouth is slightly open. The kitchen has granite counters, shiny appliances, and recessed lighting. Nothing spectacular or different from either of our apartments, except on a larger scale, as there's a huge eat-at island. But what I know impresses her are the built-in bookshelves in the living room.

The apartment is spacious, much more so than either of ours. As she turns around, taking in more of the room, there's a glint in her eyes and the tiniest hint of a smile pulling at her lips. I have my arms crossed, one hand resting against my mouth as I watch her, not even listening to Paul anymore. She's completely captivating. The look on her face makes my heart race, and I can't help but smile.

I turn ever so slightly to Paul. "I think we're going to take it. Let me just check quickly."

"Sure. There's a slight process that goes into it, you'll fill out the paperwork and we'll do a background and finance check. Is this going to be in both your names? We'll need information on both of you. Former bank statements, et cetera, I can get you a list."

"I'll be backing the financing, lease in both of our names. I hope that won't be a problem."

"Not at all, Mr. Montgomery. You just let me know when you're ready."

I approach Jules slowly, wrapping my arms around her waist. She just fits so perfectly. "Well?" I arch an eyebrow, almost daring her to deny that it's perfect.

"It's expensive."

"Let me worry about that."

Her mouth presses into a line but excitement swirls through her eyes. "Really?"

I nod, unable to pull my gaze from her face, wanting to notice any shift in her delicate features.

She looks around as it sinks in. That's when I get a rare Jules smile. The ones that pull at my heart strings and make me want to drag her to the bedroom and do everything and anything I want with her. Though that last part is pretty frequent.

"So, you like it?" I'm hesitant to make it sound too much like I'm sure.

"You could say that."

"Well, would you?" I need to hear her say it.

"I like it."

"Was that so hard?"

"It was, actually." Hooking her hands under my arms and onto the back of my shoulders she leans back, the lightest smile still gracing her face.

I can't resist anymore and lean down to kiss her. Pulling away, I cup her face, pressing my lips to her ear. "When we get back to your place, I'm going to do very dirty things to you."

The shiver that runs through her as her hands tighten on my coat and her pelvis tips forward is exactly the reaction I was hoping for.

"How is that different from any other night?" she teases against my jaw.

"Are you complaining?"

"No, of course not."

"Let me go talk to Paul. Do you want to see the bedrooms first?"

"Do we really need two? Seems excessive when have no family who will be visiting."

"It's probably just a good idea." For when she kicks me out of the bedroom, or I'm too frustrated to sleep near her. Neither have happened yet but I can see both in the future. "Daphne may want or need to stay at some point, you never know." I throw this last tidbit in, knowing it may make the difference.

"I'll go look, but if they have four walls I'm sold."

"No ceiling necessary? Interesting."

"Nope. Though I guess, with neighbors, it may be needed. Anything on the top floor? That way at least with no ceiling we can see the stars at night."

With a peck on the cheek, she goes bounding down the hall toward the bedrooms and bathroom. I stare after her until she's completely out of sight, forcing myself to turn back to go over details with Paul. I notice him watching her with wide eyes, a look I recognize as wanting.

My hands ball into fists at my sides but I take a deep breath. Jules will be the first one to say she's very taken. Which she usually follows up with how strange of a thought that is. I don't especially love that he's staring at my girlfriend as she walks away. But she's gorgeous, she gets stared at constantly, so I can't exactly blame him.

It takes me a while to focus, having to ask Paul to repeat himself a few times. The gasp from down the hall as a light flicks on draws my attention. All I want to do is run down the hall and hold her, see her excitement. But I need to finish this. I'll do anything to make her happy. And the need to get her home is getting more and more pressing with each passing minute.

Chapter 49

Jules

I give a tug against the restraints that bind my wrists to no avail. Zane ripped off my shirt and bra before he quickly held my hands above my head, procuring a strap that he secured firmly around my wrists and the bed frame. I've been trying to pull at it for a few minutes. The only movement is when I pull out the slight slack.

His fingers tip beneath the hem of my pants, pulling both them and my panties right off. He's already stripped himself naked, and while I enjoy looking, I also like to touch.

He licks up my leg and starts laying light kisses along my hips. I tug again. "Zane."

"What?" he murmurs between kisses as he works his way up my torso.

"My hands."

"No." His tongue drags along my abdomen as his hands slide up and down my sides.

When his tongue wraps around my nipple, my back peels off the bed towards him, his fingers slipping inside me.

"Fuck," I breathe. "God, fuck, Zane. *Please.*"

He pulls his mouth from my nipple to look up at me as he hooks his fingers, moving them faster and with more pressure as I arch and cry out.

Moving his body higher, his face is right in front of mine. With a deep kiss and a few more hurried strokes I'm moaning and writhing beneath him. I jerk my hands again, just wanting to feel his taut muscles beneath my fingertips.

Removing his hand from between my legs, adjusting to rest on his knees, he reaches for something. "Keep complaining and this is going over your eyes." In one hand, he holds a silk, striped tie.

I hate being blindfolded. Especially when also handcuffed. To quiet myself, I pull my lips in between my teeth.

"Are you going to ask for your hands again?"

Keeping my lips tightly shut, I shake my head.

He leaves a trail of kisses from my mouth to my ear. "Good girl." *Holy fuck.*

Sitting back on his heels, his gaze rakes over me, fire flickering in his dark eyes.

Starting at my knees, he runs his large hands straight up and over my body, his flat palms rubbing light circles over my nipples. One hand continues an upward journey to wrap around my throat.

The other glides back down my stomach to give a few quick circles around my clit. My body is humming with need as I pant and whimper.

His mouth latches to my shoulder as he eases himself into me, agonizingly slow. Once he's pressed all the way inside me, he gives two small pumps and digs his teeth into the sensitive skin of my shoulder, causing me to arch and yelp.

Keeping one hand tight around my throat, he pushes up, eyes swirling with desire which sends an extra pulsation to my clit. Leaning down, he gives me a deep kiss, tongue sweeping across mine.

Pulling away, he starts slamming into me, without restraint. My whole back lifts off the mattress as I arch toward him, moaning loudly. It causes his hand to be tighter around my throat as I try to breathe in tiny increments.

"God, you feel so fucking good, Jules. Goddamn." I can barely even hear him over the sound of skin slapping skin and blood rushing through my body.

I'd be breathing heavily if I could take deep breaths. It's making me slightly lightheaded.

Slowing down and adjusting his hips, he starts sliding into me slower and deeper. His hand loosens and tightens in sync with his slow thrusts. It allows me to take deeper breaths with each release.

The new angle lights up every point within me, making me whine and writhe and squirm beneath him.

I really need my hands. I need to run them down his back and across his shoulders.

"Zane. Please." I breathe as I try to move my wrists again.

He goes completely still, his eyes dark and severe as they lock on mine. It sends chills down my spine, an odd sensation against the sweat on my skin and heat tearing through the rest of my body. I swallow hard as he lets go of his grasp on me and reaches for something.

"No, wait. Don't. It's not fair," I plead with him as he holds the tie out in front of me. He shakes his head as he pulls out and straddles me, laying the tie against my eyes.

I flip my head from side to side and try to squirm away but it's futile while restrained.

"Now what kind of precedent would I be setting if I didn't follow through on my word?" he asks as he wraps the tie around my head, knotting it gently, but tightly.

"You're mean."

"You were warned." His voice is low. "Ask again and I'll put one in your mouth." His breath against my ear sends a shiver racking through my body.

I try to pull my hands free as I roll my head, trying to loosen something, knowing it's pointless.

When he moves off of me, I sit up the little bit I can, my shoulders lifting from the bed. My pulse quickens in anticipation of his return, and my ears perk up to receive any sound he makes.

"Fuck. Zane? It's not nice to move away when I can't see you or feel you."

"Who said I wanted to be nice?" He murmurs against my ear. His voice is low and husky. And fuck if it doesn't make me want to come right this second.

I feel his warmth before his body, hovering over me, the bed dipping on either side of my head as he presses down. His open lips move across my skin, leaving a trail of fire in their wake. They land on mine as he eases into me.

Gliding his hand down my thigh, he reaches behind my knee and wraps my leg around his waist as he pumps into me in a steady rhythm.

I so desperately want to see the look in his eyes right now. I can almost pull up an image behind my lids. Hooded and full of hunger is what I'd expect. Not the sweet and tender look he sometimes gets.

His lips on mine make me jump slightly, not expecting it. A hand cups my cheek, and his fingers trail down to wrap around my throat again. Moving his mouth from mine his thumb runs against my lower lip, pulling it down as he starts thrusting harder and faster.

With two of my senses dulled, my others are heightened, and in minutes I'm arching toward him, hands wrapping around the restraint and pulling, as I tighten around him and scream his name.

As I tremble through the end of my orgasm, Zane wraps his hands around my shoulders and with a few hard thrusts he groans, his breath catching as he digs his teeth into my neck as he comes.

He slows to a stop, resting his forehead against the mattress next to me as he kisses along my shoulder.

While I enjoy reveling in the post-orgasm high, I need my hands, I need to feel him. Thankfully I don't have to ask; Zane pulls the tie from my eyes before releasing my hands, which immediately find his shoulders.

Breathing heavily, his mouth melds against mine, tongue sliding in for a deep kiss. I hold onto him as tightly as I can, but he barely has to use force as he pulls away and rolls to his side.

Pushing up on my elbow I look at him, finger near his face. "Do not ever blindfold me again. Especially while I'm handcuffed."

Leaning up to my level, his dark eyes bore into mine as his lips curl up deviously. "Well maybe if you'd listened, I wouldn't have had to do that."

"If you ever want me to suck your dick again, you'll think twice the next time you consider it." That's how all this started. He was working at his desk when I walked in and knelt between his knees as I undid his pants and took him in my mouth.

He quirks up an eyebrow. "Whatever you say, baby."

"I'm being serious."

"Yeah, I hear you. I'm just not sure I can make those kinds of promises."

"Well then I guess you give yourself blow jobs from now on."

I start to roll away when he grabs my wrist and flips me to my back, sliding over me, leaning some weight on me. He holds each of my wrists in his hands next to my ears.

"Listen carefully, baby. I love you, so I don't want to cause you pain or discomfort, even mental. But there are times that I'm going to be in charge in the bedroom, and I'm going to do what

I want, within reason." I push my hands up to no avail as he leans harder on me.

His chest vibrates against mine as the words pour out of his mouth. "I will *never* do anything to hurt you or scare you. But things like tonight are harmless fun that you just don't *like*. And I promise when you're in charge, which happens from time to time, you can reciprocate."

The whole time he talks his voice is low and velvety. His eyes are locked on mine with a mixture of desire and sincerity. My jaw is clenched in anger, but I can sense a new wetness between my legs as his words wind their way through my insides, lighting little fires throughout. Having always been the dominant one in previous sexual encounters and relationships, I'd never really realized how much of a turn on it is for somebody else to be in charge. And Zane just does it so well.

"I don't like the blindfold." My voice is low, weak. It disgusts me.

"Noted." With a kiss on the tip of my nose he rolls to his back, pulling me against him. Immediately his hand starts running down the back of my hair, tangling every so often in what I'm sure is nothing more than a rat's nest.

I'm tense all over, anger roiling in my stomach. *Noted*. What does that mean? I've given up a lot more control than I'm sure I'm comfortable with already.

Hooking a finger under my chin he tilts my face up to meet my eyes. His mouth turning down, he moves his hands under my arms and pulls me higher so we're at the same level.

"Jules, please relax. I'm sorry if it bothered you. But I will never hurt you. You need to know that and trust that."

"I do." *Right?* "But you know I like to have my hands free. I like to touch you." To further my point, I run the hand not stuck beneath my body through his hair and then down his chest. "And blindfolding is even worse. I don't like it for any reason. Remember the first time you tried it?"

There was a time months ago when he'd had my hands tied with a robe belt and slipped a blindfold over my eyes. I started breathing heavily and thrashing around so much that I was able to get both off on my own. I yelled at him and pushed him away, not having sex.

"I do. And we've been together longer now. I just want you to be able to trust me and give yourself over to me completely."

"What exactly do you think I'm doing? Some things are just nonstarters, Zane. And blindfolding me is definitely one of them."

"I will keep that in mind. But maybe next time you won't run your mouth when I tell you not to." When my jaw hangs open, he squeezes my ass, a place his hand had been resting comfortably once he shifted me higher.

"You're still an asshole." I move to get up but his arm wraps around my waist as his other hand tangles in my hair, keeping me against him.

"I've never denied that. But I'm an asshole who both fucking loves you and loves fucking you. That can come with some disadvantages. Like sometimes I'm going to do things, like hand-cuffing and blindfolding, knowing you might not like it. I heard you, I'll try to refrain from doing it again. Can we move on now please?"

When I don't answer and keep the scowl on my face, he draws my mouth to his, tongue sliding along the seam of my lips. His kiss turns stronger as he's more forceful against me, fingers digging in tighter to my hair and my hip until I allow him entrance. As his tongue slips along mine and his hand massages my scalp, I melt into him.

He has such power over me, and I can't stay mad.

Chapter 50

Zane

Watching Jules sleep, I have a sinking feeling in my chest. She still doesn't trust me.

I've had conversations with Dr. Ptansky about doing things to push her out of her comfort zone to see how she copes. That if she seems to be struggling, it's the perfect time to veer her toward a positive skill.

She didn't say these things should happen in the bedroom, but she also didn't say that they shouldn't. I took it as a gray area where I could use my judgment, knowing Jules best and being the one who would be helping her.

I just hope I didn't push her too far tonight. It was a risk using the blindfold. I knew that before I did it. But I had to try. It's not even something I'm really that into. I like being able to see the way Jules's eyes change as pleasure pours over her.

I'd been prepared to help her if she started to spiral. She didn't, and I'm proud of her for that. But that doesn't change that she doesn't trust me. I know doing something she doesn't like isn't necessarily the best way to gain her trust. But she needs to know I'll protect her, that I'd never do anything that will hurt her.

I need to get her to give herself over to me completely. It's Dr. Ptansky's idea. Not mine. She thinks if she can completely let go, give me her full trust, she'll find some inner peace or something. I don't know. Something about her being safe.

When I had explained I make sure she's safe, she explained it had to do with Jules feeling safe during a low point, being able to get herself out of it by bringing a sense of calm to herself. Dr. P had said that she thinks by the way Jules talks about me in their sessions, that I might be that for her, but she won't let herself go there.

As much as I could have, and almost wanted to be, hurt by that sentiment, I wasn't surprised. I'm still not. It's how Jules is. I get her history; I get her fear of me disappearing on her. I won't, and that's part of where her trust in me fails. Fails to see that I'm different, that things with us are different.

I've told her that I don't lie, it's something I pride myself on. I've told her I'm not going anywhere. Eventually she's going to have to learn to trust that last fact, or she's going to make a liar out of me.

Chapter 51

Zane

Moving day. I've been dreading it for weeks and it's finally here. It's a stressful situation for most people, but for Jules, it could lead to serious issues.

She's already had some tough moments while packing. After the first day, she tried packing some boxes on her own, and I ended up finding her huddled in the bathroom, a fresh cut on her arm. I set some ground rules about packing together. I even took a few days off to get it done.

Looking around the room, everything is stacked in boxes, and Jules is curled up on the couch, reading a book. But she's not really reading. Every few minutes her eyes raise, and she looks around the room. The apprehension is clear, and multiple times I've asked her if she's sure she wants to follow through with this, and every time she assures me, she does.

The change is hard for her, it's going to be hard for her for quite some time, but I'm hoping she'll lean on me to help her through it.

"The movers will be here in an hour."

Though she glances up at me, I'm not sure she really *sees* me, but she nods her acceptance. I absolutely hired movers for this.

Not only is there a lot of stuff, two full apartments worth, but I didn't think it would be good for Jules to be involved in the actual physical moving in her already precarious mental state. Instead, I plan to distract her.

"We should plan to get out of here, let them do their job, not be in the way. What do you say we go to lunch?"

Her nose crinkles in the most adorable way.

"A movie?" Now her tongue sticks out. I'm not getting any verbal cues, but I'm fairly certain I'll be okay without them.

"How about a nice walk in the park?" This time she rolls her eyes at me and looks back at her book. I've effectively been dismissed, but I saved the best for last.

"Oh, wait. I know. Let's go to that new bookstore on 75th." I tilt my head slightly toward her, waiting for her response.

It doesn't take long, as her head snaps up, a twinkle in her eye and the ghost of a smile on her face. She gives a tiny nod before standing up and biting her lip as she looks down at her clothes.

"You look beautiful. Come on, let's get moving. I'm hungry, so I want to grab some lunch too. Maybe coffee somewhere."

With a moment of hesitation, she walks over and loops her arms around mine, intertwining our fingers as she leans into me. I knot my free hand in her hair and pull her in for a kiss against the top of her head.

Jules prefers to walk, so I'm thankful it's a nice day since we have several blocks to go.

While the store may be a bit chaotic since it's opening weekend, books and bookstores calm her. The only thing that's going to make it better, is that they have a café in store. I'm not sure she knows that.

This was all planned, very carefully. I kept a close eye on the opening, checking repeatedly to know when it was going to happen, to be sure. I scheduled the move for the same weekend, knowing Jules was going to need the distraction, and that I'd need a good reason to get her to leave.

Once we get to the store, it's bustling, but not as busy as I'd feared. Jules walks in and her whole face lights up. Taking my hand, she pulls me around the store. After a while, I let her roam and stand back and watch her. She's simply stunning, completely unaware of whatever chaos is ensuing around her, which, at the moment, is an exceptionally loud woman on her phone and a screaming toddler.

I plan to buy her whatever stack she picks out today, the first things to go on the bookshelves at *our* apartment.

A quick glance at my watch tells me we have at least two more hours to kill until they'll be ready for us. I've made sure that all boxes are labeled and gave specific instructions about what should end up where.

The bed from my apartment will go in our bedroom while the bed from hers will go in the spare room. All boxes will end up in their specific rooms. That just leaves the actual unpacking to us, which I can hopefully make less stressful for Jules.

"Okay, I think I'm done." She huffs a curl out of her face, and it falls right back in front of her eye as she frowns at it; I gently tuck it behind her ear before taking the pile of books from her arms.

"Just these?" With a raised eyebrow, I examine the few books I hold, expecting far more than just the six in my hands. These will be gone in a week, two tops if she picks up a few extra assignments.

A quick raise of her shoulders and tip down of her mouth, and I know she's disappointed.

"They didn't have as much as I was hoping. Could be 'cause they're new, could just be that they won't carry certain authors."

"You sure this is all you want?"

With wide eyes she nods her head, and we start walking to the checkout. It took a few months, but she finally stopped arguing when I pay for small things, like her books, coffee, and meals.

Most other things are still a disagreement, but I've gained some traction in a few areas.

The line to cash out is very long, and while we wait, Jules hangs onto my arm.

"Thank you, for today, for distracting me. I know that was your intention, and I appreciate it." She tilts her face up to look at me.

"You're welcome. I just thought it'd be better if you were out of the apartment while the moving occurred."

"No, it was a good plan. I feel better now. Which I'm sure you can tell because I'm actually verbally communicating with you." A smile pulls up the corners of my lips.

"Well, I'm glad my plan worked. But really, I'm starving. What do you want for lunch?"

She raises a shoulder as we take a few steps closer to the register. "I don't care. We're not far from that sandwich place you like."

"You good with that?"

"Of course."

I turn to face her and cup her cheek, drawing her mouth to mine. "I love you."

"I love you, too."

What awaits us at our new apartment, and the challenges that moving will surely present, are still unknown. But I'll do anything to keep this woman happy, because just her mere existence in my life makes me happier than I ever dreamed possible.

Chapter 52

Jules

It's been a few weeks since we moved into the apartment. Things are going...alright. I'd like to say they're going well, but I'd be a liar.

Unpacking brought an ease to me, knowing that all of my things had a place, even if it was new and different. But the whole experience, the newness, the loss of control over basically everything, has sent me in a bit of a spiral.

Zane swears I can do whatever I want to decorate, but part of me feels guilty because he's paying for everything. He said if it made me feel better, I could spend my money on decor, but it doesn't, because that doesn't make the apartment mine, it just makes the shit in it mine.

Because of all the change and stress, Dr. Ptansky suggested that Zane lock the knives, and any other sharp objects, away in a cabinet. It's supposed to take away the ease, if not the temptation. Daphne tried to do the same thing once.

Doesn't everybody know how easy it is to buy an exacto knife and how many places you can get one? If I really needed something, I could get it. That's one thing a lot of people don't realize. Cutters are resourceful.

Zane watched me like a hawk the first week we were here, he even stayed home from work. I wasn't allowed to cook anything, just in case. The knives are still locked up, but if I want to cook, which honestly I so rarely do, Zane is home. He keeps the key with him at all times, not that I'd try to take it, it's not really worth the effort.

The idea behind it is that I'll be in such a state that I need to utilize my tools to calm down. Instead, Zane has been spending a lot of time holding me and trying to soothe me—or distracting me. His methods of distraction are usually fun and dirty.

But part of me feels bad that I'm unable to be left alone, that I can't stop my demons on my own. As I sit and watch Zane cook for the fifth night in a row, after a few late-night support sessions for me, he looks tired and worn. I've done that to him. I'm not letting him get the sleep he needs before working fourteen-hour days.

Guilt twists in my stomach when he lets out a big yawn and shakes his head. He says he doesn't mind, and I know he really doesn't because he enjoys cooking and truly loves taking care of me, but that doesn't make it better. That doesn't mean that he doesn't deserve to be waited on now and again, that I'm not taking more from this relationship than I'm giving.

Hesitantly, I get up from my spot on the couch and walk into the kitchen. "Can I help with anything?"

Despite being worn down, his smile with me never wavers, never wanes. "No, baby, I'm good. Go relax."

"Zane, I'm okay, I can help."

"I promise, I've got it. I'm almost done anyway."

Zane makes so many concessions for me and helps me so much; I worry one day he'll get tired of always giving.

I take a step closer and run my hand through his hair while leaning against the counter next to him. "You look tired. I'm sorry, it's been a rough few weeks for me. I pro—"

He silences me with a kiss. "It's okay, Jules. I like cooking. I find it a relaxing way to de-stress after work. You know that. Don't let the voice in your head tell you otherwise." After adding some seasoning to and tossing some vegetables sauteing in a pan, he looks over at me with his devious smirk. "Maybe I'll let you do the heavy lifting tonight."

Fire courses through me, likely ending in my cheeks, which is why Zane laughs as he turns back to dinner. He rarely lets me be on top in the bedroom, and even if he does, he's in control.

With a firm finger under my chin, he tips my face up and brushes his lips against mine. "Hey. I like taking care of you. Okay? And *all* that encompasses."

"It just doesn't seem like you get much in return is all."

Strong arms wrap around me, and he pulls me into his chest. "I do. Trust me, I do."

I nod in acceptance and lean my ear right above his heart. There's something inside me that won't let me believe him, that says he'll get sick of me, sick of taking care of me. And while I hate that part of me, for some reason I cling to it for dear life.

Chapter 53

Jules

I'm in the middle of cooking dinner and having a hard time fighting the urge to cut. Zane and I got into an argument, something stupid I'm sure, I don't even remember what it was over or how it escalated. While he was able to keep control of himself, I'm upset, angry, and of course hating myself. It'd be so easy. Just a quick slip of the knife. I could just pull my sleeves down.

But he'd see. I'd have to tell Dr. Ptansky, and we have an appointment in two days. The one time I tried to hide it, I didn't do a very good job, constantly pulling at my sleeves, trying to pull them lower. She saw it as a tell immediately.

My gaze keeps sliding toward the knife block while I'm chopping vegetables. Sometimes I think it's a bad idea that Zane doesn't lock them up anymore. But Dr. Ptansky feels it's important that I learn self-control. For moments like right now. I'd never use a dirty knife, like the one I'm chopping with.

I can't explain why I want to. If Zane were to come ask me, I don't think I'd be able to give him a good answer. We fought, I'm mad, I hate myself. I can't ever explain it except for the deep-seated hatred for myself. The numbness I feel. Right now, it's leaning more toward me hating myself so much I want to punish myself. I'm bad, I'm terrible, I'm unlovable, I'm surely the cause of the problem. I'm angry. There's so much internal turmoil that needs an outward expression, an outward release. Hurting myself helps somehow.

The fog that I'm in is so strong, I don't even notice Zane's presence in the kitchen until his hand is over mine.

"You okay?"

"Huh?" Though I heard him clearly, it's almost like I can't comprehend what he's asking me, even though it's only two words.

"I've been watching you for five minutes. Every few seconds your eyes dash over to the knife block. Should I lock them away?"

"No." That wasn't convincing, and I know it the second it leaves my lips.

"Let me take over dinner." He's already behind me, sliding his fingers down my arms to gently try to take the knife from my hands. Instead of giving it over, I recoil. It's not exactly what I want to do, he's surrounding me, which is intentional so I can't get away from him. It's more of a folding in on myself.

"I got it," I snap, even though I don't mean to snap at him.

I feel his sigh more than I hear it. But he takes a step back anyway. There's no way he's going to leave the kitchen now. It takes all of my effort to keep cooking without looking sideways at the knife block as he moves to stand in front of me. So he can watch my eyes no doubt.

His scrutinizing glare stays on me while I continue prepping. The urge hasn't passed. If anything, with his full attention, it's making it worse.

"What are you cooking?"

What am I cooking? I have to think for a minute because it's left my mind, chopping on autopilot. Not a good sign. Of course, Zane notices, his eyes widening.

"Soup."

"So, it will be cooking on its own for a while?"

"Yeah."

"Okay. I want you out of the kitchen."

"I'm fine."

"You're not."

He's right, I'm not. Now is the make-or-break moment. Do I listen and leave the kitchen, or do I fight with him, insist I'm fine?

"Okay. I'll leave." It's a surprise even to myself. I'm usually much more obstinate, especially in matters of my own wellbeing. He was probably expecting to have to carry me out kicking and screaming. It's happened before.

Under Zane's ever watchful eye, I finish chopping and get everything going on the stove.

As soon as the burner's on, the lid is on the pot, and I've put the dishes in the sink, he wraps an arm around my waist and pulls me into the living room.

"What happened?" I haven't even finished sitting when he jumps right in.

"Nothing."

"Jules." The way he says my name is like knives to my stomach, twisting. It's pained, sad. Pleading.

"We got in a fight earlier. I feel shitty. I didn't...I didn't do anything."

"Would you have?"

"No? Yes? I don't know." My head falls to my hands. Sometimes it's just really hard having such a weakness.

Instead of responding, he wraps his arms around me and pulls me against him, leaning back into the cushions. I don't remove my hands from my eyes.

The stubborn side of me refuses to use him as my safe place, but sometimes his mere presence is enough to calm me. I could never tell him that of course. I can't let anybody know they have that much power over me, even so far into our relationship. Besides, it doesn't work *every* time.

Laying here, his strong chest rising and falling under me, his hand making repetitive strokes down my hair, I start to calm. I feel the tension releasing, the urge slipping away, the voice quieting.

"I should check the soup." Though my words indicate otherwise, I make no move to get up.

"Just sit with me for a few more minutes."

"Okay." The comfort of feeling his body against mine is more important than the hunger gnawing at my stomach. "It might overcook."

"Then we'll order in."

Despite his anger, despite our start, he's always been the calm to my crazy. I have zero doubt he would do anything for me. Yet it's still so hard to let him all the way in. Dr. Ptansky says it's because of my abandonment issues. I mean, can you blame me? Both of my parents ditched me before puberty hit. In twenty-eight years, I've had one friend stay by my side. My aunt, my savior, left me in the end too. It may not have been her choice; she died. But she still left.

I wouldn't be able to bear it if I removed the last bricks of that wall and then he also left. And really, it's just a matter of time. If I let him be my comfort, my safe place, I'll have given him every ounce of myself. I need to keep something for me, I need to keep those few bricks standing as something to hide behind when disaster strikes.

Right now, I'm letting him take the lead, decide when I'm ready to get up. I don't want to do something stupid, something I'll regret later, just to say I know myself better than he does. Especially because honestly, sometimes I'm not so sure. He can see me in a way I can't see myself.

"Where's your head at?" He asks hesitantly, not stopping the slow steady movement of his hand down my hair.

"I think it's okay." I'm truly not certain. I feel better, but sometimes I end up putting myself in a tough spot that I didn't expect. I don't want this to be one of those times where he then finds me in the kitchen or bathroom in the middle of the night.

"Want a few more minutes here?"

When I don't respond, he hooks his arm under my knees and pulls me onto his lap, kissing the top of my head. He keeps the motion down my hair, dipping lower down my back, and adds fingers tracing up and down my arms to the mixture. I try to focus on the light tickle against my skin, the rhythmic motion of it, the steady rise and fall of Zane's chest. Anything to distract me from the slight but still present call to the kitchen.

He never gets frustrated with me, never gets tired of helping me. It's been over two years, and never once has he made me feel guilty for having a bad or weak day. He'll sit with me for hours if it's what I need. Right now, he could be sighing, frustrated, ready to give up, wondering if I'll ever be able to get myself together. Instead, he's holding me, trying to calm me, breathing steadily.

One trail down my back and his hand dips lower, slipping under the hem of my shirt, fingers gliding against my bare skin, sending a strange combination of warmth and shivers through my body. His hand drifts along my back, then over my ribs, skimming along the bottom of my bra cup. He's on circuit, round and round. Every so many passes, his finger will dip under the base of my bra and run against my breast.

My arm is no longer a focus, as his hand slides up to cup my jaw, thumb by my ear while the other fingers slip into my hair. Tipping my head back, his hooded eyes latch onto mine. The darkness of his suck me in. Sometimes I feel like the color matches *my* mood, *my* mind. I get lost in them so easily it scares me.

Before I can put too much thought into it, his lips close over mine, slowly, tenderly. His tongue slips in and curls against mine, his hand sliding to the back of my head to deepen the kiss. My fingers twist and tangle into his shirt as I shift on his lap, swinging one leg to the other side of him so I'm straddling him.

He brings an arm down to rest under my ass as he stands, my legs wrapping tightly around his waist as my arms loop around his neck. I break away from the kiss and rest my head against his shoulder as he carries me, first to the kitchen to turn off the stove, then to the bedroom where he slowly lays me on the bed. He doesn't let me go, climbing on the bed immediately where he hovers over me, raking his gaze over my body. His brows knit together, creases in his forehead, his jaw taut. A few days ago, he told me he's worried about me. I'm in a bad cycle, he's worried he's losing me.

I'm worried I'm losing myself.

When his lips meet mine again, they're soft but forceful. I feel his desperation behind the kiss. He's begging me to stay with him. What he doesn't understand is he's my anchor, he's what keeps me from falling off the deep end.

I wrap my arms around his shoulders, my fingers lacing into his hair. One hand braces his weight on the bed while the other slides up my shirt, leaving a trail of heat against my skin.

He pinches at my nipple through the cup of my bra a few times before quickly folding it down, fingers on my sensitive skin. One circle with the pad of his thumb and I'm arching toward him as a moan lodges in my throat.

Zane's lips turn hungrier against mine, his hand sliding to the button on my jeans, undoing it with a mere flick of his wrist. His hand slips under my panties.

"Fuck, Jules," he gasps as he feels how wet I am, resting his forehead against my collarbone and groaning as he slowly slides two fingers in.

My chest meets his as he slides my collar off my shoulder, tenderly kissing whatever skin he can find as he hooks his fingers inside me. He's doing a good job of distracting me as I moan and writhe beneath him.

"Zane." I whisper his name like it will ground me to him. Like it's the beacon that will help me find my way out of the darkness.

Kissing down my torso, over my shirt, he slides away, hands latching onto my jeans and pulling them off with my panties in one quick movement, flying to remove his pants and boxers next.

Reaching behind his head, he pulls his shirt off, muscles flexing in a way that makes my body ache for his return. I lean up and peel my shirt off. I need to feel as much of his skin against mine as I can. While I reach around to work my bra, Zane's lips find mine again, leaning me back as one of his hands deftly unhooks my bra and slides it off my shoulders.

As my back hits the mattress, he's hovering over me, eyes meeting mine, lighter than before. His gaze drifts over me as his thumb brushes gently down the side of my cheek. He's being sweet and tender tonight, knowing I'm on edge.

His thumb rubs across my lower lip, pulling it down before claiming my mouth with his, easing into me.

My head tilts back with a moan as my hands find his back. As he starts rocking against me, it all becomes too much. The pleasure mixed with the turmoil inside my mind, plus the sweetness in his movements, make hot tears prick at my eyes.

Great. Now I'm crying during sex.

Zane's not looking at me, his head nuzzled into my shoulder, so I hope he won't notice my precarious state as I try to stifle a sniffle. But a single tear drops right onto his cheek.

Slowing to a stop, he pushes on his elbow to look at me with a scrunched brow and sheer concern lacing his features. "Jules, are you crying?"

"No," I lie.

He starts to push to his hands and slide out of me as he talks low, eyes on mine. "We should stop."

Linking my fingers behind his neck, I pull him against me, and shake my head adamantly, because I definitely do not want to stop.

Sighing, he kisses the salty tracks on my cheeks as he starts moving inside me again. With his mouth next to my ear he whispers, "You're okay, Jules. I've got you. You're okay."

The tears subside as he picks up speed, thrusting quick and hard as the pressure starts to build. Soon, every thrust brings a tiny sound from my throat, my fingers digging in deeper to his muscles.

When his lips settle against my neck, kissing and sucking, it pushes me over the edge. My nails dig into his back as my head tips back, a loud moan releasing as I tighten around him.

His breath catches in his throat as he groans into the crook of my neck and slows to a stop. He kisses from my neck to my ear, placing a tiny kiss next to it before resting his forehead against mine.

No words are exchanged. I close my eyes as I latch tighter to him, hooking my hands to his shoulders, like I'm clinging on for dear life. Maybe in some way I am. He cups my cheek with one hand and rubs his thumb over my cheekbone.

I bite back the tears that threaten to spring free. I don't want to cry again, not while he's still inside me. I'm being held together with pieces of tape and Zane's love. If I cry again, it'll be too much, and he'll leave me.

"I love you," I whisper.

He places a gentle kiss on my lips. "I love you, too." I squeeze my eyes tighter as my heart flutters.

As he pulls out and rolls to his side, I immediately miss his body against mine. Instead of folding me into him, he gives a long look, the corners of his eyes and lips down turned slightly. Then he slides out of bed, pulling on a pair of boxers. He pulls the blankets up around me and brushes my hair behind my ear before placing a long kiss against my temple.

"I'm going to go order dinner from that Chinese place you like. I want you to just rest. Please. Don't get up."

All I can do is nod as I curl my hands under my head. With one more sidelong glance, he walks out the door, shutting it slightly. I can hear his low voice down the hall but I can't make out the words. Then I hear banging around in the kitchen and the faucet. He's cleaning up the dinner I made, the mess I left when I needed to leave the kitchen.

Guilt pangs in my chest. I should be cleaning up. We shouldn't be having to order in food. I should be stronger. I should be able to get through making dinner for us without having a problem. He shouldn't have to take me out of the room and distract me so I don't hurt myself.

He should leave me.

He hates when I say it, but he doesn't need to know that I think it. The thought sets the tears free again, and they stream silently from my eyes.

I don't know that Zane has come back until I hear his heavy sigh as the bed tips down in front of me. I don't open my eyes as he climbs under the covers or as he pulls me into his chest.

Once against him, I reach my arms to hook around his neck, pressing myself as tightly against him as I can.

"I'm right here, baby." He hesitates for a minute as his arms tighten around me. "Maybe we should call Dr. Ptansky."

I shake my head vehemently. "No. I'm okay. Just...just don't leave me." It's worded a little differently, but the worry is the same.

"I'm not going anywhere. I'm here. I'm right here." I so desperately want to believe him.

Chapter 54

Zane

It's two in the morning and I'm staring at the ceiling. I can't sleep. Thankfully Jules is passed out next to me. She's tossed and turned a little but not too much more than normal. My mind is begging me to go to the gym but I can't. I'm scared to leave her. I'm scared of what she'll do if she wakes up and I'm gone. Maybe that's why I can't sleep, afraid she'll wake up and I won't feel her get out of bed.

She's struggling so much lately. I don't know what to do to help her.

She cried. During sex. And I kept going. I feel like an asshole.

Sure, I checked on her. But I should have stopped. Right? I don't even know. She used to use sex with strangers to distract her. What if that was what she needed in that moment, and I said no? Would she have found somebody else? It's not something I've ever questioned before, and yet, here I sit, bile churning in my stomach at the thought.

Using sex to distract is nothing we haven't done before, nothing I won't use to help her any other time. But this time she cried. It makes it different. Or at least, it seems like it should.

Sometimes I feel our life is so many varying shades of gray, no black or white to be found.

I feel like I'm losing her. And it scares the shit out of me. Finding her and all those feelings that came on so fast was terrifying. But now I have her, and I can't imagine life without her. The thought alone makes my blood run cold.

I cleaned up the soup and the kitchen so she wouldn't have to be in there, wouldn't be reminded of what she'd look at as a failure. She feels like her weak days are failures. They're not. Everybody has bad days, but for people like us, they can be dangerous. She doesn't want to hurt herself, she just can't control it, not yet.

Looking over at her, her chest rises and falls gently. A strand of hair moves forward and lies flat with each breath as it hangs in her face. Gently, I brush it back behind her ear. She woke up screaming once thinking there was a spider on her face. She usually tries to pull it back, but she was too drained tonight.

I held her until dinner came, which was when I slid out of bed, pulling on drawstring pants and paying as quickly as I could. That meant giving a fifteen-dollar tip. Before I was done getting the food and drinks set out, she was standing in the doorway in one of my long-sleeve shirts, looking at the ground as her fingers worked at the ends of the sleeves. The fact that she made her way out and threw a shirt on, on her own, was a good sign.

She ate, slowly, and not a lot, but she at least ate. My heart sank when she apologized, while staring at her food, for me having to clean up from dinner. I know she feels guilty, but she shouldn't. None of that matters.

"You should eat, Jules. It will help you feel better," I had said as I jutted my chin to her food. At that point she'd mostly been pushing it around.

"And you should just—" she had stopped herself, her jaw clenching for a minute before she shoved a forkful of fried rice into her mouth as my back stiffened.

But I knew what she had wanted to say. She was going to say I should leave her.

You should leave me. It's my least favorite phrase of hers. Like it's just that easy. Like it's as simple as choosing which shirt to wear in the morning. I know she doesn't want me to, she just thinks I will, that if she tells me to, it will make the blow easier to handle. It'll be like she's deciding, like she told me to go, and I listened. But I won't. I can't. She needs me, I need her.

We've been in this relationship longer than either of us have ever held onto one. When we say 'I love you' we mean it with every fiber of our being. Or at least I do. I can tell by the way her eyes glint, the way her chest rises, the way she clings to me, that she at least means it honestly. And I think that scares her. But it scares me too. It always has. Even after two years together.

But my biggest fear isn't loving her. Or her not loving me back. It's losing her. To her demons. That one day I won't be able to stop her, to save her.

Thankfully, tonight wasn't that night.

Chapter 55

Jules

Zane's thrusting into me, hard and fast, when his hand wraps around my throat. It's become a favorite move of mine since he first tried it. It had always been a thought in my mind. The one time I voiced it to a "boyfriend" he looked at me like I was crazy and told me that it was fucked up. When I left later that night, I never went back.

"Tighter." The word comes out on a puff of air as Zane slams into me, and my lungs heave.

He shakes his head. "No."

In the back of my mind, I can recognize that his hand is in fact pretty tight, that I can only breathe by taking shallow breaths. But I find myself saying "tighter," again. At his responding head shake I'm leaning up, pushing against his hold. If he won't do it for me, I'll have to do it myself.

I struggle through two breaths before he yells. "Dammit, Jules!"

When he pulls away from me, my entire body feels the loss of him, all of him. He's not just frustrated, he's *mad*, sitting at the foot of the bed, tense and tight, hands gripping the edge of the mattress.

I know that stance, it's not good. I pushed him too far.

I scramble toward him before he can get up, before he can get away from me, and wrap my arms around his chest, one high, one low to cover as much skin as I can. My legs are tight around his waist and I'm pressing my cheek to his back.

He should leave me. All I do is drag him down with me.

Every muscle is tight, he's breathing heavy. "Focus on me. I'm right here. Focus on me." I dig my nails in the slightest bit, tighten my legs and arms. I've woken up sore from holding him so tightly, he's not a small man. I hope this isn't one of those nights. I hope he can forgive me. Again.

After his outburst, he chose me as his new safe place. If we're together, he needs to seek me out, get my physical input. If we aren't, he has to picture me or call me. When I asked him why he chose *me*, especially because I'm also often the reason for the spiral, he said he never wants to see that look on my face again. That it was enough to snap him out of it that day, and he never wants to be the cause of it again. This was something I had done a few times out of sheer desperation to calm him, and it had worked.

So, here I sit, pressed tightly against his back, squeezing my arms and legs tightly. When I start running my parted lips gently over his back, I feel a slight release of the tension. I keep rubbing my mouth across his skin, hot to the touch. Ever so gently, I blow against his neck.

I once asked him what he thought about when he uses me to ground him. Sometimes when I need a reminder that he loves me, I run his answer through my head. *"See, your smile. Hear, your laugh. Feel, your arms around my chest. Smell, your jasmine hair stuff. Taste, your tears."* The tears are my least favorite. But he explained that it can drag him out of the mood, they remind him of the one time he truly scared me, of how broken I am when I cry and how helpless he feels, that it gives him strength.

Sometimes I feel like I need to have a moment like that. A moment that's hard to come back from, that sticks with me, so I can stop giving in so easily.

Before I can think about it anymore, he breaks free from my hold and pins me to the bed, pushing into me without hesitation as I suck in air and grab at his shoulders. *Fuck.* He's silent for a few minutes as he thrusts into me, hard and fast.

"You need to stop using me for your self-destruction and pain." His voice is tight, strained, angry.

"Isn't that...what you're doing...right now...ahh." I can barely get the words out between breaths.

"I'm pretty sure I'm causing you anything but pain right now. And I'm your boyfriend, we're in our home." I hate that he's not even out of breath as he talks to me while slamming into me so forcefully the bed creaks and the headboard bangs against the wall. "You're not going to wake up not knowing where you are and regretting things."

No, I certainly won't. I've regretted a lot of things in my life, a lot of men. But never once have I ever, or could I ever, regret being with Zane.

Focus, Jules. Focus on the perfect body moving above you. Focus on the feeling of him inside you. Mmm, it's delicious.

"Mmm, don't stop." It comes out a commanding whisper.

He latches on my neck as he groans and starts pumping faster. I start to tremble as the pressure builds, whimpering and breathing heavily.

"Don't stop, don't stop, don't, don't....ahh." I'm whispering and then I'm screaming, tightening around him and arching to meet his chest. With a small grunt, I know he's coming, too.

As he collapses and lays on top of me, I think about how differently my body has always responded to his. He always thinks it's because he's just that much better than any guy I've ever been with before him. Dr. Ptansky thinks it's because he's somebody I'm actually happy with, versus just killing pain and time. I think it's because I'm comfortable enough to be myself. Maybe we're all right.

Rolling to his back next to me, I notice his breathing has already started to level out. Running five miles a day will do that to a person. Even when we met, three years ago, Zane was fit. But once he started running and hitting the gym as a way to focus his anger, use it in another way, his body transformed into what I can only think of as godlike. I try to pay homage to it every single day.

As he turns to look at me, his eyes are dark and filled with fire.

"You need to stop pushing me."

"I'm sorry."

"That's the problem, Jules. You're not."

"No, I am. Really, I am. I just, I can't help it sometimes."

"I think you need to go back to group. Or pick up a second session. Something. What you're doing isn't working for you. It's not working for us." My stomach rolls. Group was hard enough the first go around. "I can't. I can't go back to group. The only good thing that came out of it was you." I want to reach out and touch him, but I'm afraid it's not the right move. I'm not sure I can take his rejection right now.

"Well, you need to figure something out. If the coping mechanisms you're using aren't working, you need to find other ones."

"Maybe you should just leave me." It comes out a whisper, and I regret it the second it registers with Zane, my eyes fluttering closed so I don't see the hurt on his face.

"I've asked you to stop saying that." His voice is low and cold. It makes my breath seize in my chest.

"I know. But all I do is drag you down. You deserve better."

"I don't care what you think I deserve. I *want* you."

"Maybe you shouldn't."

"You're right. I probably shouldn't. But that doesn't change that I do." My eyes peel open at just the right moment to see his chest rising and falling slowly. "You need to figure out how to work through your shit without involving me. I can't be your escape and your hero."

"I'm not asking you to be either."

"But you are. You ask me to cause you pain, whether you realize it or not. I have to help you when you're in the kitchen in the middle of the night having a staring contest with a knife. If you're late, I have to worry about where you are, what you're doing, who you're doing it with."

"I have never once cheated on you. Or wanted to. I've never even thought about it." Ouch. That one hurts.

"I like to believe you on that."

Pressing myself against him, I put my hand against his cheek and make sure he's looking right at me. "*Never*. Never have I, never could I. If you believe nothing else I tell you ever, believe that."

"You need to find a better way."

"I never asked you to be my hero."

"That's what you get, Jules. When you have a boyfriend who loves you, you get a hero. You get protection and love and devotion. Somebody to save you from the outside world, from yourself. But I can't also be the one who helps you feed your demons and avoid your issues. I'm trying to give you a little bit of what you want in a safe way. You want a little pain with your sex. Fine. But *I* get to decide how hard, how tight. Not you. You've proven you don't know your limits, don't know how or when to stop." The anger seethes through his words, his glare.

He's right. I once asked him to squeeze tighter and tighter until I passed out. I'm lucky he even indulges me anymore.

"I'm not strong like you." My voice is a meek whisper.

"You think I'm strong? Fuck, Jules, why the hell do you think I workout for three hours a day? Because it's fun? No, it's because I found something that *helps* me. You haven't, and you don't try. But you do drag me into it, and I'm sick of it. And I swear to God if you tell me to leave you again, you're not going to be able to calm me by wrapping yourself around me."

Sometimes I hate how well he knows me. Frequently I think he has a direct link to my brain, almost like he can turn the channel in his head to tune into mine.

"And that's another thing. You refuse to let me be the calm for you until I'm physically restraining you because nothing else has worked. You can't let me be that for you, and I don't understand why. If I'm at work and some client pushes me to the edge, I hang up, close my eyes, and focus on you. Anything and everything I can until I feel myself calm down. Why can't you do the same?" This time, pain laces with his anger.

Because you'll leave me someday. Everybody always does. "I just can't."

The bed rises as his weight no longer presses it down. He rips his boxers and athletic pants on. "You better fucking figure it out, Jules." Tearing open his drawers he yanks on a white T-shirt.

"Where are you going?"

"The fucking gym."

I flop backwards onto the bed as he storms out. He spends three hours at the gym on a *good* day. Bad ones, or days I really push him, like tonight, he'll be there even longer. Right now, at eleven at night, is why a twenty-four-hour gym was a must.

Keep going and you're going to push him away.

That's what I want.

Is it really?

No.

I don't wait up for Zane when he's at the gym in the middle of the night. I have no idea how long he could be. Sometimes he stays until his body is ready to give out.

He hates me.

Somewhere deep, deep in the recesses of my mind, I know he doesn't hate me, not even a little. Every day, he shows me, and tells me, exactly how much he loves me. Men have left me for putting them through far less than what I put Zane through on a daily basis. And he's stuck around for two years.

That's part of my problem though. That negative voice drowns out everything else. If I were to compare it to the devil and angel on my shoulders, the devil would be the size of the sun and the angel would be smaller than Pluto. The point of the coping mechanisms, the grounding, is to find a way to let a rational thought in. To slow down, to find level ground when the negative voice has sent me into a tailspin. To give time between the thought and the reaction, which could be as simple as not telling him to leave me, and as big as being able to control the urge to cut.

I named my voice Hecate, for the goddess of the underworld and demons. Dr. Ptansky doesn't think it's funny.

I don't hear voices, it's more the inner monologue in my head, the one we all have, the one that points us in certain directions, to do certain things. Mine just happens to be dark and sinister and filled with self-doubt. It likes to tell me that everybody hates me, that everything I do is wrong. The shiny sharp knives kill the numbness by causing pain and that I'm a truly awful person that should harm myself because I'm not worthy of anything better.

It's confusing, and I don't understand it. Dr. Ptansky says I don't have to and the things we do don't always make sense. It makes things harder for me. If I don't understand the why, I feel like I can't figure out how to stop. And if I can't stop, I really will push Zane away. Forever.

Chapter 56

Zane

My feet have been slamming the treadmill for an hour. This is after half an hour of lifting and over half an hour of taking it out on the bag. Over two hours and I still haven't calmed enough to go back, but I'm exhausted. It's one in the morning. I'm supposed to be at work for a conference call in six hours, up in five. Not only am I awake right now, I'm beating the hell out of my body.

Why is it so hard for her to accept that I love her? That I'm not going anywhere? It's been two years. I mean, I know why, I understand it, understand her life. Mine's not all that different. But I've let her in, all the way in. She's my safe place, until she pushes me too far, like she did tonight.

Slowing the treadmill to a walk and then off, I flick my towel across my face, through my hair. I'm aware of how long it's been since I've had a haircut as a few pieces fall back into my eyes. Jules had commented on it the other day as she brushed some wisps from my forehead, smile on her face, telling me she likes it. The last time I had these thoughts were after my outburst. After that, I mostly kept it trimmed, but it's grown out a bit longer again.

Sure she's asleep, I let myself in as quietly as I can. My initial thought is confirmed when I slip into the dark bedroom.

God, she's stunning.

Making sure the door closes quietly, I turn on the shower. Pressing my hands against the wall, I let the water run over my back, water dripping into my face, falling in droplets from my hair.

Jules's hands slide around my middle and startle me. I didn't hear her come in. Any residual anger leaves my body as I feel her tighten her grip on me, my hand moving to cover hers. Slipping around me, she presses her chest flush against mine, cheek to my chest, hands reaching up under my arms to latch onto my shoulders.

"I'm sorry." She doesn't need to voice it. But it's nice to hear.

"I know."

"I love you."

"I know."

Taking her chin in between my thumb and fingers, I tilt her face up and close my mouth over hers, leaning forward to block the barrage of water from falling on her. Releasing her from my grasp, I slide my hand slowly down her slick back, wrapping to her waist and holding her tight as my tongue slips along hers.

A hand tangles in the back of my hair, tugging gently. I move away from the wall, turning to push her against the side, water falling between our chests and pooling between her breasts.

I ache for her, throb for her, in a way I never have for another soul. My cold, hard persona has been completely broken apart by this woman.

When she wraps her hand around my cock, it triggers my need for her. Losing my hand in her hair, I tug her head back, latching on her throat, kissing, biting, sucking down her neck, across her shoulder, skimming my teeth along her collarbone.

When she sighs a low "please" I pull from her grasp and slide my hands under her thighs, lifting her up and holding her against the wall. The ensuing moan as I push into her is almost my undoing.

"Fuck, Jules."

She owns me, wholly and completely. But I don't own her.

Chapter 57

Jules

It's the middle of the day and I'm on the couch reading a book. I don't have any work assignments at the moment, and the apartment is clean. Looking around, I double check.

I've been trying really hard to stay on top of the chores since Zane is paying for the apartment, and especially since I've been struggling so much lately. Though I offer to cook more, he enjoys it, so who am I to argue, especially since I hate it.

I shouldn't feel bad reading in the middle of the day. But somehow, I do.

I'm reading the same paragraph for the fourth time when Zane walks in the door. Immediately, I throw the book down and jump up, walking around the couch toward him.

"Oh. Hi. I wasn't expecting you home yet. I, uh, have no work so I was just—" he interrupts me by pressing his mouth against mine as one hand cups the back of my head and the other settles on my lower back.

I expect a simple hello kiss, maybe a bit more passionate than most, but when Zane deepens the kiss, sweeping his tongue across mine, I melt into him. My body presses to his from my chest to my pelvis, hands sliding up his strong chest to wrap around his neck.

He walks me backward to the table, putting his hands on my hips and lifting me seamlessly onto the edge. With a strong arm around my waist, he raises me slightly off the surface, pulling my pants and panties off.

There's a sting of cold against my bare ass, and I'd be thinking about the unsanitary aspects of this if Zane wasn't running his large hands up my thighs as he spreads them, pulling me right to the very edge of the table.

He still hasn't said a word, but his eyes have said a million. And they're all different kinds of hungry.

Kneeling between my legs, he loosens his tie as he kisses from my right knee to right up to my pussy, his warm breath sending a shiver down my spine.

I gasp as he slides his tongue along my wetness, a low growl rising in his chest. My hand finds his hair as the other grips the edge of the table, white knuckled, as Zane swirls his tongue around my clit. A whimper releases from between my lips as I tug at his dark strands.

The gentle pull against him has his hands rising to my upper thighs, digging in as he pulls me closer to him. His tongue slides up and down, looping around with varying pressure and urgency, every few circuits pressing into me. Within minutes I'm moaning and bucking against him.

With a deep groan, he slips two fingers inside me, and I fill our apartment with the sound of his name roaring from my mouth. He slows as I tremble beneath him, trailing his tongue down my thigh and kissing back up.

Standing, he undoes his belt and pants, freeing his prominent erection. He still says nothing but locks his eyes on mine, asking for my approval. He doesn't need to ask, he never needs to, the answer is always yes.

As he presses into me, I fling myself forward, latching onto him as my fingers twist into the back of his shirt. I'm already panting as he slides his hands soothingly up and down my back.

When his lips are resting right against my ear, I think he's finally going to say something, but instead I just hear his slightly ragged breathing. He keeps his mouth there as he pulls out slowly and eases back in, air hissing through his teeth. Despite the lack of words, it's irresistibly sexy to hear.

Unhooking my hands from around his neck, he holds them with just one of his, leaning me back until I'm flat against the table. While holding my wrists, he starts pumping into me.

Trailing his hand down my arm, he stands, stopping to cup my breast, fingers running over my hardened nipple through my shirt. When he gives my nipple a pinch I yelp as my back arches.

He latches onto my hips with a firm grasp as he thrusts into me without reservation. It's hard and fast, my body sliding along the table. As the pressure builds in my lower belly, I wrap my legs around his waist. The groan that catches in his throat has me grabbing at his forearms, holding on as firmly as I can, nails digging in as I tighten around him.

Slowing his movements, he pulls me up to sitting. I wrap my arms around his neck as he rests his head on my shoulder. Kissing from my neck to my lips he cups my cheek before resting his forehead against mine.

"I've been thinking about doing that all day." I'm surprised to hear he's breathless. It usually takes more. Though I guess he did walk home, up a few flights of stairs and then fucked me senseless.

"What, sex on the table?"

"No. Having you for a snack on the table." The way he says it is almost a possessive growl.

"Did it live up to the fantasy?"

"Oh, so much better. Nothing can compare to the real, live Jules."

Tipping forward, I place another small peck on his lips and feel his dick pulsate inside me.

"I mean, I'm game if you want." I'm teasing him, but not exactly lying either.

A smirk plays on his face, and he drags his thumb along my lower lip. "Let me get changed and we'll see what the rest of the night brings us." Squeezing my hip, he pulls away and walks down the hall to get changed from work.

With a quick hop off the table, I put my pants back on. I grab a disinfectant wipe from the kitchen and clean the table; it's where we eat, after all.

Tilting my head, I look at the table with down turned lips. I miss my centerpiece. It was a beautiful square vase, a shade of transparent teal, with sea glass inside. I often had fake flowers sticking out of the top. I had to get rid of it when Zane and I got together. I did it for him, happily, so he'd be comfortable in my apartment. But I miss it.

He said I could find something again, maybe not *quite* as breakable as that, but something. I've been too nervous. I think it's just easier to not have projectiles around. Even though Zane only truly lost his temper the one time—and has been doing so much better—that one time was more than enough.

Wrapping an arm around my waist, Zane leans down to kiss my neck. "I told you to get a new one," he murmurs against my sensitive skin.

"It's okay. I don't need one."

"But you *want* one." He shifts to rest his chin on my shoulder as his other arm encircles me. His hands lock on his forearms, effectively caging me in.

"I want you to feel comfortable in *our* apartment. I can live without it."

"Jules, if you want a centerpiece, get a damn centerpiece." There's not even a hint of irritation in his voice.

Pushing against his arms slightly, they loosen so I can spin around to face him. "And what happens if you want a *snack* again? If anything had been on that table, it would have fallen right off."

Brushing some hair behind my ear, his gaze roams my face. "I just want you to be happy, or whatever your version of happy is these days. You make a lot of concessions for me."

"I do it willingly, Zane. You make plenty for me. And you pay for the apartment, so you can decide what we have and don't have in it."

"Stop bringing that up. I don't care about who pays for it. This is *our* home. Yours and mine. Not mine and you're my guest until I decide otherwise. Got it?"

All I can do is nod. I don't trust myself to say the right thing. Because I'll never believe that he's not going to leave me someday. Or more likely, kick me out.

"Stop." His voice is low against my ear, his hands tucking into my back pockets as he pulls me flush against him. I have to say his distraction tactics are very good.

"What?"

"You're thinking about me kicking you out. It's not going to happen, Jules. You're stuck with me. Get used to it." He runs his nose along my jaw, nuzzling into the soft space between my neck and shoulder.

"It's not me being stuck with you I'm worried about. It's you being stuck with me."

Instead of answering he cups my cheek with one hand while squeezing my ass with other as he presses his lips to mine, sliding his tongue into my mouth. A gentle moan rises in my chest as I wrap my arms around his neck and forget all about centerpieces.

Chapter 58

Zane

Rolling over, my hand hits a cold pillow. I'm immediately jolted awake and out of bed. I almost trip, catching myself on the doorframe, as I pull on drawstring pants.

My neck is jumping with my elevated pulse as I take big strides through the apartment to find Jules. She's been in a bad place lately, I've already stopped her from hurting herself a few times this week.

Today seemed different.

I find her in the kitchen and flip the light on. My finger stills on the light switch, frozen by the sight in front of me.

Jules is sitting on the floor, folded together with her knees pulled tightly to her chest and the heels of her hands pressed tightly against her eyes. What makes my blood run cold is the knife sitting next to her on the floor.

I force my self to snap out of it, ungluing myself from my spot in the doorway to kneel in front of her. Wrapping my fingers around her wrists, I pull them out, inspecting her arms as I turn them from side to side. A sigh escapes as relief washes over my body. Not a mark in sight.

Still, I have to ask. "What happened? Are you okay? Did you cut?" It pours out in hurried questions. My pulse is still quickened, thoughts racing.

"No. But I want to." Her voice comes out a low and broken whisper that chills my bones and crystallizes my blood.

I pretzel her arms to her chest as I curl around her, pulling her into my lap and wrapping my arms tightly around her. I try to be aware of how hard I'm squeezing, I don't want to hurt her, but I so desperately need to hold onto her.

"It's okay. I've got you." I murmur right against her ear, hoping she'll hear me, believe me, come back to me.

She's tense under me, her head shifting slightly every few seconds. I hope she's trying to get out of her head, out of the darkness. When a shudder racks her body, I'm not so sure.

"Are you doing your grounding exercises?" She's supposed to close her eyes and go to a safe place. She mostly refuses to do that one.

"It's not working." The fear in her voice heightens my urgency. I bite back a shiver, taking a deep breath to try to slow my racing heart.

I have a decision to make and not a lot of time to do it. She's losing her battle right now and I can't let that happen. Distracting her is the only option I can think of.

"Focus on me. See, hear, smell, touch...and taste." Tucking my finger under her chin, I tilt her face up, melding my mouth to hers as I push it open, sliding my tongue in. Her hand splays open across my chest and my heart pauses at the sensation.

We've done so much to make the apartment safe for me, but I feel like I've failed to make it safe for Jules. Dr. Ptansky had us lock away the knives at first because Jules was struggling with us moving in together, relinquishing control. When she seemed to be doing better, she had us leave them out on the counter, hoping Jules would reestablish and strengthen her self-control.

It was only a few weeks ago that we took them out. And Jules is failing. What's worse is she knows it, and that makes her struggle more. The other night she said she feels like she's failing *me*, and I almost broke along with her voice as she said it.

When I notice she's barely reacting to me, I pull back and look into her vacant eyes. "Jules." No answer.

"Jules," I try again a little louder, wrapping my hands around her shoulders.

"Jules!" I'm practically shouting as my fingers dig into her skin. I don't want to hurt her but I'm trying to hold her to me, keep her here, keep her present.

"Huh?" She looks dazed, confused, her voice is distant.

When she tries to shrug me off, my grip tightens more until she winces and I loosen, realizing I'm squeezing too hard. Fear has overtaken my body, and I'm having a hard time controlling my strength and need to keep her with me.

Maybe it's good that it hurts. "Feel the pain, Jules. Focus on it. Let it be enough." Please, for the love of God, let it be enough.

She closes her eyes, and my hands lift slightly with her deep breaths. As her shoulders slowly lower beneath my palms, I start moving my fingers in slow circles across her soft skin.

Shifting one of my hands up her neck, I lose it in her hair, massaging her scalp. This usually helps calm her, and also loosens her up a bit. She always loves when I play with her long tendrils.

As a tiny moan rises from her throat, I can't help myself, not sure she's distracted enough. I twist my fingers into her locks and tug her head back gently, closing my mouth over hers. If I can distract her enough, she'll lean into me, give her body and mind over to me. She'll be safe, for tonight at least.

It's not the best trade off, using sex to distract her. But if it works, I'll take it. She used to do it for fun when having a bad day, it was a problem. It's not anymore, but I can still use that impulse to my advantage tonight. At some point she'll get to a place where she doesn't need anything but her thoughts to get her over a rough day. That time feels so far away tonight.

Please, Jules. Give yourself to me. Trust me. Come out of the darkness.

It's a silent plea I say with my lips moving against her, my hand sliding up her shirt. She turns in my lap, straddling me, and I push away from island, bringing her with me until my back is flush against the refrigerator.

I move my other hand from her hip and slide it to join the other under her shirt, cupping both her breasts and massaging lightly. I kiss a trail from her mouth to her neck, sucking lightly with each one. A tiny whimper escapes her lips.

"If I get up, will you follow me to the bedroom?" I need to have her right now.

"Yes." It takes her a second to answer. It doesn't seem like I've distracted her as much as I thought.

"You hesitated." I need to point out the obvious. I need to keep bringing her focus to here and now. I pull her hands from behind my head, grasping her wrists tightly. When she leans in to kiss me again, I pull back. "It's not worth it, Jules. Whatever you're thinking, it's not worth it."

"You don't know that."

"I *do* know that." Oh, how I know. "Don't do it. Come to bed with me, let me distract you. Feel me, not the pain." Please, Jules. Please. I'll go excruciatingly slow just to draw it out, to exhaust her so she has no choice but to fall asleep when we're done.

She nods, and I take it as her being ready. "Okay."

Sliding her off my lap, I loosen my grasp on her wrists, trusting her to come with me.

It's a mistake.

She pulls from my hold on her and lunges across the room, grabbing the knife and dragging it across her fair skin. Blood immediately pools and pours out from the wound as the knife clangs to the floor.

I barely hear it as I scream her name and rush to her side, grabbing the towel off the dishwasher handle and holding it to her arm.

"Jules, baby. Can you hear me?" Her head is lolling to the side. I don't understand. It's bleeding, a lot, but she hasn't lost so much that she should be passed out. Not yet at least.

Keeping one hand pressing the towel to her arm, quickly wetting through, the other reaches frantically across the counter, searching for the cool rectangle.

Finally, my fingers wrap around it, and I pull it down, calling 9-1-1 and giving them the address and a quick explanation.

It's all hazy from there. I try to wake her up, get her attention, but I can't. I want to scoop her in my arms, but I know I shouldn't move her. Hot tears prick my eyes seeing her like this.

One question stands in my mind the whole ride over the emergency room. The paramedics ask me if she took anything. I don't know. I have no idea. She's never been into drugs, I'm sure she didn't go find some. But I don't know that she didn't take some sort of over-the-counter medicine. She'd been having trouble sleeping, talked about getting sleeping pills. I never checked if she did.

This is my fault. I wasn't paying close enough attention. I wasn't doing a good enough job to help her. I didn't protect her. I've failed her.

I can't make sense of any of the words being said to me, my sole focus on Jules and her beautiful face. I hold her hand between mine when they let me, wait and watch from out in the hall when the nurses and doctors need their space. She needs stitches, she'll have a scar.

At some point, I'm handed a scrub top that I automatically slip over my head, forgetting I didn't have a shirt on. A nurse urges me to wash my hands, and when I look at them, I notice that not only are they trembling, but they have dried red splotches all over. Blood.

"Why isn't she awake?" I'm not talking to anybody specifically, just out loud as I stand near the wall looking at her. She's blurry through the moisture in my eyes. A hand picks at my lip.

She looks so small, so frail. Nobody else is in the room right now. Just me and Jules, she's still sleeping. I don't know why. I'm scared to touch her. Afraid to break her more than I already have.

She's already been moved upstairs for observation. I paid for a private room. She can yell at me for it later. I hope.

Glancing at the clock I see it's three in the morning. It's been ninety minutes since I found her.

"Mr. Montgomery?" Turning, I see a short balding man in a white coat stepping into the room.

"Yes. Hi. Can you tell me why she passed out? Why she's still sleeping?"

"Short of the results from her blood where we checked for anything that shouldn't be there, there could be a number of reasons. Extreme fear, severe pain—that would have been a painful experience for her—" At his words I turn to look at her as my chest aches at the thought. "A drop in blood pressure, all things she likely experienced. As time went on, blood loss became a factor.

"She's likely still sleeping from exhaustion, both due to the hour and your report of how long she'd been awake, and the physical toll it took on her body and mind. She'd probably wake if you tried to rouse her, she was lucid and coherent when they were working on her downstairs. Her body needs rest."

He's silent for a minute as I keep my eyes trained on her. I'm sure there are a million questions I should be asking, but I can't think of any right now.

"You should get some rest yourself Mr. Montgomery. You can leave a phone number at the nurses' station that we can call you at if anything should happen. You're welcome to stay as well. She'll be staying for twenty fours at least while we watch her, she'll have to speak to somebody from the psychology department."

Of course. She's going to hate it. I want to tell him she's not suicidal, she made a mistake. But right now, I'm not entirely sure myself. And that sends fear to settle into every single nook and cranny of my body.

"I'll stay, if that's alright. Thanks, doc."

With a tight smile and bow of his head, he's off. I settle in a chair next to the bed. Ever so gently, I pick up Jules's hand in both of mine. She has a bandage on her wrist, an IV in her other arm, for fluids they said, but that's it. Her chest gently rises and falls. And with it, a few tears silently spring from my eyes.

There's only one thing left that I can do for her. I've tried to be present, I've tried to distract her, I've tried to save her. She hasn't been the same since I lost it and threw things in her apartment. That was the night I lost her, and it's taken me until now to see it.

It wasn't complete, it wasn't apparent. She never shied from my touch, my embrace. But there was a shift I hadn't picked up on. I tried to change, to be better. It hasn't helped. Nothing has helped. I can't save her from herself. Only she can do that.

My only choice left is to leave her.

Chapter 59

Jules

S lowly, my eyes flutter open. The brightness streaming in through the window in long rays makes me squint. My arms both hurt.

Looking down, I see why and my stomach slides from my body, my heart stopping completely.

I had hoped it was all a bad dream. But looking around at the white walls and machines, I see that it wasn't. Especially when my eyes connect with Zane's. They're bloodshot and red rimmed. His hair is standing up in a million different directions and his face is haggard.

I did this to him.

Guilt nestles into any hole it can find in my body.

"Hi," I say as I sit up. It comes out cracked and whispered. My throat and mouth are devoid of any moisture.

Without hesitation, Zane reaches over and picks up a cup of water, holding it near my mouth so I can suck some liquid up through the straw.

"Hi." I try again. It comes out smoother this time.

But Zane doesn't return my greeting. He doesn't say anything. Just looks at me with the glare that I haven't seen in over a year. He's all hardness right now.

"I'm sorry. I'm sorry I scared you. I'm sorry I failed." I surprise myself at the strength of my voice when I'm feeling anything but.

When he still doesn't say anything, I reach for his hand, but he pulls away. My eyes flutter closed as they flood.

"I can't do this with you anymore, Jules. I just, I can't. You don't trust me. I scare you." His words hit me like a slap in the face and a punch to the stomach at the same time. I may actually wince in pain. His voice is calm, sad, which makes it worse.

"You don't scare me." I try to talk with validation but come up short, my voice sounding shaky. Not because of the words, but because of the pain in my chest.

"I did. I did once. And you've never been the same since."

"That's not true." I can't tear my gaze from my hands, twisting the scratchy sheet over my lap.

"It is true, Jules. And I hate myself for it. But you won't let me be the safe place you need. Because you don't feel safe with me."

My chest hollows at his words. How can I tell him that with him is the *only* time I feel safe? I can't. Especially not now when he'll think I'm only saying it to keep him from leaving me. But that's what people do. They leave me. Why should he be any different?

"I love you, Jules. God, I love you so much this is killing me. But we're not good for each other. I'm not good for you. I'm holding you back."

"No, *no.* It was a mistake, a stupid mistake." Now my eyes lift to his, his face blurred.

"Maybe so. But you were with me. You were right there, with me. I tried Jules, I tried so hard to get you to focus on me, to come back to me. And you wouldn't, you couldn't. That doesn't work. It's not what you need. You need somebody you can feel safe enough with to let go. Somebody who can distract you, who can save you from yourself when you can't. I thought I could be that person, sometimes I thought I was that person. But it's painfully obvious I'm not."

I'm shaking my head before he's finished, tears flowing out of the corners of my eyes as a vice closes around my heart.

He's on the edge of the bed, taking my hands in his, the second my tears register with him. With one hand reaching behind my neck, he pulls my forehead against his.

"I love you, Jules. I love you so much. I'm doing this *because* I love you. It'd be easy to stay, but we'll just keep going round and round in circles until one of us finally does something that goes too far, something we can't come back from. I can't do that to you. I can't be the one who hurts you, and I can't let you bring yourself to that point. I have to let you go so you can figure yourself out.

"When I'm weak, you're strong, when you're weak I'm strong. It can't be like that anymore Jules. We both need to be able to stand on our own. I've become a crutch and an unhelpful one. I allow you to be weak by picking up the pieces and that doesn't help you." Pausing, he squeezes my hand, running his thumb over the back.

"I've been trying to protect you against everyone and every-thing, including yourself. That was wrong of me, and I didn't realize it until it was too late. The only person who can protect you from yourself, is you. And I'm standing in the way. You'll never truly be okay until you learn to take care of yourself. Learn to work your tools to the fullest. We found each other at hard points in our lives. If it had been different, well, maybe we wouldn't be here."

"Please don't leave me." It comes out a desperate whisper. But he can't leave. He can't. I won't make it without him. I should have told him, I should have told him every single day how much he means to me, how much I love him. I should have let him be my safety. I should have let all of my walls down.

"I'm sorry, baby. I'm so sorry. I know this is going to be hard for you. Please, promise me you'll go to Dr. Ptansky, every week. And go to group. Please. You need to. Group may be filled with memories, good and bad, but the terrible ones have been long gone, and though it may hurt at first, I know better than most how going and sharing can help."

He's right. I know he's right. But I don't want to if he won't be there. I don't want to if I won't have him to come home to.

"Jules, please. Promise me you'll go. I need you to promise me."

If I don't promise him, will he stay? No, no of course he won't. It will just make him feel better. As hurt as I am, I don't want him to hurt more than he has to.

"I promise."

"Please don't hate me." His words are no more than a pained whisper.

My eyes flash up to his. "I could never hate you, Zane." It seems like it's just as hard for him to be leaving as it is for me waiting for him to go. Lacing his fingers through mine, he gives my hand a squeeze and brings my knuckles to his lips before standing and placing a gentle kiss on my forehead.

Just before he walks out the door, my voice catches him. "You said you'd never hurt me, that you'd never leave. Was that just a lie?" I hate myself the second it's out of my mouth. I hate it even more when Zane turns back to me with a grimace of pain written all over his features.

"Jules. I know this hurts, it's going to, but it's not my intention. I'm trying to do this *for* you. And trust me, I'm hurting too." His hand presses to his chest. "This is what's best. For you."

He didn't say it's best for him, he knows it's not. But it's not best for me either. What am I supposed to do without him? He's been there for me for so long. I can't believe one mistake, one stupid moment of overwhelming weakness, has brought me to this point. This may be my lowest of lows. And if it's not, I never want to reach that place.

I can barely see Zane leave through the haze of tears in my eyes. The second the door is closed the dam breaks, and I'm sobbing into my hands. I start yanking at the wires and tubes on me. When my monitor starts beeping a nurse comes rushing in, followed quickly by Daphne.

Once the nurse sees nothing is medically wrong with me, she leaves, allowing Daphne to wrap me in her embrace. I tear at the back of her shirt as my tears soak the front.

"He left, Daph. He left."

"I know, Jules. I know." The only way she'd know is if he told her. He knew I'd break apart and need somebody to put me back together in his absence. "Shh, it's okay. You'll be okay."

I'm shaking my head adamantly. *No. I won't be okay. Not without him.*

"Yes Jules, you will be. I'll be here. I'll be here every single step of the way, every single day. It's always been you and me. We'll get through this together, just like we have everything else."

"No. It's not...the same." I can barely get the words out around my sobs.

"I know. I know it's not. But we'll find a way."

She holds me while I cry, her thin frame shaking with mine. I know Daphne's being strong for me, normally my tears bring on her own, and usually bigger and for longer. But she's never seen me like this over a guy before. In fact, the one time she saw me broken up at all, was when Aunt Juliette died, and that caused a fairly different reaction.

I've had a lot of loss and pain in my life. This one hurts more than any other.

Losing Zane is like losing part of myself. Not only because we were so interconnected, but because I'd given over so much of who I am. Almost every facet of my being and self were linked to Zane in some way. The one piece I held onto, is what drove him away.

If I had let him be my imagery, my place to go when things start to crumble around me, at the very least, he'd be the one holding me instead of Daphne. If I was even here at all.

Instead, I drove him away and the thing that always happens to me, happened. Zane left. He's gone. And I'm alone.

I've reached my lowest. It's time for a change.

Chapter 60

Zane

G oing back to the apartment, *our* apartment, alone is impossible. My whole body aches. I could be returning alone under very different circumstances, so I'm thankful in that aspect.

Walking into the kitchen, my stomach heaves. Immediately I throw off my coat and get out a bucket, filling it with warm sudsy water I clean up the dried blood from the floor. It's not something Jules should have to come home to.

I barely slept last night. I called Daphne, late, or early maybe, I'm not really sure, it's all a blur. I told her what happened, where we were, and what was going to happen. Not knowing what time Jules was going to wake up, I just asked her to be there in the morning. She promised to keep me apprised of the situation and when Jules will be home.

I plan to be gone before then.

Packing my things is miserable. I told her I'd never leave her. I told her I'd never hurt her. And I'm doing both of those things. But I'm trying to do it for her, breaking my own heart in the process.

I called Brian on my way home. He wants me to come in. Like that's going to happen. The *last* thing I want to do is sit on his couch and talk about my feelings. They're bad, I feel like shit. That's all there is to it. I have zero interest in sitting in his insipid office and hashing out the whats and the hows. I don't have any urgency or desire to break something, I've done enough of that already this morning.

It's enough to last a lifetime.

Within three hours, I've been able to pack up my things, taking only my clothes, toiletries, and anything else that is unequivocally mine.

Doing a last quick walk through to make sure I didn't leave anything, something catches my eye. It's a framed picture of me and Jules. We don't see other people often, holing in on ourselves and locking ourselves away in our apartment. But for the holidays my company had a party, and being higher in the ranks, I had to go. Jules wore a breathtaking red dress that instantly made my cock stand at attention.

Sinking to the bed, I hold the picture in my hands. Jules isn't a smiler, but she can fake it when she needs to. I'd never taken the time to really *look* at this picture. The smile in it isn't fake. It's full toothed, real, and makes her eyes shine. She's standing at my side, one hand pressed against my chest, looking up at me. My smile is equally as bright, looking down at her, one hand around her waist resting half on her ass while the other is in my pocket.

No wonder she wanted to frame it. She doesn't use the word *happy*, the day she used the word in terms of being with me, I just about died of shock. I'd come to accept I'd never hear that word come from her mouth in regards to herself. And there it was. But this picture, it shows it clear as day.

With shaky hands, I set it back on her nightstand, straightening it so it's prominent. For a minute I think about hiding it, sliding it in a drawer or the back of the closet so she doesn't have the startling reminder the second she walks into our room...her room. But I don't want her to forget about us. That's not the point. It's not to forget, it's not to cause pain.

It's so she can see herself clearly. Find out who she is and how to be okay on her own. I was never supposed to be there to protect her, I wasn't supposed to be helping her. I became a crutch that stopped working. If she can figure out how to do this on her own, then I'll just be added support.

The thing is, I don't want to leave. I can't imagine not being with Jules again. But I have to so she can be strong, so she can stand on her own. Then, and only then, will there be room for me in her life.

Chapter 61

Jules

I'm sitting in the too brightly lit group therapy room as Paul talks about the upcoming weekend and the anxiety he feels to go to a family member's birthday party. I've been back at therapy for three weeks now, five weeks after Zane left. They welcomed me back with open arms, still the same crew, nobody new.

"Thank you, Paul, for talking about your troubles. Does anybody have anything to say to Paul?" Layla looks around the room.

Tentatively, I raise my hand and am met with silence. Looking away from the group, I see Layla's stunned face. I'm not terribly surprised since I've almost never spoken in group.

"Uh, yeah, Jules, go ahead." I'd decided to come back this time with my real name. I don't want any pretenses, nothing to hide behind.

"Um, well, first of all, Paul, it can be really hard. I have issues with social situations myself. In fact, at first, I really didn't want to come to group therapy because it was going to be a room full of strangers and that's not really my thing. But I've found that sometimes if I almost force myself to go to the party, I end up actually having a good time.

"But Layla, I was hoping it would be alright for me to share?"

A stunned silence falls over the group. It seems a little dramatic. I know I don't share much but honestly.

"Of course, Jules. Go right ahead."

"Well, as most of you know, Za—Flynn and I met here and started dating after a few weeks. About six weeks ago, I had a horrible moment of weakness. He tried to help me out of it, tried to restrain me, get me to focus on him, anything he could think of. But it wasn't enough.

"I ended up cutting myself, but because I was, I don't know, hurried, I cut too deep. I ended up in the hospital. I needed stitches and lost a lot of blood, it bled quickly. Flynn was there for the whole thing. He stayed by my bedside until I woke up. Then he broke up with me. He felt like we weren't good for each other, that we were going to drag each other down. He's made amazing progress. His tools are working so well for him. He'd had one problem about a year ago which he told you about. But nothing big since. Barely anything small, really. But he thought I didn't trust him anymore after that." I take a deep breath and swallow around the lump building in my throat, willing the sting behind my eyes to go away.

"It was so far from the truth, but I hadn't ever really told him. I was scared to let him be my safe place, scared to let him all the way in, even though I loved him...*love* him. And now he's gone, and I'm sad and lonely and hurt. I'm trying not to hurt myself but it's hard, it's so hard. I hate myself for not giving him more, not giving him that validation. I hate myself for being weak." My gaze has been on my lap since I started talking, playing with the cuffs of my sleeves. I can't bear to look around.

"My psych says I need to keep working my tools. I want to use Flynn as my safe place. My place to go, my place to focus on.

But I'm scared that if I do that while he's gone, it will be worse as opposed to better."

When I finally stop talking and glance up, I see tears in Layla's eyes. Mary reaches over and squeezes my hand. She and I have become even friendlier in the past three weeks.

Levi, somebody who I've almost never spoken to or really heard speak, pipes up. "I think if he's truly your safe place, you need to use that. Trust the process. Trust that it will help you, not hurt you. But if it does make it worse, be aware, be ready to change again. And I'm sorry. You guys seemed happy together when we saw you here."

"I agree with Levi." Mary squeaks out next to me.

Everybody else throws in a 'me too.' It makes my decision easier. For the first time, I understand the purpose of group therapy. Dr. Ptansky has had her own thoughts and opinions on the matter, which very much echo that of Levi.

"Thank you all. I appreciate it."

"You're welcome, Jules. That's what we're here for." Layla has to wipe at her eyes before speaking.

Hearing so many people agree that I should lean into the instinct is reassuring, but it's still a little terrifying.

The hard times and dark days are coming more frequently with Zane gone. Sometimes I almost forget and expect to hear the door opening after six. I wake up most mornings confused about being alone in bed, the other side cold. If I could afford to, I'd move. It's enough that Zane paid for the whole year.

The next time a bad moment comes, I'm going to take the advice given to me and focus on the man I may have lost, but still very much love.

Chapter 62

Zane

My leg bounces incessantly, and my gaze keeps wandering to my phone on the corner of my desk. A headache burns behind my eyes and the orbs themselves feel like they've rolled in the Sahara.

One word can be used to describe my demeanor and outlook lately: miserable.

With one final glance up, I snatch the phone and hastily open my contacts, typing out a quick message. *How is she?*

The response comes back rather quickly for the late hour.

No different than when you asked a few days ago Zane. And if you care so much, maybe you should come back.

Me: You know I can't do that Daphne. Jules needs to learn to stand on her own two feet, to stop relying on me to be her savior.

Daphne: I'm aware, and for what it's worth, Dr Ptansky agrees with you and I think on some level, Jules does too. But you left.

Rolling my eyes, I press the phone button and move the device to my ear.

"You know why I left, Daphne. You know it's not so cut and dry." I speak before she even says hello.

"That doesn't make it easier, Zane. Did you know that she still cries? A lot."

Her words are like a burning sword, slicing through my very soul.

"Maybe you need to stop checking in on her so frequently."

"I miss her, Daphne. I'm still in love with her."

"I know, Zane. I understand why you're doing this. But if you want to let Jules move on, if you want her to be able to do this on her own, then you need to give it more time. It's only been a few weeks and you know as well as I do that these kinds of things can take months, if not years."

My fingers move to my forehead, then pinch the bridge of my nose. Being without Jules for that long causes an ache to settle in my chest and a weight to fall into my stomach. And let's not forget that the risk here is that I lose her forever.

I knew the choice I was making, I knew the possible end result was to end up without her, but I can't let go, not yet.

"She doesn't know we talk, right?"

"No, Zane, she has no idea. And I'm going to keep it that way. Look, I think it's good you check in, I appreciate it, and it shows me you love and care about her and are serious about her getting better, because you're right, she wouldn't have been able to do that with you around."

Silence fills the line for a minute as we both think about what she just said.

"She's doing well, Zane. I promise. I see progress being made. It's slow, but it's there. I've been with her to one or two meetings with Dr. Ptansky, and she sees the progress too. It's just...it's slow. But she's doing it."

Even though she can't see me, I'm nodding. "Does she...um..." I shouldn't be asking, and maybe that's why I can't.

"Jules still talks about you, Zane. All the time. It's clear she misses you, and even still loves you, a lot. But she also knows she dragged you down to a low, that she hurt you and scared you. So, while she's getting stronger for herself, I think she's also doing it for you, whether you'll see it or not."

Whether I'll see it or not.

What an awful possibility. It's already been twelve excruciating weeks. Twelve weeks and four days to be exact. Because yes, I am absolutely counting. For what, I'm not sure, but counting all the same.

"I'll keep you up to date, Zane. But know that it's only because I know how much you two still care about each other. If that changes, if there's anything that makes me think you've stopped caring, I stop answering."

"Understood. Thank you, Daphne."

She doesn't respond before the line beeps that she ended the call. I know this isn't easy on her, especially because she's surely lying to Jules in the process.

The day after I moved out, I called Daphne and told her I planned to check in regularly. That I need to know what's happening with Jules and know she's okay. While Daphne nearly bit my head off, she also understood. I had called her to let her know, I had told her Jules was going to need her and why, but I understood that after a day of watching her best friend bawl her eyes out, it took a toll that made me evil.

And I was the bad guy, I *am* the bad guy in all of this. I'll gladly take on the role if it means Jules gets better.

The thing Daphne doesn't understand, that she couldn't possibly begin to comprehend, is that I'll never stop asking after or caring about Jules. Even if she moves on, even if she's married. I'll continue to reach out to the one person who has yet to not answer my inquiry. And my need to do so will continue until Daphne says she no longer speaks of me.

But until that day comes, I can't give up hope that someday, there will be a place in her life for me again.

Chapter 63

Jules

It's been five months since I've seen Zane. Everyday I miss him more than I had the day before, even though everyday I feel like it's not possible.

We chatted every so often at the beginning, a text here or there to check in. He would ask if I was okay, if I was hurting myself. No and no. I didn't want him to feel bad though, so I told him that no I wasn't harming myself anymore—which was and still is true—and that I was okay but missed him terribly. I've never lied to him and none of those things have changed, though I haven't heard from him in at least four months.

So, imagine my surprise when I walk out of my building one Saturday morning, on my way to meet Daphne, and almost bump right into him.

"Zane." Seeing him is like finally being able to breathe again. "What are you doing here?" I fight every muscle in my body to not throw myself into his arms.

"I came to see you."

"How'd you know I didn't move?"

"You would have told me." He's right. I would have. Immediately. Probably before I even packed a single box.

"Can we—can we talk?" There's hesitation in his voice, halting his body from moving an inch.

"Uh, I'm on my way to weekly coffee with Daph." I bite my lip, foot tilting to the side as a battle begins inside my body. Every single molecule in my body is pulling like a magnet toward him, but I can't ditch Daphne without utter guilt.

"I know. That's why I came now. I hoped to catch you before you left. Or after you got back."

"Wait, after I got back? But that can take—"

"Hours. Yeah. I know." My heart skips a beat.

We stare at each other in silence for a few minutes. There are so many emotions in his eyes. Love, longing, desire, worry. I'm not sure if it's worry that I'll turn him away or if I've been with somebody else, maybe both. It wasn't something we talked about. For all I know, he's here to tell me he had a whirlwind romance and wants to propose but that he needs to close up this chapter of his life first. Or to remove my name from the lease.

Jutting my head toward the door, he steps closer. I hadn't realized how much distance there was between us until his sandalwood scent wafts into my nose and his warmth wraps around me.

Once we're upstairs and I'm unlocking the door, he makes the distance zero as he presses against my back, his hand trailing down my side to rest at my hip. My breath catches and a shiver runs down my spine, my head instinctively tilting to his shoulder as his breath caresses my cheek. God, I missed him.

My fingers are shaky with him so close, it takes me an extra few seconds to get the door open. But once I do, I spin to face him, grabbing him by the collar to pull his mouth against mine and into the apartment. His hands find my hips as he follows me, kicking the door closed behind him.

The second it's latched, he spins me around and pushes me up against it, his lips hungry on mine as his hands reach down to my thighs and he lifts me off the ground. My legs wrap around his waist as my fingers twist into his hair, pulling him closer. It's shorter than the last time I saw him.

Everything about him feels warm, comfortable. Like home.

But then my thoughts get the better of me, and I tilt away from his kiss.

Breathless, he leans his forehead against mine. "What's wrong?"

"What's wrong is I don't even know if you have somebody else in your life right now, and we're kissing like we need the oxygen in each other's lungs."

"I'm not seeing anybody, and I do need your oxygen. I need you, all of you, everything you'll give me. I always have, Jules."

"Put me down." By some miracle, I'm able to keep my voice incredibly even.

"What?"

"Put me down."

"Why?" There's fear clipping his voice. It's almost unde-tectable, but I know Zane better than anybody.

"Because I need to tell Daphne I won't be meeting her this weekend."

The smile that spreads across his face turns my stomach upside down and sets free a swarm of butterflies in my chest. He lets me down but loops his arm around my waist, sliding his hand into my back pocket and pulling me against him, kissing up and down my neck.

"She said I owe her extra long next weekend."

"Mmm, fine. You'll have plenty to tell her anyway." He says 'fine' as though he's giving permission. Are we getting back together? Or is this some sort of 'I missed you, I need to fuck you' thing?

The way he's kissing and sucking on my neck, I don't even care. I'd always wanted more with Zane, even from day one, though I denied it until it was impossible to ignore. But at this moment, I'd let him use me. The thought is absurd though, because that's not Zane.

A tiny moan escapes my lips, and that's it. Zane's done in, and he yanks me up again, mouth crashing to mine as he carries me off to the bedroom, leaving his shoes by the door as I work mine off behind his back.

Sliding his hands to cup my head and back, he lowers me slowly to the bed, leaning over me. With his bottom lip caught between his teeth, he runs his palms down my sides as he backs away, his hands giving my ankles a quick squeeze before he glides them back up, tucking into the waistline of my pants and pulling them off in one quick movement.

Before they hit the ground, he's ripping his shirt off. My tongue pokes out to slide across my lower lip at the sight of his chest.

"God, I missed that sexy mouth of yours." I glance up to see Zane looking at me with pure hunger in his eyes.

Leaning up toward him, I reach for his belt, undoing it quickly and tossing it to the floor. As my fingers work the button on his jeans, he pulls my shirt over my head, finishing what I started at his pants and stepping out of them, boxers too, as he climbs over me, tipping me back down to the mattress.

He starts laying slow, sweet kisses along my chest, working across one collarbone to the other before making his way down. His lips trail along the top of my bra, running an open mouth over the cup to tease my nipple, a tiny yelp escaping as he sinks his teeth in.

There's no chance to appreciate the warmth of his breath on my skin, the tingling rushing through my body, the sparks his fingers leave where they touch before his hands are diving to my panties, sliding them off and throwing them over his shoulder, pulling me up so he could unhook my bra in the next fluid movement.

When we're both completely naked, I assume he's just going to dive into me. But he doesn't. He takes a few minutes, leaning back on his elbow, to trail his fingers up and down my body, eyes following the track. He's quiet, gentle, tender. Like he's reacquainting himself with the lines and feel of my body.

I watch him with curiosity. I missed the way he admired my body, and I have zero regard for the way I'm drinking in his, including his pulsating cock.

My vision gets cut off when his hand slides down my hipbone and between my legs. He lets out a low groan as his fingers slip along my wetness and his mouth wraps around my nipple.

When he slides two fingers inside me, I let out a loud moan, my head tipping back, as I grip his hair. The way his fingers and tongue work together have always been nothing short of amazing. He certainly knows how to work them, or at least how to work *me*.

My arms wrap around his head, pulling him closer, causing his fingers to move faster, his mouth to turn hungrier. Within minutes I'm writhing beneath him, whimpering and whining.

It's like an exorcism is being performed on my body as my back peels off the bed and I start to buck against him. "Zane. Don't stop." He groans against my chest but keeps going until I'm screaming and yanking his hair.

As he releases my nipple, he sinks his teeth into the top of my breast, causing me to shriek. Instead of continuing, he slides up next to me, leaning in and kissing me.

"I missed hearing you say my name like that."

"Like what?" I'm somewhat breathless as I ride the high.

"Breathless and begging." His voice is filled with grit, and it sends a shockwave straight through me.

I lace my hands around his neck and pull him down against me, our mouths colliding with a force that should hurt, but I have such need coursing through me that it doesn't. Pulling my mouth from his but keeping a strong grip around his neck, I speak low, quiet, begging. "I want you. I need to feel you inside me."

He groans as his head dips to my shoulder, hair gently brushing my skin. Every noise, every movement, sets off fireworks inside my body. I'd missed it all so much. My need for him only grew over time. I should have let him in sooner.

Without hesitating, he pushes into me, causing my head to tip and my chest to press against his as he finds my throat with his lips.

My entire body is lit up, every nerve ending responding to his every touch, every movement.

Cupping my cheek, Zane rests his forehead against mine. "Jules," he whispers against my lips. The way he says my name is filled with love, desperation, longing. It seeps in my ear and straight through my veins.

"Zane." I hope the way I say his name comes across with the meaning behind it. Need. Not just physical, but eternal.

He keeps his forehead pressed against mine as he starts moving inside me, slowly and sweetly. It's unusual for us, but it's the perfect reconnection. Neither of us came into this relationship with any expectations except that we'd found somebody we connected with. Instead, we found love. Stronger and deeper than either of us have ever felt.

Deep down, he may be an asshole, and I may be a pain in the ass. But we fit together. We were made for each other.

"Fuck, Jules. You may feel better than I remember."

"You definitely do. *Fuck*." Does he ever. All the times I went over it in my head, dreamt about it at night, thought about it while alone, had somehow lowered my memory of how he feels instead of built it up.

As Zane keeps his movements slow and steady, I know he's taking his time, savoring every second.

"God, I could just be lost inside you forever."

"Mmm, I'd probably let you be." Sex has always been the one place Zane and I never had any complications.

Groaning he pushes up on his arms. "Enough of this." Taking my legs as he sits back on his knees, he slides my hips higher as he wraps my ankles around his neck and starts thrusting into me hard and fast.

After a quick tilt of my head and a scream, I'm able to turn back to him with a smile on my face. "There he is." The Zane I'm most used to.

One corner of his mouth ticks up as his eyes darken, and fire tears through them. My insides liquefy as I realize things are going to get interesting.

Pulling away and lowering my legs, he licks from my knee up to my hips, sliding in to swirl his tongue around my clit a few times as my fingers lace into his hair. With two quick flicks he moves back to his heels, grabbing my waist and flipping me to my stomach.

I shriek when he sinks his teeth into my ass before he licks up my spine and pushes my hair from my neck, where he places another bite. Slipping his fingers along the wetness between my thighs he leans against my back, lips next to my ear.

"On your knees, Jules." A shudder runs through me, and I feel Zane's responding smile against my ear.

A slow, deep groan comes from Zane as I pull my knees under me and push up on my hands.

Running his hands from my ass up my sides and down again he murmurs, "So perfect," under his breath.

Settling behind me, he eases himself in as I clench the sheets and gasp for a breath. One hand grabs firmly at my hip while the other twists into my hair, tugging as Zane slams into me.

Leaning over me, he gives a firm yank of my locks to tip my head back as his mouth closes over mine, tongue gliding in effortlessly. He never loses his momentum, thrusting harder and faster each time, my entire being ready to burst into flames.

I tear my mouth from his as a moan forces from my lips.

Moving to my ear, Zane's breath sends shivers through my body. "Let me hear it, Jules. Nice and loud for me." His voice is deep and husky. God, I missed every single thing about him.

"Fuck. Zane." Three more thrusts and I all but shatter the windows with my voice. Zane slows as my body trembles and my arms weaken, making me fall to the bed, trying to fill my lungs with air.

He rubs small circles on my hips before his large hands roam up my body, his chest flattening against my back. Warm puffs of breath tickle my ear before a grumble rattles from his throat straight through me. "Good girl."

Hot fuck.

Blowing a trail of cool air down my spine, he moves away from me and to the head of the bed, settling against the headboard, his legs spread, devilish smile on his face, and dick pointing straight up.

Long ago did I give up the desire to hold out on him, to have any pushback about his requests, commands, whatever they would be considered. And especially now, after months apart, I won't delay either of our pleasure.

Getting to my hands and knees, I scramble up the bed, throwing my leg over his lap and settling my hands on his shoulders, while his slide down my back and hold my waist.

My eyes meet his, a gorgeous shade of blue today, and we stay locked in a staring contest as I lower myself onto him. Being the same height right now doesn't intimidate me. It doesn't make me feel powerful. It feels right. Like things are finally clicking back into place, rearranging themselves how they should be.

I'm completely unable to tear my gaze from his, even as my fingertips traipse down the ripples of his abs, even as he slides his hands down to cup my ass and tip me forward and down, repeating the motion a few times.

As he continues the movement, a sigh pulls from my lips and his part, his gaze dropping to my mouth momentarily.

We're taking our time, savoring every second of our bodies reconnecting in the way only ours can.

I'm drinking in every tiny detail about him, from the layer of stubble on his jawline, to where his hair falls against his temples, down to the feel of him inside me. It's almost like I need to make sure he's really here and this isn't an elaborate dream my mind conjured on a not-so-great day.

As though he can tell what I'm thinking, one hand slides up my back and gets lost in my sea of curls, crashing my mouth to his. Our lips part and tongues tangle, breaths are exchanged like we're keeping the other alive. Maybe in some ways we're breathing life back into one another.

I grind my hips against his a few brief times before he raises to his knees and plops me on my back, driving into me with newfound vigor and lost restraint. It would almost hurt if it didn't feel so Goddamn amazing.

My hands wrap to his shoulders, nails digging into soft flesh covering tight muscles. The feel of them flexing and relaxing beneath my fingers sends a wave of familiarity, comfort, and lust coursing through my body.

Feeling his muscles tense while he moves over me and inside of me has always been one of my favorite things.

"Jules." The way Zane says my name, full of grit and need, pulls me from my reverie of remembering all the ways he can bring sheer pleasure to my body. I don't ever want to go without hearing him say it like that again.

Or without feeling the incredible way he hits every possible pleasure point in my body. There's not a single way he can fuck me that isn't just absolutely amazing.

A light sheen of sweat coats both our bodies, and our breathing becomes labored as he keeps thrusting into me so hard and fast my body slides backward with each one.

"Don't stop, Zane, fuck, don't stop."

Dipping his head, he pulls my nipple into his mouth, sucking and flicking and biting at it while my back arches, and I tighten around him, screams filling the apartment and nails dragging down his back. Within seconds he groans against my breast, and I feel him pulsate inside me.

He rests his forehead against my breastbone, his hair tickling the skin of my neck, before he leaves a trail of kisses up my earlobe, which he gives a quick nibble before falling to his back.

We lay panting for all of two minutes before he's pushing his arm under my neck, pulling me against him as he kisses the top of my head. At the sound of his heartbeat, my eyes flutter closed, and a single drop slides from my eye. I refuse to burst into tears, swallowing the rest around the lump in my throat.

Of course, the tear drips right onto Zane's chest. Though he freezes for a moment, he doesn't need to ask what's wrong, he knows. He squeezes me tightly and starts running a hand down my hair, taking a deep intake of air, his breath already returning to normal. Aside from the amazing shape he's in, it's another indicator that he's still running and going to the gym.

"I wasn't exactly looking closely, being a little distracted, but I didn't see any fresh marks." It's always been somewhat strange as to how comfortably and easily our problems are to talk about. He talks about my self-harm like it's just part of life. And I guess for me it is. But he's never had any discomfort surrounding it. He's always accepted it as part of me.

"That's because there aren't any. There haven't been since...that night." My finger twirls along his chest as I talk, faltering slightly at the end.

"That's incredible, Jules. I'm proud of you. What changed?" Aside from being filled with astonishment, his voice is low.

"You left." I let it hang in the air for a second. "You know how you changed after the night of your blow up? My being scared was enough for you to make a change? You had said my face was your wake-up call that you needed to do better. Well, you leaving was mine. I see Dr. Ptansky once a week, I go to group once a week, and I have a weekly phone check in with Dr. Ptansky."

"All it took was more meetings? Me leaving?" He sounds sad, defeated, and I know he's worrying that he was holding me back.

"It took me finding a new safe place, which I did with the help of Dr. Ptansky. And group. As much as I hate to admit it."

"Wait, you actually *talk* in group now? That I'd love to see." He flinches as I pinch at his ribs. "What's your new safe place?"

"You. Seeing you, thinking about you, thinking of being with you. I just bring up images and pictures and feelings of us together, of your warmth around me. You're my safe place. I knew I might never see you again, when I chose it, but being with you is the last time I felt safe and happy and loved."

His arms tighten around me, and he's quiet for a minute.

"You told Daphne you won't be seeing her until next weekend, right?"

"Yeah?" I'm not quite sure where he's going with his thought.

"Good. Because you're mine this weekend." He almost growls it out, a deep huskiness in his voice.

Before I can answer, he's tilting my chin up, pressing his mouth to mine, parting my lips with his as his tongue slips along mine. But there's a question gnawing at the back of my mind.

When I pull back, biting my lip, his brows furrow and his head cocks to the side.

"What's wrong?"

"Has there, have you been with...um." I'm not exactly sure how to ask without sounding like I'm worried he's cheating.

"I have not touched, thought about, or looked at another woman. It's been the Jules channel 24/7. You're all I've thought about." Gently, he tucks some hair behind my ear, keeping his hand on my cheek.

"For five months?" Closing my fingers around his wrist, I tilt my face to look at him.

"For five months." I lean into his hand, turning to kiss his palm.

"Glad I'm not the only one."

"I missed you."

I snuggle deep into his side. "I missed you, too."

Instead of jumping back into sex, we lay together for a while, talking about what we did during our time apart. He'd gotten an apartment not too far from here, confirmed my suspicion that he is still running and hitting the gym, and really devoted himself to his work.

I tell him about group, things I've shared. They had all been concerned when I returned from the hospital. That was when I first dove into everything.

"Layla cried when I told them you left. They all knew we were dating, having not been to group in a long time, they assumed we were spending our time together, but Layla for some reason had invested in our relationship. But they were supportive, there for me, checking in weekly. Mary and I have actually become closer, I see her more regularly. She helped a lot at first, talked me down a few times. She was actually a big advocate for me choosing you as my safe place. I wanted to right after you left but was nervous. Afraid it'd be hard to think about you in really hard times knowing I may never see you again." My voice trails off at the end.

"I never planned to stay away, Jules. You needed time to work on yourself. Without me. I wasn't helping you. I was doing better, you weren't, and I could see how that bothered you, even if you'd never admit it. We couldn't drag each other down more. But I've been miserable without you. Not angry, no outbursts, but just incredibly unhappy. I'm pretty sure if I didn't pay Penelope as well as I pay her, she'd have quit. I wasn't sure it was the right thing, and so many times I wanted to come back. But now I know it was the right thing. You're *thriving*." Linking his fingers with mine he pulls them to his lips, feathering kisses along my knuckles.

Thriving. Is that what this is? I feel better, happier, brighter. But something's still missing.

"So, what does this mean? What happens now?" My gaze is locked on our intertwined hands. I never want to separate them again.

"What do you want to happen?"

"I want you to come home."

"Good, because I wasn't sure I'd be able to handle it if you didn't." My heart, which had started to fall into a normal rhythm, starts hammering again.

"How soon can you move back in?"

"It'll be a few weeks to officially be able to let go of the apartment. But I can move before that. And if not, I'm still spending every night with you."

"Good. Nights have been hard and lonely. Won't you have some sort of termination charge though?"

"Worth every penny."

"Oh, that's right. You're loaded. I always forget about that. Which, by the way, thank you for paying for the apartment through the year. It was very unnecessary."

"I didn't want you to worry about it on top of everything going on. And you already thanked me." When I found out that he done it, I sent him a brief thank you message.

"Yeah, but now I get to thank you in person. You've always taken care of me, even when you're not around."

"And I've always been happy to. And will continue to be happy to. I need you to know that I don't plan to go anywhere, ever again. I'm here, I'm fully committed. While I feel like I did the right thing, next time, if there is a next time, I'm staying. There won't be anything that can happen to make me leave you again."

"Promise?"

"Yeah, yeah, I promise." With a finger under my chin, he tips my face to his and presses his lips against mine.

Everything inside me melts, my muscles ease for what feels like the first time since that fateful night.

Zane's coming back, he's right here next to me, and with his arms around me and his sandalwood scent enveloping me, everything feels right with the world again.

Chapter 64

Zane

Seeing this new Jules strikes me every single day. She is glowing. While I thought Jules was absolutely stunning before, a smiling Jules is next level, and she actually does smile now. I feel incredibly lucky to be able to be here to share this with her, to see her like this.

It's been three months since I moved back into the apartment, and we fell into our same routine like not a single day had passed. Only now, I can rest easier than I had before. With my own eyes I've seen Jules get into a frantic state, one that would normally end in a night on the kitchen floor or curled up in bed, and instead of letting it get too far, she closes her eyes and takes a few deep breaths.

A few times, she walked over to me and climbed into my lap or wrapped her arms around my waist. While those things worked minimally in the past, now they seem to work completely, to the point that within a few minutes she can get up and continue about her day.

She even cooks more, but I still prefer it and do the majority. Sometimes we do it together.

Not having to worry about Jules while I'm at work is freeing in a way I didn't realize it would be. Something had shifted when she came into my life that added a layer of unease in my day.

That's long gone now, to a point that even Penelope notices the change in my demeanor, and she herself seems more pleased to be at work.

I'm even leaving early some days. Which is how I find myself unlocking the door to our apartment at five o'clock instead of six-thirty. Though I try to be extra quiet so I can surprise Jules, she hears me, and comes around the corner wiping her hands on a dish towel, giant smile on her face that makes my heart stutter.

Despite all our time together, I had somehow never realized that Jules has the hearing of an owl. There's almost no surprising her.

"You're home early." She skips over to me and presses a kiss against my jaw. Before she can settle back to flat feet, I loop my arm around her waist and tug her against me.

"I am. I wanted to see you and was able to get everything done."

"And?" This girl can read me too well.

"And I was thinking I'd go to group with you, if you're okay with it."

"I'd really like that. I think the crew would like to see you."

One eyebrow raises to my hairline. "The crew? You're calling them your *crew* now?"

She squeezes herself tighter against my chest. "Well, when you spend an hour a week with them every week, getting to know deep dark secrets, yes."

"Am I your crew too?"

"No. You're my everything." My chest inflates, and I feel like I could float away on the slightest breeze.

"Your everything, huh? That sounds like a lot of responsibility. Sure I can handle it?"

"You always have. And you don't have to do anything but be here."

Tucking some curls behind her ear, I keep my fingers in her hair and pull her mouth to mine. Part of me is hoping I can tell her with my lips and tongue that she's always been my everything, but on some level, I'm sure she already knows.

"I'll always be here for you, Jules. For you and with you."

"Good. Because I need you." Though we've been back together for a few months, these moments of admission, these words of love and adoration still take me by surprise and steal my breath.

A low growl rumbles in my chest. "Get your ass in the bedroom. We have a little time before the meeting, and I plan to make full use of it." That shiver I've always loved makes Jules tremble and a tiny squeak comes from her parted lips before she kisses my jaw and goes running toward the bedroom.

One, two, three.

Taking off at a run, I catch up to her quickly, looping my arm around her waist and scooping her up with one arm, relishing in her squeals and giggles.

Chapter 65

Jules

Seven months later

One year after the horrible night where Zane couldn't stop me from hurting myself, he wants to take me out to celebrate.

"I'm proud of you, baby. It's been a year since you've done any self-harm. You're absolutely thriving. I want to celebrate that."

"Fine." A large breath puffs out, shifting a curl. I still don't like much attention, or the population en masse. But I have him, Daphne, and I've become even closer with Mary. She's even come to a few Saturday coffee dates with me and Daphne, and we have our own Tuesday night dinner date at a local Mexican restaurant for tacos and margaritas.

It's going to be the four of us, plus Daphne's boyfriend John and Mary's husband Steve. Zane and I have gone on double dates with both couples, and the guys thankfully all get along well. Zane even plays basketball with them and a few other guys, including Shane from group.

Using Zane as my safe place has been more helpful than I ever could have imagined. We used each other when necessary, seeking the other if we were having a bad day. Penelope has been given strict instructions that I am welcome in at any time, even if he's on the phone. If he's in a meeting, she's been told to interrupt with an emergency. She gives me his weekly in-person schedule so I'll be able to hopefully avoid interrupting anything, but he wants me to know that I come first, not work.

Aside from his unwavering support, the work I do with Dr. Ptansky to figure out and work through the root of my issues, I have a scar to remind me of why I need to be strong. The few times Zane has needed to truly comfort me instead of just be present, he'll hold me tight, letting me breathe him in, and find a way to reach and gently trace the length of the scar. A subtle reminder of what can happen if I lose control.

He asked me once early on if I wanted to get a tattoo to cover it, like he's done. At the time I said no, I wanted the reminder. I still do. But I could see covering it at some point in the future.

It's a random Wednesday when we go to a bar to celebrate. It's the first time I've been in one in years, and we chose a Wednesday because we figured it wouldn't be too busy.

"I'm not sure about a bar, Zane." One corner of my mouth tips down as I look around.

"If you're going to be fucking anybody in a bathroom, it's going to be me."

He has a point. Not only would absolutely nothing happen with another guy, but taking him into the bathroom could be fun.

Everybody gathers around as Zane raises his glass. "To the most amazing woman in the world, Jules Kline, on her one-year anniversary. I'm proud of you baby."

"To Jules!" Everybody cheers.

Heat races up my neck to my face. While I hate being the center of attention, right now, it's well intentioned. Even though John and Steve know about my problems, Zane's too, I appreciate that Zane left the specifics out of his toast.

I lean my head back against his chest as we look out over our small group of friends. Sometimes in public places I like to look around and find who I think may be somebody like me. Somebody struggling with inner demons.

My gaze settles on Daphne and John, a smile spreading across my face seeing how happy she is as she stares adoringly into his eyes.

"That smile looks good on you. I've enjoyed seeing it more frequently." Zane's mouth next to my ear sends shivers through me. His very proximity keeps my body on high alert. "I'm proud of you, baby."

I tilt my head up to look at him and expand my smile. "I'm proud of me too. It hasn't been easy, but I'm happy to be where I am, to have made it this far." The difficulty of the past seven months doesn't really need to be voiced to him since he's been there for every single one. While I came close to self-harming a few times, he was able to bring me back every single time. Instead of days to weeks between episodes, there have been months.

Dr. Ptansky is proud of my progress too. Now I see smiles and hear hope from her instead of just disappointment and frustration.

Pushing on my toes, I kiss his jaw. "I love you."

He smiles down at me. "I love you, too. In fact, I love you so much, I think you should marry me."

With wide eyes, I spin around to face him. "What? Are you serious? You're not even down on one knee." He's not even standing up straight, one elbow resting against the bar.

"I'm very serious. And I can get down on one knee if you want me to. I didn't really think it was your style, but if it's what you want." While he shrugs a shoulder, he doesn't move, because he's right, it's not my style.

"You don't even have a ring, you can't—" but my words stall in my throat as he pulls a small square box out of his pocket.

He clicks it open, holding the box in the small space between us, my hands flying to my mouth. "You mean this ring?"

All I can do is nod, my eyes filling to the point where there are now a dozen sparkling diamond rings in front of me.

"Marry me, Jules. We belong together. It's been clear since day one." His voice is low and sincere.

"Yes. Of course, absolutely. Yes!" There's zero doubt he's who I want to be with.

He slides the ring on and links his fingers between mine, pulling me against him and crashing his mouth to mine.

Daphne and Mary come running over, Daphne spinning me around and grabbing my hand as it drops from Zane's.

"Let me see, let me see!"

Zane squeezes my hip. He'd insisted they come so he could propose and let me celebrate with them immediately. It's suddenly abundantly clear of his intentions.

"Holy shit, Jules, that's huge! Nice job, Zane!" I've barely gotten a chance to look at it myself, but the ring hardly matters to me. Being with Zane forever, that's what matters. "We're doing shots!"

"What? Daph, no."

"Oh, absolutely, yes!"

"Why no shots?" Zane's voice sends shivers through me again, even though it's not against my ear.

"She gets a little crazy when she has tequila." Daphne winks as she speaks, a devious grin spanning her mouth as her tongue peeks out of the corner.

Zane's eyebrow quirks up, and I immediately know what he's thinking. "I'd like to see that."

"Me, too," Mary finally pipes in. She's a little quieter by nature, and it can be hard to get a word in edgewise when Daphne's around.

"Fine. *One* shot." I acquiesce but am sure to put firm emphasis on 'one'.

"Sure, sure, one." Daphne throws me a wink, and I know I might be in for a long night.

"I sure hope you don't mind carrying me home if you let Daphne keep the drinks flowing." Leaning back, I look over my shoulder at Zane.

"Oh, I'll make sure to cut you off before that. I have big plans for you when we get home."

I raise an eyebrow. "Oh, really?"

Zane pulls me against him so fast I almost lose my footing. "Yeah, very big." He smirks as he presses his pelvis into mine, and I feel his erection pushing against my thigh. "That ring looks very sexy on you. I'm thinking I'll need to see how it looks all by itself, no distracting clothes in the way."

"Mmm, that sounds nice. I guess it'd be rude to leave my own celebration?" Though rudeness is really the last thing from my mind.

"Your celebration, you can choose how you do that. If you want to leave, we can leave."

I turn around to see Daphne and Mary laughing as they await our shots, quite possibly about me and some embarrassing story Daphne is telling her, she certainly has plenty. Before, that would bother me, now, not so much.

"Let's stay a little longer."

He leans in and places a tender kiss on my lips, cupping my cheek. As he pulls away, he runs his thumb over my bottom lip. "Whatever you want, my love."

A shot is unceremoniously shoved into my hand, and John and Steve have returned to join us. Once all shots, and limes, are passed out, Daphne raises hers. "To my best friend in the entire world and her engagement to a man who I truly think is perfect for her in every way. Cheers!"

"Cheers!"

My mouth twists as the liquor burns on the way down.

"Another one!" Daphne screams.

"No! No more, Daph. One is plenty." I wave my hand at her.

"Oh, come on, you're no fun."

"You go ahead. I'm done."

"How many more would it take to make you crazy?" Zane's voice in my ear makes warmth spread through me and settle between my legs.

"Has there ever been a problem with me being crazy?"

"Fair point."

"You own me, Zane Montgomery. You always have. And now you always will." My hands slide up his chest to wrap around his neck as I pull him into a kiss.

Epilogue

Zane

S ome people think the second before getting home is the last chance to breathe before chaos ensues. That's part of life with two kids under four. But for me, it's the opposite. It's like I'm about to take my first breath of the day.

Jules breathes that into me, even in her exhausted and often flustered state. She always has, and adding our kids to the mix has only increased that.

Having such horrible parents, Jules was worried about how she'd be as a mother, especially with her propensity toward anxiety and depression. I took several weeks off work after Julietta and Carson were each born to watch extra closely for any signs of postpartum depression or anxiety and continue to do so to this very day.

Our kids mean the world to me, but Jules is everything. I almost lost her once, I can't ever risk that again.

Shutting the door behind me, four feet come thundering through the apartment with happy shouts of "Daddy!" My lips perk up at the corners.

Kneeling down, I pull my amazing children into my arms and kiss their heads, a hand splayed on each of their backs as I give them a quick once over. Their happy faces send my heart racing. They both have Jules's thousand-watt smile that makes my world turn on its axis.

It takes me a moment to realize Jules isn't following behind them like she usually is. And she's not in the kitchen.

"Hey guys. Did you have a good day? Where's Mommy?"

"She's in her room laying down."

My heart drops instantly as my smile fades. Jules is mostly better, despite having two kids, she hasn't fallen deep into anything, but she still fights daily. My immediate thought is that her depression has raged back, that I missed something, key signs, anything out of the ordinary that I should have known was off.

"Okay guys, I'm going to go check on Mommy." Part of me is wondering where they've been playing, what they've been doing, and for how long, but my main focus right now is making sure Jules is okay.

Walking into the room, my body freezes, ice coursing through my veins. She's curled up in a ball under the covers, her hands under her cheek. She looks so small.

Shaking myself out of it, I quietly walk to the edge of the bed and kneel down, running a hand down her hair.

"Hey baby," I say quietly when her eyes flutter open.

I'm greeted with a tiny smile as she moves a hand from under her and cups my jaw. "Hey."

"What's going on?"

"I'm just resting. I'm tired."

My brows scrunch together as I take in the dark circles under her eyes. Have I been missing something? How could I be so blind?

"Is something wrong, Jules? The kids were alone when I got home."

"Just tired, Zane. And they've been in here with me since I laid down, I've been awake. I let them go to see you when I heard the door."

"Maybe we should call Dr. P, make sure this isn't a resurgence of depression. Or Dr. Narusso, make sure it's not some sort of late onset postpartum issue."

"Zane."

"I can call now, no wait it's after six. I can stay home and call tomorrow, make sure we can get you in as early as possible." My hand is running frantically down her hair, and I can hear the panic in my voice, feel it knotting in my chest. It's not just me that needs her now, there are two other souls who need her almost as much as I do.

"Zane."

"Or maybe we should call Daphne, see if she can take the kids for a few hours and go do something fun, something to cheer you up. You've been wanting to go to that new bookstore uptown, maybe we can do that this weekend. Or a trip, maybe we can take a day—"

"Zane! Baby, please listen." She pushes herself up to sitting on the edge of the bed and I immediately move between her legs, resting my cheek against her chest and wrapping my arms around her waist. Her fingers play in my hair as I let her consistent heartbeat calm my own.

"Zane, I'm not tired because I'm depressed. I'm tired because I'm pregnant."

I blink quickly a few times before I push back to look at her, hands holding her hips. My brows are raised to my hairline as she smiles and nods.

I tackle her down to the bed and pepper kisses along her face and neck. Her resounding laugh lights my soul on fire. Covering her lips with mine, I cup her cheek as my tongue sweeps into her mouth.

Jules's fingers twist into my hair when I'm suddenly being climbed on. Breaking the kiss, I don't move from my spot hovering over Jules, creating a barrier over her to protect her, because I will *always* protect her. Pressing my forehead against hers, I take a moment to breathe her in. She still smells like jasmine. So familiar, so warm. She's home, and absolutely everything to me.

"I love you," I whisper it across her lips.

"I love you, too."

Another baby, another little mix of us, like the two wildlings using me as a jungle gym and laughing hysterically. Doing some quick math, I realize that Julietta will be five and Carson will be almost three when the new baby comes.

Dipping down to press my lips against hers, I roll the kids off my back. "Come on guys, let's let Mommy rest. You can help me make dinner!"

"I don't want to eat dinyer!" Carson's whine has Jules shifting to get up, but I put my hand on her hip to stop her. "I want to play twains."

"I don't want to play trains, I want to play princess."

"Well, what if I'm a princess train conductor who also cooks dinner?" Jules rolls her eyes as she smiles, surely thinking they'll never go for it. It's a risky choice, but the one consistency in her pregnancies, is that Jules is always exhausted in the first trimester.

The kids seem to think it's a good enough idea, as they jump off the bed and go running for their rooms to get what they need.

I take the opportunity of a few minutes alone to rest a little of my weight on Jules. "How are you feeling?"

"Just tired."

"Were you going to tell me?"

"At some point. I just took the test this morning. You didn't exactly give me a chance to figure out what to do, being all panicked." She has a point.

"Alright, I get it. I worry about you."

"I know. But I always come to you. And I know that you worry that one day I won't, that I'll pull into myself and disappear, but until that day comes, don't let it consume your thoughts. I'm happy."

Just the word uttered from her lips makes my heart soar. "I'm going to change quick, go play, and cook some dinner. I want you to rest, take a nap. I'll get you when dinner's ready."

She snuggles back into the pillow and closes her eyes. "Mmm, sounds good." Her voice is already thick with sleep.

One last kiss to the forehead and I shift off the bed, pulling the blankets up to her shoulders. She likes to have the covers on year-round.

Before I step into the bathroom, I freeze in the threshold, hand on the doorframe. Somehow, despite the shitty childhood, and the rage issues I never thought I'd control, I ended up with the most amazing life. And I owe it all to her.

Epilogue

Jules

Happy. Not a term I ever used to describe myself—at least not for most of my life. But then Zane came along, and everything changed.

With him, I did find happiness, or at least some semblance of it.

Fifteen years after we met and I can truly say I'm happier than I've ever been and ever could have dreamed I was capable of being. Zane still makes me smile daily, and we have four incredible children.

I always felt like I needed to keep a piece of myself for just me. But the moment I let Zane all the way in, lightness started to chase away the dark. I let him own me. Not just my body, but my mind, my soul—my heart.

There's still a darkness that encroaches, anxiety that cripples me. But Zane is always there, sometimes before I ever realize I need him. He has this way of reading me, he always has.

And just like always, he can make the darkness recede, let the light in. At one point in our relationship, I thought the color of his eyes was associated with his mood. At another point, I thought it was related to *my* mood. Now I know it's both.

When I'm in a bad place, they're that harsh slate. But as the darkness gives way to light, so do his eyes, clearing like the sky after a storm.

It's incredibly fascinating to watch, and exceptionally endearing. When I told him my revelation, he shrugged and said that we're connected, in a way he never knew two souls could be.

I don't see Dr. Ptansky anymore. She said that I "graduated" from needing her, but she still checks in regularly. At one point in my care, after letting Zane in, I let down more walls with Dr. P too, and she became more like family toward the end of my visits with her. In some ways, I think she always had been.

After Zane proposed, things moved quickly. We had a small wedding at town hall with Daphne, Mary, Penelope, Doctor Ptansky, and one of the guys Zane plays basketball with, followed by dinner at a fancy Italian restaurant.

Julietta was conceived that night.

It was mostly accidental, and the nerves immediately set in. Neither one of us had a good example of what parents should be. Would our problems carry over to them too? Would they have the same struggles? Would I be a good mom?

But as he had been for the past several years, Zane was the calm to my crazy. He came with me to every appointment and held my hand, he made sure we read all the books, asked all the questions, and just listened to my fears.

Now, as I lean against the doorframe of our three-thousand-square-foot colonial in Westchester, watching ten-year-old Julietta help two-year-old Jackson build a Lego tower, and seven-year-old Carson help four-year-old Danielle color a picture, I know we did a good job.

A strong arm wraps around my waist as a warm, hard chest presses against my back and sandalwood envelops me. Safety surrounds me like a blanket.

"They're really something, baby. And it's all thanks to you."

I spin around in Zane's hold and rest my palms against his chest as I look into his stormy eyes. "Me? Why me?"

"You're home with them. You give them your all. Even when you had that one bout of depression, we got on top of it, and you still gave everything you could. You're kind of amazing, Jules Montgomery. And the very center of the universe for all five of us. Mine especially." No part of me could ever get tired of hearing him use his last name in reference to me, or our family. I took it willingly and quickly, taking the name change papers home the same day we got married.

"Maybe I should learn to shine brighter then, since I'm in such a central role."

"Trust me, baby, you shine plenty bright." Zane closes his mouth over mine, and just as I'm about to part my lips, a chorus of "Mommy" tears us apart.

All four kids come running up to us, taking our hands and pulling us into the playroom.

"Look what we made you, Mommy!" I'm dragged to a tower that's almost as tall as Jackson, who I scoop into my arms for a baby snuggle while I still can.

A paper is thrust in my hand before I can tell them how wonderful it is. "And we made this!" Carson and Danielle beam at me.

Lowering to one knee, I prop Jackson on my leg and pull the others into my arms, giving them a huge hug.

"Thank you all. I love it. Just like I love all of you, so very much." I look up to meet Zane's eye and find him looking down at us with joy scrawled across his face.

My heart has never been so full, and never in a million years did I dream my life could be so complete.

There were times I almost let the voices win, times I surely thought they would, and it was only a matter of time before they got the better of me.

But I'm so glad I never let that happen. That at one point I made the choice to listen to the one voice that has always had my back, always supported me, and always helped me. Zane's. Without him and his belief in me, I would have lost my fight long ago.

If my kids ever struggle like I have, my advice to them is going to be to trust the process, to give themselves over to it completely, as hard as it may be and as weird as it may feel.

And I'd tell them I know it's worth it, because it gave me the life I have today.

THE END

If you or someone you know suffers from suicidal thoughts, please seek help.
National Suicide Prevention Lifeline: 1-800-273-8255

If you or someone you know is a victim of rape or sexual assault, you are not alone.
National Sexual Assault Hotline: 1-800-656-4673
Please also look into www.rainn.org for other resources.

Playlist

For Own Me, I wanted to do something a little different and create a playlist. These are songs that made me think of this book when I heard them.

Checkout this playlist on Spotify.

Switchfoot-I Won't Let You Go
Dirty Heads-Rage
Linkin Park-Breaking the Habit
Skillet-Monster
Motion City Soundtrack-Everything is Alright
Christina Perri-Human
Serotonin-Girl In Red
Secondhand-Fall For You
Skillet-Hero
Skillet-Comatose
Hoobastank-Reason
Senses Fail-Bloody Romance
Lauren Daigle-YouSay
Something Corporate-Save You
Crossfade-Cold
Linkin Park-Crawling
Glass Animals-Heat Waves
Bring Me The Horizon-DiE4u
Em Beihold-Numb Little Bug
Mayday Parade-Hold Onto Me

Coming Soon

The following is an unedited preview and subject to change.

Off Limits

C hapter 1

Lochlyn Reynolds is the one boy I want to date. But I can't, because he's my best friend's brother. He's the guy I want to share my first kiss with. But I can't, because he's my best friend's brother. He's who I want to be with. But I can't, because he's my best friend's brother.

Maybe if I tell myself enough times, I'll start to believe it. I'll stop dreaming about his hands on me. Stop drooling over him as I watch the rivulets flow down his impeccable, toned chest and abs as he climbs out of the pool. So far it hasn't worked. I resolve to keep telling myself. *Nothing can happen with Lochlyn. He's your best friend's brother. Her very, devastatingly handsome and sexy, older brother.*

I shake my head. Already I'm losing resolve.

Humid July air wraps its thickness around us on this starlit night. Eyes glued to the crackling fire, Lochlyn slouches in his Adirondack chair to my right. He's been home from Cornell for eight weeks, and though we see each other almost daily, this is the first time we've been able to get time alone together. Time I cherish.

Chelsea, my best friend and his sister, left for bed hours ago. She's never been a night owl, ready to go to sleep by ten o'clock but up by six every morning. I'm the opposite, up late, wanting to sleep all day.

We'd spent the day at their house swimming and lounging by the pool, coming back to my house for Chinese food and a fire. I expected Lochlyn to leave when Chelsea did, but he's made no move to rise from his chair. I appreciate the company, especially *his*.

"So how are you? Really?" Lochlyn's feet almost reach the fire pit as he stretches out his six-foot-two frame. I'm acutely aware of exactly how close his chair is to mine, that I could slide my hand and touch his. But I can't do that. Because of Chelsea, and she's been my rock for the past year, my best friend for fifteen. Not to mention, I'm sure he doesn't see me that way, his younger sister's best friend.

"I'm okay."

He tilts his head, frowning. One thin lock of his light brown hair falls into his eyes. The sides are still cut short, but the part on top looks like it's grown a little longer than he usually keeps it. "Shay. Come on."

I release a long low breath as I pull at a string on the hem of my shirt. My mouth twists in a sad way that I try to fight around everybody else. "I don't know. Every day is different. I didn't just lose my dad. I lost my family. I basically never see or talk to my mom anymore. If I do, it's about the store, while at the store. We're like passing ships in the night. And I miss her, which I hate to even admit because what eighteen year old misses their mom? Especially because she's still here, she's just not *here*."

My dad passed away a year ago come September. It was one week and four months before I turned eighteen. Lochlyn had come home from college for the funeral, staying six days instead of the one night I'd expected. He and Chelsea spent that time with me, keeping me from being alone. Lochlyn sat with me, talked to me, let me cry. Unlike Chelsea, he never tried to cheer me up or take my mind off it. He let me lead.

Those few days he was home was when I started having *real* feelings for him. I'd always had a crush, always appreciated how gorgeous he is. That week changed things. We'd always spent a lot of time together, he and Chelsea have a close sibling bond.

Close enough that she told both of us when she lost her virginity at sixteen, which in hindsight was a mistake because he got very protective and angry.

What changed things was his gentleness with me, his overwhelming sense of calm. It certainly helped when he pulled me against him after the funeral. Lochlyn and Chelsea had me sandwiched between them on the porch swing as I bawled. When Chelsea got up to get me a water, Lochlyn had leaned me into his toned chest and held me.

Tucking one of my dark brown curls behind my ear I continue. "I haven't even heard from Logan in months, let alone seen her. It's not like we were that close but she's my sister."

Shaking my head, willing away the tears, I go on. "I don't feel like I'm on a good path. I delayed Cornell. My dad had been so happy when I applied. *My baby going to my Alma Mater, nothing would make me happier.* That's what he said when I filled out the application. And now? I should be packing my things and leaving in a couple weeks. Instead I'm staying here, going to community college and working at my parent's store. The one thing I swore I'd never do."

"You'll get to Cornell. It's temporary. You're doing it for your family."

I scoff. "What family?" I mutter under my breath as I slouch slightly in my seat. How can what we've become constitute as a family anymore? I spend more time blocking out the pain of losing all my blood relations in one day than I care to admit. Especially because two of them are still alive, choosing not to be available.

Filling my lungs, I speak louder, "I'm just afraid I'll get stuck. That I'll get stuck here, working at the store, going to community college. That's not what I want for myself. And I'm dragging Chelsea down with me." I've never admitted that to anyone. I've barely admitted it to myself.

The feeling of Lochlyn's hand on mine causes me to startle, tingles pinging through my entire body. Turning to look at him, his blue eyes, which appear darker in the night, are fixed on me. "You'll get out Shay. And Chelsea made her own choice. You didn't ask her to stay. She did that on her own."

"Yeah but she did it for me. And your parents were so mad." Chelsea had delayed her acceptance to Cornell as I did.   "She didn't have to. She could have kept on the straight and narrow. But Chelsea doesn't have a path. She zigs and zags. While she may be using you as an excuse to stay, I could have seen this happening without you. And my parents will get over it. If they wanted more say, they could be around more." He says the last part with a bite to his tone.

But he's right. Chelsea does zig and zag. Her grades almost weren't good enough to get in to Cornell. It's just another glaring reminder of how starkly different Chelsea and Lochlyn are. Aside from their looks, Chelsea being much fairer than Lochlyn with hair so blond it's almost white, Lochlyn's exceptionally smart. He graduated top of his class in high school, in a group of over two hundred, and from what he says, is doing very well at Cornell. He studies, but not nearly as much as Chelsea needs to. Things come easier to him.

It's just one more thing I find attractive about Lochlyn. Looking at him you'd be sure he's just a pretty face with those startling blue eyes and sharp cheekbones. But his intelligence shines through in a simple conversation.

"Aside from worrying about Cornell and Chelsea, how are you? How is Shay?" I must not have given him enough since he's pressing about *me*. It's a thing he does, checks in about me specifically, he always has.

How do I answer that? "Honestly? I don't know. I kind of feel lost. Like I don't have direction, like I don't know where I belong. Before my dad got sick it was pretty clear cut. Get good grades, get into a good college, and go. Now? It's not clear at all."

I hesitate. "Sorry, I know that was more about college. I guess it's just at the forefront of my mind."

"It's okay. Whatever you're thinking, you can talk to me."

My eyes fall to my hem where I start picking at my shirt again. "I don't know. The anniversary of my dad's passing is coming up in two months. It sounds far away, but it's almost still surreal that he's gone at all. I can't explain it, it's a really weird feeling.

"My mom's still so broken. I don't blame her really, they'd been married almost thirty years. Suddenly he's just...gone." Part of me feels like I should have more emotion behind this sentiment. Instead, I feel numb. "Thank God for Chelsea, I really don't know what I'd have done without her this past year."

Feeling a squeeze in my hand, I turn my dark brown eyes to him. "What do you say we have some fun the rest of the summer? Try to take your mind off things?"

My heart flutters when he says 'we.' "Yeah, yeah I'd like that."

"What are your thoughts on things like, I don't know, skydiving?"

My eyes widen. "Um, not so good."

He chuckles. "How about bungee jumping?"

"I'm sorry, have you met me?" My eyes narrow, the fingers of my free hand pressing against my chest as I lean forward slightly in my chair.

I've never known Lochlyn to be that much of a daredevil. In fact, I can't think of a time he's done anything he shouldn't do, aside from attending a party or two. Right now, I wouldn't be surprised if he was just aiming to make the conversation light hearted.

His chuckle turns into a laugh. My pulse speeds up at the sound. "Okay, so no crazy stunts. How about the shore? Would you want to drive down to shore one day?"

"I mean, a beach day sounds great but I'm not sure I should leave my mom. I told her I'd be at the store every day to help out."

He nods, running his fingertips along his bottom lip, drawing my attention to his mouth and how much I wish he'd press it against mine. Heat crawls through my body and I just hope it doesn't reach my cheeks as I think about what his lips might feel like.

I shake my head at the thought. *Off limits.* There's also the glaring fact that he doesn't look at me that way.

Pulling his fingers away from his mouth, he throws his hand in the air. "Welp, I guess that just means we'll have to find things to do at home like lounging by the pool. Maybe a few parties? Maybe?"

One shoulder raises to my ear. "Maybe. We'll see."

He nods. "I know, you're not much of the party girl. But it could be worth trying, at least this summer while you're feeling off."

"Lounging by the pool sounds nice." Especially because then I'll get to see him without his shirt on. The tattoos he's gotten since he turned eighteen make him even sexier. Especially the lyrics he has scrawled along the side of his left rib cage. It was the first tattoo he got, quickly adding other lyrics on his inner right bicep and a sword down the back of his left forearm.

Damn it. I shake my head again, trying to shake the thoughts straight out, as though they'd tumble to the ground in chunks of words. "Okay, I don't want to talk about me anymore. Tell me about you, tell me about school."

His hand pulls against mine slightly as his shoulder rises and falls. "Not much to tell really."

"Oh, come on. You just finished your second year. What's it like?"

"It's fun. It's nice to have fewer responsibilities. My dad can't check every report card for grades or call the teachers. The freedom's nice, the parties are pretty awesome."

"And the girls?" Though I ask, I don't really want to know. I'm painfully aware of Lochlyn's reputation as being 'a sex God.' That was not self given, but a title he'd "earned" from girls at school. According to the rumors, which he has neither confirmed nor denied, he slept his way through the entire girl's volleyball and field hockey teams. I'm sure college has been no different.

My insides twist as he smirks. "The girls are nice." He shoots me a sideways glance, causing heat to rise to my face. I'm not sure how much Chelsea has shared with him in terms of my entirely nonexistent sexual history. She's told me she keeps me out of most conversations. I'm not entirely sure I believe her. Not wanting to know more, I don't press. Lochlyn and I are worlds apart in this area.

He can have any girl he wants, he knows it, and often does if the rumors are to be believed. And he doesn't want me. Why would he? I'm his little sister's best friend. She's also forbidden it. She's told us both, several times, she is absolutely not at all okay with it.

But that doesn't mean I'm not going to enjoy his presence—one that I'm acutely aware is missing when he's at college—while I have it. He is the star of my dreams, after all.

We sit watching the flames for a few minutes, the only sounds the crackling of wood and the occasional distant chirp of a cricket.

"Can I tell you something I haven't told anybody?" My voice is so quiet I'm not quite sure he heard me until he links his fingers in mine. For a moment, I stop breathing and turn to look at him. His eyes are on me, waiting for me to share.

I take a deep breath, preparing myself. "I feel horrible for thinking this, but I almost feel like it's better my dad's gone. He was in so much pain, so miserable. It was awful seeing him like that."

"I remember." Lochlyn had come by every time he was home while my dad was sick. Since we'd grown up together, our families had always been close. He came to see him before he left for school, just a few weeks before my dad passed.

Tears spill from my eyes without warning. I reach up to wipe them away but Lochlyn beats me to it, leaning over in his chair, keeping his hand in mine while also gently swiping a thumb across my cheek.

It may just be my imagination, but his hand hovers against my jaw for a moment before he settles back in his seat.

"I saw how broken my mom was, how broken she still is. Logan can't even bear to call. And somehow, I just feel at peace. I don't know, maybe I'm the one who's broken. I didn't even cry at the funeral. I mean I did after, but that was kind of it. I know I'm crying right now but it's more for feeling...guilty. That I'm not more upset. I kind of always sense it's right there, on the cusp of breaking free, but it never really does. And the times it does, it always just feels like it's something else." I shake my head, looking down at my lap. "I don't know, maybe there's something wrong with me."

"Shay. Shay look at me." I turn my face to him, his blue eyes gentle. "There is *nothing* wrong with you. I was here with you after the funeral. You didn't shed a few tears. You cried, really truly cried. Just because you weren't more upset then, that you aren't breaking down every day, doesn't mean you're broken. I know you miss your dad. He was a great man. And I'm sure you've been upset more than you realize."

He pauses, looking pensive. "You're one of the most down to earth, mature, and intelligent people I have the pleasure of knowing. I think you look at the situation differently. I think you can look at it and see that your dad was suffering. That while you lost him and miss him, he's no longer miserable. That's not being broken Shay. That doesn't mean you don't miss or didn't love your dad."

The tears are flowing freely now. I'm not sure if it's what he said or missing my dad. He's right, I *do* miss my dad, every day. My dad was always the first one up in the morning, making breakfast for everybody. Every morning he said the same thing, *"Breakfast is the most important meal of the day. It sets the tone for your whole day."*

I look up then, wiping the tears and sniffling a little. I laugh the slightest bit. "Ya know, after he died, I couldn't eat breakfast? For weeks. I just completely skipped it. I haven't had a real breakfast since then. I alternate between a piece of fruit, a handful of cereal, a granola bar. Anything quick and easy that doesn't require real cooking since I never really learned how."

Glancing over at Lochlyn, I notice he's scowling, a look usually saved for Chelsea. "That's not healthy Shay."

I shake my head. "I just can't. For my whole life my dad had always been the one to cook breakfast. By the time I get up in the morning, my mom's already gone. Seven days a week, she's at the store to open. She stays till close. The last day she took off was my graduation. And I'd wondered if she was even going to follow through with it."

"Well, I guess we'll have to teach you how to make yourself some breakfast."

I look over at him, brow furrowed. "You can cook?"

"I can, in fact."

"Huh. Who'd have known."

We sit in a comfortable silence for a little while longer, hands still linked as we stare into the low flames licking the charred wood.

When Lochlyn turns to me and smiles, my heart flutters as he says, "I'm full of surprises Shay Sterling."

Off Limits will be releasing September 16, 2022

Pre-order it here: https://www.amazon.com/Off-Limits-Book--
1-ebook/dp/B09ZKQ8DBK

Acknowledgements

W hat an amazing journey it's been to get here. With that, comes many thanks.

To my amazing husband and children:
Another book, another thank you. I still cannot begin to truly show or explain my gratitude for all that you do and all the ways you continue to support me on this incredible journey.

I truly could not do a single aspect of this without you. Having you by my side every step of the way means so much to me.

I love you!

To my amazing trio; GC, AK, RL:
You three are my rock solid team. There for any question, any confusion, any help I need, I know you're there. It's amazing to have found not just great writing partners, but friends.

To my awesome PA, Jennifer Webb:
Thank you for being my biggest cheerleader! I could not do this without your constant support!

To my incredible street team:
Thank you all for you continued support of me and my work. It's amazing to have readers who enjoy my work enough to want to promote it for others to read. I'm truly thankful for you all.

To my dear friend Sarah Lanthier:

Thank you for encouraging me to write down my thoughts and feelings while I was struggling and in a low moment. It turn into an incredible story.

To my amazing editors Zainab, Tori, and Beth:
This book would not be what it is without you and your input. Thank you for helping me learn how to be a better writer, adjusting my words, and most importantly, keeping my voice my own. And especially for your beautiful words as you read through it.

Thank you to the amazing **Shower of Schmidt Designs** for my stunning cover!

To my ARC team: Your time and effort does not go unnoticed. Thank you for reading my novel before it hit the public and for your gracious reviews. I know it's not always easy to find the words, but it's all so appreciated.

And most importantly, to the readers:
Thank you for taking a chance on a new author. I know it can be difficult to see a new name and say "hey let me try that" but it is so beyond appreciated, I cannot begin to find the words. I write because it's my passion, but I publish because I want to share my words with all of you. I hope you enjoyed reading it, as much as I enjoyed writing it.

About the Author

S hayna Astor is a romance author who loves writing sweet love stories, with a lot of spice. When she's not writing, she's probably watching The Office with a cup of coffee, spending time with her kids, or playing video games with her husband.

Stalk me for all the latest updates, teasers for upcoming novels, giveaways, and all the goods on what's coming next!

Instagram @shayna.astor.author

TikTok @shayna.astor.author

Facebook Group Shayna's Coffee Corner

Website www.shaynaastor.com

Made in the USA
Middletown, DE
27 June 2022